Robert Hellenga

BLUES LESSONS

a novel

SCRIBNER

New York London Toronto Sydney Singapore

SCRIBNER
1230 Avenue of the Americas
New York, NY 10020

First Scribner trade paperback edition 2003

SCRIBNER and design are trademarks of Macmillan Library Reference USA, Inc.,
used under license by Simon & Schuster, the publisher of this work.
For information regarding special discounts for bulk purchases,
please contact Simon & Schuster Special Sales at 1-800-456-6798 or
business@simonandschuster.com

Designed by Kyoko Watanabe

Manufactured in the United States of America

1 3 5 7 9 10 8 6 4 2

Library of Congress Cataloging-in-Publication Data is available.

ISBN 978-0-7432-2546-5

The publisher gratefully acknowledges permission to reprint the following:

"Fern Hill (excerpt)" by Dylan Thomas, from *The Poems of Dylan Thomas*,
copyright © 1945 by The Trustees for the Copyrights of Dylan Thomas.
Reprinted by permission of New Directions Publishing Corp.

"Come on in My Kitchen." Words and music by Robert Johnson © [1978] 1990,
1991 King of Spades Music. All rights reserved. Used by permission.

"In the Evening." Words and music by Leroy Arthur Carr © copyright
Universal–MCA Music Publishing, a Division of Universal Studios, Inc. (ASCAP).
International copyright secured. All rights reserved.

To the memory of my parents, Marjorie Johnson Hellenga,
who did in fact go to high school with Ernest Hemingway,
and Ted Hellenga, who did in fact bowl a perfect game in
the presence of Hank Marino, Bowler of the Half Century.

Acknowledgments

I would like to thank my first two readers—my agent, Henry Dunow, and my editor, Jake Morrissey—for their encouragement and their astute comments. I would also like to acknowledge my indebtedness to Audrey Petty and David Wright, Donald Brannon, Honoree Jeffers, Virginia Hellenga, and Happy Traum for reading the manuscript and offering valuable suggestions; to Brant Rumble for help with the dirty work; and to the following people for answering hundreds of questions about the Railway Post Office, hot combs, life in the Navy, the University of Chicago, Madison, bees, spelling bees, the blues, and other things: the librarians at the Knox College library, the Galesburg Public Library, and the Madison Public Library; the members of my immediate family (Virginia, Rachel, Heather, and Caitrine); and Roy Andersen, Caesar Akuetey, Jim Betts, Bill Brady, Glenn Duddleson, Bill Farr, Keith Hackett, John Haslem, Ted Hellenga, Jr., David Killion, Kathy Myler, Reverend John Nash, Ellyne Newton, Jean Nyman, Harry Weaver, and Ken Williams.

For practical blues instruction I have relied (for the last twenty-five years) on the books, tapes, and videos published by Stephan

Grossman (Kicking Mule) and Happy Traum (Homespun Tapes). For factual information about the blues I have made extensive use of Gérard Herzhaft's *Encyclopedia of the Blues* (University of Arkansas Press, 1997) and Robert Santelli's *Big Book of Blues* (Penguin, 1993). Some scenes in the novel were suggested by Michael Bloomfield's *Me and Big Joe* (Re/Search Productions, 1980), and by Thomas C. Schelling's *Micromotives and Macrobehavior* (Norton, 1978).

Parts of *Blues Lessons* were written with support from the Illinois Arts Council and from the John and Elaine Fellowes Fund of Knox College.

Fern Hill

Now as I was young and easy under the apple
*   boughs,*
About the lilting house and happy as the grass
*   was green,*
The night above the dingle starry,
Time let me hail and climb
Golden in the heydays of his eyes,
And honoured among wagons I was prince of the
*   apple towns*
And once below a time I lordly had the trees and
*   leaves*
Trail with daisies and barley
Down the rivers of the windfall light.

–Dylan Thomas

PART I

1

Vocation

1954

IT WAS NOT unusual for missionaries—sometimes alone, sometimes in pairs—to visit the Methodist church in Appleton, Michigan. They'd speak in church on Sunday morning and then, after the regular offering, there would be a special collection for whatever mission they were serving. These visitors were generally middle-aged, stout, and earnest, but Miss Prellwitz, who came late in the summer of 1954, just as I was about to enter my junior year of high school, was young and beautiful and lighthearted and spoke with a clipped British accent, and the stories she told on Sunday morning in church itself and the slides she showed in the evening at the Epworth League made me want to follow her into the heart of the dark continent. She was more entertaining and mysterious than the movies I sometimes saw on Friday nights at the Oriental Theater on Main Street, movies in which, after the previews, a large map of Africa would suddenly fill the screen, and then you'd see a line moving in from the coast toward the center, and later on in a jungle camp a huge spider would fall out of a tree onto the shoulder of a beautiful woman and the hero would knock it off. I pictured myself knocking a huge spider off Miss Prellwitz's shoulder.

"In my opinion," my mother said at breakfast the next morning, "these missionaries do more harm than good, though at least they're more interesting than Reverend Boomer."

"Reverend Boomsma." My father, who was on the vestry, corrected her out of habit. He had lived in Appleton all his life and accepted people on their own terms, whereas my mother, who had grown up in Oak Park, a suburb of Chicago, was often impatient and critical.

At that time my cousin Lotte, who was three years older than I, had been waiting for her vocation for almost a year, and a great deal of importance had been attached to Miss Prellwitz's visit. *"Voco, vocare,"* my mother explained. *"To call.* She's waiting for her *calling."* My mother taught Latin and French at the high school.

Her *calling?* Very mysterious. Was it like waiting for a telephone call? When the telephone rang you could hear it ring: one ring for Lotte's parents, Uncle Barent—my father's half brother—and Aunt Margriet; two rings for Uncle Piet and Aunt Sophie, next door; and three rings for our house. But how would you know when you got this other kind of call? Would a bell ring inside your head? Would you pick up an imaginary phone? And then the missionary came, Miss Prellwitz, and I began to understand.

The missionaries always stayed with Uncle Barent and Aunt Griet, who lived right on the corner of Dijksterhuis Corners, one mile straight north of the stoplight in the center of town. It wasn't called Dijksterhuis Corners on road maps or in my mother's big Rand

McNally *Atlas of the World,* but that's what everyone in Appleton called it—*dike-stir-hoice* (rhymes with *choice)*—and Appleton Road and Kruger Road were lined with my aunts and uncles and first and second cousins: Dijksterhuises (my grandmother's first family) and Schuylers (her second). Kitty-corner from Uncle Barent and Aunt Griet, my aunt Bridget, my father's sister, lived alone in the original Dijksterhuis farmhouse.

During Miss Prellwitz's visit I spent quite a bit of time at Lotte's house myself. I even ate tapioca pudding. The whole family—Barent, Margriet, Lotte, and Lotte's older brother, Willem, who had left home and was now a Methodist minister in Marquette, in the Upper Peninsula—seemed addicted to tapioca pudding, which I couldn't stand; but Miss Prellwitz said it was like a kind of gruel made from the manioc root and that the Mbuti were very fond of it. So I choked it down.

"We used to play a game called Missionary," I said one day, just as we were sitting down to lunch. It was the third day of Miss Prellwitz's visit. "When we were younger." As far as I could remember, this was the longest a missionary had ever stayed. "Corinna Williams was always the leader of the natives—she's a Negro—and Lotte was always the missionary. She'd get dressed up in an old choir robe and preach just like Reverend Boomer, I mean Boomsma. Out in a clearing in the woodlot." The clearing was also the bridge of our ship, the cockpit of our plane, the Railway Post Office car where we sorted mail like my favorite uncle, Gerrit, and staged train robberies. Gerrit had to carry a pistol when he was working, and sometimes Cory and I would ride into town with Uncle Jan, Gerrit's brother, to pick up Gerrit at the end of a run. The train would slow down just beyond the crossing and Gerrit would jump off holding his RPO grip in one hand and waving the other around in the air to help him keep his balance. Sometimes, when he saw us, he'd shake his head, and we'd know that he hadn't foiled any train robbers on this trip; but sometimes he'd pat his revolver, which he carried in a small holster under his coat, and tell us stories about the good old days when the mail trains were loaded with cash payrolls and robbers used dynamite to blow up the tracks and to blast open the doors of the RPO cars.

Uncle Jan was a Watkins dealer, and we stocked the clearing—our hospital and pharmacy—with Watkins products from his garage: herbs and spices, vitamins, bottled tonics, patent medicines. When you got shot during a train robbery, whether you were one of the robbers or one of the RPO clerks, you'd be well taken care of.

"You shouldn't call him that," Aunt Margriet said, meaning Reverend Boomsma.

"And what did *you* do?" asked Miss Prellwitz.

"I'd be a lion, and I'd start roaring out in the jungle—it really is like a jungle out back: raspberry canes and nettles and poison ivy. And then I'd attack the natives. And the missionary." I looked at Lotte, who was sitting with her hands in her lap. Lotte didn't say anything, so I didn't know if she was pleased or otherwise at this story, but I continued. "And sometimes I'd be Superman or Robin Hood or Sir Lancelot or Tarzan and rescue the natives. And the missionary, of course."

There had been no explicit sex in my fantasies at that time, because I hadn't known what explicit sex was, but I could clearly remember the little tingle I'd felt whenever I rescued Cory and took her off on the back of my steed to a place vaguely based on Sherwood Forest, where I turned into a Robin Hood figure presiding over a band of merry men, and over Cory and Lotte and my other cousins too. I hadn't understood my emotions at the time, or the damp spots on my pajamas.

"Your mother wouldn't let you wear your Superman costume on the swing," Lotte said. "She was afraid it would get caught on something and choke you. And she wouldn't let you play with your sword either after you hit Lucia with it." (Lucia was one of my female cousins—there were fifteen of them—on Dijksterhuis Corners, though most of them were Schuylers rather than Dijksterhuises.)

"I had a Superman costume," I said, since no one else seemed to have anything to say, "and a Sir Lancelot outfit, made out of cardboard and tinfoil, and a wooden sword that my dad made out of a piece of lath. My mother's English," I explained to Miss Prellwitz. "She used to read the King Arthur stories to me. We had a book of Robin Hood stories too, and she taught me how to play chess."

"Where did she come from in England?"

"She didn't come from England herself," I said, "but my grandmother did. She ran away from home when she was nineteen and came over in steerage to live with a cousin in Chicago. My dad built a little house for her next to ours, but she's dead now."

Miss Prellwitz smiled. "Would you like me to tell you a story about a *real* lion?"

Miss Prellwitz, who was a good storyteller, had seen many things in the jungle, or forest, that most people will never see. She'd seen the Pygmies—the Mbuti—drive a lion into a net; she'd seen an Mbuti warrior kill an elephant all by himself; and she'd heard the song of something called the *molimo* and seen the dance of death.

Lunch consisted of olive loaf and mayonnaise on white bread, and more tapioca pudding. I could see the little china desert bowls lined up on the counter next to the toaster. Miss Prellwitz sang two verses of "Amazing Grace" in the Bantu language, and then she prayed in English. Unlike Reverend Boomsma, she spoke simply and clearly, aiming her words directly at us, like a Mbuti warrior thrusting his spear upward into an elephant's stomach.

"Dear Lord and Heavenly Father," she said, "help us to live a life of service rather than selfishness; help us to be mindful of the needs of others. We are like the Samaritan woman at the well. She did not recognize you, but you spoke to her and she listened. Speak to us now, for you know that our hearts are restless and will not find ease until they rest in thee." She gave my hand a little squeeze to indicate that the prayer was over. We both looked up and smiled at each other; and then the others, accustomed to longer graces, looked up and smiled too.

Looking back, I've sometimes thought it was the tapioca pudding that saved me. I could imagine living in a hut made out of saplings in the Negro village on the edge of the forest, or in a leafy shelter in a Pygmy camp in the middle of the forest itself. I could imagine being tested in the hunt—if Miss Prellwitz had been invited to go along on a hunt, why wouldn't I be invited too? I could imagine singing hymns (with Miss Prellwitz) in a church built of palm logs; I could imagine eating moss and berries and wild honey and chunks of antelope meat that had been wrapped in leaves and roasted in the embers of an open fire. But the prospect of eating tapioca pudding day in and day out was more than I could handle, and when I refused a second bowl, saying that I was too full, really, they all looked at me and at one another and shook their heads, and I knew *I* wouldn't be going to Africa.

Summer was winding down. Peach season was over. The migrant workers had already started picking the early apples, Jonathans and Transparents. My mother had taken me to Niles to buy a new pair of school shoes with sharkskin toes that wouldn't scuff too badly. I had very narrow heels and couldn't wear the penny loafers that I wanted desperately. A week went by and still Miss Prellwitz, who was planning to go back to England to get married before returning to Africa with her husband, stayed on. The sense of expectancy surrounding my cousin's vocation increased. And then on Saturday night some of the members of the vestry, including Cory's dad, showed up at Dijksterhuis Corners, and we knew something was about to happen.

I could hear Aunt Else, Uncle Jan's wife, calling in Anna and Maria, breaking up the game of Red Rover that the younger cousins were playing under the yard lights by the garage. Cory and I were sitting by the well pump like two people waiting for a storm to break. We could hear the music of the pickers in the distance—guitar and harmonica and the scrape of a washboard. Soon it would be time for us to go in too, but we were hanging back. It was getting hard to see Cory, whose skin was as dark as the semisweet Hershey bars that we bought at the bowling alley when we walked home from school together instead of taking the bus, but I could hear her playing with the safety clasp of her ID bracelet.

"What do you think it's like?" I asked.

"I think it's like a woman who's going to have a baby and she's overdue, and here comes the doctor now." She laughed and pointed at Reverend Boomsma, arriving late in his old Ford coupe. His black briefcase banged against his leg as he walked to the back door of the house without seeing us.

"It will all be decided tonight," I said.

"What's to decide?"

"She must have heard her calling," I said. "That's why everyone's showing up now. She's either going to Africa to do missionary work or she's going to Albion." Albion was the Methodist college, halfway across the bottom of the state, where her brother had studied for the ministry.

"If somebody called *me* from Albion College and told me to come, I'd be there in two shakes."

"What if they called you from Africa?"

"Maybe," she said. "Someday. I'd go anywhere."

"Voco, vocare," I said. "To call."

"I know," she said. "I'm taking Latin too, remember."

"It's a *calling.* I keep thinking about that."

"I'll be lucky if Lakeside calls me." Lakeside was the new junior college between Bridgman and St. Joe. I was destined for the University of Chicago, my mother's alma mater, but I didn't like to think that far ahead.

"Do you want to go listen to the music?"

"I don't want to get a whipping, if that's what you're asking, because that's what'll happen if Mama finds out."

The picking camp was strictly off limits, doubly off limits at night. It was like the one room in the castle we weren't supposed to enter, or the magic gift we weren't supposed to open no matter what, or the one tree in the garden we weren't supposed to eat from.

"Just for a few minutes," I said. "She won't find out."

We followed the path that Cory's father had cleared, with a brush cutter, through the "jungle"—the old woodlot that separated the houses along Appleton Road from the peach and apple orchards that my dad and Uncle Piet and my grandfather had planted back in the twenties. This was the Michigan Fruit Belt, and Berrien County was one of the six richest agricultural counties in the United States— at least that's what everyone said—and our own orchards, almost two full sections, seemed to confirm this by producing between forty and fifty thousand bushels of peaches and apples every year. Cory's dad, Cap, was a kind of foreman. He contracted with an undertaker down in Georgia to put together the picking crew for the summer and helped my dad and Uncle Piet with the pruning in the winter.

We didn't speak till we came to the little clearing in the briers and nettles where Lotte had once preached to the natives. I had a clearer idea now about explicit sex than I'd had in the days of my heroic-rescue fantasies, or even than I'd had two years ago, when Barbara Kramer and Donny Holbrook had caused a minor stir by going off together at a class party out at Potter Dunes. They'd reached an age (my mother explained) when kids wanted to touch each other. It hadn't made any sense to me at the time—why would kids want to touch each other?—but it made sense now. But though my understanding was clearer now, it wasn't perfectly clear. I'd studied the two-year-old pinup calendar from the Harris Lumber Yard that I'd bought from Mr. Harris's son, Alvin, who was in my class, studied it like a detective studying the scene of a crime, looking for clues; and my father had taken me to watch Emmet Dziepak's father breed his big Poland China boar, Gunner, to Harlan Portinga's sows, but that was a mystery too. How did you translate *that* into human love? I couldn't picture Cory, or any woman, in the contraption they built for the sows to keep them from being crushed by the weight of the boar. Nor did I recognize my own longings in the little volume called *Into Manhood* that appeared mysteriously on my desk one day.

But there was another mystery, too, that was equally puzzling. As far as I can remember no one ever said anything, in all our years in school together, that might have made Cory feel at all self-conscious about being a Negro, and in fact her parents were pillars of the church—Aunt Flo in the choir and in the kitchen, Cap on the vestry and in the basement looking after the old furnace. We were not, in fact, naïve about race. My mother kept the new novels by Ralph Ellison and James Baldwin on the coffee table in our living room, and she had in fact almost single-handedly put a stop to the annual minstrel show. And yet no one was at all surprised that Cory's date for the class dances that had begun our freshman year was always a cousin from Benton Harbor. It didn't seem strange to me, or to anyone else; it was just the way things were. And that's what was really strange. I'd breezed through *Go Tell It on the Mountain* and *Invisible Man,* and I'd shared my mother's indignation at the minstrel show; but John Grimes and the Invisible Man were creatures from another world.

Cory, on the other hand, was right there in front of me—right next to me, actually—and the knowledge that she and her cousin danced with each other and no one else, and that no one thought it strange, left a taste in my mouth as mysterious and troubling as a boy's first taste of alcohol.

I wanted to dance with Cory now, jitterbug or box step, just to touch her, taste her. My hands cupped; saliva rushed to my mouth.

"Do you remember how we used to play Missionary?" I said.

"I remember sitting on a log and listening to Lotte preach. She was more interesting than Reverend Boomsma, I'll say that for her." She looked around for the log, but it was almost too dark to see it in the woodlot.

"Over there," I said.

"There" was the edge of our little clearing in the brush, hardly more than a widening of the path.

I could hear the music a little more clearly now. I'd heard it all my life, usually from a distance, though sometimes when I'd slept outside in my father's old pup tent I'd snuck over to the picking camp and spied on the migrant workers, who followed the ripening fruit crops up north from Georgia and Mississippi, and listened to the singing. I hadn't really thought of it as music. Music was something else; music was the songs we played on the jukebox in the bowling alley: "Don't Let the Stars Get in Your Eyes," "You Belong to Me," "How Much Is That Doggie in the Window?" "Vaya Con Dios," "You, You, You," "Three Coins in the Fountain." Music was the choir cantatas at Christmas and Easter, and my mother's long-playing records, and piano lessons from Mr. Haptonstahl, and then the recitals at the end of the year ("Spinning Song" and "La Cucaracha," and then, more recently, Handel's *Harmonious Blacksmith* and Chopin preludes). My mother played the piano too—lots of Brahms and Chopin—and piano lessons were non-negotiable.

I took a step toward Cory but I didn't quite know how to begin doing what I wanted to do, so I settled for taking her hand, and we followed the path to the loading dock at the back of the packing shed. We had to cross an open area where the trucks had packed the dirt so hard it didn't turn muddy even when it rained in the spring.

The dormitories for the single men and women were on the far side of the packing shed, separated from each other by about twenty shacks for married couples. We went in the back of the packing shed, around the culling table and the grader, to the big sliding front door, which was open about six inches. We were close enough to smell the remains of the barbecue, and to see the migrant workers gathered around the remains of a small fire, and to hear the music. Cory looked out the door and when she turned back to me I kissed her, not hitting her mouth squarely, but at least touching her lips.

"Marty," she said, "what's got into you?"

What had gotten into me was that I was seeing her in a strange new light; I was falling in love with her. She was my Guinevere, my Maid Marion, my dark-skinned Jane of the jungle, with untamable hair and hands so quick she could reach down and catch a mouse scampering across the floor of the packing shed. But who was I? Still the little boy who'd pushed her in the tire swing in Uncle Piet's backyard? The little boy in his Sir Lancelot getup who'd rescued her from the lion?

"You've never kissed a girl before, have you?"

"I've kissed lots of girls," I said.

"Name one."

"That would be telling."

"You haven't got anything to tell."

"I've kissed Dixie Carpenter," I protested; "and Frances Cochrane. I kissed Frances after the dance."

Cory laughed, and then pulled my face toward hers and kissed me hard on the mouth, but by the time I figured out that I was supposed to open my mouth a little so that our tongues could touch, she'd pulled away. "I've got to go back now," she said. "You coming?"

I started to follow, listening for a moment in the darkness to figure out which way she'd gone. I could hear her footsteps, and her fingertips brushing the sizing rollers on the grader; could hear her opening the door next to the loading dock and jumping onto the hard dirt, letting the door slam behind her. I started to follow her, thinking she might wait for me in the little clearing in the woodlot, but something called me back, the cry of a harmonica and a sound I'd never heard before. I know now that it was the new man, Chesterfield, who drove the tractor that pulled the wagons in from the orchards, and I know now that he was playing the ugliest guitar I've ever seen in my life, a guitar made out of some kind of metal and painted the color of a baby's diarrhea; and I know now that he was playing it with a knife that he held between the first two fingers of his left hand. But I didn't know that then. All I knew was that the music filled me up, like Miss Prellwitz's prayer, like Cory's kiss, like a wound. And I thought of the beautiful color pictures in my *Boy's King Arthur* of the king thrusting his spear into the traitor Mordred, and of Guinevere praying in the cell of the convent where she spends her last days.

I couldn't cross the lighted area in front of the packing shed without being seen, so I jumped off the loading dock in the back and scooted along the edge of the jungle till I was covered by one of the big outhouses that my father relocated every year. The sounds came into me. I breathed them, inhaled them, along with the odors of the outhouse and the smoke from the fire. Through my mouth as well as my ears. Through my eyes. Chesterfield was singing a song about love, but not the kind of love I knew about from movies and from the radio, not "No Other Love" or "Till I Waltz Again With You." This was more like someone driving nails into a piece of oak: *Moon goin' down, Lord, North star about to shine.* The words pierced me. I had to get closer. I had to *see* as well as hear: *My baby tole me, She don't want me hangin' round.* And then a hand clamped down hard over my mouth so I couldn't yell and a strong arm pinned my arms.

"Jesus, it's Marty."

There were two of them.

"Marty? Marty, what the hell you doin'?"

"Jonah, is that you? I just wanted to listen."

"Your old man know where you are?"

"Yes," I said.

He looked at me. "Like hell."

"He don't mean no harm," said the other man, whose name was Jake.

"I don't mean no harm," I said. "I was just listening."

He grabbed me by the arm and pulled me into the circle of firelight.

Chesterfield looked like he was attacking the guitar, striking it with the heel of his right hand and hitting the string with his thumb at the same time. A train pulled into the station at midnight. The singer heard the whistle blow and saw his baby climb on board.

I'd been working in the orchards for as long as I could remember. My father paid me twelve cents an hour my first year for dusting the faces of the bushels with a big paintbrush. Later I learned how to face the bushels myself and fill them and turn them in the basket turner at the end of the line. But I preferred loading them onto the big trucks that took them to the market in Benton Harbor or to chain store warehouses in Chicago and Detroit. My father didn't want me to get a hernia, but I didn't care. You didn't get as much peach fuzz on you, and it seemed more manly.

Some of these men and women I'd known all my life, but now I was seeing them for the first time. For a moment I was not the boss's son but a stranger surrounded by a circle of black faces. Soft. Not black either, if you looked closely, but chocolate, coffee, ebony, honey, red, tan, alabaster. All with large eyes pointed at me. I *was* the boss's son too.

"Run on home, Marty," said a woman named June, who worked at the culling table. "We don't want no trouble."

"Let him sit with you," Jake said. "He don't mean no harm."

"How you know what he mean?" the woman said.

"It's just a kid."

Chesterfield was doing something to the guitar, changing the pitch of the strings. My heart pounded. I wanted to hear him play. Jake was still holding my arm while the woman inspected me. Pretty soon the guitar started to cry, like a man crying, and Jake let go of my arm. The music began to fill me again. I wanted to sing, I wanted to rush over to Chesterfield and put my hands on the guitar; I wanted to touch it.

> *There was a time I didn't know your name,*
> *Why should I worry, cry in vain,*

*But now she's gone gone gone, and I don't worry,
'Cause I'm sittin' on top of the world.*

The next morning I went to see my cousin Lotte. Uncle Barent's car was gone, the kitchen was empty, but Lotte was up in her room, sitting on the edge of her bed.

"What happened?" I asked.

I was expecting her to be radiant. But she was quiet. She had been called to do missionary work in Africa, she said, about a hundred miles from Miss Prellwitz's mission, near a Belgian *station de chasse* on the Epulu River in the Congo, where her knowledge of French—she'd been in my mother's French classes—would be useful. She'd be leaving in a week for training at the missionary headquarters in Léopoldville. Her clothes had been sorted into piles on the floor. She showed me her list from the mission of things she'd need. Miss Prellwitz had given it to her.

We sat together for a few minutes without speaking.

"Are you happy?"

"Yes."

"Happy that it's over, or happy that you're going to Africa?"

"Just happy."

"You don't look happy. I wouldn't be happy," I said, "unless I could stay in a hut with Miss Prellwitz."

She gave me a look to let me know how childish I was being. "You're not me."

"Lotte, I know I'm not you. But going off to Africa? Is that what you want to do? Live in a hut?"

"Don't talk like that," she said. "There's a mission school, and houses." She showed me a picture. Three white figures posed for a photo, surrounded by about thirty Bantu villagers.

"What about the Pygmies?" I asked. "The Mbuti."

"They live in the forest," she said.

"Do you really want to leave here?"

"It's my vocation," she said.

I started to argue; I started to tell her that *I'd* never wanted to go anywhere or do anything other than work in the orchards with my father and Cap and Uncle Piet, but something stopped me. A sudden thought: "I think I've found my vocation too," I said, for I too had heard something calling me from afar. *Voco, vocare.* Something that would take me away too, maybe even farther than Africa.

2

Homecoming

1955

IT WAS DURING rehearsals for the junior class play in the spring of
1955, almost a year after our first kiss, that my passions for Cory
became seriously inflamed. We put on a performance of Ayn Rand's
The Night of January 16th, and Cory played the role of Karen Andre,
a secretary accused of murdering her boss, international tycoon
Bjorn Faulkner. (Miss Thornton, who directed the play, made us say
Buh-jorn instead of Bee-yorn, but on the last performance, on Saturday night, we all said Bee-yorn, which my mother said was the correct pronunciation.) In any case, I was Cory's defense attorney, or
Karen's. Every night a new jury was impaneled from the audience,
and at the end of the performance the jury would decide on Karen's
guilt or innocence. My own character (the defense attorney) was not
particularly exciting, but he had a great closing speech, which I threw

myself into. "Who is on trial in this case?" I would thunder as best I could. "Karen Andre? No! It's you, ladies and gentlemen of the jury, who are here on trial. It is your own souls that will be brought to light when your decision is rendered!" We put on three performances—a Thursday matinee and two evening performances on the weekend—and Cory, or Karen, was acquitted all three times.

But the really exciting thing was that the version of the play that we performed turned out to be a special version for high school performances. All the juicy parts had been cut out entirely. Frances Cochrane discovered a copy of the original in the public library—a script, actually, that had been used by the actress playing Karen Andre in a summer stock performance in Lakeside back in 1936. In this version Karen Andre, whose lines were heavily underlined, was not simply Bjorn Faulkner's secretary; she was his mistress. And not only that: Bjorn had had a platinum gown made for Karen, which he would heat up in the fireplace and then place on her naked body, her "shameless skin," as Magda Svenson, the snoopy Swedish house-keeper (reluctantly played by Frances herself, who thought she should have had the lead), testifies. "As hot as she can stand." This was big news in December 1955 in Appleton, where the nude photo of Marilyn Monroe in the first issue of *Playboy* was still just a rumor.

These lines might have been cut out of our version of the play, but I wasn't about to cut them out of my fantasies, and as I made my impassioned speech to the jury, I was imagining the platinum gown, spread out in front of our fireplace, waiting to be placed on Cory's naked body; I was imagining Cory laughing like Karen if it burned; I was imagining kissing the burned parts like Bjorn Faulkner, "wild like tiger!"

It was Cory who decided to read more Ayn Rand. She checked *The Fountainhead* out of the public library and a small group of us—mostly kids who'd been in the play and who were in my mother's

French class—passed it around, taking turns checking it out again when it came due. Cory and I were both working long hours in the orchards—she worked at the culling table, and if I wasn't loading one of the trucks, I was driving one of the tractors out in the field—but it was the summer before our senior year and we had driver's licenses, and someone always had a car, and two or three nights a week we'd drive to New Buffalo for ice cream at Piggy's or to Bridgman for pie and coffee at the Toddle Inn. And we'd talk. It was as close as any of us had come to philosophy—what my mother called "the life of the mind"—and we were thrilled, except for Frances, who was a Christian Scientist, by the fact that Howard Roark had become an architect because he *didn't believe in God*, because he didn't like the shapes of things on earth and wanted to change them. And we were disturbed but thrilled too by the contemptuous way that he rapes Dominique in her bedroom after their encounter in the quarry, and the way that Dominique poses in the nude for the central statue in Roark's Temple to the Human Spirit, and the way she marries Peter Keating and then, on her wedding night, fucks Roark in his apartment. I liked the way the *f* felt between my front teeth and my lower lips when I said "fucked," and the way the *k* turned into a *t: fuct*.

We weren't naïve; we knew that the world was full of evil seducers and weak women; but the doings in *The Fountainhead* were beyond our ken, enough to make us dizzy, and my mother actually encouraged us. At the beginning of August, just before my birthday, she drove us over to Michigan City to see the movie, which had been made in 1949. It seemed a little flat to me. I guess I wanted to see Gary Cooper do to Patricia Neal what Howard Roark had done to Dominique Francon, but of course that didn't happen.

My mother, who had enjoyed the movie, summed it up on the way home: "You have to live for yourself, heroically, if you want to achieve something for mankind." The whole thing was a little preachy, but the last scene was good: Dominique going up in the hoist, up up up, looking down on the banks and the courthouses and the churches, to join Roark at the top of his monument to the human spirit. For a while I wanted to become an architect.

At the beginning of the summer my mother and I had had a falling-out. I had wanted to stop taking piano lessons from Mr. Haptonstahl and devote myself to the guitar.

"You're playing Handel and Chopin now," she'd protested, "and we're going to learn the two-piano version of *Rhapsody in Blue*. Roy's going to pick up the music at Carl Fischer in Chicago, and he's going to have his own piano moved into the church for the recital." Roy was Mr. Haptonstahl.

"*The Harmonious Blacksmith* is too hard," I said. "Besides, it's boring. And besides again, I've found another vocation."

"A vocation? What are you talking about?"

"*Voco, vocare. To call.* I've had a calling."

My mother stubbed out her cigarette in an ashtray on the piano—she smoked French cigarettes—and ran her fingers through her hair, which she wore twisted behind her head at school but let fall around her shoulders when she was at home.

"What about the Gershwin?"

I didn't know what to say. I liked Gershwin, in fact. Gershwin and Chopin. But I liked their music because it gave me the same feeling that Chesterfield's music did, only not so intense. Chesterfield's music was like a painful longing, but it was a longing that was better than *having* something. It didn't make sense. So I didn't say anything. But my mother must have read my mind.

"You know, it's wonderful the way he incorporates so much of the Negro spirit into all his music, not just *Rhapsody in Blue*."

We were in the living room. My mother, who was sitting at the Steinway B that she and Mr. Haptonstahl had selected at Lyon and Healy in Chicago, and that was really too big for our living room, began to pick out the opening clarinet solo: *ta, ta, ta, TAAA*.

*   *   *

Every evening during peach and apple season I lugged my mother's big heavy Webcor tape recorder out to the picking camp, along with a hundred-foot extension cord—long enough to reach the packing shed—and recorded every song I could get Chesterfield to play; and then at the end of the season I gave him all the money I'd earned—money that was supposed to help pay for my tuition at the University of Chicago—for his metal guitar, which I kept hidden under the bed in my room.

"That's the ugliest thing I've ever seen," my mother said when she found it and dragged the whole story out of me; and I couldn't disagree. "You spent your tuition money for *that*? Who ever heard of a painted guitar?" She wanted my father to make Chesterfield return the money, but my father said that I'd made a deal and would have to stick to it.

There were no guitar teachers in Appleton, and the only instruction book I could find in the music store in Niles was in Spanish: Emilio Pujol's *Escuela razonada de la guitarra*. I figured out that *p = pulgar = thumb* and that *i = indice = index finger*, and so on. And I figured out the notes, which are more complicated than on the piano. On the piano the notes are all lined up in a row, but on the guitar the same notes show up in three or sometimes four different places. School started; Mr. Haptonstahl brought the two-piano version of *Rhapsody in Blue* to my first lesson, and my mother threw herself into the second piano part. I continued to take lessons without kicking up too much of a fuss, but I never learned the solo part of *Rhapsody in Blue*. Nor did I learn any of the other piano music that my mother ordered from Fischer's in an attempt to deflect my interest from my new vocation—Art Tatum, Eubie Blake, Lionel Hampton, Duke Ellington. I liked this music well enough, and sight-read my way through arrangements of "Take the A Train" and "I'm in the Mood for Love"; but my heart never leaped up to meet the more complex jazz chords, my feet didn't dance; my soul wasn't stirred by the love lyrics, which seemed bland to me compared to Chesterfield's songs, which I continued to listen to over and over, on the tape recorder, after the season was done.

> *I told you, you could go,*
> *And don't come back here no mo';*
> *It's your last time,*
> *Shakin' it in the bed with me.*

I sang along with the tape, keeping my voice down, especially on the last line, which I found terribly exciting in all its variations: "I mean twistin'; I mean turnin'; I mean doin' that monkey dog and all that slop." Though not as exciting as the mystery of the opening: Why did the singer tell her she could go? Why didn't he want her to come back here no more?

Alone in my room, I pondered these mysteries. At the time I couldn't separate them from my feelings for Cory, and in fact I've never been able to separate them. I seemed to be caught up in two different stories, but sometimes I thought that one was a translation of the other, and sometimes I thought that they were both translations of still another story that was too old for anyone to remember. Looking back, I can see that these two stories run through my life like the two rails of a railroad track, and when I stand between them and look down the track, I can see them meet at the horizon and I experience a kind of longing that almost breaks my heart, though now I've learned to expect it from time to time and in fact to regard it as the central experience in my life, something I couldn't live without. At the time, however, I thought that if only I could learn this song or that song, I'd be satisfied. And I thought the same thing about Cory: that if only I could hold her in my arms and kiss her, I'd be, well, satisfied. But it didn't work out that way, and when I hear that old song "Corinna, Corinna," I'm filled with a longing for Cory;

and when I think of Cory, I'm filled with a longing for that old song, even though I can play it in three different versions, even though I've held Cory in my arms and kissed her.

Corinna, Corinna, where you been so long;
Corinna, Corinna, where you been so long;
Ain't had no lovin', since you been gone.

It wasn't our only falling-out. A liberal Democrat in a conservative Republican town, an intellectual in a farming community, my mother tended to be critical of causes that were popular and supportive of those that were not, and she expressed her views in a weekly column that she wrote for the *Appleton River Gazette*. She was in favor of putting fluoride in the water system but opposed to the Atomic bomb tests held in the Bikini Atoll; in favor of Truman's civil rights package but opposed to Strom Thurmond's Dixiecrats; in favor of abolishing segregation in the armed forces but opposed to Senator Russell's plan to create a racial relocation bureau; she made sure that the local library stocked copies of the books of prominent Negro writers—James Baldwin, Richard Wright, Ralph Ellison, and Gwendolyn Brooks; but it was her opposition to the annual minstrel show sponsored by the Lions Club that turned people against her. It wasn't a minstrel show, really, more of a local talent show, but the men wore blackface, and the end men (Mr. Stone, who ran the hardware store, and Mr. Harrison, the Ford dealer) told an endless string of Sambo jokes that no one seemed to find offensive till my mother held them up to ridicule in her column and invited newspapers from all over southern Michigan and northern Indiana, and Chicago too, to cover the show one year.

So I was surprised at the strength of her objection to my plan to take Cory to the Homecoming Dance. I had expected, in fact, that she would be pleased, that she would be my ally.

Homecoming was a major event in Appleton, as it was in all the neighboring towns. Because it hadn't changed in a hundred years, it generated almost as many expectations as Christmas. It was our last year together, and we put our class float together, as we always did, in the garage at the Cochrane Funeral Home, featuring (as we always did) pumpkins and cornstalks and the fake grass that Mr. Cochrane laid out to cover up the raw dirt around open graves. Competition for the Golden Apple, which was awarded to the class that got the most points for demonstrating school spirit, was intense. The queen of the winning class would get to carry the Golden Apple on her own float with her own king. The captain of the football team, unless he also happened to be the king of the winning class, would ride in the back of a Ford convertible supplied by the Harrison agency on Main Street, right across from the Potter Featherbone Company.

When Cory's cousin couldn't make it for the Homecoming Dance, which was going to be held in the old opera house instead of in the school gymnasium, and I proposed to escort her myself, and she said *sure*, I knew, and I'm sure she knew too, that we were entering forbidden territory. Nonetheless, I kissed her on the way home from school. It was at Cedar Creek, which never had much water in it unless the river flooded. Someone had dumped a load of old spark plugs into the creek, right below the Spruce Street bridge, instead of taking them out to the dump. There were thousands of them. We stood next to each other, looking down at the spark plugs, and then I kissed her again. I'd kissed several other girls by that time, so I thought I knew what I was doing.

"Let's go down to the river," I said.

"Why not." It wasn't really a question. It wasn't an answer either.

"Are you mad at me?"

"No. Why?

"We could go to my house and get something to eat. My mom has a meeting after school."

"We could."

"We could do our French homework."

"On ne peut même pas sortir en hiver"—a line from our textbook.

"T'as tort, Giselle, c'est merveilleux de patiner sur la rivière lorsqu'elle est gelée." In my mother's French class Cory was Giselle and I was Jean-Paul.

"What's the French word for *spark plug?"* she asked.

"I don't know," I said.

We walked down Beech Street, on the far east side of town, and then over to Main Street, which turned into Appleton Road—our books in our satchels.

It was the autumnal equinox. According to Mr. Dutton, our general science teacher, a switch had been thrown in nature, as if the sun had hit a trip wire when it crossed the celestial equator. A hawk was drifting south, over the Dziepak barn just north of town, and beyond the hawk a skein of snow geese raveled and unraveled. My mother had started putting out food for the winter finches. We could still see shooting stars, Mr. Dutton had said, if we stayed up late enough—leftovers from the Perseid meteor showers of mid-August. And if we got up *really* early we'd see Orion rising in the east.

We went to my house and ate butter and peanut butter and brown sugar on saltines and then I poured about an inch of my mother's white wine into each of two glasses and we sipped it as we did our French homework. Junior year we'd worked our way through the first half of *L'Etranger* by Albert Camus, and this year we were reading Jean-Paul Sartre's *Huis clos,* which had gotten my mother in trouble with Mr. Collings, the principal, the only man who could make her cry. He didn't know a word of French himself, but he'd received some complaints from parents about *L'Etranger,* and during the first week of school he'd decided that *Huis clos* wasn't much better and insisted that she find another reading, and she'd come home in tears of rage and frustration, and not for the first time. But this time my father didn't bother to comfort her as he usually did. He roared off in her Chevy, which she'd left at the side of the house, blocking the drive, and when he came back he said that Mr. Collings had changed his mind. His face was red, and the veins in his neck stood out like ropes.

No one ever found out exactly what had happened—it was reported that my father had told Mrs. Henderson, Mr. Collings's secretary, to "skedaddle," and she'd skedaddled—but the episode certainly whetted our appetites for *Huis clos*, so we plowed ahead at the rate of four pages an hour, and sometimes even met in the evenings, at our house—so my mother could help with the translation when we got stuck—to read it aloud. The girls all wanted to be Estelle, not Inez. Except Cory. "Hell is other people," she liked to say, and soon that became our mantra: *"L'enfer c'est les autres."*

Frankly, I didn't see why Garcin didn't want to go to bed with Estelle, even with Inez watching. I'd have gone to bed with Cory with Frances Cochrane watching. So what?

When I heard my mother's car in the drive I quickly washed out the wineglasses, ran a towel over them, and put them back in the cupboard above the sink, upside down.

My mother, undoing the clip that held her hair in place, greeted us in French: *"Bonsoir, mes chers."* She was in her fifties, but she always looked more elegant in her soft, tailored suits than the other women teachers, who wore square-cut clothes that fitted them like cardboard boxes.

"Bonsoir, madame."

"Je suis ravie que tu sois là, Giselle."

"Moi aussi," said Cory.

"It's not really a *date*," I explained to my mother after Cory had gone home. "It's just that something happened and her cousin won't be able to escort her this year."

"What happened?" my mother wanted to know.

"How should I know? He's got some other plans."

"I just told Dixie Carpenter's mother this afternoon that you'd take Dixie." Dixie's mother, who taught English at the high school, was my mother's only close friend, except for Mr. Haptonstahl, and Alan Marckwardt, who'd turned the old depot into a used bookstore. Actually, I'd already been invited to go to the dance by Dixie herself, who was desperate for a date. She'd passed me a note in geometry class, and then her mother must have spoken to my mother at the staff meeting, and now my mother was speaking to me.

Dixie was a nice girl, large boned, loose, and elastic—she'd surprised everyone by making a convincing gun moll in *The Night of January 16th;* but I was too much in love with Cory by then and refused to cooperate.

The dance was still three weeks away, and I might have pressed my case harder; but Cory's mother, Aunt Flo, was just as opposed to the plan as my mother, and so, that was that. It hadn't really been a date anyway, and when Aunt Flo and I listened to the last game of the World Series together, neither one of us mentioned it. Aunt Flo and I were both avid Cubs fans, and the next best thing to having the Cubs win—which they never did, though Aunt Flo thought that maybe with Ernie Banks they'd have a shot at a pennant—was to listen to the Yankees lose, which they did in 1955, to the Dodgers, the first team ever to win a seven-game series after losing the first two games.

A certain amount of vandalism was tolerated and even expected at homecoming, and we were planning to paint "Class of '56" on the water tower of the Potter Featherbone Company. It was, after all, our last year together. Twelve years together for most of us. But tension was high in the funeral home garage, where we were putting the finishing touches on the class float. Jack Graham, the captain of the football team and homecoming king, was going to ride on the Lions

Club float with Lisa Baxter. Jack was dating Frances Cochrane, and the two were sniping at each other. Everyone knew that Frances should have been the queen, but for some reason the judges had selected Lisa, a new girl from Chicago, whose father was the new vice president of the Featherbone Company. Lisa reminded everyone of Frances's cousin from Detroit, who'd set us boys on our ears by pressing her large, firm breasts against us while slow dancing to "Three Coins in the Fountain" and "Hernando's Hideaway," and by sticking her tongue in our ears, and by French kissing us. Lisa was not part of the float committee. Allen Springer, who tried to keep us focused on the float, kept yelling and getting upset. If the float didn't come together we'd lose the Golden Apple to the juniors. It had never happened, but it could. Dixie Carpenter wasn't speaking to me. She was still mad because I'd turned down her invitation to the Homecoming Dance, even though she was going with a cousin from out of town, a student at Michigan State in Lansing, and I wasn't going at all. Cory and I were weaving strips of crepe paper through the wire mesh that formed the skirts of the float wagon.

When the float was done to our satisfaction, we locked up the garage, and Frances, who was mad at Jack, went into the house. We debated on whether to leave a sentry to prevent the juniors from sabotaging our work, but decided against it. We drove two cars—my mother's two-door Bel Air and Jack's dad's Town and Country wagon with wood paneling—along the tracks next to the lumber yard and then to the lot behind the Potter Featherbone Company, where there was a hole in the chain-link fence. Some boards had been driven into the ground to block the hole, but they came out easily. There were several huge buckeye trees behind the factory yard and more in the yard in the front. Cory and I had gathered buckeyes here every fall for years. Alvin Harris, whose father owned the lumber yard, had brought a can of purple paint. Alvin checked the ladder on the tower leg to make sure it was secure. Then he backed away. It was eleven o'clock; not much chance of being seen.

Alvin climbed up the ladder, ten feet, twenty feet, and then thought better of it. We stood around for twenty minutes, smoking cigarettes, waiting for someone to take the lead.

It was Jack who finally stepped forward. "Who's going with?"

The silence was painful. Embarrassing. The tower looks much more intimidating when you're standing at the base, in the dark, than it does from the school parking lot. Someone said it was a hundred feet high. Someone else said two hundred. Like a six-story building. Or eight stories. Maybe ten stories. How many feet were in a *story* anyway?

"I will," Cory said. She was standing next to me.

"Somebody give me a belt," Jack said.

"Use your own belt."

"I don't want my pants to fall down while I'm climbing. Alvin, give me your belt."

Alvin slipped his belt out of his pants and handed it to Jack, who looped it through the handle of the paint can and slipped it over his shoulder.

"You shouldn't have brought a whole gallon. We only need a quart. Hell, a pint."

"A quart can doesn't have a handle," Alvin said.

"You coming?" He looked at Cory. She was standing beside him now. "Anyone else?"

No one said anything.

Jack climbed up a few more rungs on the ladder and looked down. He was still smoking a cigarette. He spat and nodded his head as if we'd all confirmed his low opinion of us. He was the tough sergeant in a World War II film, looking for a few brave men to go with him on a tough mission. No luck.

I tried to get up my nerve—I was almost there, but not quite—when Jack flipped his cigarette butt into our midst and started climbing higher. With Cory behind him. At that moment I knew I could do it. But I also knew it was too late.

They climbed up higher and higher till we couldn't see them anymore. The moon was bright, but they were covered by the dark shadows of the huge buckeye trees. We could hear them, though, their feet on the ladder, flakes of rust dropping down like snowflakes.

Everyone was silent. We were a bunch of cowards. No one said it, but I kept replaying the scene in my imagination, trying to make it come out differently, trying to reinterpret my own role. I was Garcin. I'd flinched.

When they finally came back down, Jack still had the paint can slung around his shoulder.

"What happened?"

"Be my guest," he said.

Silence.

"There's no way to get up on the catwalk," he said.

"There's a trapdoor," someone said.

"That's bullshit, you jerk." Silence. "OK—be my guest." No one seemed to understand. "There's *no trapdoor*. It's like you'd have to climb upside down and grab on to the edge of the catwalk." But this still wasn't enough. "Be my guest," he said again.

No one said anything.

"Fuck this shit. Anybody got a cigarette?"

And then Avery, the town constable, drove by and we all scattered. Cory and I drove around for a while before heading home.

"We didn't go all the way," she said as I pulled into her driveway. "Jack was scared." I was still trying to rearrange the evening in my mind to make my own role a little less ignominious. I wasn't having much luck, though, so I was glad to hear her say that Jack was scared.

"I was coming up too," I said, "but Jack didn't want me to. It was too late."

*   *   *

On Friday afternoon I helped my dad and Cap set up the big kegs of cider in the school parking lot, where the floats were lined up, ready for the parade, pulled by tractors or pickup trucks or, in the case of the sophomores, by Frank Dunston's big Belgian draft horses. Uncle Piet and my dad donated the cider every year, and Dixie Carpenter's dad, who ran a doughnut shop in Niles, provided the doughnuts.

No one mentioned our abortive attempt to paint the water tower. From the school parking lot the water tower looked like a big tin can on four spindly legs, like something built with an Erector set.

I hung on to Cory's remark that Jack, who was sitting on the float with Lisa, the new girl from Chicago, had been scared. It got me through the parade, which seemed diminished this year, though everything was the same as it always was. The floats were all pretty much the same: pumpkins and cornstalks and crepe paper skirts. And the visiting marching bands—New Buffalo, Three Oaks, Galien, and New Troy—were spiffy, and our own band, headed up by the Schuyler twins, looked pretty good. The Schuyler twins—second cousins—had already been to State twice with their twin baton-twirling act. The village idiots were there too: Art Holmgren, who generally hung around the post office, and Pat Webster, who some-times spotted pins for my father, who was an avid bowler, on winter afternoons. And the veterans, too big for their old uniforms. Cory and Frances Cochrane rode on the float with the senior class offi-cers. Cory waved as she rode by; Frances kept looking back at the Lions Club float to make sure Jack didn't have his arm around Lisa Baxter.

That night Cory and I painted the tower. We left the football game at halftime, with New Buffalo ahead by three points. Jack had been having a good game, but he'd thrown an interception in the last minute of the first half and New Buffalo had scored. We left my mother's car in the parking lot at the football field, which was west of Main Street, on the south side of the tracks. We waited for a freight train to go by the crossing behind the lumber yard. The boards were where we'd tossed them in our hurry to get out of there the night before.

We crawled through the hole and stopped for a cigarette. I had two of my mother's Gitanes in my shirt pocket. Cory had a whole pack of her dad's Camels. The smoke made me dizzy. I tried, unsuccessfully, to blow rings.

The shadows cast by the buckeye trees thickened the darkness. Cory and I'd gathered buckeyes in mesh onion sacks and then buried them, like treasure, out at Dijksterhuis Corners. And once we planted a buckeye in front of my cousins' back door, thinking it would grow up and block the door so they couldn't use it anymore. Cory inhaled deeply and let the smoke out slowly, like Jean Harlow in *Hell's Angels*. It came out her nose as well as her mouth. She handed it to me. I took a drag and stamped it out.

The can of paint was right where Jack had dropped it, at the base of the tower, Alvin Harris's belt still looped through the wire handle.

I felt sick to my stomach, but I couldn't let Cory, who was standing with one hand on a rung of the ladder, go first.

I was startled by a flash of light. Cory had lit another cigarette.

"You're sure you want to do this?" This was *not* what I'd meant to say!

"Yeah, I'm sure, why?"

"Just asking."

"You scared?"

"I'm not scared. You?"

She shrugged. "What are you doing?"

"I'm shaking the paint." I was starting to shake too, inside.

"You don't have to come," she said.

"What are you talking about?" I picked up the can of paint and slung it over my shoulder.

"Right. What about the brush? *You* got any pockets?"

"No."

"Put the brush in *my* back pocket." When she slipped the brush into my pocket, I felt a little electric shock.

The first part of the climb wasn't too bad. It was just climbing up a ladder. But as we got higher my heart began to slither around inside me like a snake, twisting and turning and striking at the bars of my rib cage whenever I glanced down.

The gallon of paint started to swing back and forth and knock against the brush in my back pocket. My jeans were slipping down. I should have tightened my own belt. I couldn't tug them up without letting go of the tower. The can of paint felt heavier than Christian's burden in *Pilgrim's Progress*, one of the stories my mother used to read to me. I pictured Pilgrim climbing the tower, and then Cory, behind me, as if she were stalking me, a dangerous predator. I could feel her eyes on me, but I was afraid to look down.

When I finally reached the top of the tower leg I understood what Jack meant. There was no opening in the catwalk, no trapdoor, no way to get onto the catwalk except by climbing up a second ladder that tilted out from the leg of the tower to the outer edge of the catwalk. You'd have to hang on like death to keep from falling backward. My feet hurt from the rungs of the ladder. The moon was full. I wanted to yelp like one of the coyotes you could sometimes hear in the late fall, on the other side of the river.

"This is it," I whispered, my voice husky. I could hear Cory beneath me, but she didn't say anything. She'd been this far before. Almost. If she hadn't been there I'd have gone back down. I'd have said it was impossible to climb onto the catwalk with the heavy paint can slung over my shoulder. But Cory was there, and I couldn't propose a retreat. Because I was a boy and Cory was a girl; just because. I had a feeling that what I did now would shape my future, would determine the kind of man I was going to be.

When I made myself look down I could see the top of her head. She tilted her head back and looked up at me. There was no expression on her face. The leg of the tower disappeared into the darkness beneath her. My right arm was wrapped around the leg of the tower, welded to it. I put some weight on the ladder that joined the leg of the tower and the catwalk, first my left hand, then my right, and there was a great rush of wings as hundreds of pigeons, which had been roosting on the catwalk, took to the air like souls taking flight for heaven. The tank itself, which blotted out the entire sky, seemed to be tilting toward me, as if I were pulling it over on top of me. The paint can shifted, pulled me backward like someone trying to choke me. I pulled myself upward, hooking my elbows around the rungs of the ladder. I used my left arm to readjust the belt, and then I pulled again, harder and harder, till I reached the top rung.

I could hear Cory's breathing as clearly as if I'd had my head against her chest. Then it was quiet, and then my fingers were raking through the pigeon shit on the catwalk, looking for something to hang on to, and then I was scrambling over the edge and onto the catwalk. I was breathing hard too.

Cory pulled herself up behind me, breathing heavily; I gave her my hand, slippery with pigeon shit, and she grabbed my wrist and started pulling, and then we were both on the catwalk, the full shock of fear and exhilaration washing over us in a series of waves.

"You all right? she asked.

"I'm all right," I said. I pulled her toward me and kissed her neck, her forehead, her mouth. "I'm all right," I said again. She didn't pull away. I kissed her neck again, her forehead, her mouth, going in a circle, like someone lost in the woods.

"*Hsss*. There's Avery."

The town squad car cruised slowly down Main Street, past the gates of the factory. I tracked the squad car as it headed south across the Michigan Central tracks that bisect the town and come to a stop at the light at M-60, in front of the Texaco station where my grandmother's second husband Cornelis once had a Maxwell agency. The Cochrane Funeral Home is right across the street from the station, on the southeast corner.

"Remember when I had a crush on Frances?"

"Frances is a stuck-up bitch," Cory said. "I hope Jack makes out with the new girl. I hope she lets him go all the way."

In a silvery parlor on the second floor Frances and I had sat in opposite corners of the big dappled sofa and drunk tea while Mrs. Cochrane, a Christian Scientist, read aloud from *Science and Health with Key to the Scriptures* and from the testimonials in the back pages of the *Christian Science Sentinel.* Frances was a Christian Scientist too and never went to a doctor, though she'd worn complicated braces on her teeth when we were in junior high.

"Her mom says that sin and disease and death don't have any divine authority. They're illusions."

"Yeah? And what does she say about the dead bodies that *Mr.* Cochrane brings home? What does she think he does with them? Pray over them?"

"I've never figured that out."

In the room over the garage where we'd built the float, coffins were on display, like boats in a marina. And in the back rooms of the house . . . we could only guess, in whispers, at what secrets lay behind the several doors that led down a narrow hallway to the back rooms. Gilbert, Mr. Cochrane's walleyed assistant, teased us but told nothing. Not even Frances knew for sure.

"This is fantastic," I said after I'd calmed down; "It's like we're on top of the world. Look, you can see the yard lights." It was astonishingly beautiful. It took my breath away, filled me with that same kind of longing I got from Chesterfield's music. I wasn't afraid anymore.

There were no lights between the town and the moraines beyond except the high yard lights that burned all night on Dijksterhuis Corners. Appleton Road, as Main Street is called when it leaves the town, was lined with aunts and uncles and cousins, Dijksterhuises and Schuylers, who went to the Methodist Church, and Portingas, who went to the Dutch Reformed Church, and Huizingas, who were Catholics. Their lives seemed full of mystery to me, as if they were figures in an old painting: Old Mietje, my father's mother, carrying eggs in a net; my stout uncles pulling on their high-top boots; Maurinus Schuyler, who lived alone out at the dump, in his great black hat, big as a hearse wheel; Uncle Piet joking with the Negro pickers who ate at trestle tables in the picking camp, beyond the packing shed; my father, rifle under his arm, emerging from Potter's Woods, game bag bulging; my mother silhouetted at her Steinway B; the flame of a brulot bowl on Christmas Eve; Reverend Boomsma and the dominie from the Dutch Reformed Church in their black robes, joining forces to bless the harvest; a load of apples in the door of the packing shed.

A curtain of fog hung along the Appleton River, which divides the orchards from the woods beyond, Potawatomi and Ottowa territory, crowded with old burial mounds and pits for storing grain. If you tried to walk through there at night, Cory's dad said, you'd never find your way out. This was where the creator had held the earth when he shaped the world. You could see his palm print on the map, shaped like Michigan's lower peninsula.

Our house was next to Uncle Piet's, just south of Kruger Road—two rambling L-shaped houses that my dad and my uncle built themselves, with help from my grandfather.

"Fuck the yard lights," Cory said. "We don't *have* yard lights at our house."

"Cory!"

"Martin!"

"Sorry."

"You sound like you never heard anybody say 'fuck' before."

"I never heard *you* say it before."

"Well you heard me say it now. Fuck. Fuck Frances Cochrane. Fuck this town."

"Shhh. Not so loud. You can see where your house is."

"It's where you can't see anything."

The moraines were dark, but we could make out the line of the Appleton River and the hump of Poesy Chapel Hill, where we went sledding in the winter and flew our kites in the spring. The chapel itself, on a hill about two miles or so beyond the river, was in ruins, but the cemetery was still in use. My grandmother was buried there with both her husbands—Pieter Dijksterhuis and Cornelis Schuyler—and several of her children, too. And my other grandmother, the one who ran away from a wicked stepmother in England and went to live with a cousin in Chicago. Cory's older brother too, Charles, Charlie, who was killed in the Korean War. Aunt Flo never took down the gold star flag that hung from a wooden dowel in the kitchen window, and on Sundays she always set an extra place at the table for him. When my parents went to Florida in the fall of 1951, when I was in eighth grade, I stayed in Charlie's room, slept in his bed, and came down with the measles, so Aunt Flo kept the blinds closed and we listened to the National League play-offs during the afternoon—we were pulling for the Dodgers and turned the radio off right after Bobby Thomson's home run—and Cory read *The Three Musketeers* to me at night. Beyond Poesy Chapel the moraines gave way to the sand dunes that rim the southern end of Lake Michigan.

"What do you want to do?" I asked.

"I want you to kiss me again."

I was remembering the first kiss, on the way to the packing shed, and subsequent kisses: Frances, and Dixie Carpenter, and Frances's cousin, who'd brought French kissing from Detroit to Appleton. So I had a pretty good idea of where I was, but I didn't know where I was going. Those kisses had all been experimental. This one was the real thing. I could feel Cory's excitement answering mine. Standing at the rail, I kissed her again, aware of her tongue against my teeth, her arms around me, her hips dancing against mine as I tried to fix everything in my memory.

"I meant with the paint," I said, when we broke apart.

"I know what you meant."

I was imagining Bjorn Faulkner's platinum gown, how I'd slip it over Cory's head. Cory naked. Cory kissing me, "wild like a tiger!" But now I wasn't imagining it. I kissed her again, and again, letting my hands run down her back and sides and over her buttocks. She didn't stop me.

Over her shoulder I could see the lights of the football field. I couldn't see the field itself, but I could see a bit of the parking lot, and I could hear the sounds of the game. Crowd noises are ambiguous, but it sounded as if the game had just ended, and as if we'd won. When I let go of her and looked over my own shoulder, I could see the viaduct and the front doors of the gym, and the roof of the depot.

Fifteen minutes later a few cars were starting to go by, cruising, one couple in the front seat, another in the back. Oncoming cars stopped in the middle of the street in front of Harrison Ford or Deitering Electric so the drivers could to talk to each other. Some kids were sitting on the steps of the Methodist church, smoking. A handful of people stood in front of the Oriental Theater, waiting for the first show get out—*An American in Paris,* with Gene Kelly and Leslie Caron. My mother, who was always complaining about the films in Appleton, or the lack of them, had taken Cory and me to see it on Sunday afternoon. The story was pretty corny, but the score was by Gershwin and the dancing was great.

Cory took a quarter out of her pocket and dropped it off the tower.

"What'd you do that for?"

"I don't want to explain everything. Sometimes I just do something."

The paint can sighed as she pried open the lid. Purple paint. Our school colors, purple and gold. *Hurrah for the purple and the gold.*

"You need to stir it up," I said.

"There's nothing to stir it with. You already shook it a little. It'll be OK."

She dipped the brush in the paint, wiped the tip on the edge of the can, tipped it up. I looked down. Another pair of cars had stopped so the drivers could exchange greetings.

I walked around the narrow catwalk—barely two feet wide—to the other side of the tower and peed over the edge while Cory painted. The stream of piss disappeared into the darkness without a sound. The moon was full. Pegasus was climbing up over the horizon behind us. Orion and the Pleiades were hidden behind the tower.

When I came back, I looked, but I couldn't take it in all at once. I was too close. The catwalk was barely two feet wide, so it was hard to get a good view. But I finally made it out.

FUCK THIS TOWN

It took a while to register. The letters were so big, and I was standing so close.

"Cory, you can't do this."

"I've already done it."

"What about 'Class of '56?'"

She shrugged. "What about it?"

"We could *really* get in trouble."

"We're already in trouble. At least I am."

"We're both in trouble. Give me the brush."

"I'm going back down."

"I'll go first."

"You went first on the way up."

But she was already climbing over the edge of the catwalk, onto the ladder.

"Be careful, for Christ's sake. Let me hold your wrists."

"Are you crazy?"

"What are you talking about? I won't let you fall."

But her head disappeared. Then one hand, then the other. I was afraid to look over the edge. I listened for the sound of her body falling through space, but the only sound was the scrape of shoe on metal.

"Are you OK?"

"I'm on the ladder."

"What about the paint?" I said.

"Just leave it, for Christ's sake."

"Shall I close it up?"

"Just leave it."

"What about fingerprints?"

She laughed. "Yeah."

The brush was resting on the edge of the open paint can. I could hear her climbing down the ladder.

FUCK THIS TOWN

I picked up the brush and dipped it in the paint. I turned the *F* into an *E*. I made the bottom of the *U* a little pointed so that it looked kind of like a *V*. I turned the *C* into an *O* and added another *E*.

E V O K E T H I S T O W N

It was the best I could do. I looked over the edge. Cory was waiting for me, on the leg of the tower, about ten rungs down the ladder.

"I can't move," she whispered. "I've got a cramp in my leg. What are you doing anyway?"

I didn't want to tell her what I'd done. I tried to focus on her upturned face so I wouldn't get dizzy, though I was hanging on to the guardrail with both hands.

"Which leg?"

"What difference does it make?"

A tiny car drove by.

"I could massage it."

Someone stopped to drop a letter off at the post office. More cars drove by, but we were up too high for anyone to notice us.

"Can you put your weight on it?"

"No. I can't feel anything. It just wants to double up."

"*Try* putting some weight on it. Just don't let go."

"What do you do when you get a cramp when you're swimming?"

"I don't know."

I was lying flat now, just my head over the edge of the catwalk. I had a strange impulse to roll over to my left, right off the edge. Sometimes I felt this impulse while lying in bed. I always managed to stifle it, though I did roll off the edge of my bed once when I was asleep.

"I can't feel anything in my leg."

"Put your weight on your other leg. Relax the leg with the cramp. Hold it out straight."

"If I relax it just makes it worse."

"Then hold it straight out and see what happens."

"What if I get a cramp in my other leg?"

"You can't get cramps in both legs at the same time."

"Why not?"

I closed my eyes for a minute, and when I opened them, I looked up at the stars, the constellations. The moon was halfway across the sky.

"Martin?"

"What?"

"I think it's getting better. I'm going to climb down a little."

"I'm coming too."

I started down, sliding on my stomach on the slippery pigeon shit, searching with my feet for one of the ladder rungs. I got a foot on one rung, then another, then I unhooked my leg and got my first foot firmly onto the next rung down. The tricky part was getting your hands from the floor of the slippery catwalk onto the top rung of the ladder. I supported myself on my left arm and got ahold of the ladder with my right hand. And then I was embracing the ladder, as tightly as I'd embraced Cory.

"I love you," I whispered—this was the real business of the night—but I don't think she heard me. At least she didn't answer. I crawled down the ladder one rung at a time, slowly, confronting a variety of emotions.

We didn't stop running till we got to the hole in the fence, and then we stopped and kissed again. I dug my fingers into the nappy curls at the back of her neck, her kitchen curls Aunt Flo called them, and pulled her head back so I could see her face. She looked at me and smiled. I'd been worried that when the time came I wouldn't know what to do, but when the time did come, it didn't matter, because now I knew who I was. I was a hero—not Garcin, but Bjorn Faulkner making love to Karen Andre. I was Howard Roark fucking Dominique Francon. I suppose I was Lancelot too, now that I knew what all the fuss had been about with Guinevere. And then all of a sudden these fantasies parted, like clouds parting, and I was just me, and Cory was just Cory, and I was inside her and she was inside me, and somehow we'd scooted forward so that our heads were butting up against the chain-link fence. Afterward we were too wide awake to go home, so we drove out past Dijksterhuis Corners and on out to Potter's Woods—virgin forest—and necked in the car, kissing and touching each other again, but holding back a little, still a little afraid. A deer jumped across the road from behind us and disappeared into the woods. I put my hand on Cory's forehead, as if I were checking for a fever, and told her that I loved her and wanted to marry her and that we could live in the little house my father had built for my grandmother. I told her that I could run the orchards, and that she could be close to her family, that we could have a family of our own. She had her knees up and was looking out the window on her side, but she didn't push my hand away, and she didn't laugh. My imagination raced forward, then backward. "Do you remember how we used to take turns sitting on your mother's lap and pushing the lever on the mangle? I was always a little afraid," I said, "the way the sheets disappeared between the rollers; what if you got your hand caught in there?"

"That's why there're two levers—one to clamp it down and one to start the rollers."

"I always loved being at your house," I said. "Except for the buttermilk. *Warm* buttermilk."

"You drank it."

"That's because I wanted to be there. And it's not as bad as tapioca pudding."

"You think this is the garden of Eden, don't you?"

It was true, but I didn't want to admit it. "I think it could be," I said, "if you'd marry me."

We got out of the car and walked around the locked gate. It was light enough to see our way down the path to a little stream that was fed by an artesian well. We drank ice cold water coming out of a pipe, catching the water in a little tin cup that was fastened to a chain. And then we drove through town again, down Main Street, past the Methodist church, past Harrison Ford and Deitering Electric and the Oriental Theater, all the way out to Spring Creek, a mile south of the stoplight, and then back north to Dijksterhuis Corners, past our house, then Uncle Piet's, then Barent's. All back to life-size now. We turned left on Kruger Road. Aunt Bridget lived kitty-corner from Cousin Lotte in my grandmother's old house. On our right, Uncle Jan, my father's half brother. More cousins lived along Kruger Road, on the right. The Williamses' house, on the left, was set back from the road, on the same drive that the trucks used to get to the packing shed. I kissed her again, and again, and again, till she pulled away and ran into the darkness.

"How was the game?" my mother wanted to know when I got home.

"Good," I said, already halfway up the stairs. My front was covered with dirt and pigeon shit.

"Who won?"

I replayed the crowd noises in my imagination. "We did," I said. "I'm pretty sure. I didn't stay till the end."

I couldn't see my mother, but I knew she was alone in her chair in the study, doing a crossword puzzle or reading a novel. I was her Nick Adams, her David Copperfield, her Huck Finn, her *petit prince,* her count of Monte Cristo, her Julien Sorel, her Marcel.

"You didn't stay till the end?"

My father, who went to work at five in the morning, was already asleep.

What if New Buffalo had won?—though my mother never paid any attention to the games, so she'd probably never notice. "I guess I was tired."

I was still too excited just to go to bed. I hid my dirty shirt in the back of a drawer, got out my guitar, sat on edge of bed, reached up, and turned out the floor lamp. I could see a strip of light under my door. I tuned the guitar down to open-D and ran through some of the songs I'd been learning from Chesterfield's tapes. After a while I heard my mother's footsteps on the stairs, then in the hallway. I stopped playing and for almost a minute there was no sound at all as she stood outside my door, listening. If she'd tapped on the door, I would have asked her to come in; I would have told her everything. I was fully in love and the urge to tell someone, to speak my love aloud, was almost irresistible. "You know that book you gave me"—I almost said aloud—*"Into Manhood?"* But an inner instinct prompted me to be silent, and I obeyed. I waited till I heard her move down the hall, heard water running in the bathroom, and then the bedroom door closing behind her. I started to pick out an alternating bass with my thumb, and when I had a comfortable rhythm going I walked my bottleneck—I never learned to play with a knife, the way Chesterfield did—up to the seventh fret and played a verse of "Sittin' on Top of the World." I did not know at the time that all these songs—"Poor Boy, a Long Ways from Home," "God Moves on the Water," "Police Dog Blues," "Sittin' on Top of the World"—were part of the standard blues repertoire, linchpins of a tradition that went back to street corners in Dallas, Texas, and Durham, North Carolina, and to the Dockery Plantation in Cleveland, Mississippi; but I did know something that has never ceased to amaze me, that the notes of joy and sadness can sound the same, that the same physical notes can have different spiritual meanings. Like goose bumps might mean you've just seen the Holy Ghost, or just that you're chilly.

> 'Twas in the spring, one sunny day,
> My sweetheart left me, Lord, she went away,
> But now she gone, gone, gone, and I don't worry,
> 'Cause I'm sittin' on top of the world.

3

Messiah

1955–56

ON THE MORNING after we'd painted the tower—Saturday morning—I ran all the way through the orchards and down to the Appleton River. I was overwhelmed by beauty. Mr. Dutton had been right; a switch really had been thrown in nature. Canada mayflowers had turned purple; crab apples were soft on the ground; late dandelions were still blooming; a skunk had passed by earlier, and I heard geese overhead and the buzz of dragonflies. I picked up a black walnut the size of a baseball and threw it into the river. I picked flowers for Cory: a dozen of the mayflowers, their red berries flecked with purple; then goldenrod, wintergreen, purple and blue asters. And then some for my mother too.

Later on that morning I went to Cory's to take her the flowers and to drop off a load of laundry. Aunt Flo was humming "His Eye

Is on the Sparrow" as she pressed Cory's hair with a hot comb; my aunt Bridget was drinking coffee and heating a second comb on the gas stove, holding the comb over the burner, turning it this way and that, while Cory, who was tenderheaded, acted as if she was being tortured. The smells of the hot comb on the stove and the hot hair grease and the burnt hair mingled with the smell of the flowers, which I held close to my chest.

Aunt Bridget, who owned a small beauty parlor on Main Street, had been the fastest typist in the U. S. Navy at the end of World War I, and had a certificate to prove it. She'd fallen in love with a sailor, and the sailor had come to Appleton right after the armistice, and everyone had loved him; but then he'd disappeared and Aunt Bridget never heard from him again. She'd lived at home and looked after my grandmother till she died, and then my father and Uncle Piet bought the beauty shop for her.

No one in my family ever mentioned the sailor. I learned about him from Aunt Flo, who must have heard the story from Aunt Bridget herself, maybe when Aunt Bridget was doing her hair. Bridget could never get it pressed exactly the way she wanted it—but sometimes it was better than driving all the way up to the black beauty parlor in Benton Harbor; and Bridget kept her supplied with Nu Nile hair grease and Queen Helene hair spray at wholesale prices.

I watched Cory, who had her eyes closed and her teeth clenched. I wanted to know if she knew what I knew: that we had done something great, something for all time. Like Bjorn Faulkner in *The Night of January 16th*, we had seized the day, shaped our own destiny. News of the water tower had not yet reached Dijksterhuis Corners. I couldn't imagine what the consequences might be when it did, but I didn't care. Cap, drinking coffee, had the *Tribune* spread on the table. Later on we were going to dig new pits for the outhouses. He was going to let me run the backhoe. I couldn't wait. Everything had been transformed by love.

I put the flowers on the table.

"God bless you, Marty," Aunt Flo said, holding Cory's ear flat so she wouldn't burn it with the comb. "You're a good boy."

Aunt Bridget, though, must have read my mind, because she raised her hand to her forehead and pressed her temples with thumb and finger, as if she'd developed a sudden headache, and I wondered if she was thinking about her sailor, wondered if she'd felt for him what I was feeling for Cory now.

It took Cap about twenty minutes to dig a new trench for the outhouse, and it took me about two hours to pick up the fresh dirt and fill in the old trench. Cap sat on a stump and watched, smoking a cigarette now and then, as I maneuvered the hoe back and forth. I was able to set the end loader down where I wanted it, but I didn't have a good feel for the boom lever and kept spilling a lot of dirt. One of the hydraulic hoses that ran through the boom was leaking pretty badly and the controls were getting sluggish, but Cap didn't want to leave me alone with the hoe while he went into town for a replacement.

Cap was a kind of foreman, or overseer. Every spring he went down to his hometown, Claxton, Georgia, and contracted with a local undertaker for a picking crew; in the early summer he and my father and Uncle Piet did the spraying; in the winter they did the pruning. My father had met him at the Benton Harbor market just before the depression, and Cap, who was working for a nursery at the time, had grafted the whips that were used to set out the original orchards. In the summer he and my father looked after the day-to-day running of the orchards, and Uncle Piet dealt with the buyers on the Benton Harbor market and with the chain stores in Chicago and Detroit. Cap was never a big talker, but he was comfortable to be around, and he was always happy to teach me what he knew best: how to shape the younger trees so that they'd develop the right mechanical framework to hold the maximum amount of fruit;

how to prune the mature, full-sized trees in the original orchard to renew the fruiting wood; how to tell the fruit-producing spurs from the suckers; how to graft new bud wood onto the old crab apple stock; how to drive the tractor and the backhoe; how to bed the bees down for the winter so that the workers that hatched in the fall wouldn't die like the rest.

My father joined us at the end of the day. He was always pleased when I worked with Cap, and I knew that he wanted me to stay home and help him run the orchards and not go to the University of Chicago. I knew it because I'd heard him arguing with my mother about the application form she'd sent for, which had just arrived in the mail, though it wasn't due for three months yet.

Dad and Cap had a look at the leaky hose, and then we hooked a chain around the outhouse and Cap dragged it slowly with the backhoe till Dad and I were able to jockey it into position over the new trench; and then we had a snort of Canadian Club from a narrow flask that Cap had in the pocket of his windbreaker, and we each smoked one of Cap's Camels. The three of us stood there staring at the outhouse.

"It's ready to go if you want to take a dump," Cap said, wiping his high, shiny forehead with a handkerchief.

"You go ahead," I said.

Cap laughed.

"Well," my father said, "that about wraps it up for the year."

"Been a pretty good year," Cap said.

"Pretty good," my father said, nodding his head. "Pretty good."

"It's been a great year," I said.

Both men looked at me, expecting more. Once again I was tempted to speak my love. But once again an inner instinct prompted me to bide my time; to let things take their own course. I walked back to the house with my father.

*   *   *

That night, after supper, I went back to Cory's. Mr. Dutton had told us to watch for meteor showers, and we were going to watch for them together. I took my father's Bausch & Lomb binoculars with me and Chesterfield's metal guitar.

"Why you always want to play that down-home trash?" Aunt Flo asked when she saw the guitar. She rattled her copy of the *Appleton River Gazette*. "Seriously, Martin, why don't you play that piece you played at your recital last year? I want to hear it again."

My mother had given our old upright piano to the Williamses when she got the Steinway. I went into the living room and sat down at the piano and played the opening of *The Harmonious Blacksmith*. Cory was upstairs. Cap was eating a hard-boiled egg as he dealt out a game of solitaire on the kitchen table, which was covered with a piece of oilcloth, putting his cards down and dipping the egg in a little bowl of salt and pepper and Tabasco and then picking the cards up again.

"Come and take a look at this, Marty," he called when I got stuck in the middle of the second movement. He indicated a bowl of small withered apples on the table. Cap was interested in recovering lost varieties, and whenever someone came across a wild apple tree in an old woodlot or on an abandoned farm, they'd let him know, and in the late winter he'd collect a dozen or so scions and then in the spring he'd graft them onto one of the orchard trees, just to see what he'd come up with. There were trees down by the river that each had four or five different varieties growing on them, and Cap had managed to identify most of them and find out something about their histories: Baldwins, Pippins, Newtons, Cox's Orange Pippins, Golden Russets, Hudson's Golden Gems, Pink Pearls, Cornish Gilliflowers, Blue Pearmains, Canada Reds, Carpentins, Champlains.

I picked up one of the apples and held it in my hand. The dull crimson-red skin was covered with a fine gray-brown russet coat.

"What do you think?"

I studied the apple and shrugged my shoulders. "Doesn't look familiar."

"Looks a little bit like an Adam's Pearmain," he said. "Shaped like a cone. That's a Southern apple. Hard to tell with these little bitty things."

"Johnny Appleseed?" I said.

He laughed. "I didn't know he got to Michigan."

"Maybe it's right from the Garden of Eden," I said. "The original apple?"

"You never know," he said. "Get me a knife from the counter, would you, Marty? Let's cut one open and I'll show you something."

I brought Cap a small paring knife from the draining rack by the sink, and he cut the apple in half, across the stem, so the inner core looked like a star.

"Go ahead," he said. "Try it."

I took a bite. The apple was wrinkled on the outside, but the flesh was crisp and firm and had a sweet, dry, nutty flavor.

"That's a real nice apple," Cap said, picking up the deck of cards and starting to deal out another game of solitaire.

I finished the apple and washed my hands. "Maybe I'll play something on the guitar," I said. "How about a hymn?"

"Marty, you can play a hymn," Aunt Flo said, "but everything you play on that ugly old thing sounds like the devil's music to me. When I was a girl in Tutwiler we'd a got whipped if we'd gone near one of them juke joints; and now you're bringing the devil's music right into my kitchen."

"Aunt Flo," I said, "you know it's not the devil's music."

She held her newspaper up so I couldn't see her face.

I tuned the guitar and played one of the songs I'd learned from Chesterfield, a song that I heard Lightning Hopkins play years later.

> *Now it is a needin' time,*
> *Right now, it is a needin' time;*

Now it is a needin' time.
Jesus, won't you come by here,
Oh, Jesus, won't you come by here;
Jesus, won't you come by here.

"You see what I mean, Cap?" Aunt Flo said. "Listen to him. You hear what I mean? Marty can make that nice old song sound just like the blues. Why don't you play something a respectable woman could sing to?" Aunt Flo always sang the alto solos in the choir cantatas at Christmas and Easter. Cory sang with the sopranos. I was in charge of the tape recorder.

"How about 'Come On in My Kitchen'?" I asked. I tuned the guitar down to open-G. I'd never heard of Robert Johnson at the time. I'd only heard of Chesterfield.

Ah, the woman I love, took from my best friend,
Some joker got lucky, stole her back again.
You better come on in my kitchen baby,
It's goin' to be rainin' outdoors.

Cory came down after a while. She watched her father's solitaire game over his shoulder, pointing out possible plays till he covered the cards with his hands so she couldn't see them.

I'd been waiting for her with a lover's impatience, and my skin prickled at the sight of her bare feet. She'd spent her summer money on clothes—shoes, bright scarves like my mother's, loose sweaters, straight skirts that stretched tight across her buttocks. But tonight she was in a sweatshirt and an old pair of slacks, not exactly Guinevere or Isolde, but close enough for me.

"Bonsoir, ma chère Giselle."

She dangled a pair of low-heeled shoes on the first two fingers of her left hand as she bent over to get a better look at her father's cards. *"On ne peut même pas sortir en hiver,"* she said without looking up. It was a line we managed to work into every attempt to converse in French. *You can't even go outside in winter.*

"Je me demande pourquoi cette porte s'est ouverte," I replied, a line from *Huis clos.* Garcin demands that the door in hell be opened, but when it opens, he refuses to go out.

She laughed. *"Qu'est-ce que vous attendez? Allez, allez vite!"*

"Now, I have always wanted to speak in French myself," Aunt Flo said. "Just imagine it. My uncle," she said, looking at me, "married a woman from Canada who spoke in French, and he learned to speak it too. When they didn't want us to know what they was saying, they'd speak whatever it was in French. That was something. It was like a secret code. And she used to say that they must speak in French in heaven on account of it being such a beautiful language."

"Je ne m'en irai pas," I said. *I'm not going to go out.*

"Now to me that doesn't make any more sense than Cecil Bill on *Kukla, Fran and Ollie.* You remember how you and Cory used to talk like Cecil Bill: tooi tooi too tooi tooi tooi, and so on. You had your Aunt Bridget believing you were really talking; you almost had me believing it too."

"Mama, we were speaking to each other, and you did believe it."

"Now don't start up on that again."

"Tooi tooi too tooi tooi tooi," Cory said to me.

"Tooi tooi tooi tooi tooi too too tooi," I replied.

"Now what did you say?" Aunt Flo asked.

"He said there's supposed to be a meteor shower tonight and we're supposed to watch for it."

Aunt Flo looked at Cory, then back at me.

"He didn't say any such thing," Cap said, riffling the cards. "Hearts, anyone? Pinochle? Euchre? Three-handed cribbage?"

"We're going to go outside, Daddy."

It was almost nine o'clock and the moon was behind us, over the Dziepak barn. There were no clouds.

"It would be better if the moon weren't so bright," Cory said.

We were studying astronomy in general science class. A month had passed since the autumnal equinox, and the constellations were turning back. Mr. Dutton, our teacher, had assigned each of us a constellation to watch. I had Boötes, the herdsman; Cory had Pegasus, the winged horse. The picking crew had departed; Cap had turned most of Aunt Flo's garden under, except for the turnips that Cory liked and the brussels sprouts that she didn't. (My mother had a garden too: flowers and a few herbs that she like to use in her cooking—basil, tarragon, flat-leaf parsley, marjoram, rochette. She didn't see any point in growing vegetables when no one knew what to do with the flood of tomatoes and zucchini and sweet corn that inundated us every summer.) The woodlot was free from nettles now; the poison ivy had disappeared. It was cold, but I didn't put my jacket on. The cold felt good.

The grass was still high along the drive. Cap came out and began to tighten the tarps he'd stretched over the brush cutter and the wood he'd split with a mechanical splitter he'd built himself from some pipes and an old axe blade. There was no horizon. The woodlot consisted mostly of second-growth trees: scrub oak, elms, shagbark hickories. There were some walnut trees and some sugar maples, and a few big oaks too. We walked to the clearing behind the packing shed.

"Do you want to walk down to the river?" I asked.

"We can see the sky better from here," Cap said. He offered me a cigarette. I said no. He tapped one on the back of his hand before putting it in his mouth.

The gravel in the clearing had been packed hard by the trucks. We didn't see any shooting stars, but we could hear something. Cory looked through the binoculars but had trouble focusing. "I can see something," she said. "Like something flying in front of the moon."

"Quiet," Cap said.

We listened. Above us we could hear a high twittering.

"Little birds," Cap said, "passing overhead. Migrating. You can't see them. Thousands of them. They travel at night. Little sparrows and finches."

I looked through the binoculars and handed them to Cap. "You can see them," I said. "Like little dark specks. I never knew . . . I thought it was just geese . . . At night? How do they find their way?"

"It's a mystery," Cap said.

"How come nobody knows about this?" I asked.

Cap shrugged his shoulders. In the distance a freight train blew its whistle as it approached Brinkman's Crossing; then two more long blasts and a short as it went through town.

My mother had gone to school with Ernest Hemingway in Oak Park. Hemingway had been one year ahead of her, but he'd been in two of her classes, algebra and Latin, and they'd both worked on the school newspaper, the *Trapeze*. She'd heard him read his first stories to a group of fellow students in his workshop on the third floor of the big house on Oak Park Avenue, and he'd signed her copy of the 1919 senior *Tabula*. She followed his career and kept all of his books—including copies of the *Tabula*—in chronological order on a separate shelf next to the piano, along with a newspaper photo of him after winning the Nobel Prize in 1954 and a copy of his acceptance speech, which, because he'd been ill at the time, had been read by the U.S. ambassador to Sweden. She'd read the Nick Adams stories aloud to me, and her favorite of the novels, *The Sun Also Rises*. I'd been too young to appreciate it, but I know it was her favorite because it was set in Paris. At least the first part.

She'd been planning to go to work as a file clerk after high school, for the Western Electric Company on Cicero Avenue, but she'd been such an outstanding student that her teachers at Oak Park High School got together and raised enough money to send her to the University of Chicago. Every year when my folks and I went into Chicago to the All-Star Bowling Tournament, we'd have dinner at George Diamond's steak house and then drive along the lake to Hyde Park and then stop for a minute in front of the house where she'd lived, which was near the Midway Plaissance. One of her professors at Chicago knew the superintendent in Appleton and lined up a job for my mother. Four years later she married my father.

She wanted me to go to the University of Chicago too. I see now that she wanted it with all her heart, wanted me to attend a great university; wanted me to become passionate about art and literature; wanted me to read Balzac and Stendhal and Proust; she wanted me to grow a beard and sit up all night drinking coffee and smoking cigarettes, talking about politics and philosophy; she wanted me to think for myself, to think critically and not just accept whatever ideas were being passed around. She'd given up on the two-piano version of *Rhapsody in Blue,* but she wasn't about to give up on the University of Chicago, and she kept after me to fill out the application. It wasn't due till January, but she wanted it done before Christmas. She couldn't understand my reluctance, and I couldn't explain it either.

Cory and I had tried to go back to being who we were before—before homecoming weekend—but being who we were before wasn't possible. I thought of myself as an explorer who'd discovered a new continent or the lost land of Logres, but who couldn't tell anyone about his discovery. I was bound by an oath of silence; but I'd been there; I'd *seen;* I *knew.* I wasn't ready to go back yet, and I didn't mind waiting. It seemed like the right thing to do. But I was planning to return; I was thinking about the journey all the time.

My father rarely opposed my mother's plans, but he took my part in our dinner table discussions of my future. "The University of Chicago," he said one evening, "is a Baptist seminary where Jewish professors teach Roman Catholicism to a bunch of atheists."

My mother was starting to clear the table. "That's ridiculous," she said. "Where on earth did you hear that?"

"The *Reader's Digest,*" my father said.

My mother rolled her eyes.

That night I heard them quarreling in their bedroom. This was a new experience for me. In the 1950s in Appleton, Michigan, grown-ups rarely disagreed and they never quarreled. At least I had never heard grown-ups quarreling; and this quarrel, even though I could not make out the actual words, stuck in my imagination like a splinter in a place on my foot that I couldn't quite reach.

In the end my mother filled out the application for me; but she couldn't write the essay that I was required to submit. She wanted it in the mail before Christmas, she said, because she didn't want to have to nag me about it during the holidays. She wanted me to write about some of the books we'd read together, or some of the books I'd read over the summer with Cory and Frances and the other kids from her French class. I dragged my feet as long as I could, but when I finally sat down to write I surprised myself: I wrote about climbing the water tower—how at first everyone had suspected Jack, the football captain, and that he hadn't denied it, but then everyone figured out that Cory and I had done it because we were the only ones who hadn't been at the dance. We were heroes, and we deserved to be because we'd done something great, like Howard Roark in *The Fountainhead.* I compared the water tower to the Wynard Building. From it you could look down on everything: the bank, the churches, the Texaco station, the funeral home, M-60, the Michigan Central tracks . . .

And I wrote about how beautiful the little town looked from the catwalk. How beauty took away fear. And that even if I'd fallen on the way down, it would have been worth it.

Words poured out of me onto a large yellow pad of legal-sized paper. I wrote with the Waterman fountain pen that my mother had given me for my seventeenth birthday, wrote till I ran out of ink. My hands were shaking and I almost knocked over the bottle of ink when I refilled the pen.

I was reckless. Just when I thought I'd done the greatest thing—

climbing the tower—something even greater came along: making love to Cory. I've blocked the exact words out of my memory, but I know that I didn't restrain myself. I said that Corinna hadn't needed a pillow under her butt—something I'd read in a Hemingway story—and I quoted the famous earthmoving scene in *For Whom the Bell Tolls*. I couldn't find the part about not needing a pillow under her butt, and I didn't want to ask my mother to help me find it; but my mother's Scribner's first edition opened right to the page where Maria tells Pilar that the earth moved, and Pilar tells her it will move only three times. I thought the earth had moved for me.

I didn't bother to type the essay, even though I'd won the typing award at school my junior year and my mother had given me a very expensive Olympia portable typewriter. I just folded the legal-sized sheets in half and tucked them sideways into the big University of Chicago envelope and sealed it up so that my mother couldn't read it. I was worried that she might open the application, so I took it into the post office and mailed it myself.

It never occurred to me that I might see it again, but when my mother and I went up to Chicago in January to meet with an admissions counselor, the oversized yellow pages were sticking out of a manila folder on the counselor's desk. My mouth dried up. The walls of the small office closed in on me. The counselor tapped the folder with her finger. I didn't know what to expect. She wore a real poker face too, wasn't giving anything away. Was she going to denounce me? Was she going to whip the essay out and hand it to my mother?

"This was a very unusual essay," she said, opening the folder. And waited. "Tell me a little bit more about your interest in Ayn Rand." She was younger than my mother, but a little drab by comparison, in a straight skirt that covered her knees.

"It was our junior class play," I said. *"The Night of January 16th.* I was the defense attorney."

"I was thinking more of *The Fountainhead,* actually. In your essay you seem to be an admirer of Howard Roark." (She pronounced it *Rork*). "Maybe you could elaborate a little. Would you say he's your hero?" She took my essay out of the folder.

My mother was appalled: "You didn't even type it?" she said to me.

"That's all right, Mrs. Dijksterhuis," the counselor said. "A little unconventional, but not a problem."

"One of them," I said, meaning Howard Roark.

"And the others?"

"Sir Lancelot," I said. "Beowulf. D'Artagnan. Edmond Dantès."

"Good grief." She started to laugh and had trouble stopping. "Now that's quite a collection. And how did Howard Roark manage to find a seat at this table?"

"Well, he stands up for himself," I said. "He never gives in. And he never makes excuses."

"That's certainly true," she said, "but he's very self-centered, don't you think? Doesn't Sir Lancelot spend most of his time helping other people? And even Beowulf—doesn't he sacrifice himself?"

"He gets killed by the dragon," I said.

"But he saves everyone else, doesn't he?"

"That's right."

"Edmond Dantès?"

"He was the count of Monte Cristo."

"Of course. I'd forgotten the name. He's out for revenge, isn't he? But Howard Roark—and it's been years since I read *The Fountainhead*—do you agree with Ayn Rand that selfishness is a virtue? That self-sacrifice can only break a man's spirit? That the man who works for others is a slave? And what about his relationship with women? Is that something you admire?" She held up my essay and scanned it as if she were looking for something.

"He's a man of rational self-interest," I said. "He's self-sufficient. He doesn't rely on anyone else. He doesn't *need* anyone else. And I like the way he blows up his own building when Keating breaks his promise about not making any changes."

She laughed again. "You'll do well at the University of Chicago." She folded up the essay and replaced it in the manila folder. "Now," she said, "do you have any questions for me?"

"Have you read *The Night of January 16th*?" I asked.

"No," she said, looking a little surprised. "I don't know anything about it except what you wrote in your essay. You played a defense attorney, and your friend Corinna played the defendant, isn't that right?" She smiled.

I knew I was approaching dangerous territory—a hole in the ice that I might just fall through—but I couldn't stop myself. "Yes," I said, "and she got off every time. There was a new jury all three nights, and they all voted to acquit her."

She picked up the file folder with my essay in it and tapped it against the desk. "You must have been very persuasive." Every time she tapped the folder the yellow pages of the essay poked out a little farther.

"It was a lot of fun," I said, backing away.

"Martin," she said, putting the folder down on the desk, "we're always looking for students who are willing to take chances. Seriously. When your mother called to set up an appointment she said she'd been happy here, and I think you'd be happy too."

I almost believed her.

My mother, looking pleased, asked a few questions about the curriculum, and then the interview was over. We put our coats on, shook hands, said good-bye, and took the elevator down to the first floor.

"What did she mean," I asked in the elevator, "when she said I'd do well at the University of Chicago?"

"She challenged you a little and you pushed back. That's what they're looking for. That's what your classes will be like. Your professors will challenge you to think." The elevator door opened. "What did you say in your essay anyway?"

"Just some stuff about the play, and about *The Fountainhead*."

"It's an interesting novel," she said, "but the characters are all cardboard figures."

"Actually," I said, "Howard Roark was a jerk, wasn't he?"

She laughed.

"And Gary Cooper looked pretty stupid sitting behind a desk pretending to be an architect."

We walked across the Quadrangle to our next appointment. It was cold and the students and professors were all bundled up in winter coats. I watched for beards but didn't see any. My mother talked about Robert Hutchins, who'd started the great books approach at Chicago—Hum 101. I'd be reading Plato and Aristotle. And she reminisced about some of her own classes, in the days before Hutchins: Professor Whitford, who looked like an owl and who made her memorize French poetry. *Commit* was the word he used. "I want you to *commit* Baudelaire's 'Correspondances,'" or, "I want you to *commit* Jacques Prévert's 'Déjeuner du matin.'"

A student guide took me to visit one of the dorms—Foster Hall, right on Fifty-ninth Street, which had once been a women's dorm—and then my mother and I ate lunch in the C Shop, and then on the way back to the IC station we walked down Blackstone and stood for a few minutes in front of the house where she'd lived when she was a student, and she pointed out, as she always did, the window of her room, up on the third floor. She wanted to knock on the door, introduce herself, and see if we could have a look at her old room, and at the kitchen where Mrs. Stoddard had taught her how to thicken a sauce with egg yolks and how to pound pike fillets in a mortar to make quenelles. But when I started to protest, she took my arm and steered me north on Blackstone.

"It doesn't matter," she said. And then she said: "I was never a popular student, Marty; but it didn't matter. I had such wonderful friends. Alice Parker, and Marjorie Phillips, and Hannah Friedman, and Jessie May Stewart, who lived with the Partens over on Wood-lawn and then went to live in Paris. We saw a lot of each other. I was so happy, Marty. I want you to be as happy as I was then, to enter into friendships that will carry you through the years."

"You never saw Ernest Hemingway again, did you?" I said. "I mean, after you left Oak Park?"

"No," she said, as we turned on Fifty-seventh Street. "He went to Kansas City and then he joined the Red Cross and went to Italy. He was wounded at Fossalta di Piave in 1918 and taken to Milan. When I first came to Appleton your father reminded me of Ernest, always trying to prove himself with games and guns; but Ernest was full of self-pity when I knew him. All his early heroes are defeated and sad, don't you think? And later on he made a profession of alienation. Your father liked to hunt and fish, Marty, but he's never been alienated."

We walked east to the Fifty-ninth Street station and took the IC back downtown; and then we took the South Shore to the shops just outside Michigan City, where my father was waiting for us.

The next day Cory and I helped Cap clean out the tractor shed, and then Cory and I took a load out to the dump—the old hoses from the backhoe, worn-out brake shoes from Cap's old Packard, some damaged bushel baskets and apple crates, half a dozen Christmas trees still glittering with strands of tinsel, and an old ten-gallon hot water heater that the three of us could barely lift up onto the truck. "When you get there," Cap said, "just roll it off the back end."

I was glad to be alone with Cory because I thought it was time to get some things settled. For Christmas I'd given her a cashmere sweater that was too expensive. She didn't want her mother to see it, so she kept it in her locker at school and sometimes wore it during the day. On those days I loved her more than I loved my mother, and everything seemed possible; but when I tried to talk to her about the future and the need to agree on a plan of action, she suddenly became much older and I became much younger, like a boy with a crush on one of his teachers. She'd touch a finger to her lips and then to mine, and I wouldn't know what to say.

The roads were covered with fresh snow and I kept both hands on the wheel of Uncle Piet's 1946 orange Ford pickup—one of the first pickups made after the war. I'd learned to drive in this truck; Cory too.

She wanted to know about my trip to Chicago.

"It was OK," I said. "The usual." Cory and I had been together on class trips to the Museum of Science and Industry, which is also in Hyde Park, and she'd come with us a couple of times to the All-Star Tournament; she'd seen the big house on Blackstone, and she'd eaten a ladies steak at George Diamond's; and once when the Midway'd been flooded, we'd stopped and rented skates and skated arm in arm with my father, who pulled us along with strong, sure strokes, while my mother, who didn't skate because of her bad knee, went to have a cigarette and a cup of coffee in the C Shop.

"Those buildings along the Midway are pretty amazing," she said.

"Like medieval castles," I said. "Like the duke of Cornwall's castle at Tintagel or Hrothgar's Heorot. Lancelot probably brought Guinevere to a place like that after rescuing her from the stake."

"What about you?"

I shrugged. "I visited one of the dorms. That was more like a prison. I don't think I could take it." I reached over and took her hand, though we both had gloves on. "Cory," I said, "we've got to make a plan."

I turned off Kruger Road onto the narrow lane that led to the dump and stopped the truck.

"What kind of a plan, Marty?" She didn't touch her finger to her lips or to mine. "Living together in your grandma Johnson's little house? It's so small. It's like a playhouse. Just like this town is like a little play town." She pulled her legs up and hugged her knees.

I felt in my pocket for a Life Saver. "It's not *that* small," I said. "What do *you* want to happen?"

"I don't want to live like the Tuckers," she said. "On that little farm way out in the middle of nowhere." Mr. Tucker, a Negro, was married to a white woman. They lived two or three miles out past the dump and their kids went to school in Galien. "No one ever looks at them. When they come into town it's like they're invisible."

"It wouldn't be like that for us."

"You'll feel different when you're at the University of Chicago," she said.

"I'm not going to the University of Chicago. That's what I've been trying to tell you."

"What's your mother going to say when you tell her you're not going to go?"

"She's going to be unhappy, but she'll get over it. She'll have to. You know what she says about clothes: 'Buy what you love or you'll have to love what you buy.'"

"What's that supposed to mean?"

"Oh, I don't know. Just that she'll have to accept it."

"You should have told her before. You shouldn't have waited so long."

"I've been trying to tell her. My dad too. She doesn't want to listen."

"It's so beautiful out," Cory said, looking out the side window. "The whole world is filled with light." She turned to look out the back window.

I took the truck out of gear, pulled on the hand brake, and slid across the seat. "Life Saver?"

She opened her mouth and I placed a Life Saver on her lips. I watched it disappear. I put my hand on her shoulder and kissed her neck. I was alive with desire. She let me kiss her neck, but she didn't respond. I tried to kiss her lips.

"No," she whispered. "I can't."

"It's OK," I said, and it was and it wasn't. "We should have gone to the Homecoming Dance together."

"That's just it," she said. "We couldn't imagine it. No one could imagine it."

"I can imagine kissing you," I said.

A car went by on Kruger Road. She pushed me away. "We'd better get going."

My uncle Maurinus Schuyler, who raised grapes and dewberries, controlled the access to the dump, and we had to stop and pay him $2. The oldest of my father's half brothers, he was a deacon in the Dutch Reformed Church and wore a big black hat on Sundays and religious holidays. Cory stayed in the truck while I went up to the house, which was cold and smelled of cats. It took Maurinus ten minutes to get his boots on and unlock the gate to let us in. He didn't trust me with the key, even though I told him I'd bring it right back before we even drove down to the dump.

Maurinus's old four-cylinder Ford tractor with a plow blade attached to the back was in the yard at the side of the house. I drove through the gate and Maurinus closed and locked it behind us. In case someone else came. There were in fact fresh tire tracks in the lane, in addition to the tracks left by the tractor. Someone had been here before us.

Schuylers Bottom, or Schuylers Dump as it was called, was not a landfill or a junkyard but a real old-fashioned dump in a big ravine where the Appleton River bent sharply to the north before heading west to empty into the lake. You could dump anything, and people did. Broken appliances and old mattresses and bedsprings humped up like whales in a sea of cans and bottles and rotting garbage.

Cory leaned over to tie pieces of rough twine around her pants legs.

"There aren't going to be any rats out now," I said. In the summer we'd park on Kruger Road and sneak back to the dump and shoot rats with our .22s. We tied twine around our pants legs after a baby rat climbed up Alvin Harris's pants leg one afternoon.

"I'm not taking any chances," she said.

I backed the truck around, but I was going a little too fast, trying to impress Cory, looking in the rearview mirror instead of back over my shoulder. The back wheels hit a patch of ice and the truck suddenly lurched backward. My foot slipped off the clutch and the truck shuddered to a halt, but I could feel the back wheels sliding down over the edge of the ravine, could feel the front end tilting up into the air till we were looking up at the tops of a row of poplar trees that Maurinus had planted as a windbreak along the vineyard. It took a while to catch my breath. I looked at Cory, but she was looking out the window. I couldn't see her face. I'd taken my gloves off and my hands stuck to the steering wheel. I started thinking how was I going to explain this to my dad. And then I started thinking about a movie we'd seen where a car goes over a cliff and rolls and rolls down to the bottom. I cut the ignition and took out the keys.

"Cory, do you love me the way I love you?"

She was about to answer me when the truck suddenly pitched back a yard or two and then stopped. Cory slid across the seat and kissed me quickly, the way a married woman might kiss a husband who's dropping her off somewhere on his way to work. My stomach was churning.

"We're going to have to get out," I said. "At the same time." I experienced the same dizzying feeling I'd had on the water tower.

"Wait," I said; she was already pulling on the door handle. "We've got to do it at the same time. I'll count to three and then we'll jump and hit the ground so the doors don't knock us over if the truck starts to slide. OK?"

But Cory never waited for anyone. She threw open her door and I threw open my door and we scooted out of the truck and hit the ground. The truck stayed put. I took a deep breath. I kept my eyes closed for a while, and when I opened them, the truck was still there.

"We've got to get my uncle," I said. "He can pull it back up with the tractor."

"We could push it over the edge," Cory said. "I bet I could do it by myself."

"What are you talking about?"

"Pushing the truck into the dump."

She had her hand on the hood ornament.

"Are you crazy? Cory, don't. I'm going to go get my uncle."

"He'll tell your dad," she said, "and your Uncle Piet, and my dad."

"I don't know what else to do. It's going to be a lot worse if the truck goes in."

She moved her hand around, as if she were looking for a better grip.

"Cory, get away from there." She turned to look at me. The sun was over my shoulder, and she raised her hand to shield her eyes. I started to move toward her.

"Don't," she said, "or I will."

"Cory, what's the matter? What are you doing?"

She didn't answer.

"My uncle—Maurinus, not Uncle Piet—is such a tight old bastard," I said. "Maybe I could pay him not to tell anyone." She was looking down into the dump. "The main thing," I said, "is to get the tractor so we can pull the truck back up. Then it won't matter."

"It really is beautiful," Cory said, turning toward me again. "Snow over everything. Even the dump. I can't get over it. *'Où sont les neiges d'antan?'* They're right here. You should have brought a camera." We'd been studying poetry in French class.

"I'm going to go get my uncle."

"Go ahead."

"Stay back from the truck."

"Will you remember me when you're at the University of Chicago?"

"I keep telling you I'm not going to the University of Chicago. I'm going to stay here and work in the orchards. We can get married, but we've got to have a plan; we've got to present a united front."

"You can do anything you want to," she said.

"That's what I'm telling you."

"That's the difference between us."

Cory, even in her heavy winter coat, had never looked more beautiful. "Come *with* me," I said. "We've got to get my uncle."

She looked puzzled, as if Miss Buckholdt had asked her a difficult question in geometry class.

"Cory?"

She didn't move. "Can you feel something?" she asked.

"Feel what?"

"Fate. Destiny. Closing in on you?"

"Stop it. There's no such thing as fate. There's just what we choose." It was an old argument from the days when we'd been reading Sartre and Camus and Ayn Rand.

She turned and leaned her weight into the front of the pickup. When it didn't move she began rocking it up and down, up and down. Her feet slipped out from under her on the snow, but she held on to the hood ornament. She kept rocking the truck up and down till it finally shifted.

"What the hell are you doing?" I shouted, running toward her. But it was too late: the front end tipped up, and the truck gradually disappeared over the edge of the ravine, like a ship sliding into the water, with hardly a sound.

"What the hell did you do that for? Jesus Christ, Cory, I mean . . ."

She shrugged her shoulders. "Sometimes I just want to do something, Marty, and that's what I wanted to do."

"It doesn't make any sense."

"It's not supposed to make sense. Like Meursault shooting the Arab at the beginning of *L'Etranger—un acte gratuit.*"

"An *acte gratuit*? Are you out of your mind?"

She just stood there looking down over the edge. I was angry, but only for a moment. The world *was* full of light, and the brightness was becoming brighter, as if the sun had come out from behind a cloud, though there were no clouds in the sky. I heard the sound of another truck coming down the narrow lane, but that too was part of the snow-covered beauty of the morning. The moment was overflowing with love and life. It was a miracle. Suddenly I understood everything, could see the shape—like the clear shape of the trees we'd been working on in the orchards. The extraneous branches had been pruned back, opening up the central leader to the light. "Cory," I said, "you're pregnant."

She nodded.

I looked over the edge of the ravine. The pickup had slid down about fifty feet and then dug into the trash without flipping over.

"Je me demande pourquoi cette porte s'est ouverte," I said. *"The door is open."*

The top button of Corinna's coat had come undone and the tip of her blue scarf was peeking out like a little bird. She tucked it back in and looked up. *"'Qu'est-ce que vous attendez? Allez, allez vite! What are you waiting for? Go! Go!'"*

"No, no," I said. "We've got to go through it together."

"Are you going to tell?" she asked.

I took her hand and we started down the little road to tell Uncle Maurinus about the truck. "No. I'll just say we got too close and when we got out the truck slid on over. I think it's great."

A hawk circled overhead; a rabbit crouched in the ditch at the edge of the lane; a squirrel scolded from the branch of an oak tree. They were all waiting, as I was, to see what would happen next.

When Corinna didn't show up on the corner to wait for the school bus on Monday morning I thought she must be sick. But there was no one home when I went over after school, and when my mother came home, I could tell from the expression on her face that something had happened. No one said anything while we ate club steaks and boiled potatoes. My father's hair was turning lighter, pale, blond. He parted it in the center. He ate his salad at the beginning of the meal; my mother at the end. I didn't eat any salad. This was what I'd been waiting for, but I was afraid, too. Compared to this, Uncle Piet's truck was nothing. I'd called my dad from Maurinus's and he'd called the Texaco station and Ray Thompson had come out with the big tow truck. It had been easy enough to winch the truck up. If there were new dents, it was hard to tell them from the old dents. The worst thing was that I had to climb down the side of the dump to hook the cable around the front axle; the next worst thing was that Maurinus wouldn't let my dad in with the tow truck until he paid the $2 dumping fee.

After supper I helped my mother with the dishes, waiting for her to say something, afraid to speak myself. But she didn't say anything, and when the last dish had been dried and put away and the counter wiped off, I went up to my room and lay down on my bed.

I had a new Philco radio in my room, and it was time for *The Lone Ranger,* but *The Lone Ranger* had gone off the air last year; *Captain Midnight* too, though the high cabinets over the sink—too high for my mother to reach—were full of unopened, unmarked jars of Ovaltine. I hadn't liked Ovaltine, but I'd needed the labels for a secret decoder.

When I finally heard my mother on the stairs—because of her knee she had to put her right foot first on each step—I took my guitar out from under the bed and started to play.

My mother came into my room without knocking, sat down at my desk, and lit a cigarette. "I spoke to Mrs. Williams this afternoon," she said after listening to me play for a minute. She leaned forward, crossed her legs. She was having trouble speaking. "At school."

There was a coffee cup on the desk that I used to hold pencils. My mother took out the pencils so she could use it for an ashtray. The smell of the broiled club steaks was still in the air, along with the smell of her cigarette. I held the guitar in front of me like a shield.

"Mrs. Williams was waiting for me at school today," my mother began again. "She said that Corinna's expecting a baby." My mother tapped the ashes of her Gitane into the coffee cup. The smoke curled up to the ceiling. "She hasn't told her mother who the father is."

Silence.

"Martin, do you know anything about this?"

Embracing Corinna, that night after climbing the water tower, I'd been embracing *life itself.* We made love only once, but once was enough, and maybe that's why this memory was fixed so cleanly in my mind: because it was uncontaminated by additional experiences. Even as my mother was speaking to me I evoked the image of the little town seen from above, like a tiny toy town that I was seeing for the first time; and my arches ached from the pressure of the rungs of the ladder; in no particular order I heard the sharp spit of my own zipper coming down and the sigh of the paint can and I smelled the fresh purple paint and tasted Cory's tongue between my lips; Cory lifts up her hips so that I can pull her underpants down, and for a few minutes we're weightless, as if we've both let go of the ladder at the same time and are floating upward through empty space, as if we're being gathered up into the night sky like a new constellation.

"Yes," I said, with some difficulty. "I'm the father."

She didn't understand me at first. "Your father's gone to bed," she said.

"No," I said. "I'm the father of the baby. Corinna's baby."

I played an Am9 chord on the guitar. It was the most complicated chord I knew, musically; but it was simple to play. Two fingers, on the fifth and seventh frets of the two middle strings. I moved my thumb pick across the strings slowly. I could see my mother collapse inwardly. Her hands were shaking and she knocked the coffee cup onto the floor when she tried to put out her cigarette. I picked it up and put it back on desk.

"Mom, it'll be all right, I promise." I'd promised Cory too, but what had seemed so clear to me had seemed fuzzy, out of focus, to her, like the slides of mitochondria we'd been looking at in general science. You'd get them into focus so you could see every detail perfectly clearly, but you couldn't adjust the microscope so that someone else could see what you saw.

"How'll it be all right?"

"We'll get married, we can live next door, in Grandma Johnson's old house."

"What about the Davidsons?" That's what Cory'd wanted to know. Ralph and Peggy Davidson, who ran the local weekly that published my mother's columns, had been renting my grandmother's house for several years, ever since her death. *Cory, the Davidsons are not a problem. The problem is not that the house is too small. The problem is we have to decide what we we're going to do and then stick together. I love you; you know that; that's not going to change.*

"They can find a place in town. There are plenty of places . . . Cory can work for Aunt Bridget at the beauty parlor; she's already started, two afternoons a week."

My mother lit another cigarette.

"Mom, I know that I love her. That's not going to change."

"Love is when you grossly overvalue another person. Besides, you're only seventeen years old."

I'd never heard her talk like this before. I'd never heard anyone talk like this before. Her hand was shaking and the smoke from her cigarette made a jagged line in the air.

She propped her foot on an apple crate that I used as my dirty clothes hamper.

"How can you be sure you're the father?"

I thought she was asking if I knew how babies were made. "I know because we made love, Mom, in the back of the Featherbone Company."

"How can you be sure you're the only one?"

"That's insulting."

"You're too young to get married, Martin. It's out of the question. You can't go to the University of Chicago with a baby in tow."

"I don't want to go to the University of Chicago."

"Oh, Martin, you don't know what you're saying. You don't want to live in this town. There's nothing here for you."

"You're here."

"Thank you, Martin, but that's not what I mean."

"The orchards are here," I said.

"There's so much more, Martin. You can't see it now. You can't see it from here. This is a little village, Martin. People here think it's the hub of the universe, but it's not. It's not a terrible place, I don't mean that. But it's provincial. No one here's ever been to Paris or Rome. *I* haven't been to Paris or Rome. In class I try to open a window, Martin. A little window on another world. You don't want to settle for so little."

"You live here; *you* settled for this."

"I know I did, Martin; and that's why I don't want you to. I want you to be a citizen of the world, not a citizen of Appleton, Michigan."

"Is it because she's a Negro?"

"Who?"

"Who? Corinna, Mom. Who do you think we're talking about?"

She paused. "You know that isn't so."

"Isn't it?"

"No, of course not. But it makes things so much more complicated. It's hard on the children."

"Is it hard in Paris?"

"What?"

"Is it hard for Negroes?"

"James Baldwin and Richard Wright live in Paris right now, Martin. Because they feel more at home there."

"That's not what I'm talking about. Say a Frenchman wanted to marry a Negro?"

"You don't need to deal with this now, Martin. You've got your whole life ahead of you. You don't want to throw it away."

"I'm not throwing it away."

"Corinna deserves better too."

"Better than what?"

"Better than bake sales and potluck suppers at the Methodist church and listening to Reverend Boomer's dreadful sermons. Better than working for your aunt Bridget."

"You never told me about Aunt Bridget," I said.

"Never told you what?"

"That she was in love with a sailor; that everybody loved him, and then he just disappeared."

"Oh, Marty, that's such a sad story; but it was before my time."

I wanted to ask more questions, but I didn't, because it wasn't my aunt Bridget I was thinking of; it was my mother. Had her story been a sad one too? This life? In this time and place? I wanted to know, but I was afraid to ask.

Cory wasn't in school on Tuesday. She had disappeared, I soon discovered, just like Ruth Davis, who'd been in the class ahead of me. Just as surely as if she'd been sent off to boarding school, or to prison. Aunt Flo said she'd gone to visit her aunt, but she wouldn't let me into the house, wouldn't open the door no matter how hard I pounded. Her anger was like the steam that came out of the mangle, from between the rollers, but I didn't back away from her, didn't turn mopey and shamefaced, because I didn't feel myself in the wrong. An inner light seemed to illuminate everything, like a flashlight on the narrow path through the woodlot to the orchards. There was no missing the way.

"Aunt Flo," I shouted through the closed door—I could hear her on the other side—"I've got to talk to Cory. You've got to tell me where she is."

"Looks like you done more than talk to her, Marty."

"Aunt Flo, don't you believe me?"

"Oh, I believe you, Marty."

Finally, at the end of the week, she weakened. The door opened;

a pile of damp clothes steamed in a basket on the floor; the mangle gave off heat.

"You've got to tell me where Cory is, Aunt Flo. I've got to talk to her. We'll talk in the kitchen, the three of us."

"We have to work something out, Marty."

"That's what I'm talking about. We can work things out together. Right now. We can talk things through."

"She's not feeling too good right now. That's why she went to stay with her aunt."

"Of course not. I'm not feeling too good either. That's why we've got to talk. I love her, Aunt Flo. You know I do. We could live in Grandma Johnson's old house. We'd be right here."

"And what happened to the University of Chicago?"

"I don't care about the University of Chicago. I care about Cory. I care about the orchards. This is where I belong, not in Chicago. I've known that all along. I just didn't realize it, do you know what I mean?"

"I know what you mean, Marty. Now I want you to run along home, I got work to do."

I tried to force my way into the house, past Aunt Flo, but she blocked my way. "Now look here, Marty, that's enough, you hear?"

"I hear something," I said, "but it doesn't sound like the truth to me."

"My lord, Marty," she said, "what's come over you?"

"Nothing's come over me, Aunt Flo. I just want to know where Cory is."

"Well, Marty," she said, softening a little, "I know you didn't intend no harm, but now there's no help for it."

"What do you mean there isn't any help for it?"

"It's as plain as the nose on your face."

"It's not plain to me."

"Someday you'll understand it, Marty. By and by. But now I got to get back to my work." She closed the door in my face.

*　　　*　　　*

I watched Cory's window to make sure she was really gone, staked out the house every day after school till it finally began to snow. There were no leaves on the trees now, so I had a clear view of Cory's empty window. I wrote letters to her and put them in the mailbox. I skipped school to watch her window one afternoon, in case she moved around in the daytime when she thought I wasn't there to see her. Nothing was doing in the orchards, and there was no sign of Cap either.

My mother knew I'd skipped school, because I wasn't in French class. My father found me in the tree, watching the window and blowing on my hands.

"What's going on?"

"That's what I'm trying to find out."

"Martin, come down from there." He was smoking one of my mother's cigarettes.

"I don't want to come down."

He had two guns with him and his ferret, Ernie, in a gunnysack. I could see Ernie twisting around.

"You'd have saved yourself a peck of trouble if you'd used a rubber."

I didn't say anything.

"Let's go get a rabbit for supper. Ernie needs some exercise. You're going to freeze up there."

I climbed down. I hadn't seen any signs of life in Cory's room. I knew she was really gone.

My father was an ally. It was good to be walking together.

"I don't get it," I said. "Don't *you* want me to stay in Appleton? What's going to happen to the orchards when . . . if I don't . . .? Uncle Piet's talking about retiring. You're going to buy his half, aren't you?"

"Looks that way. David's not coming back, that's for sure"—my cousin David was a lawyer in San Francisco—"and Griet and Barent've got the propane business."

"Well?"

"Marty, it's not so simple."

"What isn't so simple? It looks pretty simple to me."

"Well, it doesn't look that way to all the parties involved."

"Why can't I talk to Corinna?"

"Corinna's not here. That's one reason."

"Where is she?"

"She's gone to stay with her aunt."

"Her aunt? Where?"

"I don't know."

"You don't know, or you just aren't telling?"

"I don't know."

"When's she coming back?"

"I don't know that either."

We walked past the packing shed, through the migrant camp, and along the first row of Red Havens till we came to a rabbit hole. My father adjusted Ernie's muzzle and turned him loose. I checked the safety on my .22, and we waited in silence.

"Marty," my father said after a few minutes, "I haven't been able to give your mother . . . everything she needs."

"What does she need? She's got her books, her music, her cross-word puzzles." I was repeating something I'd heard my father say more than once.

"You remember when she and Mr. Haptonstahl went into Chicago to pick out the piano at Lyon and Healy?"

"Sort of."

"I thought that that piano would make her happy. It's a Steinway, a Steinway B. That's the top of the line. I gave her a blank check for her birthday. I told her to pick out a piano, and she picked out a good one. And Roy Haptonstahl went with her. It took them three days to make a decision . . . They stayed in the Palmer House, so they could be close to Lyon and Healy, where they were trying out the pianos. I paid the bill for separate rooms; but she fell in love with him. It lasted about a year. She doesn't know that I know."

The idea that my mother might be carrying a torch for Ernest Hemingway had always pleased me, and I think it tickled my father too. I think that's why he named his ferret Ernie. But Ernest Hemingway was a mythological figure who lived far away, in Italy or France or Spain. That was one thing. The idea that my mother might have had a real lover, someone we knew, Roy Haptonstahl, who lived on Sherwood Street and came to our house for my piano lessons and told me to practice slowly and to count out loud while I was practicing, and who played Chopin's "Ocean Étude" with his small hands, was another thing entirely. If you asked him how he did it he'd say he didn't play the piano with his hands, and he'd point to his head, and then to his heart. I wasn't worried about divorce. As far as I knew no one in Appleton had ever gotten a divorce. Divorce was for people like Rita Hayworth and Aly Khan. But I thought I knew something about love, and I thought it was absolutely impossible that Roy Haptonstahl could ever have felt about my mother the way I felt about Cory. I knew that my parents wanted different things out of life: my father wanted meat loaf and mashed potatoes and my mother wanted to cook the French dishes that she'd learned how to make when she was living with the Stoddards in Hyde Park; my dad wanted a snort of whiskey out in the garage or in the packing shed at the end of a long day; my mom wanted a glass of wine with dinner; my dad liked to sing "Home on the Range" and "Little Brown Jug"; my mom played Debussy and Chopin; my dad read *Field and Stream* and *Hunter's Digest;* my mom read Flaubert and Proust; my dad went bowling on Thursday nights and to church on Sundays; my mom—my mom couldn't bowl because of her bad knee, and she liked to stay in bed on Sunday mornings; my dad had only one suit; my mother's closet was full of clothes that she bought at Marshall Field's in Chicago. She bought only what she loved, and she loved ivory silk blouses and high heels and touches of bright color. I'd known these things for a long time, of course; but the possibility that my parents didn't love each other—that my mother had loved another man—it was as if the ladder on the water tower had given way and I was falling like a stone, still holding on to the bottom rung.

"Why are you telling me this? I don't want to hear this."

"I don't know why, Marty. I'm sorry. It's just that—it's just that things can be so complicated. They're never what they seem. This isn't the life your mother dreamed about."

"It's the life I dream about."

"It's the only life you know."

"What about you?"

"It's the only life I know too. That's the problem."

"What are you going to do?"

"Going to do? That was years ago, Marty; I'm not going to *do* anything. There's nothing to be done."

The rabbit finally shot out of a hole about twenty feet in front of us. I picked it off with my .22. My father waited for Ernie to come out of the rabbit hole and then muzzled him and put him back in his sack. When we skinned the rabbit, the cavity was full of little balls of shit. My mother cleaned it out and prepared something she called a *ragoût de lapin*, but I wasn't hungry.

I didn't want Cory to be one of those girls who disappeared and never came back, or who came back shamed and subdued. I laid siege to the Williamses. I tried to get Cap alone so I could talk to him man to man, but he was gone most of the time. I wrote more letters, letters to the entire family, and put them in their mailbox, letters explaining everything. But Aunt Flo didn't want to talk to me; she continued to block the door when I came over.

I no longer took our laundry over. My mother had begun sending it to a dry cleaner, who picked it up in his truck every Thursday afternoon.

"Just let me come in for a minute," I begged her. "Just let me talk to you."

Finally I asked for something to drink, and she relented.

"It's too cold," she said, taking a pitcher of buttermilk out of the refrigerator. It was beyond her range of belief that someone wouldn't want his buttermilk warmed up.

Her large brown face was smooth and soft, but formidable.

"Where's Cap?"

"He had to go up to Benton Harbor to take care of some business."

I was prepared to deal with anger, but she no longer seemed really angry, and I'd already used up my arguments. Even so, it still seemed too clear and easy to me. Aunt Flo's laundry baskets were stacked up in a corner, empty. The mangle was cold.

"We expect to read about you in the papers one of these days."

"You think I'm going to commit a crime?"

She gave a kind of laugh. "I expect you to invent something or discover something or write a book about something."

"If I write a book it'll be about Cory," I said, "and you."

In March Aunt Flo and Cap disappeared too. I went over to check the house after school one day and they were gone. The door was unlocked, and the house was empty except for the mangle. I sat down on a broken chair and turned on the switch at the side. The electricity was still on. I waited for the mangle to heat up, and then I took off my shirt and fed one of the sleeves into the big rollers. I'd watched Aunt Flo do it a thousand times, but the sleeve came out all wrinkled. I did the other sleeve, and then I fed in the lower part of the shirt, below the sleeves, and reversed the rollers. The shirt was very hot, but I put it on. It was still warm when I got home.

I heard from Lotte, in the Congo, and I heard from the University of Chicago—there was no mention, in my letter of acceptance, of my application essay—but I never heard from Cory. Every day when I came home from school I would ask my mother if a letter had come from Cory, and I could see that this pained her. "There are plenty of fish in the sea," she'd say. "You'll meet lots of girls in Hyde Park, you'll see."

There were sixty-seven Williamses listed in the Benton Harbor phone book, and I called every one of them from the pay phone in the bowling alley, but I couldn't track down the elusive cousin who had escorted Cory to our class dances. I checked regularly with other kids in the class, but none of them ever received a letter either. I hadn't been singled out. On Decoration Day I staked out Poesy Chapel Cemetery—lying on my back behind the big Potter family mausoleum—in case Aunt Flo came back to tidy up Charlie's grave and leave some flowers.

My father, unlike my mother, seemed to share my disappointment. Hearing him moving around in the kitchen one night, I went downstairs, and we had a drink together. I could see that he'd had several drinks already. I didn't care. He was drinking Canadian Club. I'd never seen the whiskey bottle out on the table before.

"Sometimes things don't work out," he said.

"They can't just disappear," I said. I could feel the warmth of the whiskey in my cheeks.

And then my mother appeared at the door in her robe, her hair down. She didn't have her glasses on, but she was holding a crossword puzzle book in one hand, folded around her finger. She had a cigarette in the other hand: "You should be ashamed of yourself," she said to my father. "Leave him alone, for God's sake. You'll only make things worse."

The next morning things were back to normal. My mother continued to talk as if the matter had been settled. "I want you to be happy," she said; "I want you to be as happy as I was then. You'll meet lots of girls in Hyde Park," she said for the twentieth time. "There are plenty of fish in the ocean. You'll see. You don't have to worry about that, a good-looking guy like you."

You need only three chords, the I, IV, and V^7—the tonic, subdominant, and dominant seventh—to play a thousand folk songs and a thousand hymns. And if you play a pentatonic scale over these same three chords, you've got the blues. The pentatonic scale is the same five-note scale that moviemakers use to introduce Oriental themes: ta-ta-ta-ta ta-ta ta-ta *ta*. It's like a major scale with the second and sixth notes left out and the third and seventh notes flatted. C, E-flat, F, G, B-flat, and back to C. The flatted third and the flatted seventh—and sometimes a flatted fifth—are the blues notes. They clash with the notes of the major chords, and that gives you a bluesy sound—something in between major and minor. On a guitar you can pull on the string to change the pitch of these blues notes. Then you get an even bluesier sound. I tried to find these sounds on the piano, but they're right between the cracks of keys. You can't get at them.

In your basic twelve-bar blues you start with four measures on the tonic chord. Then you create some tension by moving to the subdominant for two measures and then you come back to the tonic for two measures. Then you create even more tension by moving to the dominant for one measure; the subdominant for another; and then you come home to the tonic for the final two measures. It's that simple.

I'd take Chesterfield's guitar and sit on the edge of my bed and play the three chords over and over, and I'd sing a pentatonic scale over those chords. I'd just make up something off the top of my head, like this: "I woke up this morning," I'd sing, "put on my travelin' shoes." And then I'd sing the same thing over again—call and response—only I'd start out with the subdominant chord on the guitar, and that would give the melody a different feel. "I woke up this morning, put on my travelin' shoes." And then I'd hit the dominant, move to the subdominant, and then come on home: "I said, 'Roll over, baby, I got them low-down travelin' blues.'"

Would *you* hear what I hear, if you were sitting on the bed next to me? Would you hear something different? What did my mother hear when she played Chopin? Sometimes it sounded to me as if Chopin was trying to get at those blues notes in the cracks between the keys, and sometimes he'd come awfully close; so maybe my mother was listening for the same thing, even though it didn't seem that way. And what had my cousin Lotte heard that had called her to Africa? Whatever it was, I didn't think it had made her happy. In the letters she wrote from Camp Putnam, in the eastern part of the Belgian Congo, she sounded more like she was homesick and was trying to put a good face on it. But then, I thought, maybe that was the same thing too.

> *Corinna, Corinna, way across the sea;*
> *Corinna, Corinna, way across the sea;*
> *She don't write no letter, she don't care for me.*

In the first week of May, on my way home from school, I saw a swarm of bees hanging on the branch of a lilac bush, like an old sweater. Normally Cap would have snapped the swarm off the branch and into an empty hive while I sprinkled water over it, to make the bees think it was raining—bees don't work in the rain; but Cap, of course, was gone. I ran into the toolshed and found the smoker and a box of kitchen matches and a pair of gloves, but I didn't bother with Cap's bee suit. I stacked three apple crates under the swarm, put an empty bushel basket on top of the crates, lit the smoker, which was already stuffed with burlap and sawdust, and worked the bellows till I had a smudgy fire going. The smoke calmed the bees, which suddenly became quiet. I put the smoker down and knocked the stirring swarm loose with one hand. Most of the bees fell into the bushel basket. As long as the queen was in the basket, it would be OK. About a third of the bees had fallen outside the basket, and I thought they might be angry. I hoped they were; I wanted them to sting me; I wanted to thrust my whole body into the fire; but they had gorged themselves on honey before swarming and were not in a fighting mood. I blew some smoke at them and they flew into the basket, which I dumped into an empty hive.

I did get a couple of stings, though, and by the time I'd capped the hive my left eye was swollen shut, and when the mail came I let my mother read the letters that had arrived that morning from the University of Chicago. She opened them with her fingers. The first was my dorm assignment—I'd be in Foster Hall, the dorm I'd visited, second floor, room number 16; my roommate would be Josh McKinnon, who was planning to be a doctor and who played the marimba. The second was from the admissions office. I had received a scholarship that would cover more than half of my tuition.

In June I learned from Aunt Bridget, who'd gotten it straight from Aunt Flo, that my parents had *paid* the Williamses to move away. This news was so stunning that at first I refused to believe it, but Aunt Bridget and Aunt Flo had always been close, and Aunt Bridget had no reason to lie. I sat on this information for two days, observing my parents from, as it were, a great distance. It was the middle of June. The Williamses had been gone for two months.

I confronted my father at the end of a long day of spraying—we'd been spraying the apples with naphthalene acetic acid to shock the trees, knock off the non-king blooms so you don't wind up with dwarf apples. I'd been driving the tractor and my father had been working the hose.

"How much did you pay the Williamses to leave?" I asked as he was checking the level of acid in the tank of the spray rig, trying to keep my voice level, as if I were asking if he was going to fill the tank that evening or wait till the next morning.

At first he didn't say anything, and then I saw him collapse inwardly, the way my mother had collapsed when I told her I was the father of Corinna's baby.

"If you say anything to your mother," he said, "it will break her heart."

"Where are they?"

"I don't know, Martin. I swear to God I don't know. We sent the money to a special account in a bank in Benton Harbor, that's all I know."

"How much money?"

"It was a lot, Martin. I couldn't pay it all at once."

I'd never seen my father cry, and I didn't want to, so I turned and left him standing alone by the big John Deere tractor. And I didn't look back.

I didn't say anything to my mother—at least not then—but I broke her heart anyway, disappointed her just as she had disappointed me. Instead of going to the University of Chicago and reading all the great books, I signed up for a three-year hitch in the Navy, and a week after I was mustered out of the Navy in the summer of 1959 I got my uncle Gerrit to take me up to South Bend to take the civil service exam, *even though I could have taken advantage of the GI Bill, could still have gone to the University of Chicago,* as my mother kept pointing out. I wanted to work for the RPO—the Railway Post Office—like Gerrit. Jobs were hard to come by, but Gerrit, who was getting ready to retire, was a clerk-in-charge on the Buff and Chicago and knew how to pull a few strings, and six weeks later I was called up. I dumped mail for three months at the Chicago terminal and then subbed for three months on the Chi West Lib and Omaha, and then I came back to work on the Buff and Chicago, where I made regular after six months. I could have lived at home in Appleton, like Gerrit, and deadheaded from Niles into Chicago for my runs, but it was too late for that too. I worked six and eight on the RPO, six days on the road and eight days off. On their weeks off most of the men on my crew went home to wives and children. I stayed in a hotel in Chicago that catered to RPO men—the Hotel Antlers on South State—and took as much overtime as I could get, often working all the major holidays: Easter, Fourth of July, Decoration Day, Thanksgiving, Christmas. I got a library card at the Chicago Public Library on Randolph Street and did a little reading while I was on the road, mostly detective novels, but for the most part on my weeks off I studied RPO routes and schedules during the day and went to blues clubs at night with another RPO clerk on my crew, Jack Skeffington, who, like me, was tired of the Kingston Trio and the Brothers Four and Peter, Paul and Mary. Some of these clubs were in rough neighborhoods where there was more or less open warfare between blacks and whites, but Jack was a tough Irish guy, about ten years older than I was, who knew his way around the South Side, and I always felt safe with him. We listened to the new Columbia release of the Robert Johnson sessions in San Antonio; we even talked about going down to Mississippi to look for Chesterfield, who hadn't come back to Appleton after he'd sold me his guitar; but we settled for Theresa's, on Indiana Avenue, where a framed poster of Martin Luther King near the cashier signaled that whites were welcome, and Pepper's Show Lounge, on Forty-third, where the women would sometimes raise their skirts up over their heads while they were dancing, and sometimes the Purple Door, on Fifty-seventh, by the University of Chicago.

When Jack got married and transferred to the Bluffs, he gave me his record player, a four-speed Fisher in a beautiful cherry cabinet. He said it was like the one JFK had in the White House. I listened to records, and I kept on going to the clubs. In the forties and fifties these clubs had been very popular with whites from the North Side, but in the sixties there were only a handful of white faces in the crowd, and sometimes Muddy Waters would invite us to stand up, and sometimes he'd invite this little Jewish kid, Michael Bloomfield, to come up on stage and play his guitar—Muddy's own red Telecaster with the action raised way up high. Bloomfield went on to become one of the first great blues-rock guitarists. I met him a couple of years later in the Fret Shop in Hyde Park, and I heard him at Big John's when he started to play with the Paul Butterfield Band, but it was astonishing to see him up on the stage at Theresa's—he couldn't have been more than fifteen or sixteen—riffing with Otis Spann at the piano and Elgin Evans on the drums while Muddy took a little break.

I envied Bloomfield his chutzpah, but in fact the urban sound wasn't really what I was listening for. Muddy Waters had amplified all the guitars, and Little Walter had amplified the harp, and the Fender basses and the drums had taken charge of the beat, so the first guitar got stuck playing rhythm patterns while the second guitar soloed. I loved the power of Muddy Waters's solid-body Telecaster and the shout of John Lee Hooker's thinline Epiphone and the scream of Little Walter's electric harp; but what I was always listening for was the sound from my childhood, the sound I used to listen to in the migrant workers' camp behind the packing shed. What I was listening for was the sound of one man and one guitar—a simple sound that spoke directly to the heart, like the voice of someone you love, calling your name from the window of a train that's pulling out of the station.

I was trying to drive out thoughts of Corinna. I'd written to her once a week—from boot camp at Great Lakes, and then from the ship, and then from Guantánamo Bay, where I was stationed—letters so full of grief and love that I don't know how I managed to seal them up. I sent them to her in Appleton. I didn't put a return address on the outside of the envelopes, though, maybe I knew enough to know that I didn't want the letters coming back. I stopped writing when I went to work for the RPO, but I watched the letters that passed through my hands, always thinking I might find one addressed to her. It wasn't impossible. Chad Clark, who worked the Michigan case with me, had found a letter addressed to himself one day, and Jimmy Purchase, who usually worked the pouch rack, said that he'd once intercepted a letter from his ex-wife to her new lover. First he claimed he'd sent it on to Greenville, Indiana, instead of Greenville, Michigan; but later he admitted that he'd taken it home and read it himself. If anyone had told Chappie, our foreman, Jimmy would have lost his job. Maybe worse than that—it was a federal offense. But no one said anything. I never intercepted a letter to Corinna, however. It was time to put Corinna behind me. But I kept my eyes open as the letters passed through my hands.

I got used to being on the road, and when I was off duty I missed the sway of the cars and the feel of the road beneath my feet, the way I'd missed the sway of the ship—an old can called the USS *Brady*—and the feel of the ocean when I'd left the Navy. I enjoyed packing my road grip before a run: tags, slips, revolver, holster and shells, schedules and schemes, badge and manual, goggles, pencils, labels, stamps and pads, travel commission, revolver permit, money. I liked the camaraderie and the cribbage games in the grip room before a run, and sometimes afterward, and the feel of the little .38 snubnose snug in its drop holster—all the RPO clerks were required by law to carry loaded revolvers while on duty. I liked setting up the cases and the pouches, making coffee with the copper coil that was hooked into the steam line in the bathroom at the end of the car. I liked the rush you got when the engineer pulled back on the throttle and eased the big F9 diesel out of the station. I liked knowing the names of every single town in Michigan and Illinois and northern Indiana and Ontario, and I liked throwing thirty letters a minute into the big Michigan case, little packets of other peoples' joys and sorrows, money, and love. I liked making the catch and locking out the pouches at the end of a run.

But I missed home too and would always try to make the catch at Appleton, which was a nonstop, when we were heading west into Chicago. I'd put on my goggles and raise the catcher arm at Brinkman's Crossing and make the catch just opposite the depot, which was on the south side of the tracks, and then I'd have about eight or nine seconds to take it all in: Dewey Cannon Park, where President McKinley had given a speech at the end of the Spanish-American War; the Oriental Theater, where Cory and I had seen *Sharad of Atlantis,* and *The Invisible Man,* and *Forty-Ninth Parallel,* and *Another Dawn,* and *Abbott and Costello Meet Frankenstein;* then a straight shot north down Main Street to Dijksterhuis Corners, then the Potter Featherbone Company coming up on the left, just a glimpse, as we left the town, and I could look back at the water tower that Cory and I had climbed, and then I'd lower the catcher arm and pull in the pouch and hand it off to the pouch-rack man and go back to sorting the U.S. mail.

PART II

4

Sweet Home, Chicago

1964

It wasn't till my father's death, in March 1964, that I learned where the Williamses were living—or at least I got a clue. Aunt Bridget had received a Christmas card from Aunt Flo saying that Cap had died and that she was keeping busy but was lonely too and missed sitting with Bridget in the kitchen. Aunt Bridget gave me the card after the funeral. There was no return address on the envelope, but the postmark said Madison, Wisconsin. The card would have come from Madison to Chicago on the Twin Cities 400, and then from Chicago to Appleton on the Twilight Limited. It might have passed through my hands.

I was sitting on a chair at the end of the breakfast nook, a little alcove off the kitchen with a U-shaped bench surrounding a built-in table. The table was painted deep blue, my mother's favorite color. A window at the far end of the table opened on the backyard. You could see the garage and the brush beyond, snow-covered. My mother was poaching eggs. I had my guitar in my lap.

I'd played my father's favorite hymn at the funeral, "Nearer My God to Thee." I played it again while my mother poached eggs:

> *How like a wanderer, the sun goeth down,*
> *Darkness be over me, my rest a stone.*
> *Still in my dreams I'll be, Nearer, my God,*
>   *to thee,*
> *Nearer, my God, to thee, Nearer to thee.*

I played it in a dropped-D tuning, with a good steady bass.

"That's a nice arrangement of that song, Marty," my mother said. "It doesn't sound so much like a hymn the way you play it."

The visitation had been at the Cochrane Funeral Home, but the funeral itself had been held in the Methodist church. Lots of people had come to pay their respects: hunting and fishing friends, the entire Lions Club, people from the church, orchard men, and men from the big farmers' market up in Benton Harbor. My father had lived here all his life. His father too, Pieter, and his mother, Mietje, who'd raised two large families.

We still had an old-fashioned toaster with sides that pulled down. You could toast only one side at a time. My mother plugged it in each time we used it. Then she cleaned it and put it away.

"How does Janis like her eggs?" she asked. "Maybe I'd better wait."

"She doesn't usually eat much breakfast," I said. Janis, the woman I'd been living with for almost a year in Hyde Park, was asleep in the guest room upstairs. She was a graduate student in economics at the U of C. We weren't exactly engaged, but we had an understanding, and my mother and I were both glad that she'd come down with me. Janis represented the future—marriage and family, continuity, getting back on track—and my mother had been doing everything she could to make her feel welcome.

"I'll put them in a bowl of hot water," she said. "They'll stay warm."

"It was a nice service," I said. She shrugged her shoulders. At the funeral I'd felt numb rather than grief-stricken. My father, who'd been pleased when he finally learned that Cory and I had been the ones who'd painted the water tower, hadn't been himself the last few years. He'd let Uncle Piet and my cousin Wim manage the orchards and my mother manage the household. In the evenings he drank a little whiskey and read Zane Grey novels till he fell asleep on the davenport. He'd been vaguely apologetic for not taking my side when I'd wanted to marry Corinna, for being weak; but this was a conversation I didn't want to have, so I never gave him an opening to say what he wanted to say. In another sense, though, the old-fashioned house, which he and my grandfather had built, had spoken for him: the hardwood floors, the double-glazed windows, the mantel over the fireplace, the wainscoting in the dining room, the bookcases he'd built on the west wall of the living room to hold my mother's books and music, the beautiful old-fashioned tile stove that heated the kitchen, the extra-wide eaves, so you could leave the windows open in the rain, the extra-large windows in the sun porch upstairs, everything still plumb and square after all these years. Even the new fixtures in the upstairs bathroom, which I'd helped him install just before I'd left for basic training at Great Lakes—the walk-in shower, the stool, the sink—marked him as a man who took pride in his work. It had been easy, as I'd pointed these things out to Janis—taking her hand from time to time, or putting my hand on her shoulder—to imagine living in this house, living the life that my father and my grandfather had lived before me.

"I've tracked down the Williamses," I said, suddenly, surprising myself as well as my mother. My mother didn't ask how, and I didn't say anything about the Christmas card. Aunt Bridget had asked me not to.

After a long silence my mother sighed, "Oh Marty, oh Marty. After all these years."

"Why don't you just tell me what happened?"

"Marty, we did what we thought was best for you. That's all. You were only seventeen. You couldn't have married *any* girl and raised a child. You were too young. You had your whole life ahead of you. Do you see? All we wanted was what was best for you."

"I see." I did see.

"How much?"

"How much?"

"How much money did you pay them?"

"It was quite a lot, Marty. Your father sent quite a lot of money."

"How much? Do you know?"

"No, I just know that it was quite a lot. Your father fretted over it, and you know he didn't fret over money."

"Well, however much it was, it probably wasn't enough."

"You see, we thought that Cory had—well—put herself forward so that you'd feel obligated."

"I see."

"You do see, don't you? We just wanted what was best for you."

Janis and I had ridden out from Chicago on train number 356 the afternoon after my father died. My mother had insisted on meeting us at the station in Niles, Ring Lardner's hometown.

She lifted the eggs out of the saucepan with a slotted spoon, dipped them in a bowl of warm water to rinse off the taste of the vinegar she always put in the water to keep the whites from spreading out, rolled them on a dish towel to dry, and put them on pieces of toast. Two for me, one for her. Two for Janis in the bowl of hot water. Little bits of gray or silver sparkled in her dark hair.

"I suppose it *was* a nice service," she said.

What could I say? "Yes."

"Your father kept to himself, you know. These last years. Ever since he got the cancer."

I nodded.

"He missed you."

I seasoned my eggs with salt, pepper, and Tabasco. The Tabasco was so old it had turned dark brown.

"People when they get old . . . ," she went on.

"Mom . . ."

"It's all right. I just want you to remember."

"I do remember, Mom, it's just . . ."

"I know it's just . . . , but it can't be helped now."

I plunged a fork into my egg.

"I don't know how you can eat it with all that Tabasco."

"Some like it hot."

"Some like it cold." She waited for me to say the next line. I waited too, and then I said it.

"Some like it in the pot."

"Nine days old."

"Do you remember how we used to go out on the porch and look at the clouds and be silly? Do you remember how I taught you to say 'Humpty Dumpty' in French? You were only five years old and you could say it."

I nodded.

"Say it for me, Martin."

"I don't want to say it in French."

"Please, Martin. We'll say it together."

"How does it start?"

"Boule, Boule sur la cuillère . . ."

> *Boule, Boule sur la cuillère*
> *Boule, Boule tombe par terre.*
> *I'y a nul homme en Angleterre*
> *Qui l'œuf puisse refaire.*

*   *   *

At the time I met Janis I was still sorting mail on the Buff and Chicago, six days on the road, eight off, still living in the Hotel Antlers on South State Street, still hitting a club or two after a run, still listening to old seventy-eights, which I bought at Sam's Record Emporium in the Melrose Brothers' old music store, next to the El station on Sixty-third and Cottage Grove, where the aisles between the bins were too narrow for two people to pass, and the wooden counters were piled so high with old albums, some not in their sleeves, that you seemed to be in some kind of labyrinth. I'd clean the records carefully and then listen to a song over and over on Jack's hi-fi till I had every note locked up in my imagination, if not in my fingers. It was a good time, in fact, for country blues. There was a bit of a revival—part of the folk music craze—and quite a few old bluesmen had been discovered by young white blues enthusiasts like me: Mance Lipscomb in Navasota, Texas; Lightning Hopkins in Houston; Son House in Rochester, New York; Bukka White in Aberdeen, Mississippi; Sleepy John Estes in Brownsville, Texas; Mississippi John Hurt in Avalon, Mississippi—men whose records I'd been collecting but whom I'd thought of as separated from us by the mists of time, like the mythological figures in my mother's stories, Odysseus, Heracles, Beowulf. With a little help from Sam Leiner, who owned Sam's Record Emporium, I'd "discovered" an old bluesman of my own, Reverend Nehemiah Taylor, who lived in a big house over on Grand Boulevard, the first major street west of Cottage Grove. Reverend Taylor hadn't actually wanted to be discovered, however.

It was Janis who'd opened the door the first time I rang the bell on Reverend Taylor's front porch. As far as *she* knew, she said, Reverend Taylor didn't play the guitar, but she'd ask him anyway. Could I wait a few minutes, because Reverend Taylor was busy at the moment but would be free in half an hour?

I waited in an old-fashioned parlor that was all done up in chintz and silk—mauve and gray; carpeting, sofa, armchairs, drapes—like the inside of a coffin. No books. No magazines. No record player. No radio. No plants. No pictures on the wall. No guitars.

It was eight-thirty when Janis came back and asked if I'd like to come into the kitchen. I followed her through a formal dining room, through a butler's pantry, into the kitchen, where Reverend Taylor, dressed in a suit and wearing a tie, was standing with his hands behind his back.

"Reverend Taylor," I said, "I can't believe you're really alive."

"Sometimes," he said, "I have trouble believing it myself."

"Sorry," I said. "I didn't mean . . . I mean, I've got six of your records, and—"

"Then you got six more than I got," he said.

The kitchen floor had been retiled with deep red Italian tiles, but the moldings hadn't been replaced; the appliances were fairly new—a six-burner restaurant stove and a huge built-in refrigerator—but there were no cabinets. You could see where the old cabinets had been ripped out, but now everything—cereal, flour, sugar, a box of raisins, vinegar, salt and pepper, dish soap, canned tomatoes—was jumbled together on the kind of metal shelves you'd expect to find in a basement or a garage. Along with two green cans of Quaker State motor oil, a big container of special powdered soap for mechanics, and a small TV.

"I just picked up 'Mr. Jelly Roll Baker' and 'Sun Don't Want to Shine' at Sam's over on Sixty-third Street. Do you still play?"

He shook his head. "Not for years."

"Would you *like* to play sometime?"

"I don't know," he said, "if I could remember a thing."

"It's like riding a bicycle," I said.

"I never rode a bicycle," he said, "but I rode a mule." He held a pair of imaginary reins in his hand.

"Well then," I said, "it's like riding a mule."

"It would have to be in my case."

"'She used to live out on Indiana Avenue,'" I said; "'moved to Sixty-third and Cottage Grove'—that's where Sam's is. 'She took all of my money, stole all of my clothes.'"

Reverend Taylor laughed. "I wrote that song about my wife," he said—"my first wife. We didn't see eye to eye after the Lord called me, I can tell you that. Come down in the morning with a towel wrapped round her head. I started wrapping a towel around my head too so I wouldn't have to listen to her. You want a cup of coffee? Janis, get Mr. . . ." He paused.

"Dijksterhuis," I said. "Rhymes with *choice*."

"Get Mr. Dijksterhuis a cup, would you?"

Janis got a glass out of the cupboard. A lime green electric percolator was plugged into an extension cord that dropped off the table and ran across the beautiful tiles on the floor to an outlet that didn't have a cover plate over it.

"No more for me," Janis said, putting her hand over her cup. "I've got problem sets to do and I don't want to get *too* wired."

Reverend Taylor poured coffee into our cups and unplugged the pot.

"Seriously," I said, "if I brought my guitar over, would you show me a few licks?"

"What did you say your name was?"

"Dijksterhuis," I said again.

"My wife—my second wife—would turn over in her grave."

"Mr. Leiner says you played a Martin 000–45," I said. "That's kind of like the holy grail of guitars."

"It had twelve frets," I remember.

"Mr. Leiner says they stopped making them in 1934."

"Is that right? I had an old twelve-string Stella too, but I kept it tuned up to pitch, and one day it just collapsed in upon itself. I believe my wife kept the other guitar when we separated."

"You could still give me some pointers," I said. "Maybe I could come by tomorrow?"

He laughed. "You're in a big hurry." He shook his head. "Can it wait till next week?"

"Next week I'll be on the road," I said.

"On the road?" he said. He fingered his empty cup and looked at Janis, who was sorting through some papers and putting them in different envelopes. "Now what do you know about being on the road?" he asked. "Are you some kind of itinerant musician?" He laughed. "Dijksterhuis. That's some name for an itinerant bluesman."

"I work for the RPO, the Railway Post Office," I said. "I work the Twilight Limited, between here and Detroit."

"Is that so? I had a cousin worked for the post office in Atlanta, in the dead letter office they called it."

"It's called the mail recovery center now."

"That's something, isn't it, when you think about it? Letters going every which way all over the world, connecting everybody, carrying love and sorrow, binding everybody together. And to think that some of them never get through. You got your love letters and your letters in time of trouble and your invitations. Think of all the misunderstandings and broken hearts. Course you got your telephone now. But tell me something I've often wondered about: what do you do with a letter to a foreign country? How do you know what to do with it? Say you get a letter to Paris, France. Such-and-such a street. How do you know what to do?"

"If I were working Michigan," I said, "I wouldn't *get* a letter to Paris. The mail we get on the train has already been sorted at the local level. The only raw mail we get—unsorted mail—is what we pick up at mailboxes at the stations. Actually, there's a slot in the side of the mail car for letters, but nobody ever uses it."

"So you *could* get a letter to Paris, France. From one of those station mailboxes."

"Yes, I suppose so."

"So say that you *did* get a letter to Paris, France. What would you *do* with it?"

"It depends on which way we're going. If we're heading east out of Chicago I'd put it in the case for mixed states and foreign mail. We'd dispatch it in Detroit and the next crew would take it to New York. From New York it would go by ship to France."

"You don't have to know the street where the person lives?"

"They'd figure that out in France. I do for Chicago city and Detroit city, though."

"You know every street?"

"I'm supposed to."

"Then tell me, where is Freemont Street?"

"That's down in Rosemont. That'd be supplied by the Chi and Carb—Chicago and Carbondale—or the Chi and Evans—Chicago and Evansville."

I sipped my coffee.

"How about Chambers Street?"

"There's a Chambers Street in South Chicago and another one up north. They'd both be distributed out of Chicago Station on Chestnut Street."

"That's pretty good." He set his cup down. "You know them bags that got the letters in them?"

"Pouches."

"They pick them up with a hook, isn't it?"

"Yes, at nonstop stations. A yardarm by the side of the track. One time we pulled a circus car from Ann Arbor to Battle Creek, between the engine and the RPO car. When I went to make the catch—you have to set the catcher to pick up the pouch; it's a big iron hook that you raise up with a wooden handle; you raise it too soon and you may hit something, like a bridge; too late and you get a demerit for missing the pouch—one of the elephants had his trunk sticking out the window of the circus car. Whap, he hit that pouch, so I couldn't make the catch. I had to send a slip back saying I couldn't make the catch because an elephant got in the way. The station manager telegraphed that he wanted the whole crew to take a sobriety test."

Reverend Taylor and Janis both laughed, but they both narrowed their eyes too, not sure if they should believe me.

Janis was good looking in a University of Chicago sort of way—long, straight, dark hair, jeans, sandals, a man's white shirt with the sleeves rolled up, hardly any makeup, oversize leather briefcase. A little intimidating. She had the manuscript of her dissertation in her briefcase, she told me as we walked back to the campus. She never let it out of her sight. We walked down Cottage Grove, past the abandoned Trianon Ballroom, on the way to Harper Library. The dissertation was on mathematical models of integration, she explained. "You start with some givens. Assumptions. About white tolerance for Negroes and vice versa. Say that a Negro family can tolerate white neighbors on five out of eight sides, but that a white family can tolerate Negro neighbors on only two sides."

"How do you get eight sides?"

Janis shifted her briefcase. "Think of a checkerboard," she said. "Any given square, except the edges, borders on eight other squares. You see what I mean?"

I saw what she meant. I listened to her explanation, to the sound of her voice. At first it seemed simple, but then it got more complicated.

"People don't live on checkerboards," I said. "They live in rows, on streets. They've got neighbors on two sides, not six sides."

"*Eight* sides," she said, "in my model. But I guess it all depends on how you define *neighbor*. The two-neighbor model would be too simple. The *whole point* of the model is to show that the sum of individual behaviors can lead to results that are counterintuitive."

"Oh."

We'd turned east on Fifty-ninth Street. The university buildings loomed ahead, north of the Midway, like a row of mighty fortresses.

"Did an elephant really hit the mail pouch with his trunk?"

I shifted my guitar again and kicked a stone, making it skitter down the sidewalk.

"Yes," I said, but she must have heard something in my voice, something I probably wanted her to hear.

"And you *saw* it?"

"Well, I didn't actually *see* it."

"Who *did* see it?"

"It's an old RPO story, actually. I heard it from my uncle Gerrit."

"Like the story about the young couple traveling around Germany with their fat aunt who dies at a scenic turnoff and they can't get her into the back of their VW so they wrap her up in a blanket and tie her on top of the car, and then someone steals the car?"

"I thought it was their grandmother in Mexico."

She kicked the stone that I'd kicked before.

"Look," I said, "I'm sorry. I was trying to make myself more interesting."

"You don't have to do that," she said. "You don't have to be more interesting."

"You mean I'm interesting enough?"

"I mean . . . you don't have to apologize for working for the RPO. I think it's great that you work for the RPO. You're a genuine proletarian."

"My *mother* went to the University of Chicago," I said, defensive.

"You don't need to *do* this," she said.

"Do what?"

"Try to make yourself more interesting."

"But it's true."

"Like the elephant?"

"*Not* like the elephant. Really true. I mean, the elephant is true; I just didn't happen to see it, and maybe it happened between Kalamazoo and Niles, or maybe it happened out west. It depends on who's telling the story. But you can look my mother up in the alumni records. She sends money every year. Her name was Rita Johnson."

"I'll bet there are a hundred Rita Johnsons."

"Her married name is Dijksterhuis. How's that?"

"You're serious."

"Class of twenty-two. She lived in Oak Park. Went to school with Hemingway."

"Martin, I can't believe this. She went to school with Hemingway? *Ernest* Hemingway? Not some *other* Hemingway?"

"*Ernest* Hemingway. She worked with him on the newspaper; he signed her yearbook."

"Do you have it?"

"You want proof? I'll get it. My mother's got it, at home. Her teachers at Oak Park High School got up the money to send her to the University of Chicago."

Janis turned to face him. "That's fantastic," she said. "If it's true."

"She lived with a family on Blackstone. A sort of live-in baby-sitter. Professor Stoddard. At the university. Mrs. Stoddard was French, and I think he taught sociology."

Janis shook her head. She didn't know the name.

"It was a long time ago."

"Do you know which house?"

"I think it was on the corner of Blackstone and Fifty-eighth."

"You *think*?"

"It was on the corner."

"Which corner?"

"Toward the lake; away from the Midway. I'm not very good at directions."

"Northeast."

"Right."

"Do you want to go see it?"

"Sure, why not? But don't you have to study?"

"I've got time."

We walked down Fifty-ninth Street. Blackstone was farther than I thought, though I didn't know the area very well.

"We used to drive by here," I said. "Once a year. When we came into Chicago for the All-Star Bowling Tournament, which was always held downtown at the Chicago Auditorium." We turned left on Blackstone.

"The All-Star Bowling Tournament?"

"Yeah. My dad was a good bowler and we used to come in for the tournament every year. I've got autographs of a lot of the great bowlers—Don Carter, Buddy Bomar, Marion Ladewig, Lou Campi, from Milwaukee, who finished on the wrong foot."

"I'm impressed," she said. "Are you a bowler too?"

"I used to bowl. You?"

She shook her head.

"After the tournament we'd have dinner at George Diamond's. Have you ever eaten there?"

She shook her head.

"It's a steak house, on Wabash."

"Sorry."

I set the guitar down on the sidewalk and looked up at the house my mother had lived in. Like many of the houses on Blackstone, it was huge, a castle. Through a lighted window on the first floor we glimpsed a room full of books and paintings. Over the fireplace a large square painting seemed to open up into another room, another dimension, in which a naked woman was sitting on a bed with a child. The child had clothes on. A very long black limousine passed in front of us and stopped three or four houses down. A man got out, said something to the driver, and went into one of the houses. The limousine waited, blinkers flashing.

Janis said, "You know, Reverend Taylor invented the stretch limousine."

Now it was my turn to be skeptical. I made a face.

"I'm serious," she said.

"You're kidding me?"

She shook her head.

"Then why isn't he rich?"

"He *is* rich."

"Reverend Taylor?"

"You saw his house, didn't you? He's rich as Croesus."

"Who's Croesus?"

"He was a very rich guy, the richest guy in the world. King of Persia—no, Lydia."

I shook my head. "He doesn't *look* rich. Well, actually, he does, now that I think of it. That was a nice suit he was wearing. And it is a nice house. But the kitchen . . ."

"They were in the middle of remodeling it when his wife died; he just left it. But you should see his cars."

"Like what?"

"Like a 1956 Rolls-Royce Silver Cloud saloon car." Janis held up an index finger.

"What's a saloon car?"

"I don't know, but it's big, and the steering wheel is on the right-hand side."

"You're kidding."

"Like a 1957 Rolls-Royce Silver Wraith convertible, which is the finest car ever made." She held up a second finger

I tried to whistle but couldn't get any sound.

"I'm not kidding."

"Where does he get the money?"

"He and his wife—his first wife—used to run a house for parties on Indiana Avenue. Then he got the call of the Lord, and she didn't. That was toward the end of the Depression. He went out east and worked for the Rolls-Royce Company in Massachusetts, except it wasn't the Rolls-Royce Company anymore. They changed the name before they went bankrupt. You'll have to ask him. He'd worked for them earlier, before the Depression. They brought over a bunch of English workers in the twenties to build Rolls-Royces in the U.S., and they were mostly Methodists. I guess that's how they got together. When he went back he worked for someone named Clifford till the end of the war. Then he and his second wife came back to Chicago and he hooked up with a guy he used to know in the auto body business, and they started customizing cars for rich people—the Swifts and the Armors and the Potter Palmers; bullet-proof cars for gangsters too; that sort of thing. It was right after the war and I guess car sales were really taking off, but there wasn't a lot of choice, so people wanted to do something to make their cars special."

I nodded.

"Somebody'd come in and they'd put in a gold gas pedal, or put diamonds around the speedometer, or cut the car in half and make it longer, whatever the person wanted. That's how the stretch limo got started. Now he runs an auto restoration business. People bring cars from all over the country."

"And you believe this?"

"I've been to the shop."

"Mr. Leiner said something about it," I said. "Over by the Oakwood Cemetery?"

"It's huge," Janis said. "There's a metal fabrication shop and a body shop and a paint shop and an upholstery shop."

"What kind of cars?"

"All fancy. There's a 1936 Bugatti that's been there over a year, and lots of Rolls-Royces. I've *driven* the Silver Wraith. It's a red convertible, and it's pretty small, for a Rolls-Royce."

"He let you *drive* it?"

"He let me *borrow* it when my car broke down. I picked up my mom at Midway."

"I'll bet your mom was impressed."

She laughed. "I told her it belonged to the guy I was dating."

"How did you get to know him so well?" I asked.

"I taught him how to read."

I must have looked incredulous.

"At the Blackstone Public Library—my second year here. The first year I didn't have any life at all, just problem sets due every Friday; but after that I wanted to do something, so I volunteered for the literacy program. After his wife died he decided he wanted to learn to read. His wife always read everything for him. He told me that Mr. Clifford and his wife were the only ones who knew he couldn't read, so don't say anything."

"He couldn't read *at all*?"

"He could read the signs that said 'Whites Only,' but that was about it. He had all kinds of tricks. When he went to a restaurant he'd just ask for the same thing that someone else had ordered, because he couldn't read the menu. Or he'd pretend he'd forgotten his glasses and couldn't see. We really had to start with the alphabet at Blackstone. Now he's working on his adult Bible studies certificate at the Moody Bible Institute. He just took a chapter test tonight. I have to proctor the exams. When he gets his certificate he wants to buy a church."

"I didn't know you could *buy* a church."

"I guess you can buy anything if you've got enough money. He's pretty much retired now; he's still the president of the company, technically, but he's turned everything over to his employees."

"But who would you buy it *from*?"

"I don't know. You'll have to ask him. He wants to have a church where black people and white people can come together, so he wants something that's kind of along the border."

"Between Hyde Park and Woodlawn?"

"He's got his eye on a couple of places."

"What kind of reverend is he anyway?"

"He did some preaching in Massachusetts, right after he got the call of the Lord; but he hasn't for quite a while. He wants to get his certificate first."

"A lot of the old bluesmen did that," I said. "Back and forth. They'd get sanctified, and then they'd go back and play the devil's music. What about the house for parties?"

"I guess they did everything. Gambling, cards, craps, drinking. Probably a lot of hanky-panky too, though he didn't tell me about *that.*"

"Hanky-panky," I said out loud. The old-fashioned word carried a slight erotic charge.

"Craps," she said. "You ever play craps?"

"You don't *play* craps," I said, "you *shoot* them."

"What do you shoot them with?"

"It's like bowling. You don't *play* bowling; you bowl."

"So you don't *play* craps, you just *crap?* "

I started to explain, but she nudged me. "It's a joke, Martin." I liked the way she said my name. Stern and playful at the same time. We started down Fifty-eighth Street.

"So he got the call of the Lord and went to Massachusetts, and then he came back to Chicago, and now he's got a car restoration business, and he can't read?"

"He can read now," she said; "but he still has a lot of trouble. It's hard to know when we read the Bible, because he's practically got the King James Version memorized. I had to switch to a different translation. This way." Janis took my arm and we turned under an arch and entered a large courtyard. When we got to the entrance of Harper Library Janis climbed the steps and turned to say good-bye.

"I guess he didn't need to know how to read in order to fix cars," I said, still puzzling over Reverend Taylor.

"He invents things too," Janis said. "That's where the real money comes from; but he's always involved in lawsuits. Every time he invents something, some big company changes it a little and tries to get around the patent."

"I don't know what to say," I said, "except that I enjoyed this."

"I did too, Martin."

"I'd like to do it again."

"I would too," she said, holding the door open.

"Good night."

The door closed behind her, softly but decisively, like the door of a Rolls-Royce; and I watched through the glass as she climbed the stairs and disappeared into a world of books I'd never read and mathematical models I'd never understand.

After we finished our eggs—Janis was still sleeping—my mother and I walked out into the orchards. The ground was covered with a thin layer of snow, and my mother slipped some boots on over her open-toed shoes.

We walked through the woodlot and on past the packing shed. She pointed out recent improvements, but I saw that a pruning saw had been left on the ground at the base of a tree, and that some of the young trees had been headed off too severely. We hadn't talked about my mother's plans yet. She was sixty-four years old. The Latin program at the high school had been dropped, though my mother had been a popular teacher; and the principal wanted to replace French with Spanish. We'd circled around and were coming up over a rise, but we didn't need to reach the top for me to see the Williamses' old cinder-block house, empty now. I knew every inch, every tree. I could see it with my eyes closed. This was home.

"We're going to bulldoze the old plot of Pippins." It was her way of letting me know that she wasn't going to put the orchards up for sale. But I didn't know whom she meant by *we*.

"There's no market for them. They've no shelf life, and the color's not what anyone wants today."

"They taste good."

"But no one wants them."

"You could save a few of them, I suppose," I said.

"I'd save them all if I could. I may plant more Delicious."

"Too mushy," I said. We'd had this conversation before. "No good for pies either."

"I won't argue about that. I could make a tart tonight, though. We could pick some Northern Spies."

"We have to leave, Mom," I reminded her. "We have to catch the seven-forty-eight in Niles."

The old path through the brush had not been mowed this summer.

"Uncle Piet wants to sell his share in the orchards. He assumed Dad would buy him out, but now, who knows?"

"What's he asking?"

"Well, it depends . . . Marty, we thought you might want to come back home. You know how you loved working in the orchards. There're plenty of colleges around here where Janis could teach."

"It's too late, Mom."

"Well, that's what I told your uncle. But I told him I'd ask you." She wasn't crying, but I put my arm around her.

"Besides, she's got an offer from Kalamazoo College, and she's waiting to hear from Princeton."

"Kalamazoo's right on the New York Central line," she said. "You wouldn't have to change trains."

"Kalamazoo was one of her backup schools, but she really liked it. Now she's thinking she'd like to teach at a place like that, where the emphasis is on teaching. But maybe it's because she had such a great dinner. Some kind of pasta with Italian ham and green peppercorns. You'll have to ask her about it. And then a venison roast. The professor who gave the dinner shot the deer himself and butchered it in a special way."

My mother took put her arm through mine. "I just wish your father could have met her."

"Well, everything is on hold right now," I said. "We'll just have to wait and see what happens."

"It would have put his mind at ease. After . . . everything that happened. To see you with someone like Janis."

"Dad didn't want the Williamses to leave, did he?" I said. She shook her head. "And it wasn't just the money. He and Cap were good friends. Cap could have run things by himself. Maybe not the marketing end, but everything here. If he were still here, you wouldn't have to worry. You wouldn't have a pruning crew leaving equipment out in the weather. You wouldn't have those trees butchered like that."

She didn't say anything for a while, and then she said: "You're not going to try to contact her, are you?"

"Corinna?"

"Yes."

"I don't know. Why?"

We were at the northeast corner of the apple orchard, the lowest point of the moraine, which had been tiled and retiled to improve the drainage. My father and my uncle had planted a few older varieties, just for the family. Apples that tasted especially good, like Pippins, but didn't travel well—Baldwins, Ben Davises, Northern Spies. We walked north between two rows of high-headed Golden Delicious till we came to the top of the moraine. There was nothing more to say, no answer to the question, so we turned back.

When we came in Janis was eating the poached eggs, cold now, that my mother had left on the table for her. She hadn't dried them off on a dish towel, the way my mother did, so there was water on her plate. My mother asked her about the dinner in Kalamazoo, and Janis told her how the professor who'd cooked the dinner had left only one slice of the venison roast for himself, and she'd offered to give him one of her slices, but he'd said no. It was sooo good, she said; not at all gamy—even better than the filets she and Martin had eaten at George Diamond's on her birthday.

My mother brought out her senior *Tabula*—the one Hemingway had signed—and copies of other *Tabula*s with some of Hemingway's earliest stories, and the two of them compared notes on the University of Chicago, and my mother got out a checkerboard so Janis could explain her thesis on mathematical models of integration. My mother couldn't find the checkers, but between them they had enough dimes and pennies to set up a hypothetical situation.

"We'll start with everything even," Janis said. "Like this."

	D	P	D	P	D	P	
D	P	D	P	D	P	D	P
P	D	P	D	P	D	P	D
D	P	D	P	D	P	D	P
P	D	P	D	P	D	P	D
D	P	D	P	D	P	D	P
P	D	P	D	P	D	P	D
	P	D	P	D	P	D	

"And we'll say that if a dime has only one neighbor, that neighbor has to be a dime or he'll move. And if a dime has two neighbors, one of them has to be a dime or he'll move. If he's got three to five neighbors, two of them have to be dimes or he'll move. And if he's got six to eight neighbors, at least three have to be dimes or he'll move. That's a tolerance schedule. For starters we'll use the same schedule for pennies."

"Now let's make it interesting by opening up some space at random. You *should* use a table of random numbers, but that doesn't matter for now." She removed about twenty coins.

	D		D	P	D	P	
D	P		P	D	P	D	
	D	P		P	D		D
D	P				P	D	P
P	D	P	D	P	D	P	
D			P	D	P	D	
		P	D	P	D	P	D
	P	D	P				

"Now let's plunk a dime or a penny, it doesn't matter, down on the board and see what happens."

My mother was quicker than I had been to grasp the purpose of the model, and once she started moving dissatisfied dimes and pennies around she found it hard to stop. It was like a game of checkers, but less predictable. You'd start over with the same initial situation, and then make a few moves, and everything would be different. After a few moves dimes and pennies might return to a stable integrated equilibrium—living happily next to each other—or a chain reaction might cause them to cluster together in segregated neighborhoods. The patterns became even more counterintuitive as Janis proposed different tolerance schedules for dimes and pennies.

My mother shook her head. "Can you give me your thesis in one sentence?"

"Aggregate results aren't necessarily a reliable indicator of individual prejudices."

"Is that good news, or bad news?" my mother asked.

"It's good news, Mrs. Dijksterhuis. Don't you think?"

My mother thought about it for a while. "Yes, I guess it is," she said.

That evening my mother repeated herself at the station while Janis was in the rest room. She had driven us to Niles. We were standing on the station platform waiting for the train out of Detroit.

"We just wanted what was best for you, Marty," she said, as if she'd been thinking things over. "That's all." She didn't mention the University of Chicago. "And now I'm so glad you've found Janis. She's really a lovely person, and so smart. I'm glad she came down with you. It means a lot at a time like this."

The train was late. "You don't need to wait for the train," I said. "It's getting dark."

"Don't grudge me this little time, Martin."

"I'm sorry, Mom. I didn't mean . . ."

I put my arms around her. I could see Janis pushing the station door open, looking around for us. My mother saw her too.

"It's all right," my mother said. "Everything will be all right. I just wish your father . . . I just wish your father could have met her, that's all," she said again. "It would have eased his mind."

A blat on the loudspeaker above our heads indicated that the train was approaching. People started coming out of the station. Lovers hugged, kissed, parted; high school sweethearts, parents and children; old friends. I can still feel my mother's arms around me; she doesn't want to let go.

We took the IC from downtown to Hyde Park, and on the way back to our apartment we walked east on Fifty-ninth Street till we got to Blackstone. We both had small suitcases, and Janis had her briefcase. The house where my mother had lived was on the corner. There was a light on in one of the third-floor windows; I thought it was her old room. Either that one or the one next to it. She'd been happier here than at any time in her life.

I tried to imagine her as a student, a girl, younger than Janis. Maybe reading in bed, her head propped up on two pillows, the way she read at home; her book tipped up on her stomach. Or writing a letter to one of her friends, someone who'd gone on to do all sorts of wonderful things in wonderful places, like Jessie May Stewart, who lived in Paris and who'd been to all the places where famous writers had lived—Hemingway and Fitzgerald and James Joyce and T. S. Eliot and Gertrude Stein—and who wrote to my mother in French. She kept all her letters in a four-drawer file cabinet in the guest room, along with carbon copies of her own letters. What was important was the life of the mind. What was important was that she'd learned to see the world through other eyes, not just her own eyes. What was important was that she had a place to stand outside the modern world. What was important was that she had a place to stand outside our tiny little Midwestern town, which, I knew now, she hated—though she'd never said so—even though it had always seemed like the most wonderful place in the world to me.

5

The Devil's Music

1964

A WEEK AFTER my father's funeral Janis got a letter from Princeton saying that the position she'd applied for had been filled. The next day she accepted the job in Kalamazoo. All of a sudden the future seemed real, and we let ourselves fantasize a little: about getting married in the little pavilion out on the Point; about our life together, and our six children, the books Janis would write, the Victorian house on a tree-lined street. And the best thing was, Kalamazoo was on the New York Central line, exactly halfway between Chicago and Detroit. I'd have to rearrange my schedule a little, but I wouldn't have to put in for a transfer, wouldn't have to learn any new states.

For the most part the Ph.D. candidates in econ dated each other and roomed together and spoke their own language, but I bought a little paperback called *Ideas of the Great Economists* so that I could take part in the conversation when we went out to drink beer at Jimmy's or at little graduate student dinner parties, where we ate lots of chicken that tasted as if it had been dunked in *vin,* and drank lots of *vin* too; and in fact I became something of an expert on the early socialists—without actually reading their works, of course. It didn't matter, because no one knew any more than I did about Babeuf or Cabet or Saint-Simon or Fourier, who published a notice in the Paris newspapers that he would be waiting at his apartment in the Thirteenth Arrondissement every day at noon to meet with any wealthy men who might be interested in financing his utopian scheme. Actually, I think Janis was on the same wavelength as Fourier. At least she tried to interest the university in using her mathematical model of integration for its new housing projects; and she even tried to talk Reverend Taylor into buying a block of apartments in order to put her thesis to the test. But in Chicago it was still the war of all against all—Hobbes, not Fourier.

Janis was working night and day to finish her dissertation, which I was typing for her on my Olympia portable, which worked better than her full-size Underwood. I was an excellent typist, like Aunt Bridget, and when I got going the typewriter sounded like a machine gun. The dissertation office at Chicago was extremely fussy. One of Janis's fellow graduate students had had to have his entire dissertation retyped because the margins were too narrow. Any page with more than three corrections would be thrown out, as would any page in which footnotes or tables were not spaced just so. I'd also taken over for Janis as Reverend Taylor's tutor—in exchange for some tips on playing the guitar. I hadn't told Janis about Aunt Flo's postcard. I'd never told her about Corinna, in fact. And I hadn't told her I'd hired a private detective in Madison to track Corinna down.

The detective didn't sound at all like Nero Wolfe or Travis McGee.

"Who's she fucking?" he asked, rhetorically. "That's the sixty-four dollar question, isn't it?"

"I just want an address," I said, "and some basic information. It can't be that hard to find her." I was calling from a public phone booth outside the Hyde Park Bank Building, about six blocks from our apartment. Through the window of the booth I could see the parking lot and Lake Park Avenue and the IC tracks.

"I mean, everybody's fucking someone," he said. "It's human nature."

"I don't want to know," I said. An operator interrupted us and I jammed two more quarters into the slot.

"Sure you want to know; that's human nature too."

"She's not my wife, you know."

"She married?"

"I don't know."

"A lot of guys want me to break down motel room doors; they want flagrante pictures, proof positive. I tell them, you see them kissing in the parking lot, then you see them go into the motel; you see the lights go on; you see the lights go out. You've seen enough. That counts as proof in a court of law, by the way. Most people don't know that. They want justice—not mercy—like little children. They want somebody to be punished. That's how I have to treat them, like little children. I have to psychologize a little. 'She's in love,' I say; but it doesn't do no good. 'She's happy; she's excited; she's alive. Do you really want to kill that?' I say the same thing to everybody, all the guys. But nobody ever listens. I guess that's human nature too."

Reverend Taylor was beginning a new Moody Bible course: *God's Plan for Your Life.* At our first session we went through the first lesson—"God Has a Plan for Every Life." Even after three years with Janis, Reverend Taylor had not learned to read easily and confidently, and sometimes when he ran into a difficult passage in the lesson he would revert to old habits, like a swimmer who's perfectly capable of swimming the entire length of the pool but who panics when he realizes he's in deep water. He'd forget to sound out the words. Instead of slowing down and breaking them up into their component parts, he'd speed up. On the other hand, he had learned most of the Bible by heart, simply by hearing it read aloud in church when he was a boy in North Carolina, and had no trouble with the passage he was supposed to memorize, Psalm 32 in this case. The general point of the psalm was clear enough: "I will instruct thee and teach thee in the way which thou shalt go; I will guide thee with mine eye." But I was more interested in one of the earlier verses: "When I kept silence, my bones waxed old through my roaring all the day long."

"Now what on earth does *that* mean?" I asked.

"It means if you don't confess your sins to the Lord, then you're gonna be groanin' and moanin' all day long."

"Oh," I said.

"But in your case it probably means that if you don't get your guitar out pretty soon and play me a song, your bones are gonna start roarin'. But we got to do this self-check test first."

The self-check test consisted of ten true-or-false questions:

> God's plan for us cannot include a life of toil and obscurity. *True or false?*
> We have a part to play in working out God's plan for us. *True or false?*

And so on.

Page references were given, so that if you didn't know the answers, you could look them up in the book, but Reverend Taylor didn't have any problems.

As soon as we'd finished going over the self-check test, I took my guitar out of its case. Reverend Taylor made another pot of coffee while I checked the tuning. It was the first time I'd played for him, and I was nervous. His kitchen chairs were just a little too high to hold the guitar comfortably. When I put my foot on the floor, my knee was too low; and when I hooked my heel over the chair rail, my knee was too high.

"That ain't sheet metal like you told me," he said, putting a finger on the lower bout of the guitar. "That's galvanized steel, one of them old garbage can guitars that they was too cheap to plate, so they painted it."

I played a chord.

"Sounds like an old garbage can too," he said.

It sounded good to me, but I didn't say anything. I put my foot down on the floor, and then back on the chair rail.

"Just sit up straight, Martin, and play me a song. We ain't cuttin' heads here. You got nothing to be afraid of."

The first song I played was one of the songs he'd recorded in a Paramount session right here in Chicago in 1933: "Sun Don't Want to Shine." My fingers weren't quite under control, but they were still functioning. I played the song just the way he played it on the record, in an open-D tuning with four different guitar breaks. I had a version for each break that was not exact, but close enough.

> *Looked out my window, Lord, about the break of*
> *day;*
> *Looked out my window, Lord, about the break of*
> *day;*
> *Sun don't want to shine since my baby she gone*
> *away.*

I held Corinna in my imagination as I sang—not the vague protean image that had been serving as my muse for the past few years, but a sharp color photo of her in the bright light out at Schuylers Dump, right at the moment I realized she was pregnant—and in spite of my nervousness, once I got through the first break I poured my whole soul into the song.

Reverend Taylor listened with his eyes closed, his lips pursed. Did the song bring back memories?

> *Dark last night, thought I heard my baby call my*
> *name;*
> *Dark last night, thought I heard my baby call my*
> *name;*
> *Moon ain't gonna shine till my baby come back*
> *again.*

"You sure can play a lot of notes," he said when I finished the song and put my guitar down on my lap.

"Thanks," I said, but my heart sank because I knew it wasn't a compliment, and I knew that what I really wanted was not criticism but praise. More than praise, really. I was applying for my blues license. I wanted Reverend Taylor's stamp of approval, like a driver's license or a pilot's license.

"You really got the feel for the blues," he said, and I started to puff up a little. "Of course," he went on, "you don't need any extra special feelings to play the blues. You already got all the special feelings you need. Any person alive in this world has all the feelings it needs to play the blues. What sets a blues musician apart from other people is not special feelings. It's the ability to play the music, to pick the guitar or blow the harp. You don't need any rarefied feelings for that. What you need is talent, and a little bit of talent will take you a long ways. But you got to relax a little. Makes me tired just to look at you work so hard. You got to let the big levers move the little ones instead of the other way round. Let the power flow from your body into your fingers. To get your speed what you got to do is practice slow, real slow, and plant your fingers before you pick a string, so you're not waving your fingers around in the air like you do, hoping they're gonna land in the hole between the strings when the time comes. To get a nice tone you got to take care of your fingernails with a good fine emery board. Don't go cuttin' at them with one of them clippers. And then file them down with some real fine sandpaper. I know you don't believe me. But I'm telling you what I know. Folks was always asking me how I got such a nice tone out of my cheap old Stella, and when I told them I take care of my fingernails, they didn't want to believe me." He shrugged. "I suppose you don't believe me either."

I *didn't* believe him, but I didn't say so.

"You *don't* believe me, do you?"

"I believe you, I believe you."

He made me hold out my hands so he could inspect my nails. He pulled out an emery board from his shirt pocket and worked on my nails, like a manicurist. "Don't go sawing back and forth," he said. "That'll make them split. Go up from the sides to the center. See? Like this."

I didn't know how to react. I couldn't imagine Robert Johnson or Son House whipping out an emery board.

"Now let me hear you play a G with your first finger."

I played a G. He worked on my nail a little more.

"Now plant your finger right down on the string. Your *first* finger. Don't swing at it. You don't want the string to go back and forth. You want it to go round and round in an oval. That's why you got to push down a little from the top. Try it again."

I sounded the G again.

"Just let the string ride up your nail," he said. "There. Now don't that sound better?"

But by this time I couldn't hear whether it was better or worse. "You want to show me?" I offered him the guitar but he waved it away. "Maybe I should just sell my soul to the devil," I said.

"Humnph," he said. "That might not be a bad idea. But you might get you some emery boards first."

"I think the devil'd probably do more for me than offer me an emery board, or tell me to practice slow."

"You think the devil don't use an emery board to take care of his fingernails? And you think the devil don't practice slow?"

"You seem to know a lot more about the devil's personal habits than I do." He didn't answer. "Were *you* ever tempted?"

"Was I ever tempted to what?"

"To sell your soul to the devil."

"Course I was tempted," he said. "I was more'n tempted, but it weren't at no crossroads, if that's what you're askin'. It was a whole way of life that the devil offered me: wine, women, and song. Drinking. Gambling. Lots of women. The women always favored a man who could pick the guitar. I's always havin' to fight them off, and sometimes I didn't fight too hard. But then you got to fight the mens too. Wasn't only once I got shot at and knifed and handed a glass of poison whiskey. Don't ever take no whiskey when you ain't seen it come out of the bottle, when you ain't seen the government label on the bottle being tore off. Better tear it off yourself. Better yet, don't drink no whiskey or no peppermint schnapps at all. I used to drink peppermint schnapps, but I don't no more. But I never did that crazy stuff, playing the guitar behind my back, throwin' it up in the air, because I thought that was disrespectful of the music. You want to let the music speak to the audience. You don't want to put yourself in the way of the music by too much clownin' around. Clownin's what you do when you can't pick good enough to satisfy people's minds."

"But did you really sell your soul?"

Reverend Taylor rolled his eyes. "Course I sold my soul to the devil. Old Nick. Old Baggy Pants. Old Mustard Butt. That's what everybody did: Tommy Franklin, Robert Johnson, Bukka White, Elmore Davenport, Tommy Johnson, Juke Phillips. It was what you had to do if you wanted to play the blues. Especially if you couldn't play too good to begin with. Otherwise nobody'd take you serious. They'd figure you was just an amateur. You know what I'm sayin'?"

I nodded.

"Blind Lemon was about the only one sufficient to make it on his own. He died in a snowstorm right here in Chicago, just before Christmas. Froze to death. Just before the Depression."

"How did you do it? I mean, how did you go about . . ."

"Ain't hard at all."

"I mean, do you have to go out to a crossroads?"

"Crossroads would be nice. Very convenient. You comin' down one way, Devil comin' up the other. You meet and take care of your business and be on your way, nobody be the wiser."

"Robert Johnson . . ."

But Reverend Taylor didn't want to hear about Robert Johnson. "Man knew two, three riffs, maybe half a dozen. He thought Chicago was in California. And where is he now? He's dead, that's where he is. Somebody poisoned him in Greenwood, Mississippi, not in Arkansas or Texas like some folks was sayin'. In 1938. I was working for Mr. Clifford at the time. We was building bodies for Phantom III chassis."

"He died in Greenwood."

"That's what I said," Reverend Taylor said, "and I'm here." He lowered his head. "You *are* lookin' to sell your soul, ain't you?"

"That's what I just said," I said. "I'd sell it if I could play like Robert Johnson."

"Man knew two or three songs," Reverend Taylor said again; "half a dozen riffs." Reverend Taylor mimicked the famous opening of "Crossroads" (and of a dozen other songs) by keeping his lips together and making a buzzing sound. "He thought Chicago was in California. You'd be gettin' a bad deal, like selling your songs to the white man for twenty dollar a side who might sell a hundred thousand copies and still begrudge you your twenty dollar, if he ever give it to you in the first place. Or the last place."

"But how did you sell your soul? Did *you* go to a crossroads?"

"Martin, you're a very smart boy, and I respect that, and I appreciate your help to me, but you're too serious. Sometime I got to have a little fun with you. If you want to play the blues in a juke joint in Clarksdale, Mississippi, or in Durham, North Carolina, where I hail from, you *got* to tell people you sold your soul to the devil. That's what they want to hear. It adds a little spice to your performance. They want to hear a story about a lonely old crossroad and it's midnight and it's dark, just a sliver of moon so you can see the devil stepping out of the tobacco row or out of the cotton row. You see what I mean? And the devil'll come and tune your guitar for you, you know, and after that you can play any song you want, stuff like that."

I didn't know what a tobacco row or a cotton row looked like, but I could picture the devil all right, just as I could picture the private detective I'd hired to track down Corinna.

"It's just a joke?"

"Not exactly a joke. But like something in between, if you know what I mean. It's part of the aura." He hefted the electric percolator to judge how much coffee was left, then poured us each another half cup and unplugged it.

"I think so," I said. "At least I've got the idea."

6

Corinna, Corinna

1964

I MET CORY, face-to-face, in Madison, Wisconsin, about month after Janis and I had left my mother standing on the station platform in Niles, Michigan. We met in a small bowling alley on US 12, just south of town.

I sat in a red Naugahyde booth and listened to the familiar sound of balls striking pins on the alleys, which were divided from the lounge by a row of planters filled with green plastic plants. I wasn't hungry, but I ordered a Pepsi and a hamburger, which I finished before Cory showed up.

"Closure," I'd said on the phone, trying to explain what I wanted. It was a word I'd learned from Janis. "The fact that you just disappeared. I've never gotten over it. You were my best friend. How could you do that to me? You didn't even say good-bye. I'm coming up to Madison. I've got to see you."

We were both twenty-five years old. I knew from the private detective that she worked in a beauty salon in the Negro section of town, but I wasn't prepared for her hair. It was my first Afro: round and black as a bowling ball, but bigger. It was tremendous. It said, *Look out, I'm comin' through.* I wadded up my napkin and the waxed paper from the hamburger and shoved them into my Pepsi cup, which was still half full of ice cubes.

She slid into the booth across from me, and I knew from the first moment what I'd already gathered from our telephone conversation: that she wasn't sure she wanted to be there with me.

"You know, Martin," she said, "I never asked you for support. I never asked you for a penny."

"Support? What are you talking about? You're not going to say hello? You're not going to say you're glad to see me? Even if you're not?"

She leaned forward and looked me in the eye. I looked away. "It's just . . . awkward, do you know what I mean?"

"I suppose I do, but I wish you *had* asked for support. You know I would have given you anything."

"I guess I didn't want to be beholden," she said.

"All these years, Cory. I didn't know where you were; I had no idea. No one knew. Eight years. Till my father's funeral. Aunt Bridget got a Christmas card from your mom after your dad died. I hired a private detective . . . But all the time, Cory, you knew where *I* was. You could have written to *me.*" I waited for a letter, every day."

She leaned forward and took my hand. "This has cost me too, Marty. You were always my true friend and I'm sorry I didn't write to you. I didn't know how. I didn't know how to explain, Marty, because I didn't understand it myself."

"But now we're here," I said.

"Yeah."

"In Madison, Wisconsin."

"Right. It's a pretty good place. The black community's not too big, but Mama's got her church, with four different choirs, and Cozy's going to a Catholic school. The nuns run a pretty tight ship."

"And you look good," I said. "You look great. But I have to admit, I've never seen hair like that."

"You haven't, but you will. It may take a while, but you will."

"It makes me a little nervous."

"That's the idea."

"Does your mom do your hair like that?"

"*This* hair? Are you crazy? She thinks Satan's taken over my head. She'd straighten it in my sleep if she could figure out how to do it! Cozy's hair too. She doesn't want Cozy to wear cornrows because it's too down-home; and she doesn't like the Natural either. She's been straightening hair all her life, but as far as I'm concerned, that's ancient history."

"Who's Cozy?"

"My daughter."

The waitress came to clear the table and to see if we needed anything. I ordered a beer, Cory ordered a Pepsi. It took a minute to register: Cozy was my daughter too.

"So let's get on with this closure you were talking about," Cory said.

"We could still get married," I said. "That would be one way to get closure." I spoke it in an offhand way to show I was joking.

She laughed.

"You're not married," I said.

"How do you know?"

"Seriously. Is there somebody else?"

"Somebody *else*?" She shook her head. "'If you mind your own business then you won't be mindin' mine.'"

"Hank Williams," I said, "and it's 'bidness,' not 'business."

"Well, it's about the best piece of advice I ever got," she said.

"But listen, Cory," I said, "if you could go back to one moment in time, what would it be?"

"I'm not looking back, Marty. I'm looking ahead, do you understand?"

"But if you could?"

"If I could, I wouldn't."

"I'd go back to the night we climbed the water tower. Looking down on everything. That was the greatest night of my life. It was like I could see everything clearly."

"I saw things clearly too, Marty. But I already told you: we didn't see the same things. Our fantasies never matched up. You've got to acknowledge that. You wanted to stay. I knew that night I wanted to get out. Maybe I'd known it all along, but that night I knew it for sure."

"But afterward, Cory? I think our fantasies matched up then. For a little while. I can remember every little thing, Cory. All I have to do is close my eyes and I can hear the sound of my zipper coming down, and the way you raised your butt up so I could pull your underpants down."

"I guess you always remember your first time. You were so scared, Marty. You didn't know what to do. You didn't even know enough to move in and out. You just lay there on top of me."

What could I say to this? "It was your first time too," I said.

"It's different for a girl."

"Why's that?"

"A girl doesn't have to do anything."

"I'm sorry," I said.

"I mean, not the first time."

"It doesn't matter *now*," I said.

"Marty, I am sorry. I'm sorry about what I just said; that wasn't fair." She touched my arm and took my hand between her hands. "But it's hard, Martin. You can't go back to the old days, sitting in the kitchen with Mama and me."

I wanted a beer, but I didn't want to get up to get one.

"How's *your* mom anyway?" she asked.

"It's going to be hard for her," I said. "After my dad died Mr. Collings—you remember that moonfaced son of a bitch—talked the school board into dropping French and offering Spanish instead, so she's going to retire. She may put the orchards up for sale, but she may try to run them herself. Kind of hard to imagine."

"Why's that?"

"Appleton was never *her* Garden of Eden, and now she's stuck there. She's got nowhere to go. She had a sister out in California, but she was a lot older and she's been dead for years.

"She was a good teacher, Marty. No nonsense: *Je suis, tu sais, il est, nous sommes, vous êtes, ils sont. On ne peut même pas sortir en hiver. Je me demande pourquoi cette porte s'est ouverte.'* And remember all those articles she wrote for the *Gazette*? And the stink she made about the minstrel show? She was an old-fashioned liberal, but she couldn't imagine you and me together."

"No," I said, "she couldn't." I reached across the table and put my hand on hers. "Remember Humpty Dumpty?"

"Sort of: *'Boule, Boule sur la cuillère . . .'"*

"That's it," I said.

> *"Boule, Boule sur la cuillère*
> *Boule, Boule tombe par terre.*
> *I'y a nul homme en Angleterre*
> *Qui l'œuf puisse refaire."*

I guess we can't put it back together again, though."

"Martin," she said, smiling, "you've got to pull yourself together. You've got to let go of the past. You've got to let go of me too, Marty."

"What about the little girl? Cozy you called her?"

"Carolyn. We call her Cozy."

"Do I have to let go of her too?"

"You never had ahold of her to begin with. I'm not blaming you for anything, Marty, but Cozy was my ticket out of there. You've got to understand that. I didn't understand it myself at first."

"You mean the money from my folks."

She nodded.

I waved my hand in front of my face. "It's kind of a shock."

"What?"

"The fact that I'm a father."

"You knew I was pregnant."

"I know, but I never really thought of it before. Like this, I mean. It's going to take some adjusting." I felt uncomfortable, as if my whole body were trying to adjust to the fact of fatherhood.

"What's she like?"

"That's an impossible question."

"Does she know about me?"

Cory shook her head and picked at some stuffing that was poking out of a tear in the Naugahyde. Pins exploded in the background.

"She must suspect."

"Why?"

"Because she's light skinned?"

"How do you know what she looks like?"

"I'm just guessing," I said. "But she's a mulatto, so . . ."

"Martin, listen to you; do you know what that word means?"

"One parent's white and one's Negro."

"It means *mule*, Martin. *Little mule*. Besides, she's a mulatt*a*, not a mulatt*o*."

"Sorry."

"If she does, she's never asked. Would *you* ask?" She raised her hands and carefully patted the circumference of her hairdo.

I nodded yes. "I'd ask. I'd want to know."

"She's not so light that anyone suspects anything."

"Suspects anything?"

"Marty, if you're black you've got black friends to watch your back against the white folks; if you're white, you've got white friends; but if you're mixed, you haven't got anybody."

"So that's why you don't want me hanging around."

She nodded.

"You never wanted other children?"

"Wanting and having are two different things. Besides, I'm only twenty-five, Marty; it's not like I'm over the hill."

"I see."

I didn't know what to say. I felt overwhelmed, too, as I counted back in time on my fingers: 1963, 1962, 1961, 1960, 1959, 1958, 1957, 1956. She would be eight years old. I could imagine the tears welling up inside me as I dropped her off for her first day of school.

"I love her too," I said.

"You don't know her. You barely know her name."

"Carolyn Dijksterhuis," I said. "Cozy."

"Williams, Marty. Her name is Williams."

"I just wanted to see how it sounded. She's my own flesh and blood, you know."

"I realize that, Martin, but—"

"What do you want to happen? With Carolyn—Cozy? With your life? What are you looking forward to? What does it all mean? Do you know?"

"Martin, there's something else you've got to understand. You've got to stop feeling sorry for me because I'm a Negro. I like being a Negro. I *like* my life. I can't imagine being a white person"—she laughed—"feeling guilty all the time and not knowing what to do about it." She waited for a minute. "It's a joke, Martin."

"Cory, I'm glad to see you so—I was going to say 'happy,' but I'm not sure that's the right word."

"What did you expect? I'd be waiting for you to rescue me?" She looked at her watch. "Sorry, Martin, I shouldn't be so rough on you. Tell me about yourself. How was the University of Chicago?"

"I never made it to Chicago. At least not to the university."

"You didn't? What happened?"

"I joined the Navy. Spent six months at Great Lakes, six months on a destroyer, and two years in Guantánamo Bay. 'Gitmo' we called it. Elvis was king, and everybody was in a dither till he went into the army in fifty-eight. I didn't have my guitar with me, but I borrowed one from a guy on the base so I could play a little. That's where I was when Sputnik was launched, and when Castro invaded Havana."

"And now?"

"Working for the Railway Post Office, sorting the U.S. mail. Playing the blues. Learning some of the old songs. Writing them down."

"You mean like the songs you learned from the old guy out at the orchards? Chesterfield. You mean down-and-out, hard-times-knockin'-at-yo'-door songs?"

"Yeah. I found another old guy in Chicago. A friend of mine taught him how to read; now he's working on his Moody Bible Institute certificate. I go over there once a week. I've got my guitar in the car."

"You brought your guitar?"

"Yeah."

"Are you kidding me? You brought your guitar up here? Why? What are you trying to prove?"

"I thought I might get a chance to play. You never know."

"For me? Marty, black people don't listen to that stuff. It's too down-home. It reminds us of stuff we'd just as soon forget."

"It's my vocation, Cory. Like Lotte getting called to go to Africa. Remember that night?"

"But it's not real, Marty. The only people who listen to that stuff are white college kids. Maybe you can fool them, but you can't fool me."

"How do you know? You haven't heard me play. It's been eight years. You used to like it when I played for you out at the Corners when all I could do was strum a few chords."

"It's like someone trying to speak a foreign language."

"What's wrong with trying to speak a foreign language?"

"You've always got a funny accent."

"That's no reason not to speak it. You can still communicate. Besides," I said, pressing my advantage, "I'm not trying to *fool* anyone. I'm just trying to hang on to something. There aren't many of the old bluesmen left. Five years, maybe ten, and most of them will be gone. There won't be anyone left to speak the old language, like that Eskimo language there was just something about in the *Trib*—Tlingit—that only three hundred people speak. All these old songs ought to be written down on scrolls, like the Jewish Torah."

"And that's what you're doing?"

"I'm trying—in regular notation and in tablature. But it's hard to get it down right."

"What's tablature?"

"Instead of just notes, like regular music, you show a diagram of the six strings. Here, let me show you."

She looked through her purse and came up with a ballpoint.

"That's a big purse," I said.

"I've got a lot of stuff."

I drew six quick lines with the ballpoint. "Instead of your staff lines," I said, "you've got six lines for your six strings. Then instead of notes, you write in numbers. Right on the lines." I wrote in a two on the fifth string. "That means you put your finger on the second fret of the fifth string, OK? That's a B." I added another two on the fourth string, a one on the third. "Now you've got an E major chord," I said. "And if you add a three on the second string, you've got your E7."

I handed her back the pen.

"What about the key signature? What about the rhythm?"

"You've got your regular staff line up above the tab."

"You write all the notes down by hand?"

I took my own fountain pen out of my pocket and sketched a guitar on the napkin and signed it and slid it across the table to her. The ink from my pen bled into the napkin, but you could still see the shape of the guitar, and you could read my writing: "Love, Martin."

"You think I'm one of your fans asking for an autograph?" She laughed, but she folded the napkin in half and put it in her purse.

I could feel my face heating up.

"Let me get this straight," she said. "Basically what you want is to play the guitar and sing like an old black man? Is that it? That's your mission in life? Apart from working for the post office?"

"That's probably not the way I'd put it."

"It's a cultural thing, Marty. You take away a black audience and what have you got? You've got just another consumer option, cut off from its roots. You could wind up like one of those pathetic white people who want to hang around black people all the time—'cause of our natural rhythm and our noble suffering." She leaned forward: "Do any black people come to hear you play?"

"I don't actually perform," I said. "I'm more like an archivist."

"So you haven't even got the nerve to put your behind out where folks can lay some fresh hickory on it if they don't like what they hear?" She laughed, but I didn't think it was funny.

"God damn it anyway, what the hell are you doing that's so great? Working in a beauty parlor?"

"I *own* a beauty *salon*, Marty. Mama and I."

"OK, so you *own* a beauty *salon*. Maybe the music I love is too down-home for you, but at least it's art, something you can put your whole soul into. But doing women's hair? This is how you want to spend your life? Come on."

"You don't know a damn thing about it, Martin Dijksterhuis." She slapped her hands back and forth to emphasize her determination. "All that torture. That's what it was. Torture. Hot-comb torture, and now they're starting a new kind of torture, with chemicals. Beautiful Negro women wanting bone-straight hair. Deep-fried, pan-fried, processed hair, I call it. They call them *relaxers*, but you might as well slap an old-fashioned conk on your head. It got into their psyches, and I'm going to get it out. I'm giving them their own natural beauty back. I'm telling them their head's a sacred place. But it's part of the belief system that you've got to straighten your hair to make it look like white people's hair. It's hard to get through to some black people. Like Mama. They've got hard heads."

"You've convinced me," I said.

She laughed again. "I guess I get carried away sometimes."

"Do you do your own hair? I mean . . . whatever it is you do to get it like that?"

"A lot of women want to know that. All you've got to do, I tell them, is let it grow out and then let it get wet. Of course it won't look nice, like this. That's why they need *me*. You've got to trim it and shape it and blow it out. It doesn't just happen by itself."

"It's striking."

"This is just the beginning. I'm going to Los Angeles in a week; there's a woman out there who's teaching people how to do traditional African hairstyles. If things work out I might even be going to Africa too."

"Where?"

"Probably Dakar."

"Dakar? In Senegal? Then you'll have to speak French, won't you? Another language."

"I suppose."

"You think you can order a cup of coffee?"

"Marty, that I can handle: *Un café au lait, s'il vous plait. On ne peut même pas sortir in hiver!*"

"*You can't even go out in winter!*" I laughed. "I'm glad you remember. How about dinner in a restaurant?"

She nodded. "I think I can handle it."

"What about your accent?"

She smiled. "How old are you, Marty?"

"We're the same age, for Christ's sake."

"Sorry."

"You want me help you out?"

"Help *me* out? You're not listening to me, Martin."

"With Carolyn. Cozy. I mean financially."

"No, Martin. I already told you."

"Is there anything I *can* do?"

"There's one thing, Martin, and I know you're not going like it."

"Try me."

"Don't interfere, Martin; don't upset the apple cart."

"Interfere?"

"With our lives."

"I just want to help."

"I know you do, Martin. But I've got enough trouble with Mama watching every move I make, making sure I don't come home with my panties in my purse. Oh, I'm sorry I'm being bitchy. Mama means well, but she's so old-fashioned, and sometimes it's hard."

"You have relatives here?"

"We stayed with my aunt in Milwaukee for a couple years. Actually, Milwaukee wasn't so great; it's not a good town for Negroes—too many Polacks and Bohunks and Germans, you name it. That's where I had Cozy, in Milwaukee County Hospital, but when my aunt got married again and moved back down to Georgia, we came up here."

"I know; I had a lot of trouble finding you. Your mom wanted to let Aunt Bridget know when your dad died or I never would have. How's your mom doing?"

"Yeah," she said, "Daddy's dead—he didn't want to leave Appleton—but Mama's still kicking. She helps out at the salon. She takes the bus down to Milwaukee two or three times every summer when the Cubs are playing the Braves. She likes to watch Ernie Banks. She was glad to get out too."

"She left the mangle behind."

Cory shook her head. "I think she said she gave it to the Salvation Army, but I don't remember. I think she'd had enough mangling."

"Cory, listen. I am what I am. I grew up in a certain place at a certain time, just like everybody else. About a hundred yards from where you grew up. I fell in love with a certain kind of music. I heard something. That's my calling. I used to sit in the kitchen with your mom and listen to Arthur Godfrey and *Just Plain Bill* while she worked the mangle. I can still taste that goddamned buttermilk and smell the hot sheets. I liked the smell of the sheets, though. *Hot sheets*. That'd be a good name for a song. And I fell in love with you. Right at the same time. That was the night I heard Chesterfield. You and I climbed the water tower and then we made love at a certain time in a certain place, and you had a baby. We had a baby. Now she's eight years old.

"Now we're living at a certain time in a certain place. Madison's supposed to be a good place; probably the most liberal place in the country right now. People are coming together. I think we could come together too. I know we could. If you wanted to."

"You're kidding me?"

"I'm not kidding. Dead serious. Why not? You're doing well. I'm doing well. I could move to Madison."

"I can think of a million reasons."

"I know, but I had to say it. Because if I didn't say it, I'd never know, would I? For sure?"

I waited. She didn't want to speak. Finally she said, "Martin, it's hard enough . . ."

"What's hard enough?"

She shook her head. "You still trying to save me, Marty?"

"Cory," I said, "I don't want to *save* you. I want to come on in your *kitchen*, taste your sweet jelly roll. Is that better?"

"It's better."

I looked at her. "But not enough?" She shook her head, but I didn't know if this meant that I'd guessed right or that I'd guessed wrong. "Be with you?" I said. "And with Cozy. She is my daughter too, you know. That's it; the end of the line. She needs a father."

"Have you been listening to me, Martin? It's just not that simple. You never even gave her a thought till tonight. You said so yourself. Besides, she's got my mother; that's all *any* child needs."

"Not the same."

"Close enough. Marty, it's good to see you again, it really is; but I've got to run."

I almost panicked; I wanted to hold on to her. "What about Carolyn? Cozy? I'd like to see her."

She began to look for something in her purse.

"She's got to find out sometime," I went on.

"Why, Martin? Why does she have to find out?"

"Because it's true."

"There's different kinds of *true.*"

"Cory, look at me. It's me. Marty. Remember me? Your old pal? We carted buckeyes out to Dijksterhuis Corners and buried them in our hideout? You read *The Three Musketeers* to me when I had the measles? Then we were in the play together? I was your defense attorney? We read *L'Etranger* and *The Fountainhead* and *Huis clos*?" I waited for Cory to say something. "Well?" I said, finally.

"Well," she said, "every black parent in this country has to sit down and have the same talk with his kids, about how to get along in this world. The white world. Daddy had that talk with Charlie, and Mama had it with me, and now I've got to have it with Cozy. I've been putting it off. It's harder than the sex talk, believe me. The sex talk is a cakewalk by comparison. But now she's eight years old. If I thought you could tell her everything she needs to know, I'd take you home with me right now. I'd say, 'Cozy, your daddy's here and he's got something to say to you, and I want you to pay attention.' I'm sorry, Martin; it's not your fault. You were sweet, and you wanted to do the right thing. You didn't run away. I'll give you credit. But it's hard. Some things you just can't explain. At least I can't. And you can't either." She pulled a photo out of her purse. "I've really got to run. Here, you can have this."

I slipped the photo into my pocket without looking at it. Cory was already sliding out of the booth. She stood beside me for a minute and ran her fingers through my hair, as if appraising it professionally, and then she was gone.

The teenaged waitress came back with the check. I paid at the register and ordered another beer, walked back to the alleys, and sat down to watch the bowlers. It was an old-fashioned bowling alley that hadn't been modernized yet. It did not have automatic pinsetters and I could see the legs of the pin boys in the pits.

I had the picture in my shirt pocket. The shirt was new and hadn't been washed and the collar was beginning to irritate the back of my neck. I wanted to look at the picture, to study it; but at the same time I was afraid; I had to prepare myself, like a man who's caught a glimpse of the truth but is afraid to look it in the face. I'd planted my seed. Sperm and ovum, seed and egg. A man knows when he plants his seed. I closed my eyes and felt the familiar pressure of the ladder rungs on my feet and the sensation of falling I'd experienced when I pulled Cory's underpants down.

Mixed doubles is usually more relaxed than league play, but there were some serious bowlers competing that night. By the time I'd finished a third beer a man on lanes five and six had put together a string of eight strikes. I wondered if my guitar was safe. It was in the trunk of Janis's new Volvo Amazon. I'd thought I might have a chance to play it for Cory. I decided to leave, but people were starting to watch the bowler on lanes five and six, who had rolled 192 in his first game and 240 in his second. His partner, a small blond woman, looked good too, with scores of 202 and 185. They were clearly the pair to beat. The atmosphere was changing: the noise level had dropped; more and more people were watching; the players on the adjacent lanes were making a point to yield the right of way.

He had the classic Dick Weber stance and delivery that my father had taught me—no wasted motion in his smooth five-step approach—but between frames he walked up and down in front of the scoring table, rubbing his hands on a towel with a red stripe down the center. His name, which appeared in small letters on his league shirt under "Ray's Body Shop," was Gabe. His partner's name was Alice. I didn't think they were married, and I thought that he was more in love with her than she was with him, though she kissed him on the mouth after each strike. He was trying to be nonchalant, throwing himself down carelessly between frames, his arm out on the back of the bench. But then he'd get up and start pacing again.

In the ninth frame Gabe stepped up to the approach, took his stance behind the second set of dots, and put one right in the pocket for a strike.

He wasn't too demonstrative, didn't use a lot a lot of body English. But some. You could see him tense almost involuntary, driving the ball into the pocket, giving it a little help.

The noise level went back up while the man from the other team bowled, followed by the two women. People went back to their own games. A baby cried. A woman laughed. But everyone was waiting, and on the tenth frame they were gathered three deep on either side of lane six. I had a good view, directly behind lane five, a good angle, especially when he was bowling on lane six. A large man on my left kept leaning over in front of me. He was wearing a league shirt too, but his match was over.

I'd once seen my father bowl a three hundred game in the presence of Hank Marino, who'd just been voted the Bowler of the Half Century. It wasn't in league play, so it wasn't official, and my father did not receive a three hundred ring. But it was a great moment anyway. We'd stopped at a bowling alley Marino operated out in Berwyn or Cicero, I don't remember. But I remembered how I'd begun to get nervous as the strikes added up. Six, seven, eight, nine. My father always recommended a five-step approach to others, the first step being just a little push-off; but he used a four-step approach himself. I sat on the bench next to Marino and kept score. Marino, who had bowled his share of three hundred games in league play, was a nice man, and I could tell that he wanted my father to strike out. He seemed almost as tense as I was when my father picked up his ball from the rack to start the tenth frame.

Gabe came up for the tenth frame, lined himself up, took a deep breath, pushed off, and leaned into his approach. He knew as soon as he'd delivered the ball that it was another perfect strike. He turned and walked back to the scoring table and didn't turn till he heard the ball slam into the pocket.

"A rocket to the pocket." The name on the shirt of the man sitting next to me was Connie. "You know," Connie said, "the tenth ball is harder than the twelfth. Most people don't know that." I didn't say anything. "You know why?"

"Because after the ninth frame you've got to sit around while everybody else bowls. You got too much time to think."

"Right," Connie said. "The pressure's different. You got to go with the pressure, learn to enjoy it."

"Have you bowled a lot of three hundred games?" I asked.

"If he strikes out," Connie said, ignoring the question, "he'll have something to tell the kids."

"If he doesn't he'll still have something to tell the kids. The sun will still come up tomorrow. The trains will still run."

"Yeah, but . . ."

The bowling alley was now perfectly quiet. There wasn't even any noise coming from the lounge.

Gabe stepped up and threw a strike. The spotter rolled the ball back and set the pins. No one else was bowling now. The big moment had arrived, bowling's equivalent to the full count with the bases loaded in the bottom of the ninth inning, or football's long pass with the clock running out; the critical free throw at the end of a basketball game.

I remembered sitting on the hard wooden bench as my father

prepared for his last shot. I could see him pick up the ball with two hands and carry it to the approach. I could see him move into his stance, slightly crouched, supporting the ball in his left hand, a little below chest high. He lined up his shot, but he was taking too long—you can be *too* careful—and he froze. He couldn't move. Marino walked out to him, pulled him back to the scoring table, and set the ball down on the floor. Then he picked up the ball again and handed it to my dad, who went back to the approach.

"All he's got to do now," Marino whispered to me, "is stay down with the shot. He's moved a little to the right, you see that? He's compensating for the adrenaline rush. Your dad could have been a pro. He knows he's going to throw the ball harder; he can't help it. The extra speed will cut down his hook and he'll get a light hit. He's compensating by moving to the right." I looked at Marino and then back at my dad. "He's nervous as hell," Marino said, "but he's *thinking* like a pro. He knows he's got a problem and he's dealing with it. *Take a deep breath,*" he said under his breath, "*and then just let the ball go.*"

"You ever bowl a three hundred game?" Connie asked.

"No, but my dad did."

Gabe waited a second too long for me, shifted his weight to his left foot, began the push-away, let the ball fall into the downswing, but he was forcing it. He speeded up; instead of letting the ball swing freely at the end of his arm, like the weight on a pendulum, he forced it back and then had to pull forward; going into his slide he dropped his shoulder and then set the ball down short. Instead of following through smoothly, he reared up and turned away in disgust. His big moment had come and he'd choked. The ball broke hard and went right through the nose.

"Railroad," Connie said. And I had to agree. But the gods were kind to Gabriel. The pins exploded. The six pin stood for a moment in the right-hand gutter and toppled over slowly to take out the ten. The deck was clear.

A moment of silence, and then applause. A kiss from Alice,

Gabe's partner, and a round of drinks on Gabe, who kept wiping his face with the towel as if he was trying to wipe away the big grin that was spreading out of control, but I was afraid I was going to cry, because it was the first time I'd let myself grieve for my dad. We'd never gone hunting again after the Williamses disappeared; we'd never bowled another line together; never walked home together from the packing shed after a long hot day. I'd punished him for being weak, for not standing up for me.

"Not exactly a rocket to the pocket," Connie observed.

"Connie," I said, "I want to show you something." I pulled the picture of Carolyn out of my pocket and showed it to Connie. "This is a picture of my daughter." Connie looked at the picture and then at me and then back at the picture. "You're a lucky guy. Me, I got no kids. Never got around to tying the knot." I looked at the picture for the first time. She was beautiful, of course. But you can't describe beauty. You can just point at it. I pointed. "Her mother's a beautician," I said.

"Looks like she's been doing some experiments on your daughter's head."

I looked again. A great burst of hair shot upward out of my daughter's head, like water shooting up out of a fountain."

"How did she *do* that?" I asked out loud.

"Let's get a beer," Connie said, waving at someone who was passing out bottles of beer. "Looks like Gabe bought about two hundred bottles of beer tonight."

But I was already high without another beer. I studied the face in the photo, looking for Cory, looking for myself, looking for something I hadn't known was lost.

If I'd had a box of cigars, I'd have handed them out. But I didn't have any cigars. I managed to shake Gabe's hand before leaving. He was high, and I was high too, even though I'd already realized that sometimes finding something can be as painful as losing it.

7

Careless Love

1964

IT WAS AFTER eleven when I got back from Madison. I could hear the sounds of Mozart's *Requiem* coming from behind the bathroom door. Janis was reading a book in the tub. When I opened the door she looked up and covered her breasts with her book. A scented candle was burning on the little stand next to the tub. She put the book down and smiled. Her breasts were soapy. "Martin," she said, "you're home," and everything suddenly went back to normal. Almost. Everything *could have* gone back to normal. I was glad I hadn't said anything about Janis to Cory.

"Why don't you turn that off?" she said, indicating the little radio on the wicker hamper, "and you can tell me about your trip." I'd told her I was going up to Madison to see an old friend from Appleton.

It would have been easy and sensible: to accept this invitation, to return to the path after a little detour. But I declined.

"I'm tired," I said.

"Marty, what's the matter?"

I didn't want to explain, but my feelings were chaotic and I needed to give them some kind of shape or form. I took Cozy's picture from my pocket and handed it to her in the tub. She held one corner between thumb and finger. I soaped her back while she looked at it.

"I don't get it, Martin. What am I looking at?"

"My daughter."

She looked up at me, her face white, her lips pressed together. She looked back at the picture and then back at me again, taking deep breaths, rocking a little in the tub, making gentle waves.

"You had your hair cut," I said, pulling her hair back into a pony-tail. The ends were wet.

"Just trimmed the ends a little. I needed a break this afternoon. Cathy did it."

"How's the proofreading going?"

"OK. I got through another twenty pages today. But two of the graphs have to be done over, and there are some small corrections."

I took the picture back and wiped the corner on a towel and put it back in my shirt pocket.

"This is big news, Martin. I don't know how to react."

"I don't either."

She got out of the tub, and I told her the whole story while she was drying herself off. It took less than three minutes to get through it. "That's it. That's my story."

"That's not your *only* story, Marty. You've got a lot of stories."

"Well, this one is special."

"You know you didn't have to lie to me about it."

"I didn't lie."

"I mean, you didn't have to keep it a secret. Did you think I wouldn't understand?"

"I don't understand myself. I didn't even know I had a daughter till tonight. I mean, I knew Corinna was pregnant—but I never thought about the baby. I just thought about Corinna."

"Why don't you take your clothes off and get in the tub?" she said. "I'll run some more hot water."

I was tired, and the tub looked inviting. But once again I resisted an inner impulse, declined a generous invitation, shook my head, and let Janis pull the plug. She got out of the tub and I helped dry her off.

"Glass of wine?" she asked.

"Sure."

"Stay right here. We'll have a glass of wine in the bathroom, where it's nice and warm." She brushed past me, holding a big fluffy towel around her waist. "I'll be right back."

While Janis was getting the wine I peed and flushed the toilet. The tiles of the bathroom floor were tiny white octagons, like the tiles on the floor of Aunt Bridget's beauty parlor in Appleton. The toilet flushed like a hotel toilet—a chrome handle sticking out of the wall. The mirror over the sink was all steamed up and I couldn't see my face. I put the toilet seat down and sat down and listened to the water swirling down the drain and the clink of glasses in the kitchen.

I moved the radio off the hamper so she'd have a place to sit. When she came back with a half bottle of wine and two glasses she was wearing a robe and had white socks on her feet. She sat down on the hamper, poured the wine, set the bottle down on the floor, handed me a glass.

"Thanks."

"What's her name?"

"Cozy. Carolyn, but they call her Cozy."

"To Cozy, then." She lifted her glass.

"I'll sleep on the couch," I said.

"You don't need to do that, Marty."

"I thought you might want me to."

"We could adopt her."

"Who?"

"Who? Who've we been talking about? Cozy. Your daughter."

"Adopt her? What about her mother? Don't you think she might object? Or do you think her mother's not fit to raise her?"

"I'm sorry, Marty. That's not what I meant."

"She's not one of the dimes or pennies on your checkerboard." If I was angry, it was only because I'd had the same thought—alone in the car on the way home from Madison, trying to understand what it meant to have a child.

"Martin, I'm sorry. I shouldn't have said that. But don't punish me. I didn't do anything wrong. We don't have to quarrel, Marty. I'll try to understand. But it—I don't know, I guess it hurts."

"I'm sorry. It was a long time ago; that was another world."

"I'm not sorry about a long time ago, Marty. I'm sorry about tomorrow, and the next day, and the day after that."

"What are you talking about?"

"What are you going to do?"

"I'm not going to do anything. She told me she doesn't want me hanging around. I don't know."

"Let's not worry about the future, Marty."

"You're the one who brought it up."

"I know I did, Marty. It was a mistake. Let's just think about tonight tonight."

But it was too hard to think about tonight tonight. We lay down together in Janis's double bed like an old married couple, careful not to touch each other.

I continued to tutor Reverend Taylor on Saturday afternoons, but I didn't take my guitar, and my heart wasn't in the lessons: "The Threefold Rule of Earth's Wisest Man," "Bible Prophecy," "What

Does God Expect of Us?" I had a case examination coming up, too, on lower New York State; but instead of studying I sat on the sofa and put my feet up on the soft leather-covered ottoman that sometimes figured in our lovemaking and watched Janis's TV in the living room with the volume turned down low: *Andy Griffith, Gunsmoke, Beverly Hillbillies, Bewitched, Ozzie and Harriet, Bonanza, The Addams Family, Candid Camera, Dr. Kildare, Ed Sullivan, Gilligan's Island, The Tonight Show*. Janis proofread her dissertation in the bedroom with the door closed. Every so often she'd bring out a page with too many errors and I'd retype it—a burst of machine gun fire—on the Olympia at the desk in the living room.

In mid-March her parents stopped on the way from Boston to California. They were staying over one night in Chicago and then taking the California Zephyr to San Francisco. We went out for a late dinner at La Boulangerie, a French restaurant near the Palmer House. It was freezing outside, but we were seated at a table in a huge indoor atrium, with palm trees thirty feet tall. I was wearing a new Italian silk tie that Janis had given me that was every bit as elegant as the tie that Janis's father was wearing, except that the knot on mine was a little lopsided. Janis's father laid out some change on the table, but he didn't have enough and he asked the waiter to change a five-dollar bill: pennies and dimes.

"It's all right, Papa," Janis said. "You don't have to do that. There's not room on the table." But now Princeton University Press had expressed interest in publishing a revised version of the dissertation, and she was pleased to talk about it.

"You say it comes out different every time?"

"Once you get an unstable situation," she said. "You can change the definition of *neighborhood,* and you can alter the tolerance schedules." But the waiter had come to take our order.

Janis's father asked us what we wanted for our first course, and then ordered in French. Janis's mother and I had the specialty of the house, *coquilles St.-Jacques.* Janis and her father had lobster soufflés.

The white wine Janis's father had chosen was really good. I hadn't realized that wine could taste so good. Every time I picked up my glass, the saliva rushed into my mouth, and I wished that my mother could taste it. The scallops were good too, but not as good as the scallops Janis and her parents had eaten in a little restaurant on the Grande Corniche, just above Nice, a meal so expensive that Janis's father had asked if the price included the silverware. The menu I'd looked at didn't have any prices on it, which made me think he might want to take the silverware at La Boulangerie too.

Janis hadn't told me that her father was Hungarian and that they'd spent three years in Rome when she was in high school. He'd been an architect at the time, working on a project in Saudi Arabia. No one had wanted to live in Saudi Arabia, so they'd set up their headquarters in Rome. Later they'd been forced to move to Cambridge.

For the main course Janis's father ordered a roast tenderloin of beef with stuffed mushroom caps and braised lettuce, which we ate family style.

"My mother went to the University of Chicago," I said, cutting a mushroom cap in half. I told them about my mother going to school with Ernest Hemingway and about how her teachers had got up the money to send her to the University of Chicago. Before I finished the story I realized that they assumed I was a graduate student too, at the University of Chicago. And that Janis had let them assume this. I tried to catch her eye as I fended off probing questions about my future plans, but she kept her head down.

"Actually," I said, "for a while I thought about becoming a bluesman."

Janis's mother looked alarmed. "Do you play an instrument?"

Janis was still looking down at her plate. I was not her pearl of great price but something she'd been willing to settle for. I experienced a little flush of anger.

"I used to play the guitar," I said. I hadn't touched my guitar since the trip to Madison.

Janis looked up. "He plays really well," she said.

"Reverend Taylor's the one who really plays well," I said.

"He's the one with the Rolls-Royces?" Janis's father looked at her. She nodded.

We ate our salads last, the way my mother did at home, and after the waiter cleared the table we chose our desserts from a pastry cart, and then Janis and I walked her parents back to the Palmer House. Janis's father gave her money for a cab back to Hyde Park, but we took the IC instead: Van Buren, Roosevelt Road, Eighteenth Street, McCormick Place, Twenty-seventh Street, Forty-seventh Street, Fifty-third Street. It took about twenty minutes to get to Hyde Park. At each stop I resolved to speak, to say something that would break through the veil of politeness that separated us. I wanted to propose, to say, *Marry me, marry me, Janis.* I knew she'd still say yes. But on the station platform at Fifty-ninth Street I said, "Are you ashamed of me?"

She didn't protest, didn't pretend not to know what I was talking about.

"Are you embarrassed that I'm a proletarian?"

She still didn't say anything. We walked back to her apartment in silence. Her keys jingled as she unlocked the three locks and opened the door. The walls of the apartment were a depressing gray, lavatory gray, except for the bedroom, which Janis had painted a light yellow, with dark blue trim.

"Before you say anything more," she said, "let's sit in the living room and have a glass of wine and you can play your guitar for me. You haven't played it since you saw your old girlfriend."

"I can't play the guitar," I said, "not after the way Cory talked. You should have heard her: *What are you trying to prove? Black people don't listen to that stuff. It's too down-home. Reminds us of stuff we'd just as soon forget . . . It's not real . . . The only people who listen to that stuff are white college kids. Maybe you can fool them, but you can't fool me.'* What am I supposed to do, play 'I Want to Hold Your Hand' and 'I Feel Fine'?"

Janis smiled. "Those are nice songs, Martin. You're so funny. And stubborn. I'll dance with you if you'll dance with me?"

"The Beatles?" I said, but I had to smile too.

She nodded. "I'm sorry, Martin."

I slipped my shoes off. "Yeah," I said.

She put on her new Beatles album and we danced to "Roll Over, Beethoven" and "Thank You Girl," and then we had a glass of wine and then we danced to "You Can't Do That." Janis was a good dancer, but I always had to concentrate to count three against four, and I worried about getting splinters in my feet. As we danced we tried to rekindle the fantasy of the Victorian house on the tree-lined street in Kalamazoo, and the six children; but Janis put in her diaphragm before we made love—for the first time since I'd gone up to Madison. She spit in the palm of her hand and rubbed herself between her legs and climbed on top of me.

"You're thinking about *her*, aren't you?" she asked after a few minutes. There was no point in denying it. I didn't say anything. "It's all right, Marty. Everybody thinks about somebody else when they're doing it. It's all right," she said again after a few minutes; but she was crying. It wasn't all right. She leaned forward so that her breasts were in my face. "I don't know why, Marty, maybe it's just the way we're made. But it doesn't make any sense. I try to understand, but I can't."

"Do you think about somebody else when we do it?"

"Sometimes," she whispered in my ear. I could feel her cheeks wet with tears.

"Paul McCartney? John Lennon?"

She straightened up so she could see my face, and shook her head.

"Are you thinking of somebody else right now?"

A little smile broke through and then disappeared again. She nodded. "I can't even remember his name, Marty. It was a long time ago, but you'd think I'd remember his name."

I pulled her down on top of me and tried to kiss away her tears, but there were too many of them, and I knew that someday, doing it with somebody else, I'd think of Janis, and Janis, doing it with somebody else, would think of me.

A week later I rented a car—I didn't want to borrow Janis's car again—and made another trip to Madison, driving up through Beloit. Cozy was eight years old. I had the home address from the private detective who'd tracked the Williamses down in the first place, but it took me a while to find the house, partly because I don't have a very good sense of direction, and partly because "the Bush," as the detective called it—"colored, Italians, Greeks, Jews, whites, a little bit of everything"—was not identified as such in my guidebook. I parked two houses down and read a copy of the *Capital Times* that I'd picked up in a gas station on Highway 51: a man had been photographed while picketing the IRS office; Khrushchev had lashed out at Trotskyites; Governor Stratton of Illinois had been indicted; Rachel Carson had died; a Top-Farmer contest had opened; T-bone steak was on sale at Kroger for ninety-seven cents a pound; Governor Wallace of Alabama had received 25 percent of the vote in the Democratic primary in Wisconsin, but that was because the Republicans crossed over and voted for him; and police had been summoned to an East Side diner to rouse a man who'd fallen asleep in a booth. The man said the service was so poor he'd dozed off before the waitress had come to take his order.

The weather was bright and sunny but cold, and I'd turn on the engine and run the heater for a while and then turn the engine off again. The houses on Cory's block were small but attractive, some with fake-brick siding. The front of Cory's house had been painted gray, the shutters black. Iron railings kept you from falling off steps that led up to a screened-in porch. A small ornamental plum tree barely reached up to the big front window, which was full of plants,

plants almost as big as the plum tree. I got out of the car and walked down the street to stretch my legs. Other houses had plants in the windows too. The front yards were small but well kept. I went back to the car and then got out and walked down to the corner again. The front door opened at quarter to eight. I couldn't really recognize Cozy, who was bundled up in a red coat, but I recognized Aunt Flo on the step, in a housecoat, hugging herself against the cold, bending over to tell Cozy something. To warn her? Against what? Against me—a strange man hiding behind a newspaper in the front seat of his car, like a spy? Aunt Flo waited on the steps, her hand on the doorknob, and Cozy waltzed around till an older girl with two other kids in tow came around the corner, swinging a green book bag. I watched from behind the paper till Aunt Flo went back inside and then I followed the girls, staying on the opposite side of the street, till they arrived safely at St. James Catholic School, which was only three blocks away. I watched to see if Cozy would be joined by any friends, but she stood alone for a while, holding her little arms down stiff at her sides. She looked too thin to me, even in her heavy coat. When she pulled her hood back, her hair splashed out in all directions.

A bell rang, and all the children swarmed into the school, like a colony of bees swarming into their hive.

I made another trip up to Madison at the beginning of April, this time in Reverend Taylor's Silver Wraith. I staked out St. James Catholic School for a while and watched the kids play at recess. The playground, which was on the opposite side of the street behind the school, had a fence around it that must have been twenty-five feet high. And then I drove downtown and parked in a lot near Corinna's beauty salon, which was called Chez Corinna. It was in a wedge-shaped building on State Street at a three-way intersection, only a block from the capitol. I sat in a bus kiosk on the opposite side of State and watched the women coming and going. And then I drove back to the school. I'd bought a little Minox spy camera—the kind James Bond used—and I used it to take a picture of Cozy walking down Charter Street to Mound. She wasn't wearing the red coat she'd worn at recess and she kept jumping up and down and slapping her arms to keep warm as she waited for the light to change.

I'd asked the detective to follow Corinna's property trail and to get Cozy's school records and a school calendar. Corinna and her mother were holding two mortgages: one on the house on Mound Street, and one on Chez Corinna. Business was good at Chez Corinna, and Cozy was doing well in school.

I made another trip in April and two more in May, and each time I followed Cozy after school. Usually she walked home with an older girl, but once Aunt Flo came to meet her and they took a bus downtown to Chez Corinna and then walked to the public library, which was just a block away; and once she went on a school trip to the State Historical Museum. I almost got arrested on my sixth trip, in fact, for loitering near the school playground; but by this time I had some good pictures: Cozy holding up a dead snake; Cozy jumping double Dutch at recess, encircled by the ropes like a bird in a cage; Cozy sitting next to a boy on the steps of the State Historical Museum; Cozy sharing a candy bar with another girl on the edge of the school grounds. Fragments. Mysteries. Had she forgotten her sweater, or had someone stolen it? What was she saying to the boy next to her as they sat on the steps of the museum? She's just said something, because he's laughing. Had they enjoyed the visit, or were they glad to be released from a numbing infusion of culture? Had she found the dead snake on the sidewalk, or had some boy tried to frighten her with it? Was she best friends with the two Negro girls twirling the ropes and chanting something that sounded like "Strawberry, strawberry, cream on top / Tell me the name of yo' sweetheart. Is it A–B–C–D . . . ?"

I made one last trip, at the beginning of June, just before school got out. Aunt Flo and Cory walked down to the bus stop on Regent Street. I drove downtown to stake out Chez Corinna. Shampooing, drying, cutting were done in the back, which looked like a conventional beauty parlor, like Aunt Bridget's beauty parlor in Appleton. I could see chairs that tipped back over sinks, chairs with the big hoods for drying, and magazines spread out on little tables. Cozy and Aunt Flo stopped at Chez Corinna for a few minutes. When they came out I snapped a picture. They were looking right at me, but they didn't see me. They headed down Fairchild toward the library. I was about to head home. It was almost four o'clock and I'd gotten what I'd come for. Cozy and Aunt Flo would probably stay at the library till six and then ride home with Cory. But as I was heading down Dayton, to the lot where I'd left the Silver Wraith, I looked back and caught a glimpse of Cory's Afro. I followed her all the way down State Street—a street of small shops, restaurants and cafés, record stores, an Orpheum Theater, just like the Oriental Theater in Appleton—to the UW campus, to the Memorial Union, to the Rathskeller, out onto the Union Terrace, overlooking Lake Mendota. There were sailboats on the lake. On the terrace, which was crowded, people sat in brightly colored chairs at white tables. Some of the tables had big umbrellas, but not the ones on the upper terrace, which were shaded by big oaks and lindens. No, not excited, agitated. I knew I was about to cross a line. I tried to pull back—my foot was suspended in the air for just a moment, and then I put it down. There was no turning back. Corinna sat at a table on the upper terrace, under a large oak tree, where she was joined by a man, a black man with a briefcase that must have had a broken handle, because he carried it under his arm. A professor? That's what he looked like to me. It was almost five o'clock. I went back into the Rathskeller and watched them through the leaded glass window. They talked for over an hour, talked the way I imagined lovers talking in cafés in Paris, their heads nodding, almost touching, their bodies leaning back and laughing. I pretended to look out at the lake, at the sailboats luffing in the sharp breeze, while I took a few pictures, though my hands were shaking and I couldn't hold the little camera steady. Leaning forward, their foreheads touched, and they kept them together for a while. The man left, but he didn't take his briefcase with him. Corinna took a letter out of her purse and read it. When the man came back she read it aloud to him, and they talked some more and then they walked to the parking lot next to the Union, where he locked his briefcase in the trunk of his car, a beautiful sky blue Buick Riviera. They walked back down State Street and ate at a Middle Eastern restaurant. I had a beer at a place across the street, and then another beer. When they came out I followed them to a small hotel that was fancy enough to have a maroon awning in front but not a doorman. They stood under the awning for five minutes, maybe ten. I stood in the entryway of the Badger Music Company, pretending to look at guitars. Finally the man hugged her, just the way the detective had predicted, and gave her a kiss. It was a long kiss, but I was still staring at them when the man looked up, over Cory's shoulder. He looked right at me. Our eyes met, and he smiled a big goofy smile, like Gabe's smile after he'd bowled the last strike of his three hundred game. It was an extraordinary, totally unself-conscious smile. Like an invitation. I was looking, staring, right into the face of joy.

He took her arm and they disappeared into the hotel. I waited, waited for the lights to go on and then off. Of course I had no idea where their room was, so I just waited. For what? Was this their first time? I was sure of it. But what had they been talking about in front of the hotel? What had Cory told Aunt Flo? *"Mr. Jelly Roll Baker, let me be your slave, when Gabriel blows his trumpet you know I'll rise from my grave, for some of your jelly, some of your sweet jelly roll; you know it's doin' me good, way down deep in my soul."* Did she like to do it dog fashion, like Janis? I could picture Janis bending over the leather ottoman, her bare bottom a primitive invitation, deeply satisfying. Would the earth move for Cory and her lover tonight? If it moved, would I feel it where I was standing? I could still remember the earth moving for Cory and me, under the buckeye trees in the back of the lot of the Potter Featherbone Company, though I guess Cory remembered it differently. I'd learned a few tricks since then, mostly from Janis, but not how to make the earth move whenever I wanted it to.

There was a guitar in the window that was almost as ugly as my guitar. A Gibson Nick Lucas, made in Kalamazoo—where Janis was teaching—about eighty miles east of Appleton. It had a price tag on it, but the tag, hanging from a string, was turned so you couldn't see it from the window. I looked at it from every possible angle.

I stood in the doorway for almost two hours, imagining the lovers entering each other's orifices from every possible angle. Finally I had to pee. I walked back to the men's room at the Rathskeller. On the way back downtown I stopped in the Union parking lot to write down the license number on the man's Buick Riviera. And then I drove back to Chicago. It cost me $50 to learn that the man's name was Monroe Franklin; that he was a visiting professor of political science from Columbia University in New York; that he was married and had two kids; that his wife was a pediatrician at Columbia Presbyterian in Washington Heights.

Janis received her Ph.D. at the end of the second week in June. Her parents came out from Cambridge. Reverend Taylor came with us to the commencement ceremony in Rockefeller Chapel, and afterward we ate lunch at Tai Sam Yan, on Sixty-third Street, and then that afternoon Janis and her parents left for a monthlong trip to Rome—Janis's graduation present. They were going to stay with friends in a palazzo on the Esquiline Hill. They were going to leave Janis's Volvo in Kalamazoo, take the train into Detroit, spend the night, and fly out the next evening: Detroit-London-Rome. After lunch Reverend Taylor and I walked down Sixty-third Street, past the little Episcopal church that he had an eye on, past the drugstore where Bobby

Franks's father had waited by the telephone, with $10,000 in a cigar box, for instructions from Nathan Leopold and Richard Loeb, past the Illinois Central station where Muddy Waters had gotten off the train in 1943. We cut through Jackson Park and walked all the way out to the Point, where we sat on a bench and kept an eye on the lake and thought our own thoughts till the sun started to go down behind us, and then we walked back.

I'd bought most of Janis's furniture, including the double bed and the TV, but she was taking the ottoman with her. In the morning, after they left, I stacked the leftover boxes of clothes and books for Kalamazoo College by the door. I was going to mail them to Janis at Kalamazoo College when she got back from Italy. And then I went down to the shooting range at the police station on Eleventh and State. I had to qualify once a year for the handgun that I had to carry on the train. The range officer checked my gun, which I'd cleaned and oiled the night before. I stepped up to the firing line. My father had taught me to shoot rats out at the dump with a nine-shot .22 pistol, and I was a pretty good shot.

The gun was a .38 double-action snubnose revolver known as a banker's special because it had once been favored by bank messengers. It was designed to shoot someone who was standing right in front of you—a train robber coming down the narrow aisle of the RPO car—but I still had to qualify at fifteen feet, at thirty feet, and at sixty feet. We used cardboard bullets at fifteen and thirty feet, and live ammunition at sixty feet. The closer targets were regulation bull's-eyes, but the sixty-foot target was a human silhouette. We used a one-handed target-shooting stance: *front sight, squeeze the trigger*. The .38 rose automatically to eye level and aimed itself, like a Zen gun, directed solely by some spiritual force within my body, or that had taken over my body, but as the sight came on target I could see a human face smiling at me: Monroe, giving me that big goofy whole-body smile of joy, of ecstasy that simply can't be contained. I held my stance for ten seconds and then let my arm drop.

I walked back to the counter where the range officer was checking my scores with a spotting scope. "You're doing fine," he said.

"I can't do it," I said. "When I sight in the target, it looks like somebody I know."

"I know what you mean," he said. "Sometimes it looks just like my old lady. I usually just blast away. Sit down a minute, grab a cup of coffee. I got some here."

"I think I'm just going to go home," I said.

"I can't fill out your form till you finish with the sixty-footer," he said.

"That's all right. I'll come back next week."

"And I got to have the wad cutters back," he said.

I swung open the cylinder and pushed the plunger to release the flat-topped bullets into my hand.

Back in my apartment I took my shoes off and lay down on the bed and played a Beatles album that was on the turntable. The Beatles sang "I Want to Hold Your Hand" and then "Can't Buy Me Love." I turned the record player off and waited for Janis to come home from the library. And then I remembered that Janis wasn't coming home from the library. She wasn't coming home at all. The door of the big Victorian house on a tree-lined street in Kalamazoo was closed and locked. I'd closed it myself, turned the deadbolt with my own hand.

8

God's Plan For Your Life

1964

REVEREND TAYLOR took the last exam in *God's Plan for Your Life* at his kitchen table. It was the middle of May. I'd put water on to boil for tea. Reverend Taylor had installed new cabinets and replaced the moldings around the baseboards. The metal shelves were gone. I got two dark blue mugs out of one of the cabinets and put them on the table.

"This is the last exam in this course," he said. "Two more courses to go: *The Doctrine of the Holy Spirit* and *A Holy Life and How to Live It*. I better get a move on, 'cause I still got my eye on a church on Sixty-third Street that we walked past, not too far from that Chinese restaurant where we ate dinner with Janis and her folks. I think it's gonna go under."

"Reverend Taylor," I said, "I don't think you've missed a single question on any of the exams so far, so I wouldn't worry."

Reverend Taylor put the Moody course book on the table and laid out the exam, his King James Bible, the Scantron answer card, and two yellow pencils. I picked up the test and glanced at the first question:

> 1. Some Christians live disappointed lives because
>   *a.* God planned no great work for them.
>   *b.* their circumstances prevented them from doing what they wanted to do.
>   *c.* they made wrong choices and missed God's way.
>   *d.* they failed to follow good advice.

What the hell! I thought. Had God planned a great work for me? I didn't think so. Had circumstances prevented me from doing what I wanted to do? Well, I *could* have gone to the U of C, *could* have run the orchards after my dad died, probably *could* have married Janis. But that wasn't what I'd wanted to do. On the other hand, you might argue I'd made wrong choices all along and missed God's way. That seemed like a real possibility. Still, what difference would it have made to God one way or the other if I'd gone to the U of C or stayed home and run the orchards or married Janis?

The teakettle began to cheep a little, and I fussed with the tea bags and warmed up the cups with hot water from the tap. I put a tea bag in each cup and poured boiling water over them and added a tiny bit of sugar to Reverend Taylor's, and then I washed up some dishes while he took the exam. The exams consisted of multiple-choice questions on each lesson, followed by true-or-false questions. My job as proctor was to make sure Reverend Taylor didn't look at the textbook or the Bible while he was taking the exam.

When he finished I sealed up the color-coded Scantron card—tan for the last exam—in its envelope before asking him how he'd answered question number one.

He said the correct answer was *c,* and when I started to protest, he laughed. "It don't have nothin' to do with Janis," he said, "though I don't understand how you let that girl get away from you."

"Then what *does* it have to do with?" I said, impatient.

"Martin," he said, "why don't you tell me what's eatin' at you?"

And I did. I told him about Corinna and Cozy, told him the whole story, right from the beginning: childhood, working together in the orchards, the junior class play, Latin and French classes, reading Ayn Rand and Camus and Sartre, climbing the water tower, Cory's pregnancy, the Williamses' disappearance, discovering that my parents had paid the Williamses to disappear, Aunt Flo's postcard, hiring a private detective to track Cory down, meeting her in the bowling alley in Madison, "shooting" Monroe in the police shooting range.

I waited for him to say something, waited like a coiled snake, ready to defend myself. But he didn't say anything. He just put a little more sugar in what was left of his tea and stirred it.

"According to the book here"—he tapped the dark green Moody course book, *God's Plan for Your Life*—"the answer to every problem ever faced by the human heart can be found in the Bible. If you're absolutely honest with yourself and with God, then God won't leave you in the dark. The problem for most people is not finding the answer, it's acting on it by submitting their own will to God's will."

"Is that what *you* believe?"

"Yes it is, Marty."

"Then what's the answer? You want to look it up for me? You've got your Bible here. I'm serious. Really."

Reverend Taylor picked up his Bible and paged through it, and then put it back down.

"When I got out of prison in east Texas," he said, "there weren't but two ways to go, south to Waco or north to Dallas. I wanted to get out of east Texas."

"I didn't know you'd been in prison," I said.

"Yes," he said, "I stole a car from a colored undertaker in

Durham. I guess cars was in my blood, that's how bad I wanted it. It was called a Moon and it was made in St. Louis and it had a regular steering wheel, just like a car today. I didn't mean to steal it, you know. I was just going to take it for a drive out by the tobacco house at the edge of town, but when I got out on the main road I couldn't stop. I drove all the way to east Texas before the police caught up with me. I can still get that same feeling when I hit the Edens Expressway or the ramp for the Skyway. There's nothing like it.

"But I don't broadcast it around," he went on. "I mean, that I was in jail. Just like I never told anyone I couldn't read. Mr. Clifford at the Rolls-Royce Company in Springfield was the first person I told; and then my wife, my second wife—my first wife, she never knew; and then Janis. And now you.

"But I was sayin' . . . You had to walk up a dirt road, wide for the trucks, to the main road. There was a man waiting on me. He shook my hand and said, 'Nehemiah, I been waiting on you a long time.' And I asked him how long and he said, 'All your life.' That man's name was Mr. Jesus Christ. He said he would go with me wherever I was going, but I said I was going to go by myself. I was going to go to Chicago. I told him I'd been a nigger in North Carolina and I'd been a nigger in Texas, but I be damned if I'd be a nigger any longer. 'Well,' he said"—Reverend Taylor pronounced the word well so that it rhymed with whale—"'I hate to say it, but you're gonna be a nigger in Chicago too. But I'll go with you,' he said, 'if you want me to.' I told him no, I wanted to go by myself. There was a bus that took you to Lubbock. I had enough money for a ticket from Lubbock to Chicago. That was in 1927, just before the Depression. I didn't have but one little grip and my guitar, which they left me. That was the old Stella I told you about. I left him standing there in the Greyhound station. I was no better than Jonah when the Lord called him to preach to the Assyrians at Nineveh."

"I thought you got the call of the Lord when you were running a house for parties on Indiana Avenue?"

He looked surprised. "Janis tell you that?"

I nodded. "Yeah."

"That was later, during the Depression. The first time was in 1921. I was working for a Cadillac dealer on the West Side; I got into a little trouble here in Chicago and decided to try my luck in New York, and then Boston. That's where I met Mr. Clifford. He carried me with him to Springfield. They had brought all the trained experts they need from England to make Rolls-Royces in Springfield, and their wives and families too. A lot of them was Methodists, and I caught the fire from them. I started out as a janitor, but I loved cars, and I knew a little something about cars, and Mr. Clifford encouraged me to learn all I could and even introduced me to Mr. Henry Royce. I worked for the Brewster Company, they called it, and then it was Rolls-Royce—right up to the Depression, and then they changed the name again to Springfield Manufacturing Company, because they didn't want the name Rolls-Royce on a company that was going bankrupt. They had to rent the plant out to what they called cottage industries. That's when I come back to Chicago."

"That's when you ran the house for parties?"

"That's right. I had some money that I'd saved, and I hooked up with a woman I knew from before and we bought us a house on Indiana Avenue. We put in a big horseshoe bar and tables for playing cards. Nice tables everywhere. Music for dancing. I used to play my guitar. It was a party every night. Every kind of card game you could think of. And beds upstairs, too, if you know what I mean. I started drinkin' a lot myself, and gamblin', and dancin'. I was a dancin' fool. But then the Lord called me again and told me I ought to make myself useful, like Nehemiah, my namesake, and after that I couldn't carry on with that life. My wife was very sociable. I told her we could have friends in to talk and socialize but that I wasn't gonna do no more drinkin' and gamblin'. That was over. The Lord told me clear as a bell. But she didn't hear what I heard, and when I tried to talk to her she'd wrap a big towel around her head so she couldn't hear a word I was saying. She wasn't too happy with me and said she'd go get her a divorce. I told her that was up to her. I didn't think she was serious, but she was. I told her I didn't want no lawyers burning up all our money, so she could have whatever she wanted. She said she wanted everything. I told her she could have everything. She didn't believe me. So she went and got her a lawyer, and he asked if I'd sign the agreement for everything. House. Cars. All our money we had in the world. And I said I would. And I did. And afterward I felt so hurt I had to leave town. That's when I went back to Springfield. Mr. Clifford had taken over the old Brewster Building and was doing coachwork. I went to work for him.

"That was the second time I got the call, so I guess I was worse than Jonah."

"How do you know when you get a call like that?"

"How did Abraham know that God wanted him to leave Ur and go to Canaan?"

"I don't know. That's what I'm asking you. Did you hear a voice? Like someone on the phone?"

"Not a voice exactly."

"Like getting a letter in the mail?"

"Not exactly that either."

"A telegram?"

"That's enough, Martin. It wasn't no telegram either. It was more like you walkin' down the road and you come to a fork, and you know you got to go one way or the other, and you yourself don't know which way you're gonna go, to the left or to the right, just like you didn't know whether you was going to marry Janis or not, but at the last minute a voice inside you must have told you something. Unless it was a voice inside Janis."

"What about Cory?" I asked.

"Your friend was like me," he said. "She was a nigger in your little town, and she's probably a nigger up in Madison, and she'll be a nigger till she stops running away."

"I don't think she's a nigger up in Madison," I said; "I think she's stopped running."

"Well then, good for her."

"What about you?"

"I stopped running a long time ago."

"What happened?"

"I told you, Mr. Jesus Christ was waiting for me in Chicago; and then he was waiting for me in Springfield, only I didn't recognize him. It was Mr. Clifford who reached out to me, treated me like a man, introduced me to Mr. Royce like we was all in the same club, if you know what I mean. Invited me into his home."

"Reverend Taylor," I said, "I don't want to rub you the wrong way, but maybe you could explain something to me."

"I will certainly try."

"Why is it," I said, "that in the Bible Mr. Jesus Christ is so eager to divide people up into sheep and goats, and to send the goats off into everlasting fire? Or the wise virgins and the foolish virgins, and then the foolish ones get locked out? Just because they forgot their oil. I mean, isn't that what our society has done? Divide people up into sheep and goats, whites and blacks, and send the blacks into slavery, or slums, which are about as bad as Gehenna? I mean, isn't that the problem? Divide people up so one group can lord it over the other. Like the Jews in Germany. It's the same thing. Isn't that why Corinna's a nigger? Isn't that why I couldn't love her the way I wanted to? And it's not the bad guys who are doing this, it's Jesus. Why is he so eager to give pain? Look at the wedding guest. He wears the wrong clothes, so they should tie him up and throw him in the dump?"

Reverend Taylor's face looked ashy. I turned on the ceiling light. The water was boiling in the teakettle on the stove. I was sorry now that I'd spoken. I emptied our mugs, rinsed them out, put in new tea bags, and poured the water.

"I don't know that I can satisfy your mind," he said, stirring some sugar into his tea, "but I believe that in Palestine they used to graze the sheep and the goats in the same pasture, and I believe that you take your sheep to market in the early spring and you leave the goats for a while longer because the goats crop the grass closer than the sheep, if you know what I mean; just like sheep crop the grass closer than cattle."

"I do, but you don't send the goats to everlasting fire; you take them to market, right? And you sell the meat for food and the skins for wine bottles, all that stuff."

"Martin, you don't want to take it too simple. It's like a metaphor. Jesus isn't talking about sheep and goats; he's signifying about people who fed the hungry and took in strangers, and people who didn't feed the hungry and closed their doors to strangers. It's what you choose, Marty. It's what you turn yourself into. It's the same way with dividing people up. People divide themselves up. People choose what they're going to be. That's the problem with stealing. You can steal something without getting caught; but you can't steal something without turning into a thief."

"How do you know all this stuff?" I asked. "I mean, about the sheep and the goats in Palestine?"

"Martin, Janis and I been studying on it for almost three years. You see that stack of books on my shelf."

I looked at the stack of books on the kitchen shelf, next to a bottle of Murphy's Soap. There were ten or a dozen of them, all different colors, stacked on their sides.

"You read it all in books?"

"Why're you so surprised? Ain't that what books are for? But tell me something, Martin. Are you telling me that you quit playing the blues because some old girlfriend poked some fun at you about it?"

"It was more than poking fun. She was right. Black musicians have moved on. It's only guys like me who can't get enough of the old down-home stuff. We write it down, try to play it note for note."

"So are you saying that I should have checked answer *b* on that first question?"

"Which one was *b*?"

"Your circumstances prevented you from doing what you wanted to do."

"Except I didn't want to do it anymore."

"Martin, you told me the blues was your vocation. Those were practically the first words out of your mouth when you come into my home. That means a *calling*."

"I know what it means. I just don't want to make a fool out of myself, like those white women who are always throwing themselves at the musicians, just because they're black. I saw that everywhere I went, in all the clubs, I mean."

"If you're afraid to make a fool of yourself, then you're afraid of life."

"It's not my music, Reverend Taylor."

"Are you saying that colored people have a special blues gene, like they got a special dancing gene? Or like Italian people have a special opera gene? Or Jews have a gene for making money?"

"No, Reverend Taylor, I just don't want to make a fool out of myself."

"Then there's your problem, like I just said. It ain't circumstances prevented you from doing what you wanted to do, it's your own fear of looking foolish."

"So?"

"So like I told you, the right answer is *c*: you made wrong choices and missed God's way. Just like I told you in the first place."

I made my last RPO run on Friday, June 26. I was playing cribbage with Hugh Green, who'd worked registers on the Buff and Chicago for twenty-five years, in Union Station in Detroit. I was holding a pair of sixes and a pair of threes and the starter was a nine, when Chappie Hendricks—foreman of my crew and the best cribbage player on the New York Central—came into the transfer office to sign us out. I led with a three. Hugh put down a six, but Chappie didn't give us time to play out the hand.

When we went through Appleton at 9:53 I pulled the catcher back against the rubber stopper and made the catch for the last time. The White Sox were playing a night game as we came into Chicago. Someone hit a home run and the scoreboard was popping and fireworks were going off as we went under the Thirty-fifth Street viaduct. We dumped over five hundred pouches that night between Detroit and Chicago and the register clerk worked over a thousand registers.

I almost choked up in the grip room in the La Salle Street station as the men in my crew shook my hand or clapped my shoulder and wished me well, but it wasn't nostalgia I was feeling; it was fear, panic, a nameless dread. I wasn't looking back; I was looking ahead. I was giving myself three years to make it as a musician, as a bluesman.

The next day I drove up to Madison and bought the Nick Lucas I'd seen in the window of the Badger Music Company. After all, Reverend Taylor had never stopped complaining about my old garbage can guitar. I could use the old guitar for open tunings and bottleneck and keep the Nick Lucas in regular tuning.

The guitar wasn't in the window anymore, and I started to panic—I'd made another wrong choice and missed God's way again—but it hadn't been sold after all. Mr. Steckeley, the owner, had been putting new strings on it. It was a small guitar—mahogany and spruce with a rosewood fingerboard—but deep bodied, warm and rich and powerful. The inlays on the neck were beautiful, and the purfling around the body and the sound hole were beautiful; the sunburst finish, on the other hand, was almost as ugly as Chesterfield's guitar, but I didn't care. I spent an hour pretending to look at a dozen other guitars and then offered the owner two hundred fifty for the Nick Lucas. He was asking three fifty, and we settled on three hundred. I could have saved the Wisconsin state sales tax by having it shipped to Hyde Park, but I didn't want to wait.

I propped the guitar up in the passenger seat and then put the top down—there was no electric motor, but the gear mechanism was so fine that you could do it with one hand. I drove by Chez Corinna. I was ready to let go; to wish the best for her, and for Monroe too—if she was still seeing him—though I knew that trouble and heartache lay in that direction: Monroe's wife, his children. I hardly knew what to wish for. I drove past the school on St. James Court. I thought about waiting for Cozy to come out—it was a little before three o'clock—but decided against it. I came back east to Park and then followed Park out to the Beltline.

I badgered Reverend Taylor till he agreed to go with me to the Newport Folk Festival, which was held in the last week of July. We drove out in his big Silver Cloud.

"There are two kinds of bluesmen," Reverend Taylor said to me as we were crossing the Newport Bridge, "and you're gonna meet both kinds tonight. You got your crazy drunks, and you got your sober, decent people." We'd driven straight through, taking turns driving and resting in the back of the big car. By the end of the trip I'd finally gotten used to the right-hand drive. I was wide awake now. According to the road map Narragansett Bay was to our left, Rhode Island Sound to our right. I'd never seen the Atlantic Ocean before.

"I'd say the first group outnumbers the second."

"You're right about that. But now you're going to meet Robert Wilkins and John Hurt; you won't find more sober, decent men than that, though John likes to add a little bourbon to his coffee."

"Are you worried about me?"

"No I'm not, Martin. All I'm saying is that it's not drinkin' whiskey that makes you a bluesman, and it ain't selling your soul to the devil, like I was kiddin' you. I just want to be sure you understand that. What makes you a bluesman is playing the blues."

Reverend Taylor had taken me to see some of the old-timers in Chicago, men who looked as if they'd sold their souls to the devil without getting much in return—except for the music, of course: Redbone Parker, Jazz Gillum, Lightning Hopkins, Big Joe Williams, and Juke Phillips, who claimed to be the oldest living bluesman. I guess Reverend Taylor was afraid I'd get the wrong idea. Redbone Parker, who lived on Cottage Grove about a block south of Sam's, was too feeble to do anything but show us a picture of the gold-plated National Steel guitar that he'd pawned years ago; Jazz Gillum, who had a fire going in a woodstove, though it was ninety degrees outside, was afraid we'd come to steal his songs and wouldn't talk to us; Lightning Hopkins—at a juke joint out in the country south of Gary, Indiana—accused Reverend Taylor of trying to steal the spotlight from him. His own head was all conked up and caught the light the way a steel helmet might catch the light of bombs exploding on a battlefield, and he played James Brown funk on a deep red Stratocaster. Big Joe, at a place out on the West Side, got drunk and took his shoes and pants off onstage and threw them at a woman who'd accused him of stealing them from her husband. Juke Phillips, who was living out on the West Side with a woman named Honey from Sunflower County, Mississippi, was a complete wreck of a man with a missing front tooth. Honey gave me $2 and asked me to go out to get a bottle of peppermint schnapps. "He gets up in the morning and has to have his pint of schnapps," she said. "Then about ten o'clock he gots to have another. I'm gonna have to take him back to hobo jungle, where I found him, that big junkyard on Twenty-second Street and Clark."

When I got back with a bottle of schnapps, there were about twenty people standing around the car, the Silver Wraith. Inside, Phillips had gotten out of bed and was sitting at the kitchen table eating ribs. He dipped each rib into a jar of mayonnaise and ripped off the meat by pulling it through the gap in his teeth.

I asked him if it was true that he'd traveled with Blind Lemon

Jefferson, and he said it was; and I asked him how he'd met Reverend Taylor, and he said he'd been running around with Reverend Taylor's first wife for a while. I glanced at Reverend Taylor, but his face didn't give anything away.

Phillips unscrewed the cap on the pint of peppermint schnapps and poured some for me into a jelly glass before raising the bottle to his lips. I took the little glass to be polite. It tasted more like a warning than an initiation.

"There," he said, "now you can say you had a drink with Juke Phillips, the oldest living bluesman. Not everybody can say that."

"But a lot of people can," Reverend Taylor said. "I'd hate to have to count them."

"Tell the reverend here"—Phillips looked at me and snorted—"tell the reverend," he said, "that time has not sweetened his disposition."

Alan Lomax, the folklorist and blues scholar who was going to emcee a lot of the events at the festival, had fixed up the downstairs of the Blues Cottage, a two-story house on the edge of the fairgrounds, like an old juke joint and had stocked the bar with plenty of whiskey, but he'd forgotten peppermint schnapps, so when I ran into Juke Phillips, he wanted me to go out to buy a bottle. I was surprised to see him on his feet, looking seventy rather than eighty; even more surprised that he remembered me. He didn't like to drink whiskey, he said, because it went to his head. Reverend Taylor, who'd gotten performer's badges for both of us, had gone back to the motel for a while, so I didn't have a car, and I used that as my excuse.

I hadn't exactly expected a congregation of saints, but I hadn't expected a congregation of prima donnas either, surrounded by their admiring attendants, young white guys like me who were trying to keep them under control.

"Look at Tommy Franklin," Juke Phillips said. The gap in his teeth through which he'd pulled the barbecued ribs on the day we'd visited him out on the West Side had been filled with gold. "Man looks like a pimp, or like somebody pretending to be a pimp." It seemed to me that Juke himself looked like a pimp, in his striped shoes and snap-brim fedora and a yellow suit that he said he'd bought at Lansky's Men's Wear in Memphis, where Elvis and Carl Perkins had bought their clothes.

"What are all these girls walking around here?" Juke wanted to know.

"They're blues fans," I said.

"Looks like a goddamn whorehouse to me," Juke said. "I got plenty of money. Go get us a couple of them skinny gals, you hear. I don't care if they's black or white, just so they ain't shabby, you understand? I'll just wait here."

"Mr. Phillips," I said, "this isn't a whorehouse. It's just kids who've come to hear the music."

He motioned me to follow him outside. "You see that blind guy sittin' back there on the couch?"

"Sleepy John Estes?"

"He used to scam suckers down on Beale Street, pretending he was a blind guy. Now he's really blind. Serves him right."

"He wrote a great song about Kennedy," I said, "after the assassination."

Juke shook his head as if the thing were impossible, as if he'd just heard news of a miracle. He said he was going to go back and wait in his room till I bought him a girl. He said he'd do the same for me the next night. He had people over in Providence. We could drive over there.

"Mr. Phillips," I said, "I came for the blues festival. You're supposed to play tonight."

"That's why I'm talking about tomorrow night," he said. "Tomorrow night we'll go into Providence, have us some fun."

"Don't you want to hear anyone else play?"

"I already heard everything I need to hear," he said. He didn't have a good word for anybody. Mississippi John Hurt—who was a genuinely nice man—was a lightweight. Son House was a wet drunk. Tommy Franklin was a pimp. Reverend Gary Davis and Reverend Taylor were both hypocrites. Skip James, who'd wowed everyone with his Saturday afternoon impromptu concert on the lawn, was a mean bastard and a fool; Howlin' Wolf was a cheap son of a bitch who paid his sidemen only $12 a night. And so on.

"Well, it's up to you," I said. "But if you're going to wait here till I bring you a girl, you're going to wait all night."

Newport 1964 was the greatest assembly of country bluesmen in the history of the world. It was the high point of the country blues revival. And I was part of it. If you look at the footage that Lomax took at the festival for the Library of Congress you'll see me standing behind Reverend Pearly Brown as Bukka White chugs out his protofunk "Jitterbug Swing." A little later on you'll see Howlin' Wolf, a grown-up among children, trying to talk sense into Juke Phillips, delivering a little sermon on the dignity of the blues. Phillips is sloppy drunk, mugging for the camera, flapping his hands like flippers. Later on you'll see Reverend Taylor and me sitting on an old leather sofa. Reverend Taylor's the one playing John Hurt's Guild F-30 and singing "Mr. Jelly Roll Baker." It was the first time I'd actually heard him play.

> *Now you know I was sent up for murder,*
> *Murder in the first degree,*
> *Judge's wife cried out, "you got to let that man go*
>   *free,*
> *'Cause he's a jelly roll baker,*
> *Bake the best jelly in this here town;*

Why he's the only man around
Bake good jelly roll with his damper down."

At the end of the video you'll see me sitting at the end of a long table in the kitchen of the Blues Cottage—a white guy about twenty-six years old. It's Sunday night; the festival is over; the Blues Cottage is empty except for the garbage cans full of empty whiskey bottles; but Reverend Taylor is playing "Oh Glory, How Happy I Am" on my guitar, the Nick Lucas, which sounds just great. He just keeps playing the same thing over and over, and singing. Another white guy, sitting across the table, next to Reverend Taylor, starts to pluck his banjo and sing along. I didn't realize, till I saw the film years later, that it was Pete Seeger. "Oh Glory, how happy I am. My soul is washed in the blood of the lamb. Glory, Hallelujah."

We'd left Newport at eight o'clock on Sunday morning, and after six hours we were passing the Harrisburg interchanges on the Pennsylvania Turnpike. Reverend Taylor put his hand on my knee. "You want to stop and take in a movie?"

"Are you crazy?"

He laughed. "Might take your mind off of what's botherin' you."

"I didn't expect a man who's studying to buy a church to play the devil's music in public like that," I said. "You know, that's the first time I ever heard you actually play the guitar. And then you play the devil's music!"

He laughed again. "That's what's on you mind? Hard to believe. You tellin' me you think the Lord don't want people to have a good time? You think he don't understand what brings a man and a woman together? Praise the Lord. Maybe you ought to lie down in the backseat, rest your mind a spell."

"I'm fine," I said. It was too early to go to sleep. Besides, I wanted to stay up front with Reverend Taylor.

"Then maybe *I* will," he said, "in a little bit."

"Is it raining?" I realized he had the wipers on.

"Just a little sprinkle."

He drove for another hour or so.

"Oh Glory, how happy I am." The song kept running through my head, but I wasn't happy. I had always assumed that I would replicate, in some fashion, the life my parents had led, that at least I'd marry and settle down and have children.

We entered the Tuscarora Tunnel and when we came out the other side of the mountain, it had stopped sprinkling. It was only four o'clock in the afternoon, but the clouds on the horizon ahead of us were fire-rimmed. You could see the turnpike stretching out below us. Sunday, July 27. Cory's twenty-sixth birthday. In another week I'd be twenty-six too. Hardly over the hill. But I seemed to see my own future stretching out below me as clearly at the turnpike, curving sharply south and then heading west again. Whenever I come home, I thought, I'll be coming home, as I'm coming home now, to an empty apartment. I'll set my guitar down and open a window or turn up the thermostat and pour myself a glass of wine, and maybe I'll call a woman I know, and maybe I won't; and if she's home, maybe she'll come over, and maybe she won't. And if she comes over, maybe we'll make love, and maybe we won't.

I drove for a while and Reverend Taylor slept in the backseat. The Silver Cloud seemed to be standing still while the Pennsylvania Turnpike sped by beneath us, like the belt of a treadmill. Reverend Taylor didn't wake up when we stopped for gas in Pittsburgh. I drove all the way to Cleveland and we changed places again, and when I woke up we were going past Kalamazoo.

"How'd we get onto I-94?"

"Must of taken a wrong turn back at Toledo. We could stop and see Janis."

I looked at my watch. It was two o'clock in the morning. "Want me to drive?"

He shrugged his shoulders. I was thinking of Janis, too. She'd called when she got back from Italy and I'd sent her boxes by Railway Express.

"I thought we might go by your hometown," Reverend Taylor said. "I'd like to see it. Then I'll know what you're talking about when you try to tell me something about it."

I climbed over the seat and got into the front.

It was three-thirty when we got to Appleton. The stoplight in the center of town was blinking, orange for the highway, red for Main Street. We turned north and drove through the downtown, across the tracks; past the library and the Potter Museum, which actually had some Egyptian mummies in it; past the Potter Featherbone Company.

"This is a little bitty town, ain't it?" Reverend Taylor said. "I used to think Avalon was small."

"I thought you came from Durham."

"Grew up there when we left Avalon, after my daddy died. My mother couldn't wait to get away. It used to flood so bad every two or three years that we had to fasten our house to a big old swamp oak so it wouldn't float away more'n five or six feet from the foundation."

"Ever go back?"

"Not since my mother passed. That was in 1938. My wife and I drove one of Mr. Clifford's cars down from Springfield. Mama couldn't wait to get away from Avalon, but that's where she wanted to be buried, so that's what we did."

Dijksterhuis Corners was exactly one mile north of the stoplight. "Turn left here," I said when we got to Kruger Road. "Then right." We turned onto the dirt road that led up to the packing shed. It looked as if someone had taken the crown of the road off with a snowplow—potholes had formed where the water had puddled instead of draining off—but the shocks on the Silver Cloud smoothed out the bumps. The Williamses' old house was on the right.

"That's where Corinna lived," I said, pointing ahead.

Reverend Taylor pulled the car over to the right so the lights shone on the house. "Nobody living there now, is there?"

"No. Not since they left."

Reverend Taylor turned the big car around in front of the packing shed and we cruised north on Appleton Road, going very slowly so I could name all the houses, starting with Aunt Bridget's on the corner. When we came to our house Reverend Taylor slowed to a stop. There was a light on in my mother's bedroom.

"She's doing a crossword puzzle," I said. The venetian blinds were closed, but I could picture my mother, propped up in bed, her hair down around her shoulders, two pillows behind her back, a book of crossword puzzles on her lap, a puzzle dictionary open, facedown, on the bed where the quilt is turned back. I can hear voices in the background—the radio turned down low. Thirty-two down, seven letters: *five owls in a tree*. Like a patient hunter in a blind she waits, a hand on her cheek, for the game to come to her. With the tip of her number two Venus pencil she taps her teeth, and then she writes: SEQUOIA.

Reverend Taylor and I leaned forward, looked up at the light. I tried to recall her face. There was no one else to see her in the lonely house, no one else to see the bathroom light go on, right over the front door, and then off. Like the flatted fifth in a blues scale the light in the bedroom window stirred up bittersweet longings before it went out. My heart seized up and my hands started to tremble, and I felt a need to cry out rising in my throat, but I stifled it, and by the time we passed the water tower I had control of myself.

When we reached the blinking light in the center of town, Reverend Taylor pulled over into the Texaco station, which was closed. "There's a time to speak and a time to be silent," he said. "Maybe now's the time to speak, tell your mama about your little girl."

"Maybe so," I said. "It's just . . ."

"Just . . .?"

"I don't know," I said. "You're probably right."

"Of course I'm right," he said, and pulled out onto M-60.

An hour and a half later he dropped me off on Fifty-seventh Street. I climbed two flights of stairs to an empty apartment, opened the windows, and turned on an electric fan. I didn't call a woman because I didn't know a woman to call, so she didn't come over, and we didn't make love. But I took the Nick Lucas out of its case and sat on the edge of the sofa and played "Oh Glory, How Happy I Am," the song Reverend Taylor and Pete Seeger had played in the kitchen of the Blues Cottage. And I resolved to be happy myself, to stop fretting about Cozy and Corinna; to stop fantasizing about some great success; to stop hoping for some extraordinary happiness. Instead I was going to be true to my calling, my vocation. Maybe it wasn't God's plan for my life, but it was the only plan I had.

PART III

9

Spelling Bee

1968

I DIDN'T SEE Cozy or Cory again till the All-City Spelling Bee in Madison in April 1968, four years after our trip to Newport. During those four years Reverend Taylor and I read the newspaper every weekday morning at seven o'clock and drank coffee at his kitchen table. We'd go over items that interested him, and I would make him read aloud, and together we'd try to make some sense out of what he'd read: pacification of Vietnamese villages, the use of napalm on civilian populations, the defense of the free world, the escalating death toll, the body counts, the non-bombing of North Vietnam, the non-invasion of Cambodia, the rumors of massacres.

At home the news wasn't any better: black marchers beaten and gassed by an army of state police in Selma, race riots in Watts and

Detroit and on the west side; the assassinations—Malcolm X in New York, Martin Luther King in Memphis.

At one point Reverend Taylor found himself in the news too, accused of caching weapons and holding orgies in the basement of the church he'd finally bought on Sixty-third Street, on the borderline—a sort of demilitarized zone—between black Woodlawn and white Hyde Park. The article was a general attack on TWO. The Woodlawn Organization, which was headed by a group of Protestant ministers and a Catholic priest. He read the passage about his own church aloud three times, because he thought he must be not be understanding it correctly. I had to explain *cache* and *orgy*.

"Now where we gonna catch weapons?" he asked me. "Behind the new furnace?" He laughed, but I could see that he was angry. "Martin, you know better than that. And orgies? Sex orgies? On that new linoleum we put down? What do they think, we runnin' a house for parties?"

"It's the mayor's office," I said.

"I know that," he said. "They can't stand the fact that a bunch of niggers are doing something on their own. That man is a barren fig tree, there's no truth in him, no fruit, just chaff." We drafted a letter to Mayor Daley, and one to the *Tribune*, canceling Reverend Taylor's subscription.

After each reading lesson—we switched to the *Sun-Times*—I'd play a song for RT and he'd put his finger on the weakest passage, and we'd work on that till it became the strongest passage, just the way a fracture in a bone that's been set properly becomes the strongest part of the bone when it heals.

And then at nine I'd put the Nick Lucas in the case, and Reverend Taylor would drop me off on Fifty-seventh Street on the way to his church, which had become one of the centers for The Woodlawn Organization's job-training program, and I'd start my practicing routine: finger exercises and scales from Pujol's *Escuela razonada de la guitarra*, the Spanish instruction book I'd bought when I was a junior in high school. I kept extralight strings on the guitar, to save wear and tear on my fingers, and I damped the sound of the Nick Lucas with a rubber drain plug so as not to disturb my neighbors. In the afternoons I worked on repertoire, focusing on five different songs each week, and when my fingers were too tired to play anymore, I worked on an instruction book that I called *Down-Home Blues,* transcribing songs from the old seventy-eights I continued to buy at Sam's Record Emporium: Vocalion, OKeh, Brunswick, Paramount.

I didn't want to start playing out till I had thirty songs that I could play with cold hands in front of an indifferent audience through a cheap PA system; but I worked up an abridged version of Arlo Guthrie's "Alice's Restaurant" that was a hit at protest rallies over at the U of C; and three or four times a month Reverend Taylor would take me to different retirement homes on the South and West Sides, and I'd play some down-home blues; and the old folks, who were desperate for any form of entertainment, would take up a collection for me. I tried to protest, but it was just their way. I tried to give the money to Reverend Taylor, but he wouldn't take it either.

"Keep it," he said. "That money makes you a professional."

I did. It was about the only thing that made me a professional.

If you pursue a musical vocation long enough you'll encounter dry spells in which it becomes absolutely clear to you that your best efforts—all the long hours of practicing—will never amount to a hill of beans. Stuck on a plateau, you'll practice your mistakes, over and over. You'll take one step forward and two steps back. You'll try to force all your emotions—your unrequited loves, your memories of past happiness, your profound melancholy at the brevity of life—into the music, but it'll be like trying to put toothpaste back into the tube. You'll struggle to get your hand around difficult chords, and to keep your tone nice and fat and to fix the notes and the chord progressions in your memory, and the more you struggle, the more you'll founder.

But if you stop struggling, you'll discover that the music will hold you up, the way the ocean holds up a ship; you'll feel the ocean beneath you, and the power of the music will carry you along like a strong wind in your sails, transforming loss into longing, longing into beauty, beauty into joy.

At least that's the way it's supposed to work. If it doesn't—if you're still stuck—you can always go out and spend a lot of money on a new instrument. That will always get the juices flowing. But I didn't have a lot of money. I had mastered my thirty songs and was prepared to play them with cold hands to anyone who would listen; I was working on the next thirty. I was starting to play out at open mikes, but I wasn't making any money. By the end of March—in fact, just before Martin Luther King's assassination—I was broke and had started working for Reverend Taylor at the church as a sort of janitor, or sexton, a word that Reverend Taylor had picked up from his predecessor at the Episcopal deconsecration ceremony. The building was in bad shape, and in addition to keeping the place clean, I found myself seating new toilets, patching plaster on the walls and cement on the front steps, painting Reverend Taylor's office, tightening the risers on the stairs that went from the vestibule up to the small bell tower, and laying down new linoleum in the basement, which bore a strong resemblance to the basement of the Methodist church in Appleton. A row of narrow, round columns supported the ceiling; a Ping-Pong table at one end of the room crowded the bathroom door; a sort of stage area was framed by purple curtains at the other end of the room; and a wide Dutch window on one of the side walls opened into the kitchen. Folding chairs were stacked against one wall, along with about a dozen folding tables. In the kitchen Reverend Taylor had had a new restaurant stove installed, with an overhead fire extinguisher—all you had to do was pull a chain—and a special exhaust fan. One Sunday morning, Reverend Taylor asked me to ring the bell, and on the last ring, I held on to the bell rope and let it pull me up toward the little hole where it disappeared into the ceiling.

My mother had announced at Christmas that she was planning to put the orchards up for sale, and I was tempted to go back home, like the prodigal son. But I was pulled in another direction too, by my fears for Cozy. I no longer pined for Corinna. I wished her well, her and Monroe, if she was still seeing him. But Cozy was my flesh and blood, just as I was my mother's flesh and blood. I had resolved not to fret about her, but I couldn't help myself. The pressure of the floodwaters was too great. I couldn't hold them back. Madison might have been one of the most liberal places in the country, but it was also one of the most violent, violent enough to make the *Sun-Times*. Reverend Taylor and I read about firebombings on the UW campus; about clashes between students and the National Guard; about clashes between Black Panthers and the National Guard; about a group calling itself Students for Humane Institutions that proposed to burn down the entire campus; about police firing tear gas at students at a block party not too far from Cozy's school. Most of the protests and demonstrations began at the university, at the Library Mall, and went right down State Street to the capitol, right by Chez Corinna. I began to dream about Cozy. In the past my dreams had always been trivial, boring. I'd dream that I was walking down Main Street in Appleton and Uncle Piet drove by and waved, and I waved back, and then I went into the drugstore for a cherry phosphate. But my dreams about Cozy were more focused: I dreamed her wrapped in a blanket, beaten bloody by National Guardsmen swinging their truncheons like baseball bats; I dreamed her choking and screaming as the tear gas burned her eyes; I dreamed her in a building bombed by student revolutionaries, the smoke, the dust, the collapsing walls, the flames.

*   *   *

On the night of Martin Luther King's assassination there were riots in Madison and in a hundred other cities around the country. Reverend Taylor called me from the church about eleven o'clock, and later that night we watched the news on the small TV set in his kitchen: federal troops and the National Guard had been called out; the West Side of Chicago was up in flames. Woodlawn itself, however, remained quiet. Thanks to a truce brokered by the ministers of The Woodlawn Organization, the Blackstone Rangers and the East Side Disciples were assisting the police in keeping order. In Memphis police had discovered a 30.06 Remington rifle at an amusement company a block away from the motel where King had been shot and were searching for a man driving a white Mustang.

"When I was in prison down in Texas," Reverend Taylor said during a commercial for a new kind of shampoo, "we used to sing a song while we was hoeing, breaking up clods of dirt hard as rocks. I was always in Number Two Hoe, and we would push Number One Hoe, which was made up of lifers, and we'd sing this song. We'd sing lots of songs. That was how we survived, you know. You work twelve hours, eat on the johnny—that's the wagon they bring out in the field; no place for a man to relieve himself.

"When you got to the end of your turn row that's on the edge of the field, you might see a dead man; you might see three or four dead men, because that's what they did with the bodies when somebody collapsed and died, or when the guards killed somebody.

"I can still see the faces of some of them dead men. Looking up, like they wanted to know, why? What had happened to them?

"And that's what we're askin' now. What happened to them? What happened to Medgar Evers? What happened to the three civil rights workers murdered in 1964? What happened to them four little girls in Birmingham? What happened to President Kennedy? What happened to Pastor King? I can see their faces too, like the faces of them dead men at the end of my turn row."

Reverend Taylor was silent, and in the silence I was afraid, for a moment, that his faith had been shaken by the assassination. "What was the song?" I asked.

"Oh, the song," he said. "It was a flatweeding song. You had your leader, and he made the feeling come to everybody else. The leader would sing, 'Rise up, dead man,' and then everybody would join in: 'Help me drive my row.'"

The shampoo commercial was over. The politicians and the televisions pundits were still reaching down as deep as they could for their very best wisdom, still trying to come up with *something*; but their words seemed inarticulate and fatuous at worst, timid and facile at best, compared to Reverend Taylor's.

> *Rise up, dead man,*
> *Help me drive my row;*
> *Rise up, dead man,*
> *Help me drive my row;*
> *If you rise in the mornin',*
> *Bring judgment on.*
> *Lord, Lord, Lord,*
> *Lord, Lord, Lord.*

The next day I called the detective in Madison and asked him to collect more information for me: more school pictures, more school records, more school newspapers. Which is how I learned that Cozy'd won her school spelling bee and would be competing in the All-City Bee at the end of April. The detective also sent an article about Cory, photocopied from the *Capital Times:* she'd made several trips to Los Angeles and two more trips to Africa to learn some of the hair-braiding techniques of the Senegalese people, which she was introducing at Chez Corinna. The article included a picture of Cozy getting her hair braided by her mother at Chez Corinna. Corinna was also wearing braids—not a couple of fat pigtails, but twenty or thirty springy corkscrews.

*   *   *

On Saturday, April 26, I borrowed the Silver Wraith and drove up to Madison for the All-City Spelling Bee. I got there early enough to pick up a copy of the *Wisconsin State Journal,* which sponsored the bee. Cozy's picture was in the paper, along with fifty-one other school winners. Her name was given under her picture, along with the name of her school—St. James—and then again in a separate list that included parents: "St. James—Carolyn Williams, 12, daughter of Mrs. Corinna Williams. Mound St. Sixth grade."

Mrs. Corinna Williams? Had she married a man named Williams? It seemed unlikely.

Central University High School was only two blocks from Chez Corinna, but I had trouble finding a parking space, and the fifty-two contestants, mostly girls, were already seated in two rows on the stage when I entered the auditorium. I was familiar with the drill because Cory and Frances and I had always been among the top spellers in Appleton Junior High, though Frances was the only one who'd ever gone beyond the district bee in St. Joe to the state bee in Lansing. Cozy was number forty-eight. I recognized her braids immediately from the photo in the newspaper. The master pronouncer, who had a big round face, stood on the stage at a spindly podium under a banner that said THE WISCONSIN STATE JOURNAL. I could see Aunt Flo's white head in a seat in the back on the wall opposite the judges' table. The three judges sat at a long library table next to the master pronouncer, nodding and turning their heads this way and that. The chief judge, who had a small head and silvery blue hair, adjusted her hearing aid against the echoes of the large room. The second wore a blond wig. The third, a man, was dressed in a three-piece suit. According to the paper they were longtime Madisonians, but two of them were new to the All-City Bee.

I had never been particularly nervous at my own spelling bees.

What was the worst that could happen? You misspell a word and somebody rings a bell, and you sit down. But I was nervous this afternoon. I sucked on a Life Saver while the round-faced master pronouncer made a patriotic speech linking the fate of the nation to spelling bees, which motivate students to work hard, which promote healthy competition, et cetera. I wondered if my mother had been nervous.

The master pronouncer finally signaled the first contestant to come up to the podium, and the spelling bee got started. I'd always been a good speller, but I had a weakness when it came to the *ede/eed* words and would have been eliminated in the first round. Cozy, however, spelled *secede* correctly without bothering to pronounce it herself or to ask for a definition.

The first contestant in the second round—contestant number two, a redheaded girl who looked like an eighth-grader—asked for a definition of *kaleidoscopic*.

The chief judge, the woman with a small head, looked up the definition in a medium-sized dictionary. But she had some trouble. The dictionary gave a definition of *kaleidoscope* but not of *kaleido-scopic*. She conferred with the master pronouncer and then read the definition of *kaleidoscope*: "a tubular instrument containing loose bits of colored glass, plastic, etc., reflected by mirrors so that various symmetrical patterns appear when the tube is held to the eye and rotated."

Contestant number two left out the *e: kalidoscopic*. The chief judge rang a bell and number two burst into tears and was escorted off the stage by two helpers.

In round two Cozy asked for a definition of *loci*—plural of *locus*, "the set of all points whose location is determined by stated conditions"—and then spelled it correctly. By the end of the round, twenty-four contestants had spelled their words correctly and eight had been eliminated.

Every time someone misspelled a word, the head judge rang a

little bell and the contestant was escorted off the stage by the helpers.

In round three, contestant number thirty-eight spelled *sesamoid* with a *y* and then corrected himself, but it was too late. The bell had rung. Once you'd started, you couldn't start over.

I'd been a finalist in the all-school bee twice, in sixth grade and again in eighth grade, and had gone to the district once; Cory and Frances had both gone twice, and one year Frances won the district and went on to state, where she'd gone down on *mirador*.

There were lots of parents in the audience, mostly mothers. I kept my eye on Aunt Flo. At first I thought she was saving the empty chair next to her for Corinna, but she didn't object when someone else sat down. If my mother *had* been nervous, she'd never let it show.

Six more contestants had been eliminated by the end of the third round.

In the fourth round Cozy had to spell *pointillism*, which the master pronouncer tried to pronounce in French by making the double *l* sound like a *y*. Cozy asked for an alternative pronunciation and the master pronouncer reverted to English: *poin-tul-ism*. By the fourth round contestants were beginning to chew on their fingers or their hair, and to hold on to their chairs, as if they were about to take off (as if they were on a carnival ride—the Tilt-a-Whirl or the Whip). Many were chewing gum. (We hadn't been allowed to chew gum. In fact, Miss Thornton, who later directed *The Night of January 16th*, disqualified any contestant who was caught chewing gum.)

Number thirty-one went down on *myrrh*—which she spelled more or less the way the master pronouncer pronounced it, *mirror*—and started to cry.

In the fifth round number twenty-six asked for a definition of *cnidarian*—which turned out to be a phylum of stinging invertebrates. He asked for the country of origin. The small-headed judge looked at the dictionary again and said, "Latin." Number twenty-six thought about this. "Is there an alternate pronunciation?" The master pronouncer shook his head and repeated the word in a loud voice: *cnidarian*. Number twenty-six scratched his head. "Is there any more information you can give me?" Everyone laughed except the master pronouncer, who shook his head no. Number twenty-six gave it a shot, and spelled it correctly. He kept waiting for the head judge to ring the bell, till finally the master pronouncer told him to sit back down.

In the sixth round, Cozy spelled *cetacean* without asking for a definition. She just spelled it. That was her style.

By the thirteenth round the bee was down to four contestants, all of whom made it to the fifteenth round. They went round in a circle for four more rounds, and then number three misspelled *kylix* and number forty-two misspelled *fetiparous*. That left Cozy and number twenty-two in round twenty.

It's only a spelling bee, I told myself. I thought I would have spelled everything correctly except the first word, but my heart was on edge as Cozy and number twenty-two dueled it out for three more rounds.

In round twenty-four, number twenty-two spelled *xerophyte* with a *z*. The audience gasped. If Cozy spelled it correctly, she would win. If she misspelled it, then she and number twenty-two would go into another round. I waited for the bell to ring, but the judge with the small head asked number twenty-two if she'd spelled *xerophyte* with an *x*, or a *z*. Number twenty-two respelled it with an *x*: *x-e-r-o-p-h-y-t-e*. "Thank you," the judge said.

I was about to leap into the air, but before I could get all my energies pointed in the same direction the spelling bee went on; it was Cozy's turn.

Her word was pronounced *plötid*. She should have asked for a definition, but she didn't: *p-l-o-t-t-e-d*.

The chief judge dinged the bell. "The correct spelling is *p-l-a-u-d-i-t*."

But.

This time I did rise from my seat. "This is not fair," I said in a loud voice. I knew that Cozy should have asked for a definition, that she should have pronounced the word herself. "Number twenty-two misspelled *xerophyte*. She spelled it with a *z*. Everyone heard her."

Cozy's eyes were wide open. There was a stunned silence.

"Don't you people realize what's happened? It's not fair. Isn't anyone else going to say something?" I waited a moment before going on. "The judge had no business asking number twenty-two if she'd spelled *xerophyte* with a *z*, or an *x*. She spelled it with a *z*, and that was wrong. The judge gave it away by asking. Everyone heard her spell it with a *z*."

Now everyone was looking at me. "What are you looking at?" I said. "The judge gave it away. Number twenty-two clearly misspelled *xerophyte*. There's no question about it. Everyone heard it. You heard everyone gasp. Then the judge said, 'Spell that again for me, dear. Did you spell it with an *x*, or a *z*?' Everyone heard her. She misspelled it the first time. Cozy—contestant number forty-eight— should have had a chance to spell it. If she'd misspelled it, then the bee would have to keep going, like tennis. But if she'd spelled it right, then she'd be the winner. You can't have the judge giving someone a chance to correct a mistake. Once you say a letter, that's it; there's no going back. When she said 'an *x*, or a *z*,' that gave it away. That told number twenty-two that she'd spelled it wrong." (I couldn't stop myself.) "Don't you see what I mean? When the judge said '*x* or *z*,' that told her that she'd spelled it wrong, so she changed it. That's not allowed."

The judge with the small head was livid. She tried to speak but couldn't.

"Who's in charge?" the three-piece-suit judge asked.

"Who are you?" The round-faced master pronouncer was asking me.

Who was I? "I'm Cozy's—contestant number forty-eight's—

father," I said. I knew I'd crossed a line, like crossing the Continental Divide outside Estes Park when we'd driven out west one fall. My dad and I had both taken a leak right on the divide, swinging back and forth over the line, watering two oceans. But this line I could never cross again. Once you'd crossed it, it disappeared.

Aunt Flo was looking at me. Cozy gave me a sideways glance and quickly turned away.

"That's not the point," I said.

The master pronouncer looked at Cozy, and then at me, and then back at Cozy. "Is this man your father?"

Cozy gave me another sideways glance. The master pronouncer looked at Cozy again, and then at me. He shook his head, as if to dismiss the idea. Cozy gave me another quick glance.

"The point," I said, "is that the judge gave the right answer to a contestant after she'd spelled a word wrong. That's not right."

"I'm going to call security if you don't sit down."

"You can call security, but that won't make it right."

The parents of number twenty-two were conferring with the judges. As far as they were concerned the bee was over.

"And then *plaudit*," I said. "The way you pronounced it, it sounded like *plotted*. It sounded exactly like *plotted*, in fact." I said the two words over several times: *plaudit plotted plaudit plotted plotted plaudit*. You can't tell which is which, can you? You should have pronounced it *plawdit*, not *plahdit*."

Two security guards were coming down the center aisle. The people they would have had to climb over to get to me had already gotten out of their way. The master pronouncer went back to the judges' table. "The spelling bee is over," he said. "The winner is . . ." He gave the name of contestant number twenty-two. I didn't pay attention to the name.

"You're a stupid man," I said, "and a coward."

The security guards, one black and one white, took me by the arms. "Just take it easy," the white one said.

"You heard it, didn't you?" I said to them.

"Just take it easy, OK? Or do you want a broken arm?" The larger of the two, the white man, had my arm twisted up behind me. They marched me down the aisle and out the front door onto Fairchild Street. At first I was blinded by the bright sun. But then my eyes adjusted. I sat down, my arm throbbing.

"Don't come back."

I sat on the front steps and waited for Cozy and Aunt Flo. I waited a long time and began to wonder if they'd gone out some other exit. I sat with my back to the door, but I kept turning around as people kept coming out. Parents and children. I didn't see the master pronouncer or any of the judges.

A blue-and-white city bus passed down State Street. I counted cars on Wisconsin Avenue, telling myself that when twenty cars had passed in the right-hand lane, Cozy and Aunt Flo would appear. I had to double twenty to forty and forty to eighty before they finally came out.

The photos I had of Cozy had all been taken from a distance, using my little spy camera. Now she was right up close. I looked for my face in hers.

"Martin Dijksterhuis," Aunt Flo said, "is that you?"

"Aunt Flo," I said, "it's good to see you."

"I always knew you was gonna turn up some day. Like a bad penny."

"Why a bad penny?"

"It's just a saying, Martin. Cory's on her way. It's kind of like my rheumatics acting up before some weather. We might as well sit while we wait for her."

"You called her?"

"I don't carry no two-way radio inside my purse, do I? Of course I called her."

Aunt Flo sat down next to me on the steps. Cozy sat on the other side of her grandmother and looked around at me. Our eyes met and glanced away, ricocheting like billiard balls. I couldn't read her expression.

"You don't have to be afraid of *me*, Marty," she said. "What's the matter with your arm?"

"The security guard twisted it. She may not be too happy to see me."

"The security guard?"

"Cory."

"I wish I had a cup of coffee for you. You remember how you used to drink a little cup of my coffee that was mostly milk and sugar?"

"I remember the mangle. I remember a lot of things. I was sorry to hear about Cap," I said.

"You got good ears," she said, and I realized that Corinna had never told her about our meeting in the bowling alley.

"She's my daughter, Aunt Flo. She's *my* daughter too. I loved Cory. I would have married her. And then *she* disappeared, and you wouldn't talk to me, and then *you* disappeared. I didn't find out till 1964, right after my dad died."

"Maybe God understands everything that happened then, Marty, but I'm sure I don't."

"I think you do, Aunt Flo. It's simple: you took the money and disappeared, that's what happened. A lot of money. I never found out how much. Mom wouldn't tell me. But *you* could."

"Is that why you tracked me down? You want some money?"

"You don't believe that, do you, Aunt Flo?"

"No, I don't, Marty. I wouldn't believe that of you. Your mother was a hard woman, for all her liberal ways. She went against what she knew was right. But when she wanted something, she wanted it, and what she wanted, your daddy wanted too, whether he knew he wanted it or not. I remember your daddy going back and forth most of the night, from your kitchen to our kitchen, talking things over with Cap, negotiating till they got all negotiated out, and then your mama come by herself and your mama and me negotiated what was going to be and which way it was going to be and how it was going to be, and in the morning your daddy and Cap went down to the bank."

"And you took the money and disappeared?"

"Cozy, why don't you run into the school and see about your prize? You're supposed to get some kind of dictionary, isn't it, if you're the number two?"

"She was cheated on that spelling bee," I said to Aunt Flo. That was outrageous. *Plotted/plaudit.* And everyone heard that girl spell *xerophyte* with a *z.*"

"I don't want to see about my prize," Cozy said.

"What did I tell you about sass?" Aunt Flo said.

"Not wanting to see about my prize isn't sass."

I leaned forward, trying to see around Aunt Flo, and every once in a while Cozy leaned forward too, and then pulled back when my eye caught hers.

"Marty," Aunt Flo went on, "your mama was a tiger; she wanted what she thought was best for you. That was just her nature. It wasn't nothing else she could do. She wanted you to go to the University of Chicago, and she knew you weren't going to no University of Chicago with a colored wife and a half-caste child. Cap was content to work outdoors half a year and go hunting and fishing with your daddy and your uncle for the other half. He would have accepted the first offer your daddy put on the table. But I was a tiger too; I wanted what I thought was best for my child too. I wanted a stake for her, and I got it. How do you think we was able to open a beauty salon? I was tired of washing clothes for white folks. I was tired of sitting at that old mangle day in and day out. I wanted to be among my own kind. I had a sister and her husband lived up in Milwaukee, but Milwaukee wasn't a good town for colored, if you know what I mean, so when my sister moved back to Georgia, Cory and me come up to Madison. Maybe it ain't the land of milk and honey, but it's all right, maybe better'n all right. We been treated pretty good here."

"If you're such a tiger, why didn't you stick up for Cozy in there? Why didn't you stick up for me? You heard that girl spell *xerophyte* wrong."

"I don't know no *xerophyte* with a *x* or a *z*," she protested, "so don't put your mouth on me."

I could see I'd hit a nerve and backed away.

"And you told Cory all this?"

"Told her what?"

"About taking the money."

"I told her what she needed to know."

"So you didn't tell her everything."

"I told her what I told her, Marty. I always knowed you was a good boy. But you got to understand that it don't give you no claim on Cozy."

"Aunt Flo, my claim on Cozy is that she's my daughter."

"Not in no court of law she ain't."

"'Court of law'? Aunt Flo, what are we talking about here?"

"Maybe you should tell *me* what we're talkin' about here."

I wasn't sure in fact what we *were* talking about. What was it I wanted? What had I hoped to accomplish? All of a sudden I needed to think it all through again, but there was no time.

"I'd like to see her, that's all we're talking about. I'd just like to talk to her; hold her in my arms; be a little part of her life."

"Tell me something, Marty. I see you ain't got no ring on your finger, but that don't always mean nothing. Are you a married man, Marty?"

"No, I'm not."

"Why is that?"

"I'm not sure, Aunt Flo. It's not—it's not that I haven't thought of it."

"How old are you now? Must be thirty, same as Cory."

"That's right."

"You got a good job?"

"I'm doing all right." I said; "I worked for the RPO for quite a few years. The pay was good."

"The RP what?"

"Railway Post Office."

"Doing what?"

"Sorting mail on a train between Detroit and Chicago."

"You went to the University of Chicago so you could be a mailman?"

"I didn't go to the University of Chicago."

It took Aunt Flo a few minutes to digest this information.

"I did make something of myself. There wasn't anything wrong with working for the RPO. It was a great job."

"Well, I swan. All that struggle and your mama didn't get her way after all. How is your mama anyway?"

"She's not doing too well. My dad died, you know; about seven or eight years ago."

"I didn't know that, Marty. I had no idea. We never heard from anyone, you know. We cut all our ties. Not that we had that many, though I missed your aunt Bridget. But that was part of the agreement. A few friends over in Benton Harbor we kept up with, but they didn't know your folks."

"Mom took over the orchards, but they stopped selling to the chain stores after Uncle Piet moved to Florida. Wim's helping her. You remember Gerrit's oldest. He's kind of slow, but he's a good worker. Mom wanted me to come back."

"Your daddy did pretty well."

"Pretty well, yeah. But since Mom bought out Uncle Piet, she never had enough cash to do things right. She wants to keep all the Pippins and the Northern Spies, but there's no market for them. She may have to bulldoze the whole section into the ground and start over with something else. The Gerber baby food plant takes most of the peaches. Most of the apples go up to Benton Harbor. Other than that it's people from Chicago. They drive out, make an afternoon of it."

"And your mother's running the place? I always knew she was a tiger. And she always treated me right. Right up to—Cory getting with child, you know. It did something to her. Affected her mind. There was a certain way she wanted things to be, and most of the time they fell out that way, and if they didn't, she kept at them till they did. But in a way I was glad she did what she did. It was time to move on. If I was to see her again—I don't know—I don't know how I'd feel. But I don't wish her no harm. Not after all these years. You thinking of going back home? Helping out your mama?"

"I thought about it, but it's too late now."

"I'll bet she wasn't too happy when you went to work for the railroad."

"The Railway Post Office."

She shook her head, and I shook my head too.

"Why'd you do it?"

"Do what?"

"Go to work for the railroad—I mean the post office?"

"I don't know, Aunt Flo. It just—we were just at odds, that's all, after Cozy disappeared. After I got out of the Navy I wanted to play the blues. Working for RPO I was in Chicago one night, Detroit the next, going to clubs."

Aunt Flo laughed. "You joined the post office to listen to the devil's music?"

"I wanted to stay and run the orchards, Aunt Flo. I didn't want another life. I didn't want to go to the University of Chicago. I could have done it too. Cap taught me how to do the pruning, and when we got that new stock after the big freeze, I helped him graft the new whips. I could have taken over the marketing too. Cap would have helped me. I'd met all the buyers. I could have sold everything by the truckload instead of one bushel at a time to tourists from Chicago. If Cap had been there to help; if you hadn't disappeared.

We were shipping fifty thousand bushels of apples a year. Now it's down to about twenty. I could have married Cory too; I would have; you know it. I don't have to tell you."

"I know it, Marty. That's why we had to disappear. At least your mama and I agreed on that much."

Corinna was coming down Dayton Street. She looked like a million bucks in a lightweight summer dress, as if she'd just come from a garden party. She was wearing sunglasses, but I could feel her eyes zero in on me, trying to take me in—a pale stranger in an old-fashioned Italian suit.

"What's she going to say?" I asked, looking at Aunt Flo.

"That's always a good question. With a girl like that you never know, but now we're gonna find out. She was doing a special workshop this afternoon and that's how come she couldn't come to the bee. I hated to call her."

This was my new life; I couldn't go back now. Nothing would ever be the same. Which is, I guess, what I wanted. Cory seemed to be contemplating a range of responses, as if she didn't know herself how she felt or was going to feel. From her face I judged it would probably be somewhere on the negative end of the spectrum. But how negative? Anger? Irritation? Was she like a woman trying to decide what shade of lipstick to put on? Or a judge deciding whether to let the convicted prisoner's sentences run concurrently or sequentially? Her hair was in narrow braids that wriggled like snakes. I was reminded of the picture of Medusa in my child's mythology book.

"Martin," she said, "you could have had the common courtesy to call."

"I was afraid you—you know I couldn't have done that."

"This isn't funny. Mama says you put a big stink over everything and called a lot of attention to yourself, and Cozy, and embarrassed everyone, including Cozy. Now it's going to be in the paper."

"So?"

"Oh well, I guess it doesn't matter." She started to laugh. "I guess it is pretty funny. Cozy, isn't there something else you could do right now?"

"I told her to go and see about her dictionary prize," Aunt Flo said, "but she won't do it."

"Then why don't you go check on that, Cozy? And isn't there supposed to be a lunch for the top ten at the Downtown Rotary Club?"

I looked at Cozy, willing her to stay. "The lunch is next week," she mumbled.

"Cozy, you heard me. Mr. Dijksterhuis is an old friend from way back and we have some things to talk about privately, do you understand?"

"If he's an old friend, why are you mad at him?"

"I'm not mad, Cozy; I'm just surprised, that's all. I didn't expect— well, I'm just surprised."

"How come he said he was my daddy?"

I didn't know whose side Aunt Flo was on, but I could see that Cozy was not about to leave without a struggle.

"Mama," Cory said, "will you deal with this child? Take her to find out what she needs to know. I'll explain things later."

Aunt Flo dragged Cozy into the school.

Corinna stood three steps below me and looked straight into my eyes. "It's kind of a relief, actually. I've been dreading this."

"Me coming?"

"No, going into things with Cozy."

"Why don't you sit down?" When she sat down her tight skirt rode up over her knees, which looked like they'd been polished to a high gloss. "I'm surprised your mom didn't tell her."

"I think she let some things slip."

"Is it so terrible, really?"

"Sometimes you don't know where you stand. The hard thing is you don't know. You have to take a choice. It just complicates . . . everything. You don't know who you are. She won't know . . ."

"You mean whether she's black or white?"

"She doesn't have any choice there. One drop . . ."

"What do you want to happen?"

"Now? I don't know."

"What did you tell her about her father? About me?"

"Killed in Korea. Like my brother. It was easier when she was little. Later on she wanted to know if there were any medals, letters, papers of some kind. Anything."

"Any problems at school?"

"No, she's dark enough. It's not really a problem, yet." She held out her own arm.

"Look, she has to figure it out sometime."

"To tell you the truth, I think she figured it out a long time ago."

"Then maybe it's time to tell her the truth?"

"Maybe so," she said. "But let's just sit here till they come out."

I saw this as a good sign.

"You still working for the railroad?"

"The RPO," I said. "The Railway Post Office. No. I quit about three years ago. Just in time, actually. Everything's changed in the last couple years. They've got optical reading machines now, and facer-canceler machines that use electric eyes to locate the stamp and face all letters in the same direction. The new transportation system's tied in with the ZIP codes. It's all air mail now. The old railroad hubs are gone. There's only one RPO train left between Chicago and Detroit."

"Then how come the mail's so much slower now?"

I started to explain, but the first time I paused she interrupted: "So what are you doing?"

"I'm a bluesman."

"You're kidding me."

"I'm not kidding," I said. And I wasn't.

"You're making a living as a bluesman?"

"Not exactly a living," I said. "It's a jungle. No record deals in the jungle; no managers; no agents; no contracts; lousy PA systems; amateur engineers; a lot of open mikes and coffeehouses, no paying gigs."

"And this is what you want to do?"

"Yup. Somebody's got to keep the old country blues from going down the toilet. There's been a little revival in the last few years, but it's all been swept away by the Beatles and the Stones. Most of the old guys are dead or too sick to play. There're only a couple left, and they're lucky if they get a chance to open for a rock band. I was at Newport when Dylan went electric in sixty-five and everyone booed. It wasn't his fault. I mean, Michael Bloomfield played so loud you couldn't hear Dylan, and Dylan's the one everybody wanted to hear, but it kind of put paid to the old acoustic music."

"But why you?"

"It's my vocation."

She snorted. "More like some kind of hepatitis," she said, "A, B, or C, I don't remember which, you can control it, but you can't ever get rid of it." She looked at my finger. "Married?"

"No."

"Any prospects?"

"Not right now."

"I'm sorry, Marty."

"There's no reason to be sorry, Cory. I'm having a good time."

"You still got that old metal guitar?"

"That guitar attracts women like flies."

"What kind of women?"

I gave her an enigmatic smile. "You?"

"Does it attract *me*? Are you kidding? It always looked like a piece of junk to me."

"I mean, do you have somebody special?"

She gave *me* an enigmatic smile, but shook her head.

"I saw the article about you in the *Capital Times*," I said.

"Really?"

"Absolutely. Trips to New York; trips to Los Angeles; trips to Senegal."

"Things have been going well." She put her hand on my knee. "I want to do the right thing with Cozy, but let me handle it, OK?"

"So, you're not mad?"

"No, Martin, I'm not mad."

When Aunt Flo and Cory came up behind us, Cozy had her prize dictionary in her hand. No one said a word. Aunt Flo sat down slowly and carefully. "I wish Cap was here," she said. "What was that show we all used to listen to?"

"Arthur Godfrey in the morning," I said. "*Just Plain Bill* around supper time."

"I can't remember anything about it," Cory said, "except the name. And that voice: *Just plain Bill.*"

"I'm thinking about something else," Aunt Flo said. "That TV show that we all liked, what was that? *Kukla, Fran and Ollie.* And you kids used to talk to each other like Cecil Bill: tooi tooi *too* tooi tooi, tooi tooi *toooo* tooi."

"So it wasn't all bad, Aunt Flo?"

"Marty, I never said it was *all* bad. I don't suppose the old plantations in the South was *all* bad. But it was *de ol' plantation* nonetheless. There's no getting around it. You can't tell the story any other way; you can't make it come out different."

"What 'old plantation'?" Cozy asked.

"Nothing, honey."

"They didn't *have* plantations in Michigan," Cozy said emphatically.

"They had old plantations everywhere. Peach plantations, apple plantations, celery plantations, strawberry plantations, cherry plantations. What's the difference?"

"They didn't *have* slaves in Michigan!"

"They didn't call 'em slaves, honey, but they might as well have, come up from Georgia and Carolina every year to pick the crops, livin' in little shacks with no running water. And Martin's daddy was the *massa* and your grandpa was the colored overseer, and I did the washin' and ironin'. I guess that made me a house nigger." She laughed.

"It's not funny, Grandma."

"Naw, it ain't, sweetie, but it's the truth."

Cory threw up her hands, like a mother in a TV show, or like Karen Andre in *The Night of January 16th* when she learns that the man who's been pretending to be murdered actually has been murdered.

I resolved not to worry about appearances but to speak from the heart. "Do you remember what it was like up on the catwalk, Cory?" I asked. "Do you remember it as clearly as I do? Looking down. Climbing up wasn't so bad. But we didn't know how we'd get back down. We were afraid to climb over the edge of the catwalk. That's where we are now. We're up on the catwalk and we don't know how we're going to get back down."

"*I* wasn't afraid," Cory said. "*I* climbed over the edge."

Cozy looked at her mother.

"I should never have told you that story, honey. Maybe I wouldn't have, if I'd had some other stories."

Cozy looked at her hands in disbelief. The same blood was running in her veins that was running in mine.

"You had lots of stories," I said to Cory. "You were the class president sophomore year; you won the spelling bee; you were the lead in the junior play."

I could see her mother trying to improvise a response, trying to find the right chord. Sometimes it's better if you don't have time to think about it. You have to put your fingers down on the strings and play whatever you find. She looked at me, but she didn't say anything.

Cozy hadn't *called* me anything yet. Daddy, Papa, Dad, Martin, Mr. Dijksterhuis.

"Martin's mama's your grandmother," Aunt Flo said, "just like me. You got tiger blood in your veins." She laughed. "On both sides. I believe it, I believe it."

"*Grand*ma."

"Your grandma's just having her little wheeze." Aunt Flo settled herself. "So what are we going to do *now*?"

I wanted Cozy to set the tone. To play the new chord, resolve the discord, take us home to the tonic.

"What do *you* want to happen, Cozy?" I asked.

"I don't know."

"I think we need to ask the good Lord for advice," Aunt Flo said. "Here, let's all hold hands."

"Oh, *Grand*ma."

"Come on, child, give me your hand," Aunt Flo said.

"Mama," Cory said, "this is difficult enough, please. Don't make it any worse. People are already staring at us. Now let's go."

Cozy and Corinna started down the steps together, taking each step carefully, as if they were afraid of falling.

Aunt Flo, flustered, started looking through her purse for a handkerchief. I waited for her. Cory was waiting for us at the curb. It took a while for Aunt Flo to catch her breath when we got to the bottom.

"You got any questions, Cozy darling?" she asked—I could see that it was costing her something not to be angry—" 'cause if you do, now's the time to ask 'em."

"I can give you a ride," I said. "My car's about two blocks away."

Cozy looked at me. "Did you do it when you were up on the tower?"

Cory lowered her head and looked at her daughter over the tops of her sunglasses. "Cozy Williams! Do you want me to wash your mouth out with soap?"

"Mama, I'm just curious. I just want to know. You treat me like I'm a baby."

"Maybe that's because you're acting like a baby."

I wished someone would burst into tears, but no one did. Cory had to get back to her workshop, so I drove Cozy and Aunt Flo home in the Silver Wraith. But first we put the top down and drove around Lake Mendota, which was a very fine thing to do, though Aunt Flo fussed about the wind in her hair and scolded Cozy for sticking her head out over the side like a dog. We stopped at a diner for a bite to eat and then I dropped them off at home and went to Chez Corinna to see if Cory wanted to go for a drink. I found a parking place and waited outside in the Silver Wraith for a few minutes while the women in the braiding workshop chatted with one another on the sidewalk.

Cory had a dinner that night—part of the workshop—but she had time for a cup of coffee in the back of Chez Corinna. I told her I wanted to work something out so that I could be a part of their lives. Just a little part. I wasn't going to do anything foolish, but I had to know. I always like to get things settled. That's why I pay my bills the day they come. I want them out of the way.

I was afraid she'd tell me again to stay away, but she was expansive, generous, touching my arm, my hand, my shoulder. She was in love, she told me, and then I understood.

"With Monroe Franklin?" I asked.

Her eyes opened wide with surprise. "What are you talking about?"

"Monroe Franklin, from Columbia University, visiting professor in political science."

"Now how in the hell do you know about Monroe?"

"I have my spies."

"Martin, you're kidding me. What have you been up to?"

"I hired a private detective, just to find out some stuff about you, how you were doing, that sort of thing. Back in sixty-four, after I saw you in the bowling alley."

"I can't believe this. You hired someone to spy on me?"

"Well."

"Well, did you or didn't you?"

"I talked to a private detective. I did the spying myself."

"You spied on me? You followed me around?"

"I watched you and Monroe on the Union Terrace, yakking away. I followed you to the hotel. It was your first time together, wasn't it—no, don't say anything. It doesn't matter. I waited in the door of that music store across the street. There was a guitar in the window, a Gibson Nick Lucas. I bought it last year, the one that was in the window that night."

She threw herself back into the chair and began to fiddle with her purse. I was afraid she was going to ask me to leave, but she started to laugh. "You bought a guitar that night?"

"At the music store across the street. I stood in the door there for two hours waiting for you to come out. That was April 1964. Four years ago. I didn't buy the guitar till the middle of June."

"How much do you know?"

"I know you were happy. I know you were in love. You can see it in the pictures I took. Sitting there at a table in the Union, talking away, looking out at the lake. You were reading something too, a letter or something. You read it through, and then you read it out loud. I wanted you to be happy. I was happy for you. Sort of. After a while."

"How'd you know who it was?"

"License plate. Couple of phone calls."

"You've got a friend in the license bureau in New York?"

"Well, I had to pay a detective to find out for me. What happened?"

"You don't know?"

"No. I'd seen enough."

"He went back to New York."

"I'm sorry."

She shrugged.

"But you still love him?"

"You still have those pictures?"

"You want me to send them to you?"

She nodded and leaned forward. "Martin, you've got to promise me something."

"Of course."

"You swear to God you won't tell Mama, or Cozy, or anyone?"

I raised my hand.

"I still love him, Martin. He's going to leave his wife as soon as they get some things worked out. I'm going to move to New York." She was glowing. "You're the only one who knows, Martin. You've got to keep this a secret."

I was stunned. I counted on my fingers. "He's had four years to get things worked out," I said.

"It's complicated, Martin. I don't want to go into it."

"You've been seeing him?"

"Four or five times a year—Chicago, Los Angeles, Dakar, New York. I shouldn't have told you this, Marty, but it's a relief to tell somebody, somebody who's not going to blab it all over."

"I could see how happy you were, that afternoon at the Union. I really was happy for you. Sort of."

"Thanks, Martin. You're right, I was happy. I am happy. I'm happy now. Marty, I wish you could be as happy as I am."

"What about Chez Corinna?"

"You think they don't have black women in New York who need their hair done without all that torture? Besides, I want to get out of here."

"Just like you wanted to get out of Appleton?"

She nodded. "Chez Corinna's a success, Marty. I can taste it. I can touch it. I can feel it way down deep in my gut. I'm going to make a difference, Marty. I'm part of something. We're going to change the way black women feel about their hair, about themselves. No more torture with those straightening combs. None of these new processes either. Right now we're just a cottage industry, but we're going to be big. You know why? Because we're going to go back to a standard of beauty that's four thousand years old—braids, extensions, Bantu knots, beaded hair sculptures. But the revolution's going to happen in New York, not Wisconsin. New York and Los Angeles, where you've got people from all over Africa. Have you ever been to New York, Marty?"

I shook my head.

"It's unbelievable. It's not like Chicago, where you've got a nice little strip along the lake that's about as thick as your fingernail. In New York you drive down Fifth Avenue along the park and then you keep going till you get to Broadway and you keep going and going and going. Manhattan doesn't quit, Marty; it's unbelievable; you just keep going till you get to the Staten Island Ferry.

"What about Cozy?"

"They've got schools in New York, Marty, just like the rest of the country. Besides, Madison's not the safest place in the world."

"But New York?"

"Martin, do you know how many times my front window's been broken—here at the shop, not at home?" She held up three fingers. "Mama's afraid to bring Cozy down here anymore, and I don't blame her. I'm tired of looking out the window and seeing the students coming up State Street one way and the National Guard coming down the other way and the Black Panthers coming around the corner."

"That's the problem with these three-street intersections!" I said.

"One time during a riot there was a National Guardsman right in the shop," she said. "I had to make a deposit at the bank and I was afraid to go out by myself, so I asked him if he'd go with me."

"Did he?"

She shook her head.

"What'd you do?"

"I went by myself. I had over a thousand dollars in cash."

"But New York?" I said again. "I think you're rationalizing."

"I don't need to rationalize, Marty. I'm just going to do what I want to do. That's not rationalizing."

"OK," I said. "What about your mom?"

"It'll take her a while, but she'll adjust."

"Have you told her yet?"

She shook her head. "Not till I get things worked out."

"You think she'll turn into a Yankee fan?"

"Now that *would* be something. That would truly be a miracle." She laughed and looked at her watch. "You got a car?" I nodded. "Could you drop me off at the restaurant? They don't have a lot, and it's impossible to park."

"I'd be glad to," I said.

She got her things together, checked her makeup, locked the door behind her. She thought I was joking and refused to get in when I opened the passenger door of the Silver Wraith.

"Stop fooling around, Martin, before you get yourself arrested. I've had enough excitement for one day."

"Get in the car," I said, holding up the gold Rolls-Royce keys.

"You're a bluesman and you're driving a Double-R? You were just crying poor about living in the jungle with no record deals, no agents, no contracts, no paying gigs. There must be something you're not telling me." She patted the leather seat and ran her fingers over the mahogany dashboard. She kept glancing sideways at me and shaking her head.

"I'm going to play at the folk festival at the U of C next year, and I'm playing in a lot of old people's homes."

"Old people's homes?"

"Reverend Taylor sets it up for me. You can't ask for better audiences. You can really cut loose and nobody'll laugh. There's one old guy there who heard Blind Lemon play on the corner of Jackson and Halsted, and another one who heard Blind Willie McTell on Maxwell Street, and an old woman who was coming out of a bakery on the corner of Thirty-ninth Street and Indiana Avenue when the streetcar rammed into Elmore Davenport's empty coffin when his friends were pushing it up and down the street collecting money for his funeral. She tells that story every time I play."

"And you're getting paid enough for this that you can drive a Double-R?"

"Not exactly."

"And *exactly*?"

"Exactly? Exactly I guess I'm working for Reverend Taylor as a janitor at his church."

"Oh, Marty." She put her hand on my arm.

"It's all right. I'm going to start giving some lessons at the Old Town School, and I'm almost finished with a blues instruction book I've been working on. There's going to be a tape that goes with it too. I'll give you a copy when it comes out. That should help me break out of the local scene, maybe attract a booking agent."

"But what about the car? What's the story?"

"Let me show you my pub photo," I said. "Bruno of Hollywood. For the press kit I'm putting together. I've got some in my guitar case." I'd brought Chesterfield's guitar because I didn't like to leave the Nick Lucas in the trunk.

"You brought your guitar?"

"It's in the trunk."

"That's not what I meant."

"Let me get the photo."

We both got out of the car and I opened the sloping trunk. I had to take the guitar out of the case to get at the photos.

"That's kind of like the suit Blind Lemon Jefferson is wearing in the famous painted-tie photograph. Pinstripes. Wide lapels. Actually I borrowed it from Reverend Taylor."

"Why'd they paint a tie on him?"

"They didn't paint it on *him*," I said. "They painted it on the photograph."

"But the one in this picture's real, right?"

"Right. Reverend Taylor taught me how to tie a half Windsor knot that doesn't bulge out on one side."

She laughed. "Who the hell is this Reverend Taylor? He must be one hell of a preacher."

"It's his car," I said, "in case you're wondering."

"You know I've been wondering, Marty. I've been wondering my butt off."

"He's my guitar teacher," I said.

"Your *guitar* teacher? How much does he charge for lessons?" She studied the photo. "You look pretty good in those fancy duds." She looked at me and then back at the photo.

"That's the real me," I said. "Maybe a little exaggerated, but not too much."

"You're full of surprises, Marty," she said, handing back the photo. "Honestly."

"No, keep it. Give it to Cozy. So she won't forget me."

"I don't think she'll forget you, Marty. Not after today."

When I put my arms around her she didn't back away. I kissed the side of her head before letting go. I watched her pause to take another look at the photo and then slip it into her big purse before disappearing into the restaurant

On the way back to Chicago *I* began to wonder too—about Aunt Flo's prayer. What if I'd intervened, taken her hand and Cory's hand? Or Cozy's? What if we'd formed a little circle on the school steps? What would Aunt Flo have prayed for? What kind of advice would she have received, would *we* have received? No one would ever know now. These were just *if only*s, missed opportunities, like the magic wishes that always get squandered in fairy tales.

10

In the Evening

1971

THE PUBLICATION OF *Down-Home Blues,* the songbook I'd been working on for several years, opened some doors for me. I already had twenty advance copies by the official publication date, but I bought an extra copy at Kroch and Brentano's on Wabash, just for the pleasure of it, and then another copy at the Old Town School of Folk Music. There was no book tour; the book was not displayed prominently in store windows; there were no cocktail parties; but now when I introduced myself in certain circles, people knew who I was. And if they didn't, I could tell them. I was honing my performance skills at open mikes, and at small clubs too. I'd take both guitars with me and pretend to be one of the musicians, filling in whenever there was a spot. I wrote an occasional instruction column for *Sing Out!,* which was owned by my publisher, Irwin Silber. I'd assembled a press kit with a demo tape and some head shots and my Bruno of Hollywood photo, which I shopped around, along with copies of *Down-Home Blues,* and by the end of the year I'd collected some good reviews and was starting to land some paying gigs: I was featured at a couple of open mikes; I was a guest performer at the Fickle Pickle with Big Joe Williams; in October I played at the folk festival at the University of Chicago; and in November I cut a record with Juke Phillips for a small independent label. Juke was too dilapidated to play the guitar, but he could still sing, so I played and he sang, and after a while we got the hang of it and nobody was ever the wiser. I'd become a regular at the Old Town School, giving lessons in the afternoon, leading the sing-alongs, just hanging around and meeting the people who came through town: Paul Geremia, Dave Van Ronk, Cliff Johnson, Roy Book Binder, Happy Traum, Marc Silber, Sam Charters, Pete Seeger.

In 1970 I opened twice in Chicago for a local folk rock band called the Doves, and then again when they played a concert in Madison, in March 1971, in the Great Hall of Memorial Union. The campus had been relatively peaceful since the bombing of the Army Math Research Center the previous August. My copies of the *Capital Times* were piling up unread. I saw Corinna and Cozy and Aunt Flo from time to time, but I didn't see them at the concert, and I was slightly depressed on the Dove bus back to Chicago.

A week later Cozy was arrested for shoplifting. Not once but twice in one week. Corinna was in Africa and Aunt Flo was at her wit's end. She didn't like to use the telephone, and she didn't know how to call Cory in Senegal, though Cory had left a long list of instructions on how to reach her at the hotel in Dakar, but she called me in Chicago and I drove up to Madison in an old side-loader hearse that I'd bought from Mr. Hall at the funeral home next to the church. Reverend Taylor had had the lower panel on the sliding door replaced in the shop on Warren Street, and he'd had the whole hearse painted a rich deep green, like the Silver Cloud, with sixteen coats of paint, each one of which had been sanded by hand. He wanted to paint Chesterfield's old guitar too, but I told him I liked it the way it was.

There was room for a narrow cot in the back of the hearse, and a small Fender amp, and secure places for three guitars—the Nick Lucas, a backup guitar for emergencies, and Chesterfield's galvanized steel guitar, which was actually an early National Steel guitar. And stenciled on both sides, in black letters:

Down-Home Blues, Inc.

I stopped at the house for Aunt Flo, who wasn't crazy about riding in a hearse, and we went to pick up Cozy at the youth division in the police station on Harper Street. She'd been sitting there for four hours. The youth officer had persuaded the owner of the store, a stationery store on State Street, not to file a complaint. However, if Cozy were caught shoplifting again, the store owner would have the right to file complaints for the first two incidents as well as the third. Did Cozy understand that? She indicated that she understood without actually saying so.

When we got back to the house Cozy and I had a heart-to-heart up in her room. It was the first time I'd been upstairs. Four doors opened off a narrow hallway with pictures in thin frames on both walls, but the doors were closed. And it was the first time that I'd been alone with Cozy. It was a moment I'd been waiting for, but I hadn't imagined it like this.

Cozy kicked off her shoes and curled up in a big round chair—a sort of bamboo bowl that rested on a smaller bamboo frame; I sat on a chair at her desk. There was a large paper pad on the desk on which she'd doodled a series of water towers. Birds circled some of the towers, but not all of them. I didn't know how to begin. I was remembering the baseball cards I'd stolen when I was a boy, remembering how I'd been caught and punished, my father still demanding an explanation as we walked through the snow on the way out to the shed. And then on the next day I'd stayed home from school and my father bought a new pair of ice skates for me and we skated on the river.

"I already know what you're going to say," she said.

A large bookcase loomed over the desk. I could see some of the books I'd sent her over the past three years—*Beowulf, The Boy's King Arthur, The Three Musketeers, Wind in the Willows*—stacked on their sides.

"What am I going to say?"

She imitated her grandmother. "I don't know what's got into you, child, but in my day you'd a had your behind blistered before you could say Jackie Robinson. Yo' mama workin' and slavin' to feed and clothe you . . ."

"I think it's 'Jack Robinson,'" I said.

"Who's Jack Robinson?"

"I mean the saying is 'quicker than you can say *Jack Robinson.*' Your grandmother's right, you know."

She shrugged.

"A fountain pen," I said. "You think your mother wouldn't buy you a fountain pen?"

"I didn't want to wait in line. That's all. This stupid woman had a purse the size of a suitcase and she couldn't find her checkbook, and there were about ten people waiting in line."

"So you just took the pen and walked out?"

"Right."

"But what about the second time? Didn't it occur to you that after getting caught two days earlier, you might get caught again?"

She shrugged. "I still needed a pen."

"Don't just shrug your shoulders, Cozy. I want an answer."

"What am I supposed to say?"

"I mean, it was the same store! The same pen. A Mont Blanc pen. Those are expensive."

"So?"

"No wonder they made such a fuss. Aren't they usually kept in a locked case?"

"I've got a friend who works there. She left the case unlocked."

"Jesus, Cozy. I thought you were just in a hurry and didn't want to wait in line."

"That, too."

"Didn't they wonder how you got the pen out of the locked case?"

"My friend's white," she said. "It's her daddy's store. That's why he didn't sign the complaint."

"I see," I said. But I didn't see. I rubbed my eyes with the heels of my hands. "The problem is," I said, repeating something Reverend Taylor had said to me, "you can steal something without getting caught, but you can't steal something without turning into a thief."

"What's that supposed to mean?"

"I think you know perfectly well what it means."

"So what if I do? Didn't you ever steal anything?"

"Cozy, it doesn't make sense."

"Why does it have to make sense? Sometimes you just do something. There doesn't have to be a reason. Didn't you ever steal anything?"

"Yes I did," I said. "Baseball cards. I mean, bubble gum. The baseball cards came with the bubble gum. I stole them from a little grocery store in town. It had been there forever, but everybody called it the new store."

"So?"

"I understand some things."

"Did you get caught?"

"Your grandmother wondered how I was getting so many baseball cards. She liked them too, you know. We were both Cubs fans. The Cubs had some great players: Bob Rush, Dutch Leonard, Smoky Burgess, Phil Cavaretta, Wayne Terwilliger, Hank Sauer, Mickey Owen. I wanted to get the whole starting lineup, but I couldn't get Mickey Owen. That's why I kept stealing more cards. Your grandmother finally told my mom; then it all came out."

"What happened?"

"I got a whipping. And I had to pay for the baseball cards."

"Are you going to give *me* a whipping?"

"No."

"I didn't think so. What *are* you going to do?"

"I don't know. What do you think I *should* do?"

"I don't know. Nothing."

"You know what my dad did?"

"After he gave you a whipping?"

"The next day."

She shook her head.

"I stayed home from school and he bought me a new pair of ice skates and we skated on the river."

She didn't say anything.

"Would you like me to buy you some skates?"

She hesitated. "I've already got some skates."

"OK," I said. "I'll bet you're a pretty good skater."

She nodded.

"Is there something you want to talk about?"

"Like what?"

"You tell me." She shook her head. "Because you can talk to me if you want to."

"There's nothing to talk about."

"Have you read any of the books I sent you?"

"Not yet."

"Are you going to?"

"Stop bugging me, all right? Everybody's always bugging me. You're just like Mama and Grandma, always pushing up against me, telling me what to eat, fixing my hair, running my bathwater for me, like I can't turn on the faucet by myself."

"You want me to talk to your grandma?"

"If you want to."

"And your mama?"

"If that's what you want."

"Is that what *you* want?"

"I guess so." She kicked off her shoes and tucked her feet under her. "Did the Cubs win?"

"When?"

"When you stole the baseball cards?"

"No. I think they came in eighth."

"Oh."

"I'm going to go downstairs."

"Go ahead."

"Your grandmother's very upset."

"She'll get over it."

"All right. But no more shoplifting till your mother gets back."

"Right."

Back downstairs I called the hotel in Dakar, where it was the middle of the night. The man who answered the phone spoke in French, and then switched to English. He transferred the call and another man answered the phone in French, and then I was speaking to Cory. She wanted the details.

"Jesus, Marty. You think maybe it's just kid stuff? You and I skipped school a couple of times, and you stole all that bubble gum with the baseball cards. I picked up a few things myself at the dime store."

"If that store owner had signed a complaint," I said, "she would have been arrested. There would have been a trial. *A trial!*"

"Did you talk to her?"

"Yeah, we had a talk."

"What did she say?"

"She said everyone's always bugging her."

"What's that supposed to mean?"

"I think she just needs a little more independence?"

"More independence?"

"Maybe you and your mom do too much for her."

"Like what?"

"Like running her bathwater. She said you're always running her bathwater, as if she can't turn on the faucet by herself."

"Running her bathwater? That's what she said? She's complaining because someone's running her bathwater? Give me a break."

"Maybe she just needs to see you more."

"Wait a second, Marty. Are you telling me to stay home and baby-sit her, or are you telling me to let her be more independent? And who are you to be telling me what to do anyway?"

"I'm her father."

"Yeah. Right. I forgot."

"We need to consider our options."

"*Our* options? You mean *my* options?"

"All right. *Your* options."

"You're always wanting to *save* us, Martin. First you wanted to *save* me; now you want to *save* my daughter. You're as bad as that missionary, Miss Prell, what was her name?"

"Miss Prellwitz."

"You remember her, don't you? She sure had your undies in a twist."

"What's your point?"

"Oh, I don't know, Martin. I'm sorry. I should be thanking you for driving all the way up to Madison to help out."

"Go ahead."

"Thanks."

"I was glad to do it."

"I know you were, Martin. And I'm glad you're there. I'll bet Mama's upset; I can hear her now, banging around in the kitchen. Why don't you order a pizza? Cozy likes pepperoni and mushrooms but no anchovies. Mama probably won't eat much anyway. Get whatever you like, OK?"

"OK," I said.

"I suppose I better talk to Cozy," she said.

"It might be better to wait. She's up in her room and I'm not sure she wants to come down."

"OK. Put Mama on then. I'll tell her you're going to order some pizza."

Aunt Flo didn't want to order pizza, but she was too distraught to fix supper for us, so I ordered a large pizza anyway. Cozy ate half the pizza up in her room. Aunt Flo and I sat in the kitchen and picked at the other half. I pretended to be a little distraught too, but I was secretly pleased, like an actor who's just been given an important part in a play, or a musician who's just landed an important gig. I spent the night on the couch and drove home in the morning.

In October I played a solo gig at the Rathskeller, in the student union at the University of Wisconsin. I got a call from Stephanie Green—the events coordinator at the union—who'd heard me at the Doves concert in March. She'd had a cancellation and needed someone to fill a spot on short notice. This time Corinna promised to come and to bring Cozy. I couldn't persuade Aunt Flo, however. "You don't have to worry about the devil at your age," I said to her on the phone.

"You don't know a thing about it," she said.

On the morning of the gig I typed out two copies of my playlist and taped one on the upper bout of each guitar. I played through the two forty-five minute sets slowly.

If Cory came, it would be the first time she'd seen me perform—though in my imagination I could always see her in a booth or down at the end of the bar or in one of the back rows—or even heard me play, actually, since Appleton. I came up to Madison once a month or so and we were on easy terms. She was busy and happy—a minor celebrity in certain circles. She'd made two more trips to Senegal and regularly gave braiding workshops in New York and on the West Coast; and she didn't object to my playing the father to Cozy in small ways. Madison was full of interracial couples, at least around the university, so no one gave us a second look if we stopped for coffee or a drink at one of the cafés along State Street. If I was a little nervous it was because the two stories of my life seemed to be coming together, converging, like two highways or rivers, like US 20 and US 12 outside Gary, or like the Mississippi and the Missouri at St. Louis, or like parallel lines on a globe.

I stopped at Chez Corinna to put up a poster, right next to a picture of two Mabalantu women with hair that hung down to their feet.

DOWN-HOME BLUES
AN EVENING OF COUNTRY BLUES
WITH MARTIN DIJKSTERHUIS

What I really wanted was to make sure Cory hadn't forgotten. I sat in the back of the shop for fifteen minutes, paging through a magazine, and then I watched the braider, who worked at a barber's chair that had been set up in the front window, so that people walking by on the street outside could stop to watch. She wore a brightly colored robe with short sleeves that wouldn't get in the way of her hands, which moved quickly, gathering up strands of hair. When she'd finished a braid she'd double up a piece of wire and thread it through a loop in a piece of thread, and then twist the ends together tightly to make a kind of needle. She'd put this needle through the holes in a dozen beads, and then put the end of the braid through the loop of the wire, pushing the beads up onto the braid itself, wrapping the thread around, making a slip knot, cutting the end of the thread, and sliding the beads down the thread.

Cory came up from the back of the store and watched for a while without saying anything. Her own hair lay in tight little cornrows right against her scalp before plunging into a free fall.

"I'll see you tonight," I said. "At the gig."

"No more of those big wide parts," she said. "And you can't even see the knots." She looked at me over the tops of her new reading glasses. Half glasses. "Where the extensions are joined to the natural hair. Close your eyes. Now feel this." I closed my eyes and she guided my hand to the head of the woman in the chair. I ran my fingers down one of the braids.

"I don't feel any knots," I said.

"Good. You see?"

The young woman who worked as her chief braider had been a little standoffish at first, but now she seemed warm and friendly.

Corinna laughed when I showed her the poster. She stood with her weight on one leg. I had my gear in the hearse and didn't want to leave it too long. "I've got to get going," I said. "Sound check."

"I'll see you tonight," she said.

"And Cozy?"

She shook her head. "She's grounded."

"Another fountain pen?"

"Skipping school."

"So it'll be just you and me?"

"Unless you've got a date," she said.

I was early for the sound check, which didn't really amount to much. I was going to play from nine to eleven. Stephanie Green helped me haul my gear in from the hearse in the parking lot: two guitars and my old RPO grip with my own mikes, just in case, and extra instrument cords, microphone cords, a tuning fork, strings, a string winder. And a metal footlocker with extra instruments: kazoos, bongos, tambourine, bones, and a washboard.

We got a good sound out of the monitors right away, but when she turned the house speakers on I couldn't hear myself. I kept strumming the guitar and talking to her, using her name, trying to be funny and amusing while she fiddled with the mains and the sliders on the graphic EQ, trying to get a natural sound, and the monitors went up and down: *Sounds a little thin. Sounds a little boxy. You're getting there, Stephanie, just a little more bass. I'm going to try the vocal mike just a little closer and sing a verse of "C. C. Rider" on the Nick Lucas and then on the metal guitar, OK? Now maybe try a little more mike and a little less pickup on the Nick Lucas, but listen to each channel in the mains before you adjust the gain knob, and keep the fader at zero. There isn't any pickup on the metal guitar, so you're going to have to adjust the levels again . . .*

Her arms dropped to her sides and she started to laugh. "Martin, calm down." She wiped her forehead with the back of her hand. "Where did you learn to talk like that?"

"At the Old Town School," I said.

"Those folks at Old Town must be pretty intense. Now just give me one more chord on that ugly guitar of yours and I think we'll be all set."

"Which one?"

She laughed again. "The one that makes all the racket all by itself."

"It's a National Steel guitar," I said. "It's galvanized steel. It just hasn't been plated, that's all." I ran my thumb across the open strings; Stephanie made one last adjustment, and the sound check was over.

There wasn't any greenroom, so I changed into my stage outfit— a pinstriped suit and the Italian silk tie Janis had bought for me when her parents came to town—in Stephanie's office while Stephanie went to get a couple of sandwiches. I liked to dress up a little, wear a suit and tie when I performed, like Reverend Taylor or Robert Johnson or Blind Willie McTell, or Blind Lemon.

It was warm for November and we ate our sandwiches, standing up, outside on the Union Terrace, where I'd spied on Cory and Monroe. The tables and the brightly colored chairs were gone, and there were no sailboats on the lake. We went back to the Rat, and I waited in Stephanie's office. I was nervous, of course, and went to pee three or four times, checking the house each time to see if Corinna had shown up. There were a lot of empty tables, and I was wondering if the students milling around the bar would coalesce into an audience. Were they here for the music, or just for a quick beer?

I took the Nick Lucas out of its case, but I didn't play anything I was going to play that night because I didn't want to start second-guessing myself. I'd developed a habit of being onstage whenever I picked up the guitar, though, so I sat up straight, breathed from the diaphragm, and thought about what I was doing. I played a blues scale up and down the neck. *Never apologize; never explain. Put your stage fright to work for you. You owe your audience all you've got. They're giving you their time, if not their money. They're nervous for you. They want you to do well.* I was getting to the point where I believed this.

At nine o'clock Stephanie tapped on the door. "It's time."

"How's the house?"

"Not bad for Tuesday night."

The metal guitar was already on a stand on the stage. I was holding the Nick Lucas. The footlocker of extra instruments was behind my chair, the lid propped open. The lights went down; people cleared their throats. From the edge of the stage I looked around for Corinna but I couldn't find her. Someone was introducing me. Stephanie.

Every night, at small venues around the country, thousands of performers like me walk out onto small stages to sing their songs and tell their stories and play their instruments, and thousands of audiences decide, minute by minute, song by song, whether we're worth attending to. Sometimes we die a thousand deaths; but other times the music opens our hearts, lifts the veil of familiarity, reveals the mysterious inner life of things—raw, fresh, fragile.

When Stephanie was done I walked out onto the stage and

picked up the Nick Lucas. "Folk singers stand up," I said, leaning over the microphone. "Blues players sit down."

I sat down, listening carefully for the response, like a doctor listening for a pulse. I could hear it, firm and steady—not exactly a chuckle, but something in the breathing. "I'd like you," I said, adjusting the microphone, "to imagine you're at a party, and you've had a little beer, or a little wine, or a little Maryjane—but not too much—and now you're sitting around afterward and everyone else seems to be talking to someone else, and maybe it's time to go home, but now you hear my voice, and you feel a little less lonely.

"Or maybe you're in your car, driving across the country. Maybe you've just said good-bye to someone you love, someone you're not going to see again for a long, long time. Maybe you've just taken your youngest child off to college, and now you're driving back home, and you have a long way to go, and you know that a door has closed behind you, that an important chapter of your life has come to an end. So you turn on the radio, and now you hear me talking to you.

"Or maybe you're just alone tonight, waiting for someone who was supposed to show up a long time ago, and maybe you'd like to hear some blues."

I was stalling, waiting for Corinna to show up, but I'd run out of things to say.

Before I began to play, though, I looked at the note to myself that I always kept in the inner pocket of my suit jacket: *Don't play too fast,* it said. It was a trick Reverend Taylor had taught me. I shoved the note back in my pocket and began to play, starting with a real crowd pleaser, a song that's never let me down.

> *You can steal my woman, but you sure can't keep*
> *   her long;*
> *You may steal my woman, sure can't keep her*
> *   long.*

I got a new way of lovin', Californians can't
catch on.

Cory came in at the beginning of the second verse and sat down at a table by herself. I started to speed up—I couldn't help myself—but then I heard Reverend Taylor's voice in my ear—*Speed is not the same as hurrying*—and I slowed down. *Like you're takin' a nice easy walk on firm ground.*

I got me three wimmin', And they live on the same
old road;
I got me three wimmin', They live on the same old
road;
One does my washin', one my ironin', One I love
pays my room and board.

One's from Virginia, one's from Georgia, one I
love's from Caroline;
One's from Virginia, one's from Georgia, one I
love's from Caroline;
I got wimmin from coast to coast, and they's
always on my mind.

When I finished the song I started to laugh, and the audience laughed too.

"I learned that song from a man named Chesterfield," I said, "when I was about fourteen. Just about the first blues song I ever heard. Actually, it was probably the second or third. That was in 1953. That was the year the Braves moved to Milwaukee. It was the second year in a row with no lynchings. The first issue of *Playboy* came out that November, with a nude picture of Marilyn Monroe, and a reporter for the *Capital Times* right here in Madison tried to get people to sign a petition that was made up of a list of items from the Declaration of Independence and the Bill of Rights. People thought he was a communist. My mother wrote a column about it in our local paper.

I got into a little trouble with Blind Blake's "You're Gonna Quit Me, Baby." I hooked my thumb pick on the G string and almost heaved the guitar out into the audience; then I screwed up the first break and played it again and screwed it up again. I tried not to get agitated, tried to put my trust in my body, tried to get my thinking brain out of the way. When you're playing with a group, the group will carry you, but when you're soloing you've just got to pick yourself up and carry on. I could feel support coming from the audience; I could feel their goodwill as I played the break a third time, this time without thinking. When I came to the passage I'd had trouble with, I stepped into it, like my father stepping up to the starting line in the tenth frame of his perfect game. This time the pressure concentrated my energies instead of fragmenting them. The music was there, in my body, and the notes came out like drops of sweat.

> *Standin', standin' in the station*
> *Suitcase in my hand,*
> *Suitcase in my hand,*
> *Doggone.*

Everyone relaxed. The mistake was working in my favor. I was vulnerable, but not incompetent! Everything was going to be all right.

"The next song I want to play," I said, "is 'Corinna, Corinna.' It was probably written by Bo Carter. It's been recorded in every genre you can think of—western, country, pop, bluegrass, blues—but I'd like to sing it the way Blind Lemon Jefferson recorded it back in 1926." I strummed a chord. "Anyone here named Corinna?" I asked.

No answer. I looked at Corinna, but she didn't meet my gaze.

"Corinna, Corinna," I sang, "where'd you stay last night; Corinna, Corinna, where'd you stay last night; come home this morning, sun shinin' bright."

I sang one song after another (naturally), and chatted up the audience—a lot of singles, a few blues aficionados who nodded their heads knowingly, a few kids just there for a beer (the drinking age is eighteen in Wisconsin). Some older people too: a professorial type, probably an eccentric physicist; two women together, faculty members, I was sure of it—one had to be the chairman of the English department. And of course, Corinna. It was all coming together. I lost track of time, lost myself in the music. In other words, I let the music speak for itself instead of trying to dazzle the crowd with my virtuosity. I never consciously try to be original onstage, never try to do more than put my fingers down where the old bluesmen used to put theirs, but every now and then a funky lick will rise to the surface, like a bubble of swamp gas, or I'll get carried away on a guitar break and find myself in unfamiliar territory, wondering how I'll ever get back home to the tonic.

When Stephanie waved at me from behind the mixing board, I waved back at her. It took me a minute to realize that it was time to bring the first set to a close.

"You were right," she said, "I should have listened to the mains before adjusting the gain, but it sounds pretty good." I could feel some heat coming off her. "There's going to be a party afterward," she said.

"There's always a party afterward," I said. She made a moue. "Sorry," I said, "I didn't mean . . ." I wanted to sit with Cory for a minute, but I didn't want to explain.

Corinna'd tied some colored threads around the tips of her braids. I walked over to her table and asked if she'd like to sing a different version of "Corinna, Corinna" with me in the second set, or maybe just come up onstage.

"Are you crazy?" she said.

"Just thought I'd ask. I've got to put new strings on the Nick Lucas. I'll see you after the show."

I didn't need new strings; I'd just put new strings on the night before, but I was nervous. Stephanie brought me a shorty beer in her office, but I didn't drink it because I didn't want to lose my edge.

I checked the tuning of the steel guitar, which was in open-G, and began the second set with another song I'd learned from Chesterfield, "Moon Going Down," an old Charley Patton song. "In fact," I said, "this is Chesterfield's old guitar. I bought it from him when I was fourteen with the money I was supposed to be saving for my college education. My mother wasn't too happy, I can tell you that."

A stunningly beautiful blond woman had come in between sets and was sitting at a table in the front. She wore a straw hat and was wearing some special makeup that made her glow like a movie actress. Maybe she *was* a movie actress, an actress who'd just walked onto the set and was waiting for the cameras to roll. She was paging through a magazine when I started to play, and she kept right on paging while I finished the song and played a pair of Robert Johnson songs, "Come On in my Kitchen" and "Crossroads." When I got to the second break in "Crossroads" she got up and walked out. I wanted to stop the song and yell at her: *What the hell do you think you're doing? What did you come here for?* But that would have been too unprofessional. I was losing the audience. Everyone was following the blond woman with their eyes, and then their ears, as her high heels tap tap tapped on the hardwood floor. What was she doing? Walking in place in the hallway? Tap tap, tap tap, tap tap, tap tap, tap tap, tap tap.

I'd lost my hold on the audience, and I didn't get it back till I cranked up the energy level by getting a bunch of kids onstage and giving them instruments to play. I gave the washboard to an athletic type who looked like he could keep a beat. I asked if anyone knew what a backbeat was, and a big blond girl raised her hand, so I gave her the tambourine; and then I handed out bones, African rattles, a bongo drum, and a washboard and a metal dog brush.

I told the story about Reverend Taylor buying a church and then we played the song he'd played in the kitchen at the Blues Cottage in Newport, "Oh Glory, How Happy I Am." We were pretty ragged at first, but then we started to hit a beat, like the tumblers of a padlock clicking into place. The washboard kept us steady and the tambourine hit the backbeat, and finally I got everybody singing.

> *Oh Glory, how happy I am,*
> *Oh Glory, how happy I am,*
> *My soul is washed in the blood of the Lamb,*
> *Glory, Hallelujah.*

And in fact I was happy.

I closed the show with Big Bill Broonzy's "In the Evening." I told a story about working as a part-time janitor for a while at the Old Town School of Folk Music, setting up chairs, taking down chairs, cleaning up at night. I had keys for everything, and when I finally managed to locate Big Bill's guitar, which was kept in a locked cabinet in Win Stracke's office, I went out and got a six-pack and played that guitar all night long.

> *In the evening, in the evening, Baby, when the sun*
> *   go down;*
> *In the evening, in the evening, Baby, when the sun*
> *   go down;*
> *Ain't it lonesome, ain't it lonesome, When the one*
> *   you love can't be found.*

After the show I sat at a table in the back of the Rat, near the bar, and sold copies of *Down-Home Blues* and copies of the instruction tape I'd made to go along with it. The man I'd pegged as an eccentric physicist owned a hardware store out on the Beltline; the chairwoman of the English department turned out to be a housewife from Colorado who was visiting her daughter. Stephanie handled the money while I chatted with people and kept my eye on Corinna to make sure she didn't leave. She finally came up to the table.

"Well," I said.

"Well," she said.

"Can I buy you a drink?"

"It's late," she said, looking at Stephanie.

"She's an old friend," I explained to Stephanie. "My oldest friend. From my hometown. And it's not *that* late."

We sat at a small table under a sign, in Gothic letters, that said:

> Deines Geistes Blitze,
> schick sie in die Welt hinaus.

I was more nervous than when I'd walked out onto the stage. Cory was looking straight into me, as if she could read my thoughts. But that would have been impossible. I couldn't read them myself. I didn't have an agenda, a plan. I didn't know—really—why she'd come alone. We listened to the bar noises, student waitresses taking drink orders.

Stephanie came to the table. "Musicians drink free," she said. "Can I get you something?"

"Maybe a couple of beers," I said.

"I guess I don't need to write that down," she said.

"What does that sign mean?" Cory asked.

Stephanie studied the German words: *"Your soul's lightnings* . . . I'm not sure. *Send them out into the world?* Something like that."

She went to get our beers.

"Did you see that blond woman?" I said to Cory. "She got up and left right in the middle of 'Crossroads.' What the hell did she think she was she doing?"

"Maybe she didn't like the music."

"What'd she come here for? And why sit right up front? Besides, she was looking at a magazine right from the start. She was reading a magazine when I came out for the second set and she just kept turning the pages right up to the time she left."

Stephanie brought us two draft beers. "Let me know if you need anything else, OK?"

I was waiting for Cory to say something about the show, but her mind was on something else.

"Well?" I said.

"I don't know what to say."

"You thought it was fabulous."

"It *was* fabulous, Marty. You were really taking care of business up there. I'm impressed. You sound just like that old guy out at the orchards."

"We've already had this conversation."

"Sorry."

I hesitated to ask the obvious question, but she read my mind. "I'm going to New York, Martin, one way or another."

"Things all right with Monroe?"

"'If you mind your own business then you won't be minding mine.'"

"You really like that old Hank Williams song, don't you?" I said.

"I guess I must."

"Was that Monroe who answered the phone when I called you in Dakar?"

She nodded. "His wife," she said, "is making it absolutely impossible. First it's the money, then it's the kids."

"I'm sorry, Cory."

"It's all right, Martin. I'm negotiating for a place on a Hundred Twenty-fifth Street, about two blocks from Lenox Avenue. New York is swell, Marty; do you know what I mean? It's swell."

"I didn't think anybody said *swell* anymore."

"Sometimes it's the only word that'll do."

"I'd like to take Cozy to see her grandmother before you go," I said. "What do you think?"

"Whoa. Hold on a second."

"Why not? It would mean a lot to my mom."

"How much does your mom know?"

"Not much, really. Just that I'd tracked you down in Madison. Right after my dad died."

"You think she really wants a granddaughter?"

"She's got nothing to look forward to, Cory. That's the hard thing. Cozy might give her something to . . . a way to imagine the future. It helps *me*, I know that. Remember how she taught us to say Humpty Dumpty in French? *'Boule, Boule sur la cuillère.'*"

"You bring it up at least once every time I see you."

"Sorry. But sometimes you *can* put things back together."

"You know," Cory said, "it's too bad you didn't stay in Appleton and take over the orchards. It wasn't the Garden of Eden, but it wasn't Peyton Place either. That was the life for you. That's the sad thing, Martin. Not that you didn't marry me, but that you gave up that life. You and Daddy could have run the orchards after your dad died. That was the life for you. For Daddy too. He was at loose ends here. It suited Mama fine, but he didn't know what to do with himself." I wanted another beer, but I didn't want to get up to get one.

"I'm doing all right."

"You traveling a lot?"

"Not too much. Mostly around Chicago. Farthest I've been is Denver. I went out for a showcase three weeks ago. Waste of time, but I camped for a couple of days on the way back, up north of Estes Park, slept in the back of the hearse. I stopped at the Continental Divide on the way back, and peed on both sides of the Divide."

"But you're doing all right?"

"I'm doing all right," I said. "But it's lonely, even around Chicago. I thought I was prepared for that, but it takes you by surprise sometimes. I usually pick out someone in the audience . . ."

"A good-looking woman?"

"Yeah, like you, and I sing to her; I try to reach her, to love her, to touch her, give her a sense of what it's like to climb out of some stranger's bed at four o'clock in the morning and hit the road, drive through town when all the houses are asleep, rolling your window down out on the highway, letting the night air wash over your face, sticking your arm out the window."

She started to laugh. "You got all this out of one trip to Denver? You ought to make it part of the show."

"Actually I've thought about it."

"Do you meet any of these women in the flesh?"

"There's usually a party after the show—if it's a campus gig—and a place to crash."

"And a pretty coed to crash with?"

"That's the idea, but it's nothing personal. It's like sleeping with the white hunter. That's what one girl told me. Like sleeping with the white hunter on a safari."

"Martin"—she laughed—"why do you put yourself through this?"

"I don't know," I said. "It's not all that different from sorting mail on the night train, looking out the windows at the little towns that go by. Except you've got the music, all that richness in a little room. How can you get so much beautiful music out of three lousy chords and three or four simple patterns? That's what's amazing. And the language. It's the mother tongue, the American mother tongue: I got the key to the highway. I'm going away, Baby; cryin' won't make me stay. Come on in my kitchen, 'cause it's going to be rainin' outdoors. Now she's gone gone gone, and I don't worry, 'cause I'm sittin' on top of the world. I got me three wimmin and they live on the same old road. You know I'd rise from my grave, for some of your jelly. If I get lucky, and find my train fare home. Standin' in the station, my suitcase in my hand. I told you, you could go, and don't come back here no more. I'm goin' back home, wear out ninety-nine pair of shoes. Now it is a needin' time. Ain't had no lovin' since you been gone. I went to the crossroads, fell down on my knees. I went down to the depot, that evening train done gone. I'm a stranger here, just blowed in your town. I'm a big fat mama, got the meat shakin' on my bones. You made me love you, now your man done come. All my life I been a travelin' man. If I had a listened to my second mind. When I had money, we lived on Easy Street. Winds on Lake Michigan, Lord, blow chilly and cold. Rise up dead man, and help me drive my row. When my bed get empty make me feel awful mean and blue.

"Do you remember how my mother used to talk about a line of poetry, or a whole poem, greeting your spirit? Like that line about the tears of things, *lacrimae rerum.* That's what the blues gives us, Cory, *the tears of things.* The joy of things too. Of course, there's a lot of bad blues too. Some old guy whanging away at the guitar. But there's a lot of bad opera too, so what's the difference?"

"Well," she said, "you sold a lot of books and tapes tonight, so you must be doing something right. I started counting, but I lost track. You put on a good show, and I think the woman who brought us the beer—the one who helped you with the show—is waiting for you. Why don't you take her out, show her a good time—take her to one of those parties? Look at her—nice long legs, great big eyes, a couple of little moles on her face, like beauty spots. Her hair could use some work . . ."

"Jesus, Cory."

"Don't 'Jesus' me, Marty. Get real. I did my share of screwing around before I met Monroe. I guess it's a good thing I didn't have you on my tail back then! Mama was bad enough."

"What happened, Cory?"

"What do you mean what happened?"

"With Monroe."

"I told you, his wife . . . Oh, I don't know, Marty."

I moved over to her side of the table and held her hand and we just sat there like that for a few minutes.

"You want another beer?" I said after a while.

"No thanks, I'd better go."

"You're sure?"

"I'm sure."

"You want me to give you a ride?"

"No, I've got my car."

"What about Cozy?" I asked.

"Your mom really wants to see her?"

We walked out to the parking lot. She'd parked next to the hearse, which wasn't as impressive as the Silver Wraith but which was pretty impressive anyway.

"I haven't asked her yet," I said, "but I think it would mean a lot to her. And to me too."

"I don't know, Martin."

"Where's the harm?"

"I don't want her any more confused, Martin, about who she really is."

"Maybe you should give her a little more credit," I said. "She's tough. She can handle it."

"She's tough, all right." She laughed. "When she and Mama get going sometimes it's like two bears in a den."

"I thought I might get her that fountain pen for her birthday."

"Just a little reminder?"

"Maybe. Something like that. Maybe just a fountain pen. My mother always writes with a fountain pen. I still use the Waterman pen she gave me when I turned seventeen. You were at the party when she gave it to me. I had it in my pocket when we climbed the tower that October. It's the pen I used to write to you after you disappeared. I wrote my U of C essay with it too. I always carry it." I held the pen up for her to admire." The barrel was iridescent blue.

"It's too expensive, Martin."

"I suppose. Mom knew I wanted a guitar, but she got me the pen instead. It probably cost more than a guitar. And then I bought Chesterfield's guitar anyway."

"What happened to all the letters?"

"Dead letter office," I said. "Mail recovery center. I didn't put any return addresses on them."

"You're so funny, Martin."

"Now I better listen to my second mind," she said, "or I'll be sittin' here wringing' my hands and cryin'."

"You sound like your mom," I said, "always listening to her second mind and her third mind and her fourth mind."

"You're right, Marty; and she still hasn't gotten to the end of her minds."

"I've got to get my gear together," I said.

"You all right to drive? You could sleep on the sofa."

"I'll be all right."

From the parking lot we could see the lake, and the armory that had been firebombed a couple of years earlier.

"I guess it's so long," she said. "I'm sorry. I know you mean well; and I know you do love me, and Cozy too. I'm glad she's gotten to know you. You know that Big Bill somebody's song you sang at the end?"

"Broonzy."

"That's it."

"'In the Evening'?"

"How did that last verse go?"

"'So long, old sweetheart and pal?'"

"That's it, Marty. That's our song. Not 'I Love You Truly.' You should know that by now. You're the bluesman." She put her arms around me and kissed my neck. She had a new car, a Porsche Carrera. I opened the door for her and then closed it behind her.

When I went back inside Stephanie had collected all my gear. "You sold a lot of tapes," she said.

"How much?" I asked.

"Almost a hundred bucks. And I've got a check for you too. Everything's packed up. Who was that anyway?"

"Did you get names and addresses from everybody who bought?" (I always collected names and addresses for my mailing list.)

She nodded.

"An old friend of mine," I said, "from childhood."

"She's more than that, isn't she?" I nodded. "What about the party?"

"No thanks, Stephanie. I'm a little down."

"You shouldn't be, it was a great show." I shrugged. "Something happened, didn't it?" she asked. I didn't say anything. "I'll help you carry your stuff." It took two trips. I opened the big side door of the hearse and stowed the footlocker behind the guitars and then slid the door closed. Stephanie walked around to the other side and climbed into the passenger seat.

"Where you going?"

"Wherever you're going?"

"I'm going back to Chicago."

She was looking out the window. I wanted for her to turn and look at me, but she didn't turn. "I just want to get out of here," she said. "It's just something I have to do. I have to do something crazy every once in a while, just to—"

"You're not married, are you?" She shook her head. "Just checking. I didn't think so." I started up the hearse and pulled out of the parking lot onto Observatory. I hit three red lights in a row. At each one Stephanie turned to look at me, and then she looked down, and then she looked out the window again. By the time we got to the edge of town she got scared and wanted me to let her out at a gas station.

"I'll call a taxi," she said.

"I'll drive you back," I said. "It's no problem."

"I'm sorry," she said. "This is too embarrassing."

We argued for a while, but she wouldn't let me drive her back to campus, or to her apartment. She was too embarrassed. But she didn't need to be embarrassed. I knew just how she felt.

I took 151 out to the Beltline, and when I hit I-90 I cranked the hearse up to sixty and rolled down the windows. I sang all the songs I hadn't sung that night, and then some of the songs that I had sung. I sang "C. C. Rider" and "Key to the Highway" and "In the Evening." That was our song.

> *So long, old sweetheart and pal.*
> *I'll be on my way;*
> *I may be back to see you,*
> *Some old rainy day,*
> *In the evening, in the evening,*
> *Baby, when the sun go down.*

PART IV

11

Tragic Mulatta

1972

CORY DIDN'T MARRY Monroe Franklin, but the Williamses moved to New York in June 1972. Cory opened a more elaborate version of Chez Corinna on 125th Street, Harlem's main thoroughfare, and bought a small town house on 138th Street, not far from City College. I bought a Fodor's Guide to New York City so I could see with my own eyes how the Harlem River and the East River divided Manhattan Island from the Bronx and Queens and Brooklyn. It's a little bit like Michigan, actually, but backwards: if you hold your left hand up at a forty-five degree angle, your thumb is Manhattan and your fingers are the Bronx and your palm is Queens and the heel of your hand is Brooklyn.

At home in Chicago I settled back into my old life as June gave way to July, hot as an oven and sticky as molasses. The blues revival was winding down. You could hear Buddy Guy and Junior Wells at Theresa's, but many of the small clubs around the city—around the country, for that matter—were closing down or converting to comedy clubs. People were starting to look back on rock 'n roll with nostalgia: Don McLean's "American Pie" was at the top of the charts.

On the other hand, I was making a living doing what I wanted to do: giving lessons at the Old Town School, where I also worked as a part-time janitor; playing at the old people's homes three or four times a month; picking up some paying gigs around the city. I was doing some traveling too—mostly campus gigs—and seeing Stephanie from time to time! If I had a gig in Milwaukee or Minneapolis, she'd go with me, and we'd go out to dinner after the show and make love in a Holiday Inn or a Howard Johnson's and I'd think of Janis—Janis reading in the tub, candles burning on the sink, Mozart on the radio; Janis bending over her leather ottoman, waiting for me to pull her underpants down and enter her from behind; Janis moving her dimes and pennies around on the checkerboard on the kitchen table—and I'd look down into Stephanie's eyes and wonder whom *she* was thinking about as we drifted further and further apart into a realm where every wish was gratified before it was fully formed, till a sneeze or a growling stomach or a cramp in a leg would remind us who we were and what we were about, and we'd come crashing back together, not insubstantial fantasies but solid flesh and liquid blood, fueled by appetites, guided by the will: *Yes, that's it, move a little slower, but harder, right there, move in a circle, yes that's it, keep doing that, O God yes, O God, yes that's it, O God.*

But for the most part I traveled alone.

I sometimes dreamed about Cozy, but these dreams were incoherent and unsatisfactory. I'd see her at the bus stop on Fifty-sixth Street, for example, a satchel over her shoulder, but before I could reach her, the Jeffrey Express would stop and whisk her away; or I'd see her in the audience at Old Town, in the back row, as we sang "Michael Row the Boat Ashore" or "Waltzing Matilda," but by the time we'd finished the last chorus of the last song, she'd be gone. My memories were perfectly clear, however, and became even sharper at the end of the summer when I saw children on their way to Bret Harte School on Fifty-sixth Street or the Lab School on Fifty-ninth. Cozy was no longer a child, however. She would be starting her sophomore year at George Washington High School in upper Manhattan. I'd bought a street atlas of the city at Kroch's and located the school on Audubon Avenue.

At the end of the second week of September I bought an expensive fountain pen for Cozy at B. J. Townsend, in the basement of the Monadnock Building, where I'd once waited in the Silver Cloud while Reverend Taylor met with his patent attorney. A back-to-school present, I said to myself. I'd intended to buy a Mont Blanc—the same pen she'd stolen, twice—but Mr. Townsend admired my own Waterman Le Man so much (*a classic, a world-class pen, with an eighteen-carat-gold nib that adjusts to your writing style*) that I bought one for Cozy. I bought a scrapbook too, for the photos of Cozy I'd taken in the spring of 1964, when she was finishing second grade; and for all the school pictures and school records I'd gotten from the secretary at St. James; for the picture of her and Aunt Flo coming out of Chez Corinna on the day I followed Cory and Monroe to the hotel across from the music store; and for her spelling-bee pictures from the *Wisconsin State Journal*:—the small one on the Saturday of the bee; a larger one on the front page of the Sunday, as the runner-up; and a third one from the Rotary Club luncheon for the top ten spellers. The article about the bee said there had been some contention about the spelling of one of the words and that one of the parents had been asked to leave. *One of the parents.*

At the end of the month I received a proper thank-you note for the pen—the sort of note your mother makes you write to a maiden aunt who's given you a nice graduation present. I imagined that the note was Aunt Flo's doing. Then about two weeks later I received a postcard with a picture of the George Washington Bridge. I sent Cozy cards from Madison and Iowa city, and she sent more cards, with pictures of the Empire State Building and Audubon Park, which had once been the estate of the artist and naturalist John James Audubon.

I scrutinized these cards as if they were important clues, and I suppose they were, though they didn't yield up much information about her state of mind. She was taking geometry and biology and English and French and phys. ed. She had to take the subway to get to school. If she walked six blocks over to Broadway, on the other side of City College, she'd have to walk only one block to school when she got to 191st Street. Or she could take the subway on St. Nicholas Avenue, but then she'd have to walk six blocks to school from the 191st Station. Or she could take the IRT from St. Nicholas Avenue and transfer to the number one train at 168th Street, and then she'd hardly have to walk at all. All that information was on a single postcard. Her grandmother, I learned from a subsequent card, hadn't ridden on the subway yet and didn't plan to, and she was afraid to walk north of Broadway because of the Puerto Ricans; but on Sunday mornings she walked to the Abyssinian Baptist Church, which was only two blocks away. All the cards were neatly written with the new pen.

The postcards all seemed moderately cheerful, but in the middle of October I came home from a gig at the Carl Sandburg House in Galesburg, Illinois, and found a real letter, in a small pink envelope addressed to Mr. Martin Dijksterhuis. I balanced the envelope on my fingertips for a minute and then put it in my jacket pocket, keeping it separate from the stack of bills and junk mail that had accumulated during my brief absence. I climbed the stairs to the third floor, unlocked my door, put the guitars down on the floor at the end of the couch, and left the mail on the kitchen table while I went back to the hearse, which I'd parked in the lot at the Museum of Science and Industry, to get the rest of my gear—my amps and mikes. And then I washed my face and hands and sliced a tomato and panfried a frozen minute steak and opened a bottle of beer. I opened the letter with a Sabatier knife that my mother had given me for Christmas one year and felt a little twinge of guilt: my mother never let anyone use one of her good knives to cut paper. But the knife was dull anyway, and I didn't have a steel to sharpen it. I unfolded the letter and read it as I ate my little steak. I'm not sure what I expected. Whatever it was, it wasn't this.

November 18, 1972

Dear Daddy—

Grandma and I went to see *Imitation of Life* last week at a theater that shows old movies, and we both cried when Annie died and the actress who plays Sara Jane is really a white woman, but Grandma says she saw a different version that's even older when she lived in Benton Harbor and the actress was Fredi Washington, who really was a mulatta. My English teacher says she's a "tragic" mulatta because it's so hard for her to fit in, and there's no way she's ever going to be happy, and I know how she feels. Every time someone at school calls me nigger or zebra or oreo I just laugh and say same to you, but it's like someone's punched you in the stomach so hard you want to cry, and I can't help it. But I still don't think Sarah Jane should have pretended to be white. Miss Hanson says she sold her soul to the devil, just like somebody named Faust.

Mama says it will be better next year if I can go to Music and Art on 135th Street, which is closer to home. The brother of a girl I know got in just by playing a song called "As Tears Go By" on the guitar; but Mama and I went there in July and they said it was too late and they said they don't really want to take students for just the last year; that would be next year, so I don't think that's going to work. Besides, I like my English teacher, Miss Hanson, and my biology teacher, Mr. Jordan, and I don't think I'm the arty type anyway; I think I'd like to be a veterinarian.

Miss Hanson says that in the first version of *Imitation of Life* the characters all have different names and instead of making pancake mix Lora and Annie live in New York and Lora is an actress. She's going to try to rent the one with Fredi Washington and show it to our class, so I can compare them for my paper.

Mama bought a cassette player so we can listen to the little tape you sent. It's really nice. And Grandma says to say hello. Next summer we're going to go take the bus over to Queens to see the Cubs play the Mets at Shea Stadium.

Yours truly,
Cozy

She also included a copy of a poem in French that she'd written out in longhand. It was by Stéphane Mallarmé. I put it aside without trying to translate it.

Nigger, zebra, oreo. I felt as if I'd been punched in the stomach so hard that I wanted to cry too. My mother used to say that children were hostages to fortune, but I'd never really known what she meant till I read that letter. I pictured Cozy, thin and angular like her handwriting, with no one to watch her back or hold her hand. It was the first time she'd needed me.

"You can tell her," Reverend Taylor advised me in his kitchen that evening, "that she's one of God's children, just like everybody else. She's got the same right as everybody else to laugh or to get mad or to get happy." And that's what I told her in the letter that I sent the next day, but I knew it wasn't enough. And I also told her that people were always drawing imaginary lines and then throwing real stones at whoever was on the other side of the line.

But I knew that wasn't enough either. I had to see her, put my arms around her, tell her I loved her. So a week later I flew to New York. I wanted to see my publisher anyway. I took a Carey Bus from La Guardia to the Empire Hotel near Lincoln Center. I ate a sandwich and an apple that I'd brought with me and then walked all the way down to Washington Square, Chesterfield's guitar in one hand and my map in the other, switching them from time to time as the guitar got heavier and heavier. I wanted to hear Cliff Johnson at the Café Bizarre on Third Street. I'd met Cliff a couple of times at the Old Town School and thought I might get a chance to sit in, but it didn't work out that way. He was already stoned when he came out onstage and had lost all self-control. He was openly contemptuous of the opening act, a couple of old folkies, he called them, who sounded like metronomes and who smiled all the time and wanted everyone to like them. "To hell with them," he kept saying, "and would one of you Midwesterners from Iowa or Illinois please bring me a drink—preferably brandy?" And somebody would. I thought Cliff could have used a metronome himself. He couldn't hold a beat and he couldn't manage to get to the end of a song. He'd just stop in the middle of a song, have another drink, and start playing something else.

I sat with Herb and Mary Chappel—the two old folkies who'd opened the show. We left before the end of the first set and went for a drink at a bar where there wasn't any music, and Herb and Mary, who were in fact from downstate Illinois but who'd spent a lot of time in New York, got into an argument about the best way for me to get from Washington Heights to La Guardia the next afternoon. Herb wanted me to take the A train to Times Square, transfer to the seven out to Queens, and then take the shuttle bus from Roosevelt Avenue. Mary thought I should take the IRT to Times Square and then the R to Astoria Boulevard and take the shuttle from there. They sketched out their respective proposals on paper napkins and weren't speaking to each other by the end of the evening. I walked up Broadway, through Times Square, through the theater district, all the way back to the hotel, about three miles. I was tired, but I needed to clear my head. In front of the hotel the doorman grabbed my guitar and carried it in for me. I gave him a dollar.

In the morning at Oak Publications, on West Sixtieth Street, I met with my publisher, Irwin Silber, and with my new editor—my old editor had moved to London. *Down-Home Blues* was in its fourth printing and I wanted to negotiate a bigger budget for *Down-Home Blues II*—more money for photos and for some studio time for recording the instruction tape. The first tape, which had been recorded in the back room of Sam's Record Emporium, was fine, but I wanted to get a better sound for *Down-Home Blues II*. The meeting went well, and as I was leaving I got more conflicting advice on how to get to La Guardia from Washington Heights, first from the secretary and then from the doorman back at the hotel.

I took the IRT, missed my stop at 191st Street, rode all the way to the end of the line, which is in the Bronx, stayed on the train, and then rode back. It wasn't even noon yet. I told myself I should have gone to the Metropolitan Museum, or to the New York Public Library; that I should have walked in Central Park or taken the ferry over to a new guitar place I'd heard about, Mandolin Brothers on Staten Island. Instead I walked up and down Audubon Avenue in front of George Washington High School, carrying my guitar and my overnight bag. At one o'clock I decided I'd go into the school and ask to see my daughter, but a policeman who'd been watching me from his post at the main door looked me up and down and told me to get lost.

What was I going to say to Cozy anyway? What did I want to happen? When she saw me, would she run toward me in slow motion, a smile lighting up her face? What if I missed her after school? Why hadn't I called? Did *she* need *me*, or did *I* need *her*? I remembered watching the school in Madison, waiting with my little spy camera for Cozy to come out. I was lucky I hadn't been arrested.

I walked back to 191st Street and bought an apple and a couple of candy bars at a Greek grocery store. It was too cold to play my guitar, but I sat on a bench for a few minutes and studied my map while I ate the apple and the candy bars. I tossed half the second candy bar, a Butterfinger, to a stray dog that had decided to keep me company—some kind of mix between a shepherd and a husky. I held out the back of my hand and she sniffed it and then licked it, and then I put my hands on the thick ruff around her neck and kept them there—to warm them up. The dog followed me back to Audubon Avenue and then took off. It was cold, and I was pretty well frozen by the time school finally got out and kids erupted out of the two main entrances. I stood up on tiptoe. As long as Cozy headed for the nearest subway station, I was sure I'd find her.

A lot of the kids stopped to light up cigarettes the minute they got out the door, blocking the way for others and slowing down the exodus. Cozy was among them, in a red jacket, her head bent forward, tossing away one match, then another, then tipping her head back to let out the smoke from the first drag. I headed toward her, like a salmon swimming upstream through a river of students—a salmon carrying a guitar and an overnight bag. I lost sight of her for a minute, but then I found her again, saw her push the hood on her coat back and give her head a shake. She didn't recognize me at first and shook my hand loose from her jacket when I reached out and touched her arm.

"Cozy."

She stared for a few seconds. "Daddy?"

"Yes, it's me."

She dropped the cigarette and put her hand over her heart. "You scared me. What are you doing here?"

"I had to come to New York on business, so I thought I'd stop by."

"Is something wrong?"

"No, no. Nothing's wrong. I just wanted to see you. Well, *something's* wrong: I was afraid, Cozy. I couldn't stand to think you were so unhappy. I wanted to see you."

"I'm sorry, Daddy. Mama says I'm just feeling sorry for myself."

"Are you?"

She started to cry. I set my guitar and my overnight bag down and put my arms around her. The crowd flowed around us, brushing against us. I tried to fix her face in my mind.

"You should have a warmer coat."

"You sound like Grandma."

I pushed her away and looked at her and then pulled her back again. I kissed the top of her head, where her cornrows lay along her scalp like ropes before breaking free and curling down around her neck.

"Hold on to my arm," I said. I picked up my things and we walked back to the bench, out of the flow of students. Cozy took an envelope out of her satchel. She was going to enter a French competition, she said, a *concours*. She showed me the purple sheet with the contest rules listed on it. The winners from around the city got to go on a trip to Quebec.

"How's your paper coming?"

"Miss Hanson says that the first version of *Imitation of Life* is going to be on TV next week. It'll be on real late, but Mama says I can stay up and watch. Grandma's going to watch it too."

Do you know what really worried me?"

She shook her head.

"When you wrote to me that you didn't think you'd ever be able to be happy. Do you still feel that way?"

She put her head down but didn't say anything. I wanted to tell her what Reverend Taylor had told me, that she was one of God's children just like everyone else, and that she had just as much right as anyone else to be happy. Or to be sad or angry, or whatever she wanted to be. But I'd already told her that in my letter, and then I suddenly remembered something I'd seen on my way out to the airport.

"You want to know something I saw painted on the side of a car in Chicago?" I said.

She shrugged her shoulders.

"'Sometimes I go about pitying myself, and all the while I am being carried on great winds across the sky.'"

She stopped and looked at me. "What?"

"'Sometimes I go about pitying myself, and all the while I am being carried on great winds across the sky.' It was painted on the side of an old beat-up car, and there were two girls in the front seat. They looked like a couple of hippies. The car was painted all different colors. I drove along beside them for a while. I wanted them to look at me and smile, but they were too busy talking to each other and laughing. I fell in love with both of them. I knew they were beautiful people."

"What happened?"

"I had to get off the expressway to go to O'Hare, and they kept on going."

"Why didn't you follow them?"

"Well, I don't know. I might have if I hadn't been coming to see you."

"Do you think *we're* being carried by great winds across the sky?"

"I'm sure of it," I said.

She put her satchel down and spread her arms out, like wings. The policeman who'd told me to get lost was strolling along the sidewalk toward us.

"I'm sure of something else too," I said. "That you're my daughter and I love you. Nothing can change that."

"Did you love Mama when you—you know."

"Yes I did."

"But you couldn't get married."

"No. I thought we could, but I guess we couldn't."

"What was it like?"

"What?"

"Being up on the tower?"

"Well, it was great, really. It was fantastic. Like the poem you sent me that you had to memorize for your French class. I taped it up on my refrigerator. I couldn't figure it all out. You'll have to help me."

"*Brise Marine*?"

"That's the one. You can almost see the lake, out past the dunes, and hear the call of the sailors. But it was more than that. It was like taking my life in my own hands. It was all mixed up with the junior class play. We were reading Ayn Rand and Camus and we wanted to do something existential."

"Fuck this town," she said.

"That was your mama's idea."

"Fuck this town," she said again.

"You like saying that?"

"It feels good," she said.

The dog who'd followed me back from 191st Street came up to the bench and looked at us. Cozy reached out and scratched her ears.

"Still going to be a vet?" I asked.

"Mr. Jordan said it's really hard to get into vet school. He said I could get into Tuskegee for sure, but that I'd probably be better off at the University of Pennsylvania or Wisconsin."

"It's probably easier to get along with animals than with people."

She looked at me and rolled her eyes. "That's a common misconception about vets."

"You don't have a dog, do you? Or a cat?"

"No."

"Maybe that explains it!"

Silence. "Why do they call it a *cat*walk?"

"What?"

"A *cat*walk. You know, on a water tower. Like *cat*house, you know. It's not like it's a house for cats."

"I don't know. Maybe it's because cats are pretty surefooted."

"Did you and Mama do it up on the catwalk?"

"I don't think we should be talking about this."

"That's what Mama always says."

"Maybe she's right."

"Why did you change what Mama said?"

"On the water tower?"

"You painted over it so it said, *'Evoke this town.'*"

"Well, I didn't think that what she wrote was very nice, do you?"

"Is that why you changed it?"

"I think that's why I did it at the time. But at the time . . . I didn't understand how . . . well, that she might feel so different; that she'd see things so differently. I still thought it was the Garden of Eden."

"And Mama?"

"I think she thought that too till she got to be your age, and we started having the school dances. I think that's when she started to feel . . ."

"Like she didn't fit?"

"I suppose. But I didn't really understand that till your mama and I got together in a bowling alley in Madison. That had to be in 1964. Almost eight years ago."

"Do you still think it was the Garden of Eden?"

"It's hard to say, Cozy. When I went into the Navy I swore I'd never go back. But then I missed home. But I could never see it the same way. It was like I had some kind of double vision and I'd see the Garden of Eden and what your grandma called 'de ol' plantation.' I could never see one without the other."

"Like sometimes when you wake up and you see things double?"

"Right." I put my arm around her. "It's cold, isn't it? Do you want to go inside somewhere?" I pulled her toward me.

"There's a Greek restaurant by the subway where you can get coffee."

The policeman who'd been strolling up and down now approached. "Everything all right here?"

"Yes," I said. "Everything's fine."

"Is this man bothering you?" he said to Cozy.

"No, it's all right," she said.

"You just let out a holler if you need any help," he said, putting one hand on his baton.

We walked to the Greek place by the subway. Cozy ordered a Coke and I asked for coffee, and I got out my map and opened it up on the table. "I've got to get to La Guardia," I said. The waitress brought the Coke and the coffee. Cozy sipped her Coke. "You know that policeman couldn't see us," I said. "No one could see who we really are, or know what's really going on. All the important things are hidden. Even if they took off our clothes, we'd still be hidden, invisible. All the important things are invisible."

"They could see our skin," Cozy said. "That's pretty important."

"Hmmm," I said. "You're right; but . . ." Something in me wanted to challenge her, but I didn't know how to explain what I wanted to say. I opened up the map and began to study it. "The problem is . . . ," I said.

She leaned forward, holding her Coke in both hands, waiting for me to explain what I'd tried to explain to myself over the years. But what did I know now that I hadn't known yesterday, or hadn't known this morning? That the bonds that linked us could not be broken now? That I would always be her father? That we'd come right up to the edge of understanding and could see where we were going even though we weren't sure just how we'd get there?

"Has anyone ever told you how beautiful you are?" I said.

She looked down into her Coke glass. "Thousands," she mumbled into the glass.

"What?"

"Thousands."

"Thousands?"

"Thousands of people have told me."

"Oh," I said. I don't know why I was expecting her to say something different. "I've got to get going or I'll miss my plane. You got any theories about how to get to La Guardia from here?"

"Come with me on the subway," she said. "I get off at a Hundred Thirty-eighth Street, but you'll stay on till you get to Times Square, and then you can take a bus from the Port Authority."

On the subway she made me repeat the directions: "Get off at Times Square and walk to the Port Authority." But then instead of getting off at 138th Street, she stayed on the train with me all the way to Times Square and then walked me down Forty-second Street, looking neither to the right nor to the left at the sex shops and X-rated movie houses, to the Port Authority Terminal, where she waited with me till I was safely on the bus to La Guardia.

12

Babette's Feast

1973

BY THE FALL of 1973 I was doing quite a bit of traveling, and in December I made my first West Coast trip, working my way up from Los Angeles to Seattle. The Arab oil embargo made finding gas a little dicey, but I didn't miss any dates—twenty-two gigs in twenty-four days: coffeehouses, open mike features, small clubs, but mostly campus gigs, which paid pretty good money, though I had to do a couple of frat parties, which everyone dreads. Stephanie, who had a lot of connections in the business, did all the bookings for me, and I was giving her 10 percent of the take. My last gig was in Salt Lake City, on the way home. I didn't stick around afterward, because a cold front was moving down from Canada. I was worried about snow, so I drove all night; but I-70 was still clear when I got to the Eisenhower Memorial Tunnel, about forty miles west of Denver, and went under the Continental Divide.

My billfold was stuffed with checks, and the secret compartment that Reverend Taylor had built for me in the back of the hearse was stuffed with cash and silver from tips and cassette sales. I was pleased with myself, but I was lonely too, and about two hours later when I dozed off and almost went off the road, my heart seized up the way it had when I'd seen the light in my mother's window at three o'clock in the morning. I rolled the window down and let the cold air wash over my face, but it wasn't enough, so I pulled off on one of those ramps for trucks that have lost their brakes and waited for the sun to come up. I'm not a philosopher, but I think that some experiences offer us clues: sexual intercourse with someone you love; walking in the woods; eating the first peach of the season, or the last apple; driving across the Golden Gate Bridge, or climbing the water tower in the dark; playing the blues in front of some people who want to listen to you; or holding your daughter in your arms. But I thought that the loneliness I experienced on the road was an even more important clue. It wasn't actually loneliness, really; it was more like the two-note intervals that Reverend Taylor used to use in his guitar breaks, like double stops on a fiddle, or the drone of a bagpipe, or the intervals in a lot of medieval music. You need three notes to define a chord, and when you leave one of those notes out you can't pin the chord down anymore; you take the music down to a place where you can no longer say major or minor, four-chord or five-chord. Whatever I experienced on the road was like this. I couldn't place it, couldn't nail it down, couldn't say, "This is loneliness," or, "This is joy." I had been true to my calling, my vocation, and I thought that this loneliness, if that's what it was, was my reward. If only I could interpret it correctly.

By the time the sun came up I realized that the heater had stopped working. I was freezing. I stopped at a Chevron station on the outskirts of Denver to have it looked at. I figured a hose must have come loose, but it turned out I needed a new water pump, so I slept in the back of the hearse for four hours while the mechanic put in a new pump, and then drove on to Appleton. I'd been planning to stop in Chicago to touch base with Reverend Taylor and to check my box at the post office in case there was a letter from Cozy, who was filling out college applications. Corinna wanted her to go to City College, so she could live at home, but I was pulling for the University of Wisconsin. But it was Christmas Eve, so I just stayed on 80 till I hit 94 east of Gary and followed 94 all the way home.

My mother had sold the orchards in October, at the end of apple season. She'd gotten a good price, too. A commodities trader from Chicago had bought the orchards and a whole section—640 acres, mostly timber—on the other side of the river, land that had been in the Potter family since the early part of the century. A crew of carpenters had fixed up the big house; masons had tuck-pointed the walls of the house and the big stone wall that ran along Appleton Road. Security cameras had been installed at the main gate halfway between Kruger Road and Coop's Bridge. The new owner had been seen once or twice biking by the packing shed with his wife. But the really astonishing thing was that my mother was planning a trip to France with the money from the sale. This was stunning news. "See Naples and die," she said on the phone when I called her from Salt Lake, "only for me it's Paris." But she fretted a little about spending the money, worried about leaving a chunk for me, especially now that I was no longer working for the RPO. She couldn't believe that I was actually making a living as a musician.

She was in the kitchen when I got home. "You don't have the storm windows on yet," I said, leaning over to kiss her on the little landing at the top of the basement stairs.

"Barent's going to do it; he just hasn't gotten around to it yet." An old *Ladies' Home Journal* was on the kitchen table along with travel brochures about France. "I saved this," she said, picking up the magazine. There was a picture of Marlene Dietrich on the cover, smoking a cigarette with a long white filter. "It's from June 1950.

There's a story in it by Karen Blixen—she called herself Isak Dinesen—that I liked, about a special dinner. I've always wanted to try it, but your father was a meat and potatoes man, you know."

"They had recipes in the story?"

"No, but I've pretty well figured everything out. I just want to do a trial run on these blini tonight. I got some special buckwheat flour at the health food store in Michigan City. I got a box from the grocery store too, just in case."

"Just in case what?"

"It's got different recipes on the side. The sponge has to rise three times. I'm stirring it for the second time. It's such a wonderful story, Marty; you ought to read it. You could read it while I make supper. I thought we'd just have an omelet and a little salad tonight. I just wish you could get good lettuce around here in the winter. They should throw all that iceberg lettuce into the North Atlantic as far as I'm concerned."

"I thought I might put up the storm windows," I said.

"You don't need to do that, Marty. Barent will take care of them."

"It won't take long. Dad put those handles on them so you can put them on from the inside."

"I wanted to wash them first."

"Look, Mom, it's cold in here. You'll be a lot more comfortable with the storm windows up. So what if they're a little dirty?"

"I suppose you're right."

It took only half an hour to put up the unwashed storms, and then we ate an open-faced omelet, with some mushrooms and peppers in it, that my mother called a *piperade,* and then while I changed the furnace filters my mother made a trial run of blini. We'd never had them, so we didn't know what they were supposed to be like, but somehow I didn't think they should be so fat and heavy. Even with caviar and sour cream on top, they were disappointing. Disgusting, in fact.

At first we tried to pretend that they were OK. "Maybe it's supposed to be a combination of hearty peasant food—fat, heavy pancakes—with caviar for a touch of class." My mother had put a small scoop of sour cream on each fat blini and then a smaller scoop of lumpfish caviar. But she was disappointed too. We couldn't even finish one blini apiece.

"This can't be right," she finally admitted, more to herself than to me. "Don't you think they should be more like crepes?"

"I don't know, Mom, but they'll be fine."

In the evening, while my mother did a crossword puzzle and smoked a cigarette, I wrapped the presents I'd brought, including the scrapbook containing everything I'd collected about Cozy. Later on we played some carols. My mother played the piano and I played along on the Nick Lucas, though in almost every carol there was some funny chord that I couldn't pluck out of the air. My mother seemed to be getting smaller. She sat on the piano bench hunched forward, her bifocals on a chain around her neck. She wore a different pair of glasses, with jeweled frames, when she played the piano, which was slightly out of tune.

There was no tree this year. There was a new bookcase in the corner where we usually put the tree. I was tempted to go out and get one, but it was too late, and my heart wasn't in it. Besides, it would have seemed like a criticism. In a way I wished my mother were a religious woman; more active in the church, so she wouldn't be so alone. But she'd stopped going to church after I left home; and I'd known, long before that, that she wasn't a believer, though I was beginning to think that that didn't matter. I didn't tell her that I'd been going to the services at Reverend Taylor's church from time to time. Not because I really believed in anything, but because I wanted to affirm something, if only in a small way, if only by trying to hang on to something that was slipping away. I guess I wanted my mother to affirm something too. But maybe that's what she was doing by going to Paris.

I put my guitar away, but she kept playing while I lay on the couch and read the story in the *Ladies' Home Journal*. She played

Chopin's "Ocean Étude," which had been too difficult for me, and then she played *The Harmonious Blacksmith*, a piece I'd played at my recital my junior year. Nothing could have been further from the blues than *The Harmonious Blacksmith*, but all music has its own intensity, and when she got to the last movement, the presto, I thought about my old piano teacher, Roy Haptonstahl, who had married and moved away, and I remembered what my father had said about their trip to Lyon and Healy to pick out a piano.

A clock chimed in the story I was reading, and suddenly I missed the sound of my mother's French clock. It was a small black mantel clock with a painted panel on the front, a clock with a big sound, like the Nick Lucas. I wound it with the key, which was attached to a knob at the back with a bit of wire. I turned the hands to the correct time, 9:45, and set the pendulum in motion. At ten o'clock the clock struck four.

"You've got to set the chimes separately," my mother said. "You have to move the hands forward till the chimes are set at the right time and then move the hands backward so *they're* set right."

I fiddled with it for a while and then decided it was too much trouble.

The story in the *Ladies' Home Journal* was about a Frenchwoman who'd worked as a servant during the war—my mother thought it must be the Franco-Prussian War—for two Danish sisters in a remote part of Denmark, two sisters who'd forgone their chances for independent lives by staying with their father, the leader of a strict religious sect. It turns out that the Frenchwoman had once been the chef at a famous restaurant in Paris, and when she wins the French lottery she decides to put on a dinner for the people in this small community. The people (all members of their dead minister's congregation) decide that they'll eat the meal to be polite but that they won't enjoy it, because pleasure is sinful. Petty disagreements surface, but the food and wine are so wonderful that these differences are reconciled, and the guests can't help enjoying themselves. At the end the two sisters ask their servant, Babette, what she's going to do with her winnings from the lottery, where she's going to go. But she's not going to do anything or go anywhere. She's spent everything on the dinner.

This was the dinner that we were going to prepare.

My mother was already starting over with the blini when I came down in the morning, using the same recipe but with buckwheat flour from the box. I looked at the recipes printed on the side of the box. "You know, we could make regular buckwheat pancakes in about five minutes. They couldn't be any worse than those big fat things we had last night." But my mother wanted to give it another shot. Three risings.

I put on a pair of my father's old boots and went out to cut a Christmas tree. The weather was fair and cold—gray and cloudy behind me in the southeast, blue and clear ahead, over the lake. The straw-packed beehives at the edge of the woodlot wore six-inch lids of new snow that crested like breaking waves, and on the path through the woodlot the snow lay in drifts three or four feet deep. I waded through the drifts and then followed the tractor path across a narrow strip of bottom land that was generally planted in corn or soybeans—I could feel the corn stubble beneath my boots—and up the dirt track that angled up the outwash slope to the top of a ridge. My mother had planted the lower part of the slope with McIntosh, grafted onto semi dwarf root systems so you can get more trees per acre. The thick blanket of snow would hold in the moisture and protect the trees from meadow mice and rabbits. The far side of the ridge was planted with Granny Smiths, which were just starting to become popular. The soil was especially good for apples on the lake side of the moraine, where more sand was mixed in with it; but the slopes were steeper and unprotected from the wind. I could see Poesy Chapel Hill.

From a small stand of evergreens—light bluish-green spruces and balsam—that grew farther north between the crest of the hill and the northernmost row of apple trees, I cut a seven-foot cone-shaped white spruce. I lay down on my side and cut it with my father's curved saw, which was a little rusty but still sharp. I walked back through the orchards, which were no longer the Dijksterhuis Orchards but Sunnyhill Farms, dragging the tree behind me through the snow, careless of the new owner.

When I got back my mother told me that the new owner had flown in by helicopter yesterday morning to spend Christmas in the country. She hadn't seen the helicopter but she'd heard it. I found the stand in the basement and mounted the tree. The sponge was on its second rising. My mother was apologizing. "I didn't get a tree this year because I don't like to take it down by myself."

"I'll help you," I said. "I'll come back next week and we'll take it down together. We'll just put a few ornaments on, OK?"

"What about the lights?"

"Yes, and a few lights."

In the *Ladies' Home Journal* story the descriptions of the different dishes were provided by a visiting general—a real gourmet—who had once wanted to marry one of the sisters and who now lived in Paris.

"The first course," my mother said, "is already in the refrigerator: turtle soup. I got the turtle meat at the bowling alley. I didn't think it would be so expensive, but I didn't need that much. All we have to do is heat it up and remember to put the sherry in at the end. Remember 'The Cask of Amontillado'? Amontillado's a kind of sherry." Poe had been my favorite author for a while.

"The blini are the second course: *blinis Demidoff*. And the main course, *la pièce de résistance: cailles en sarcophage*. The quail still have to be boned."

"How are you going to do that?"

"I'm afraid my hands aren't strong enough, so you'll have to help me."

"How do you bone a quail?"

"They're not quail, actually. I got a couple of Cornish game hens. They're a little too big, but they'll have to do. *Cailles en sarcophage*. Quail in a tomb."

"You going to dig a grave?"

"I'm going to make puff pastry tombs. Those Pepperidge Farm frozen shells you can get at the grocery store aren't really big enough for game hens, so I bought a sheet of puff pastry dough from the bakery over in Harbert."

"Have you ever done this before? Boned a Cornish game hen?"

"I used to bone a chicken every once in a while to make a galantine for one of those infernal church suppers. Stuffed with tongue and ham and the chicken meat and green olives. I'd leave the legs on so it would look like a chicken, but you could cut right through it. Those church ladies, though . . . There was always a lot left. Your father didn't really like it either, but he was always polite about eating it."

She got the sheets of puff pastry dough out of the freezer. "We need to make a circle for the base, and then cut some rings to go on top. I've got an old soup can that should be about the right size for the inside of the rings, and I've got a big tomato can we can use for the outer circle."

"I'm surprised you didn't make the dough yourself."

"I thought about it, Marty. I suppose I could have done it; I've tried it a couple of times, but I never got it quite right."

"And I'm surprised you don't have a special tool to cut puff pastry rings."

"It's been so long since I did any serious cooking. Your father, you know, was a meat and potatoes man."

She sprinkled some flour on the table, laid out the sheet of dough, and surveyed it. "Big decisions!" She cut four big circles with the empty tomato can, then cut the center out of two of them with the smaller can. She moistened the third ring with her finger and placed number four on top of it. "What do you think?"

"Looks good to me."

"I think we should put another ring on top so the cases will be higher."

She cut two more big circles, then cut the centers out, moistened the additional rings, and put them on top.

"There's enough dough left for a fourth ring," I said. "You want to make it a little higher?"

"Why not?"

The oven was already on. She greased a baking sheet, put the pastry tombs into the oven, and set the timer for twenty minutes. We waited in silence.

"I suppose I should have made the dough myself," she said, "but you really should have a marble-topped table with a drawer underneath to hold ice. To keep the dough cool."

After twenty minutes she turned the oven down and reset the timer for half an hour. She was nervous. We were both nervous. It was like waiting for the jury to come in with a verdict: *How does the jury find in the case of the puff pastry tombs?*

"I've already made a cake," she says. "The general doesn't say anything about dessert in the story, so I made a Bundt cake with little frosting flowers and a lemon brandy sauce. I poured it in the center. The cake should soak it up. At least I hope so." It's been so long since I did any serious cooking. Your dad was a meat and potatoes man, you know."

"That's the third time you've said that since I got here."

"I'm sorry, Martin. I don't mean to complain."

I boned the game hens with a small Sabatier knife that no one but my mother had ever been allowed to use, following my mother's instructions at every step of the way. It wasn't that hard, actually. You cut down the back, right through the bone; then you cut along the rib cage till you get to the breastbone—you just have to be careful not to break the skin. Then you cut through the wing joints, cut off the wings, and tuck the skin inside. You can do the same thing with the legs, but we decided to leave them on, so that the game hens still looked like game hens.

My mother stuffed them with a sausage stuffing and sewed them up. "The general doesn't say anything about the stuffing," my mother said, "so I'm just using a mixture of pork and veal and apple cooked down in a little brandy."

She punched down the blini dough for a third rising, took the pastry shells out of the oven, put in the game hens, and adjusted the temperature. All we had to do now was heat up the turtle soup, add a bit of sherry, and make the blini while the soup was heating up. My mother had already made a salad and opened the wine. Two bottles of Bordeaux. (I didn't know good wine from bad, but these two bottles, with their sloping shoulders and French labels, looked impressive, imposing.) "I couldn't afford to buy all the wines in the story," my mother said, "but these should be very nice. I had to go to Michigan City to find something this good."

My mother had always kept a bottle of wine in the kitchen, but I don't think I'd ever seen two bottles together like this, side by side, like twin towers.

My mother made the blini in a crepe pan while the game hens were roasting in the oven. *"Voilà,"* she said when the second one— "you always throw the first one away"—turned out perfectly flat and thin. *"Le premier miracle de la journée."*

She topped the blini, three apiece, with dollops of sour cream and small scoops of caviar. Real caviar this time, not the lumpfish caviar we'd used on the practice blini the night before.

She spread a linen cloth over the table in the breakfast nook and arranged the silver and the glasses, one for water, one for wine.

I sat down and she served the soup.

"Bon appetit," my mother said.

"Bon appetit," I replied.

We drank a glass of sherry with the soup, and then my mother rinsed out our wine glasses and brought out the blini. She poured two glasses of the Bordeaux and raised her glass. I raised mine. "To one of the great miracles of nature," she said. I wasn't sure whether she meant the blini or the wine, but I touched my glass to hers. "As great as the miracle of photosynthesis." I wasn't used to hearing my mother talk like this. "Remember how King Arthur always waited for a miracle on Christmas day before he ate?"

I didn't remember very clearly, but I nodded. The blini were wonderful. "How much did you pay for the caviar?" I asked.

She was taking the game hens out of the oven.

"You don't want to know."

She put each game hen in a pastry shell. "They should rest a few minutes," she said. "Your father could never understand why a roast bird needs to sit awhile before you eat it."

She cleared our plates and rinsed them in the sink while the birds were resting.

I poured a little more wine into our glasses.

The game hens, in their puff pastry tombs, were gorgeous, stunning. My mother was delighted, or perhaps relieved. "Just butter and flour," she said, "and a little water. Another miracle, isn't it, Marty? Just look."

We opened our presents in the living room, in front of the tree, disposing of the predictable ones first: guitar strings, Old Spice aftershave (lime), gloves, a shirt, and a tube of some Norwegian hand lotion for me—we both developed painful cracks in our fingers during the winter months; and for my mother, a tiny bottle of Chanel No. 5 and a French scarf (from Marshall Field's), a bottle of Italian olive oil (also from Field's), a new crossword puzzle dictionary, and a book of crossword puzzles in French that I'd found at Kroch and Brentano's on Wabash.

I hadn't told my mother about Cozy, about making contact with the Williamses. I had no idea how she'd react to the scrapbook.

We'd brought our dessert plates and more of the Bundt cake into the living room with us, and my mother still had half a glass of wine. We finished the last crumbs of cake, which was wonderful, and my mother handed me my special present, which was an Omas fountain pen with a special nib for writing music. The nib was much longer and much more flexible than a regular nib, and my mother demonstrated how a professional copyist would hold it: between the first and second fingers. "It's blue celluloid," she said. "Omas lost the secret to making celluloid and then rediscovered it." She kept on talking, as if she were trying to talk me into liking the pen. "I could have gotten a round barrel, but Roy said he thought you'd prefer the faceted barrel. It's not really easier to hold, but it's got a different feel."

"Roy?"

"Roy Haptonstahl. I wrote to him in Cincinnati to ask where I could get a music writing pen, since I know you're writing down all those old songs, and you do it so beautifully." (It was true: I'd written out by hand all the music for *Down-Home Blues*.) "He got it for me, at a pen store in Cincinnati. They had to special-order it."

The pen was so beautiful it brought tears to my eyes. I'd bought the Waterman pen for Cozy, so I was pretty sure she'd spent too much for this one.

"It comes with a leather case," she said, "for carrying it in your pocket. I got some staff paper too, but I didn't wrap it up. I think I put it in the piano bench. Let me look."

"Mom, it's beautiful, but you shouldn't, I mean you didn't need . . ."

She was lifting the lid of the piano bench. "Don't scold me, Marty. I got a good price for the orchards. I wanted to do it."

"Mom, it's great. I'm overwhelmed."

"I got two bottles of special ink too. I wrapped them up, but I think I left them in the dining room closet with the wrapping paper."

And now. Now I thought that if only my mother and I could

speak openly about what was in our hearts, we could forgive each other for disappointing each other, that we could, well, maybe go on to some other place, travel down the line to the next station, where we'd dispatch the old mail and take on new.

My mother used a pair of scissors to open the package, careful not to tear the silver paper.

"This ought to be a surprise," I said.

"I don't think anything can surprise me anymore, Marty."

"I'll bet I can still surprise you."

She put that package down. "You're not going to tell me that you're getting married, are you? Janis . . .?"

"No, Mom. Not that."

"Is there anyone special?"

"No, Mom. Not now." I didn't mention Stephanie, who was spending Christmas with her parents in Iowa City, because I didn't want to get her hopes up. My own either. "Janis is engaged. Someone in the political science department. Princeton University Press published her dissertation, and she's had a couple of job offers, but she's staying in Kalamazoo."

"Tant pis," my mother said. "I liked Janis a lot, though—I don't mean any harm by this, Marty—I thought her dimes and pennies scheme was . . . I don't know. There was something not right about it. Oh, well, who am I to be disappointed? *Tout comprendre, tout pardonner.* But I guess I don't understand everything."

"Go ahead, open it."

She removed the paper and folded it, and then started to page through the scrapbook.

"It's your granddaughter," I said, not sure she understood. "My daughter." My mother covered her mouth with the tips of her fingers. Her face was pale. I suddenly had to go to the bathroom. I went upstairs, leaving her alone for a little while. There was toothpaste smeared on the sink, a few hairs, gray and black.

My mother was making coffee when I got back downstairs, in

her little French pot with little curving tubes. You put little cups on a little shelf that was part of the pot itself and the coffee came out the tubes into the cups. Her hands were trembling when she picked up the cups and put them on little saucers.

"Well, Grandma," I said when we took our coffee into the living room. "Are you surprised now?"

"I wish your father could see these."

"But what about *you*, Mom?"

"I'm sorry, Martin. I'm sorry I've been such a disappointment to you."

I thought, It's not too late to put things right. That's the goal. But what does it mean to "put things right"? What did I mean by that?

"I wanted you to be happy, and I made you unhappy. I made myself unhappy. I made Roy unhappy; I made your father unhappy."

I sat down next to her on the couch and we turned the pages of the scrapbook together. I'd added some snapshots Cozy'd sent me from New York; all her cards and letters; a postcard of the George Washington Bridge; a copy of her certificate as one of the finalists in the *Concours de français pour débutants,* and a snapshot she'd sent me from Quebec: she's standing in front of a fountain outside the train station.

"She's just had her hair cut short in Quebec," I said. "Cory was furious about her hair," I said. "It's a good thing she didn't see the photo." Cozy is holding a cigarette between her first and second fingers, tilting her head back to exhale, like Marlene Dietrich on the cover of the *Ladies' Home Journal.*

When we came to the last page my mother closed the scrapbook and held it on her lap. "Do you ever talk to her?"

"Corinna?"

"The little girl—Cozy?"

"Yes. Every once in a while. It's a funny thing—we didn't really hit it off till she moved to New York. Then we started corresponding. I think she felt vulnerable. The kids are tougher out there. She got called all kinds of names. She even thought of herself as a tragic mulatta for a while. I was a little worried for a while so I went out to see her."

"The children are the real problem, aren't they, Marty?"

"Mom, Cozy's not a problem. It's people who are a problem. It's not like she's some kind of a freak, for Christ's sake. If people get twitchy because they don't know if she's black or white, who's fault is that?"

"I'm sorry, Marty, I just meant . . ." I took my mother's hand. "When I was a little girl," she said, "my mother kept individual scrapbooks for my sister and me. Your Aunt Alice. She put everything in them: report cards, school programs, vital statistics, birthday parties, piano recitals. We had a record of everything. I always meant to do that for you, but somehow I never got around to it. My life has always been such a jumble. I started one for you; I still have it. I wrote down your first sentence—'Puppy get eggs'—but I never kept it up. And then later, after you left, we were just numb. We couldn't understand it. You could have done anything, Marty. But working for the railroad?"

"The post office," I said.

"Your dad blamed me, and I blamed him. We hardly touched each other for all those years. I was only fifty-six. Your dad was fifty-eight. All of a sudden we were old. I don't think we even kissed each other again till your dad got sick, and then when we left Dr. Arnold's office over in Niles, after we learned about the cancer, we had to wait a long time for the elevator, and your dad asked me for a cigarette. I don't think I'd seen him smoke a cigarette in twenty years, and it made him dizzy. The doctor said we could try chemotherapy, but he didn't think it would do any good. But we could think about it and let him know, and he'd get things moving. We never told you about it, Marty, because—well, I don't know why.

"We got in the car and instead of stopping when we got back home your dad kept on driving, out past the orchards, and then by

Grandpa Dijksterhuis's old place, out past the dump, and on out to the lake. It was like driving backward into the past. We went out to the dunes and took off our shoes and climbed up Old Baldy. Your dad was so short of breath I didn't think he'd make it to the top. He put one hand on my shoulder, and nothing ever felt so good. It was the middle of the week and the middle of September so it wasn't too crowded, just a few couples with portable radios necking back in the woods, just out of plain sight. We just sat there looking at the lake till the sun started going down. I rubbed your dad's back and he ran his fingers through my hair and then Glenn Miller's "In the Mood" came on on somebody's portable radio and Dad said he was in the mood too. He was sick and scared, but he was in the mood anyway, after all those years, so we found our own spot in the woods—you know, down the slope a little on the far side of Old Baldy—and took our clothes off and made love in the sand, just like that. I can still feel how the sand felt on my bottom, cool and sandy. I was sixty-one; your dad was sixty-three; and that was the last time we made love. It was wonderful, really. Better than the first time. And we talked about going to Paris. You know your dad never wanted to go to Paris in his life, any more than he wanted to learn to dance; but he wanted to go then. We'd walk in the Tuileries in the morning and browse at Shakespeare and Company in the afternoon, and in the evening we'd eat at the Café Anglais. You know, that's where Babette, the woman in the story, was chef. We could never have afforded the Café Anglais, of course. Your dad would have had a heart attack. But we could talk about it, or at least I could talk about it, and maybe that was even better.

"I think it must be the different flour," my mother said. "I did everything else the same."

"What are you talking about?"

"I mean the blini. I used flour from the new health food store for the first batch. You'd think the health food store would have better buckwheat flour than you get in the A&P."

"You know what you could do, Mom, for me, while I clean up?"

"You don't have to clean up."

"I know I don't, but I'd like you to record something for Cozy. Maybe something from *The Wind in the Willows,* or one of the Pooh stories. I've brought a cassette recorder along. You could to it in the living room and I'll wash up."

"How about *Babette's Feast?*" she asked. "How old did you say she is?"

"Seventeen last July."

"What do you think? It's too long. I guess it's not such a good idea."

"I think it's a great idea, Mom. Let's do it."

As I washed the dishes I paused from time to time to listen to the sound of my mother's voice in the living room. When my mother came to the end of the story she started to cry, and then she checked herself. She ran the tape back and erased the sound of her crying. *"Tout comprendre, tout pardonner,"* she said. I was standing in the doorway. "That's when I finally understood, Marty. When two people love each other, nothing else should matter."

I didn't quite understand her. "Would you like to see her sometime? I mean, if she came down here with me?"

"Oh, Marty," she said, "I'm so sorry. I'm so sorry."

"I could go to Paris with you," I said.

She stopped crying and started to laugh.

"You don't want to go to Paris any more than your father did."

"I do now," I said.

She laughed some more. "I don't think so, Marty. I think I want to be in Paris alone, just to see what it's like."

13

Matriculation

1974

In September 1974 Cozy took the Twentieth Century Limited from New York to Chicago—with all her stuff. She was going to attend the University of Wisconsin. I met her at the La Salle Street Station and drove her up to Madison. Her stuff included a bicycle, in a shipping box, and her big round bamboo chair, also in a shipping box, and several suitcases, so the hearse was full.

I hadn't seen her since I'd gone out to New York. But I'd seen the picture of her on the trip to Quebec, where she'd had most of her hair cut off. It had grown out to about eight inches and had been twisted into little spiky braids with little glass beads on the ends.

"Too many kids, not enough chaperones," Cozy explained when she saw the look on my face. "That's what Mama said when she saw it."

"Maybe she had a point," I said.

"And maybe not," Cozy said. "She was pretty mad."

"I know. I talked to her right after you got back."

"Um-hmm."

We had to take the bike out of the box in order to fit it into the back of the hearse with the suitcases, but the *papasan* chair was simply too wide, so we tied it on top, upside down, like a Chinese hat.

There had been a hundred kids on the trip to Quebec, she said. A hundred kids, six teachers, and only five parent chaperones, and only two of the chaperones could speak French. "Mama offered me two hundred dollars not to go."

"That's pretty funny," I said. "How much would it have taken?"

"You couldn't have paid me enough to stay home."

"Did you speak French?"

"Yeah, but they talk funny in Quebec."

"Say something in French."

"What?"

"Just something, anything."

"I don't know what to say."

"How about the poem you did for the forensics competition?"

" *Brise Marine* '?"

"That sounds right. I still have it up on my refrigerator."

" *'Mais, ô mon cœur, entends le chant des matelots!'* "

"That's it. Your grandmother would like that poem."

"Grandma doesn't know French."

"Your other grandmother. My mom."

"Oh."

"She always wanted to go to Paris. She was going to go this spring, but I don't think she's going to make it now."

"Why not?"

"She had to have a gallbladder operation in February, and she's tired all the time. She's still talking about going, but . . ." I paused. "I think it would do her good to see you. She'd like to hear you recite that poem. She could speak French with you. It would be better than a trip to Paris. Would you like to do that sometime? Drive down to Appleton? See where your mom grew up? See where your grandmother lived?"

Cozy didn't say anything. We'd crossed the state line at Beloit and were entering a system of ridges and valleys that had not been flattened out by the Wisconsin glacier. We drove for a while without speaking. Cozy kept her face turned away, staring out the window.

"Your mom and I," I said, "were in your grandma's French class for four years. Latin too."

"Yeah, but you should hear Mama when she tries to say something in French!" She made a sour face. "She's worse than the people in Quebec. When we were in Dakar I had to translate everything for her."

I was suddenly overwhelmed by a vision of my mother in Paris: I could *see* her trying to ask directions on the Champs Elysées, or trying to buy a paper at one of those little kiosks on the sidewalks, or to order a meal at the Café Anglais. I could *see* her lips move, and I could *hear* the laughter of the man on the street whom she's asked for directions, of the man in the kiosk, of the waiter. An old woman trying to make herself understood in a foreign language. I'd never been a good student, but I'd always thought she spoke beautifully, standing in front of the class saying, *"œuf, œuf, œuf,"* and making us say it after her until we got it right. *Egg, egg, egg.*

We stopped for gas at a Standard station just before the state line. I paid with a credit card and then went to the men's room. When I came out, Cozy was sitting behind the wheel, her arm out the window.

"Have you got your license?"

"Want to see it, Officer?"

"Fifty-five miles an hour, OK?"

"Right, Officer."

We drove in silence for a while, past Beloit and Janesville.

"You know what you'll be taking?"

"French, biology, physics. An elective."

"You want to keep it down to fifty-five."

"Yes, Officer."

"I'm not an officer; I'm your father."

"Yes sir."

"Can you see behind you OK? You might want to adjust the outside mirror."

"I can see OK."

"This side too?"

"OK."

"You got a sweetheart you're leaving behind?"

She gave me a sideways glance and rolled her eyes.

"It's a legitimate question."

"Do *you* have a girlfriend?"

"Sort of. She lives in Madison."

"In Madison? No wonder you wanted to drive me up. Are you going to see her tonight?"

"I might."

"You are, aren't you?"

"So?"

"Do you love her?"

"Yes I do," I said, "but I'm trying to be sensible about it instead of crazy."

"Is that good?"

"I think so. Right up there with having a sense of humor."

"Are you going to sleep with her tonight?"

"'If you mind your own business,'" I said, "'then you won't be worryin' about mine.'"

"That's what Mama always says."

"Well, your mama knows what she's talking about."

"Will I get to meet her?"

"Probably not tonight. You've got a dorm meeting tonight, and then a mixer. But soon, OK?"

She nodded. "Next time?"

We caught a glimpse of the capitol dome from the new highway across Lake Monona.

"Next time," I said. I got the campus map out of the glove compartment "We want to take Broom, and then University. University will get us in the general vicinity, and then you want to watch for Charter." I knew my way downtown and around the main campus, but I'd never been back by the women's dorms.

"I know the way," she said. "I lived here for most of my life."

"You want to drive by your old house?"

"Maybe later."

The small parking lot behind Elizabeth Waters, which Cozy called 'Liz Waters,' was crowded, but there was a lot of coming and going, and we found a space for the hearse. Cozy's room, on the third floor, did not have a view of the lake, but from the student lounge you could see sailboats and catch a glimpse of the Memorial Union Terrace.

The room was much like the one I'd visited with my mother at the University of Chicago: bunk beds, two desks, two closets with built-in dressers, two chairs with plastic cushions. We set up Cozy's *papasan* chair in front of the window and carted her bike down to a storage locker in the basement, next to a laundry room with long rows of coin-operated washers and dryers.

I made a trip to a hardware store for plastic anchors and picture hooks, so Cozy could hang her pictures, and when I got back her roommate had arrived. A large bowl of grapes was on the desk by the door. Everyone was eating them, so I ate some too.

Roommate's mother, a large handsome woman about three or four shades darker than Cozy, looked at me and then at Cozy. "This your daddy?"

"Yes."

"Honky in the woodpile." Everyone stopped eating grapes. "Y'all can laugh," she said, when nobody did.

"Mama, remember what I said."

"And what was that, honey?"

I shook hands with roommate's father, who introduced himself as Jason Moore.

"You folks from around here?" he asked.

"She's from Harlem, Jason," his wife interrupted, "up around City College. We got all that information from the school. Her mama runs a beauty salon on Lenox Avenue. But you used to live right here in Madison, isn't that right, Carolyn, honey?" I was startled to hear Cozy's given name. I'd almost forgotten it.

"Everybody calls me Cozy," Cozy said.

"We're from Philadelphia," Mrs. Moore said, looking at me, "but we get up to New York quite a bit. We wanted Samantha to come to the Midwest. Wisconsin seemed like a pretty good place. Madison's about as liberal a place as you'll find, if you know what I mean."

"It's so damn liberal they bombed the mathematics building a couple of years ago," her husband said.

"I thought we agreed not to discuss that anymore? Besides, it was the *Army* Math Building."

"I'm just saying, you can't get any more liberal than that."

"You gonna fix that toilet paper holder in the bathroom?"

"I'm sure the maintenance staff will fix it. Just leave them a note."

"Could you please just take a look at it, Jason? It's Saturday and they're not going to come today or tomorrow."

"It just needs a little set screw," Jason reported from the bathroom. "That outside holder fits over a brace that's attached to the wall. I'll have to go find a hardware store."

"I'll go with you," I said. "I know the way."

Jason was impressed with the hearse. "Down-home Blues, Inc.," he read aloud. "Sammy told me you were some kind of musician," he said, "but I didn't believe her. Got any records out that I might have heard?"

"Not yet," I said, "but I've got a deal lined up with a small label in Chicago. Actually, I cut an album for them with Juke Phillips a couple of years ago."

"Beautiful campus," he said.

"You come out to visit?"

"Yeah. Twice. You?"

"Cozy used to live in Madison."

"What about her mother?"

"We don't really live together."

"You married?"

"No."

"Sugar daddy?"

"No, nothing like that."

"How about you?"

"I'm married." He laughed. "Drainage engineer."

"You drain swamps?"

"Mostly parking lots. You take your big airports. Now JFK, you can just run everything off into Jamaica Bay; or at Philly International, you got the Delaware River. But at O'Hare, down in Chicago, you got almost nine square miles of solid concrete. When it rains, that water's got to go somewhere or you'll have yourself one big lake."

"So you put in drains?"

"Well, we don't put them in. We tell other people where to put them in, and how big they've got to be, and where they've got to go. So you've got to calculate the area, and you've got to figure your gradients—you don't want all those lots level, you want them sloped a little. Well, the angle of the slope's going to determine how fast the water runs down and where it's going to go, you see what I mean? And you've got to worry about the floodplain too. If you want to build in the floodplain, you've got to dump a lot of fill in there so it isn't the floodplain anymore, you see what I mean? You may be sit-

ting high and dry because that water's going to run down somewhere else, and that somewhere else is going to be the floodplain.
Well, if somebody else's house is in the floodplain, they're not going
to be too happy having all that water coming into their basement.
They're going to squawk to the city council or the county commis-
sioners, depending on what kind of city government they've got. Illinois has—"

"I get the general idea. Whatever you do, the water's going to
run downhill to the lowest place."

"Right, so you've got to make sure that nobody's living in that
lowest place, or they'll get flooded out every time it rains."

"Kind of like society itself."

"Exactly my point. You always got some people living in the
floodplain, and somebody's got to look out for those people."

"That's you?"

"That's me. But people are funny. All around O'Hare, say, you've
got open spaces. That's the floodplain. But then somebody starts
dumping fill in an empty lot. Well, when he gets enough fill in there,
he's out of the floodplain, but now somebody else's in it."

We were heading back to the dorm with an assortment of set
screws and a little tool kit I'd bought for Cozy. "I see what you
mean," I said.

By the time we got there Samantha's mother had replaced the curtains; the beds had been made up; two of Cozy's bird drawings were
hanging on the wall over the two desks. A red-winged blackbird and
a small finch of some kind. It was getting late and the girls were getting ready for an orientation meeting. Then dinner in the dining hall,
then a mixer in the evening. I had memorized the schedule.

I knew that when people come too close for a moment, they generally pull back, and I knew that it worked the other way around
too, that when people have pulled away from each other, they experience an inner impulse to come back together. But I didn't know
where I stood with Cozy at the moment. She and Samantha were

dressed almost identically: too tight jeans, men's white shirts with the sleeves rolled up, bright red lipstick.

"Do you want me to stick around?" I asked.

She hesitated for a fraction of a second. "Naw, I'll be all right." But that hesitation was enough to for me, and before she was even out the door I started to play it over and over in my imagination, like a new riff that I wanted to learn.

"Be sure you close the door when you leave," Sammy said to her mother, holding up her keys. "It'll lock. I'll see you in the morning." They were staying in a motel and driving back to Philadelphia in the morning.

Samantha's mother sat on the bed and cried while her husband and I fixed the toilet paper holder. The tiny set screw kept falling on the floor, but finally we got it in and I tightened it with a little screwdriver from the kit I'd bought for Cozy.

About six weeks later, toward the end of October, Uncle Barent—Lotte's dad—called to say that my mother had had a heart attack and was in serious condition in the hospital. The first thing I thought of was how Reverend Taylor and I had seen the light in her window at three in the morning when we were driving back from Newport, back in 1964. The second thing I thought of was that she wasn't going to make it to Paris.

It was seven o'clock in the evening. I called Cozy and asked if she wanted to go with me to Appleton—I could pick her up in Madison in about two hours and then we'd drive down to Michigan—but she couldn't do it. She had a midterm exam coming up; and a paper; and Alexander Solzhenitsyn was going to be giving a reading on campus.

"OK," I said. "I just thought . . ."

I was packing a few things in my old RPO grip when the phone rang. It was Cozy calling back. Her boyfriend would drive her down to Chicago. It would save time. It was the first I'd heard about a boyfriend. I finished packing and picked up the Nick Lucas, which I was going to take with me, and played for a while, and then I called Reverend Taylor.

"You want me to come with you?" he asked.

"No, no, Reverend Taylor. Cozy's coming down from Madison. She's going to go with me. I just wanted to hear your voice."

"Martin, ain't nothing I can say to you now that you don't already know, but I see that as a good sign."

"A sign of what?"

"It's just a sign, Martin; it ain't a sign something else; it's a sign of itself."

"Reverend Taylor," I said, "I know that."

I knew that Reverend Taylor would pray for my mother, but I didn't want to ask him outright.

Cozy and her boyfriend got to Chicago about eleven o'clock. I offered them a quick cup of coffee and a sandwich, but the boyfriend, who was as dark as Cory, was in a hurry to get back. Cozy leaned over, stuck her head through the window of his battered Ford Fairlane, and gave him a discreet kiss on his cheek.

"He seems like a nice young man," I said.

Cozy gave me a sideways look and rolled her eyes. "Looks like rain," she said.

We took Stony Island to the Skyway. "This is the route we used to take into Chicago," I said, "when I was a kid."

"Where are we now?"

"We're almost in Indiana. This all used to be wetlands; now it's all steel mills, but they're starting to close down.

"What are all those fires?"

"Those are the exhaust fumes from the refineries. They burn them off. Makes me think of Mordor in *The Lord of the Rings*."

"I haven't gotten that far yet," she said.

We took the toll road to 94. "Before they built I-94," I said, "we used to take Twelve and Twenty, and my dad would always say that it was the most dangerous stretch of highway in the United States. More accidents per mile."

"Is it still the most dangerous?"

"For me it's the highway that links past and present. I'm going backward now, and you're going with me. That's pretty dangerous. You know, US 12 goes all the way up to Madison. I just thought of that. The first time I saw your mom after she left Appleton was in a bowling alley on US 12. Lake Wingra Lanes, something like that."

"We had a bowling party there on my birthday once," she said, "but I don't think it's there anymore."

"Too bad."

The storm that had been threatening broke over us. The wipers couldn't keep up. I pulled off the highway at Chesterton and we waited out the storm at a Standard station, letting the rain hammer down on us. We could see a neon motel light blinking on and off, chartreuse and bright pink, but not much else.

"Does your mom know I'm coming?"

"No. I couldn't talk to her."

"Do you think she'll be mad?"

"No, I don't think so."

"Did she want me to come before?"

"I think so."

"Hmmm."

"But I think she was afraid too; afraid it would be too painful."

"And it's not going to painful now?"

"Cozy, I don't know. I've been over it so many times in my mind."

"She must have said something. When she saw the scrapbook. Did she like the pictures?"

"She liked the one of you smoking a cigarette! She always smoked, you know, French cigarettes, not Gauloises, but something pretty strong. Gitanes, something like that."

"Oh God, Mama would have a conniption fit if she saw that."

"Were you trying to look like Jean Harlow in *Hell's Angels*?" I did an imitation of Jean Harlow smoking an imaginary cigarette, drawing imaginary smoke deep into my lungs.

"Who's Jean Harlow?" she asked.

"She was in a film called *Hell's Angels*. Your mom used to imitate her when she smoked."

"I didn't know Mama smoked."

"I guess she doesn't, now."

The rain had stopped. The hearse started right up, and we were off.

It was after two when we got to Appleton. The stoplight in the center of town was blinking. Orange for M-60. Red for Main Street.

"Population eighteen hundred and sixty-two," Cozy said, reading the sign at the city limits.

"It gets smaller every year," I said. "It was two thousand when I joined the Navy in 1956."

"What do people *do*?"

"They farm—celery, blueberries, corn, peaches, and apples. There's a Gerber baby food plant. The Featherbone Company moved out about ten years ago."

"What's *featherbone* anyway?"

"Mr. Potter figured out a way to use the spines of turkey feathers to make corset stays. Instead of whalebone. It was a lot cheaper. They made buggy whips too. Potter made a fortune. During the Spanish-American War there was a competition to see which town or city could contribute the most money per capita to the war effort; Mr. Potter gave so much money that Appleton won. We got a cannon from Admiral Dewey's flagship, and President McKinley came to town.

"The farm equipment dealership on M-60's closed. The Texaco station's closed. There used to be a DX station across from the depot, but that closed before I got out of the Navy. There isn't a full service gas station anymore. The Oriental Theater shows films every night during the summer, for the tourists from the resort towns along the lake, but only on weekends during the rest of the year. Look, it's showing *Thunderball*. We could see that tomorrow night. If you want to."

"I've already seen it," she said. "When you were in the Navy did you ever do underwater stuff like James Bond?"

"I was a cook," I said.

"Oh."

"I could scramble eggs for four hundred sailors."

"How?"

"I'd break the eggs into a huge bowl, two at a time, one in each hand, and then I'd cook them in a big copper with a steam jacket. They'd get a little watery in the steam tables, and the men would complain that they were powered eggs, but they weren't; they were real eggs. You stirred them with a paddle."

She looked at me as I took my hands off the wheel and demonstrated the twisting motion you used with the paddle to scramble the eggs.

"Were you on a ship?"

"Part of the time, but it didn't matter. You cooked the eggs the same way."

She leaned forward and looked out the front window—out and up. "Can we stop and see the water tower up close?"

I pulled over in front of the Harrison Ford agency. We got out of the hearse and crossed the street. The gate of the chain-link fence was locked with a chain. The factory yard needed mowing. The buckeye trees blacked out the moon.

"It's empty," Cozy said.

"It is," I said. "The factory moved to Georgia about ten years ago. They make baby clothes now. You can buy them at Sears." We looked up at the tower. "They took the ladder down after your mom and I climbed it. The ladder up to the catwalk is still there, though. It's hard to see at night."

Cozy looked up. Much of the tower was blocked by the trees,

which hadn't shed all their leaves yet. "You can see a little better from across the street." We went back to the hearse and looked up. You could see the tank itself rising over the tops of the trees. It was too dark to see the faded letters, but I could see them in my imagination:

EVOKE THIS TOWN.

"You see the old depot?" I said, as we crossed the tracks. "It used to be full of rare books. The man who owned it was one of my mother's friends. He sold to dealers. Wholesale. Collectors. He sold his whole catalogue to Yale University one time. Someone called up and bought every book in the catalogue!"

We pulled into the drive at Dijksterhuis Corners. The big spirea hedge that separated our house from Uncle Piet's old house was bare now. The spruce trees that had been ten feet tall when I was a boy towered above the house. The garage doors were closed. A shag bark hickory next to the garage had fallen over, nicking the roof. One of the limbs was blocking the door on the right side, where my mother kept her Chevy. How long had it been there? I opened the back door with my key and climbed the three steps up to the kitchen. Everything was neat, in order. A new gas range had replaced the old electric one. The refrigerator hummed. I sat down in the breakfast nook. The table needed a new coat of the shiny deep blue enamel that my mother liked. Cozy sat across from me. In the morning I'd show her the pencil marks on the doorjamb where my folks had measured me on my birthday every year.

"It'll be all right," she said. "In the morning."

"You want something?" I asked. "Tea? Hot chocolate?" I opened the refrigerator. Only a few things: catsup, Dijon mustard, bottles of pills, vitamins, a pitcher of orange juice with a plastic shower cap over the top, a bottle of white wine on its side, the cork jammed halfway in.

"Orange juice? A glass of white wine?"

"You're tired," she said. "Let's get some sleep."

The double bed in the guest room was made up. I pulled back the ridged bedspread and fluffed the pillows.

I looked in my mother's room. Her own double bed had been made. Where had she been when the ambulance came? What had happened? Wouldn't *something* be out of order? Had she straightened everything up and then called the ambulance? Was she frightened now? I knew now that she didn't believe in God. In a town where everybody else did. But maybe they didn't either. Maybe they just pretended.

Cozy put on her pajamas and brushed her teeth in the bathroom.

"My mother used to read to me every night," I said. "I always thought if I had children, I'd read to them every night too."

"You could read to me tonight, but not too long."

"What would you like? What kind of stories do you like?"

"Just pick something."

When I came back with *The Wind in the Willows* she was asleep, but I sat on the edge of the bed anyway and read the chapter where the comforts of home are weighed against the call of the open road. "'Tis but the banging of a door behind you, a blithesome step forward, and you are out of the old life and into the new."

In the morning I spoke to my mother for the last time, in St. Anthony's Hospital in Michigan City. A Catholic hospital. Nuns. A crucifix on the wall. Why had they brought her here instead to Pawating Hospital in Niles? She opened her eyes when I told her that I loved her and that I'd brought Cozy to see her; but I wasn't sure she understood what I was saying. Her lips moved and I bent down to hear her, but all I could hear was Cozy sipping Coke through a straw.

"Say something to her in French," I said.

She put her plastic cup of Coke down on the table next to the bed. "Grand-mère," she said, *"je viens vous voir.* It's Cozy. *Votre petite-fille."*

"Take her hand," I said. Once again, my mother opened her eyes and moved her lips. "Say the poem, Cozy."

"*Brise Marine*'?"

"The one we talked about."

"'La chair est triste, hélas! et j'ai lu tous les livres.'"

That much I understood. *The flesh is sad, alas, and I've read all the books.* And I understood the lines about the steamer with the swaying masts, and hearing the song of the sailors, and leaving everything behind.

"'Mais, ô mon cœur, entends le chant des matelots!'"

And then my mother spoke, in a voice so tiny Cozy had to lean over the bed to hear her. They spoke for a while in French, and then a nun came in and shooed us out of the room so she could give my mother a shot of something.

We ate tuna salad in the hospital cafeteria, and I waited for Cozy to tell me what my mother had said. Finally I couldn't wait any longer.

"What did she say?" I asked.

Cozy's mouth was full. I had to wait till she finished chewing. "She said that she'd gone to the University of Chicago," Cozy said, "but that the University of Wisconsin was a great university too. You must have told her I was at UW?"

I nodded.

"She said I should study hard and learn all I can, and that I should read all of *À la recherche du temps perdu,* not just *Du côté de chez Swann."*

"That's it? That's what she said?"

"Pretty much."

And those in fact were my mother's last words. When we went back up to the room, she was dead. The nuns were removing the body. I held back my tears. Cozy put her arms around me.

"What comes after *Du côté de chez Swann*?" she asked.

"*Swann's Way*? I don't know," I said. "That's as far as I got."

We talked about stopping for breakfast on the way back from Michigan City, but nothing suited us. There were eggs in the refrigerator, but no bacon. I was short of breath. I started to make coffee in my mother's little French coffeepot. Cozy'd never seen anything like it, and I told her she could have it. The little demitasse cups too.

"I never drank coffee," I said "till I started working for the RPO, and then we made it by heating the water with a copper coil that was hooked up right to the steam line."

The pot began to sputter and the coffee poured out the tubes into the little cups. We drank it with lots of sugar.

I lay down for a while on my bed. Cozy came into the room and then left. I tried to read more of *The Wind in the Willows* but soon put it down. I couldn't sleep, though. I was making a list. What did I have to do? I had to call Howard Cochrane, the undertaker. He'd do the removal. *The removal.*

And then what?

When I went downstairs again Cozy'd changed into a pair of jeans and a sweatshirt. It was chilly. "Do you want some more coffee?"

"Yeah."

"I'm glad you're here," I said.

"I am too," she said.

"I don't know what to do," I said. "Do you want some eggs? Soft-boiled?"

"Sure. Want me to do it?"

I nodded.

"Do you remember Humpty Dumpty?" she asked. "Mama taught me in French."

" *'Boule, Boule'?*"

" *'Boule, Boule.'*" She couldn't help correcting my pronunciation: *bul, bul.* "I could do Grandma's hair," she said.

I looked at her in surprise. "She's dead, sweetheart."

"I know that. Mama says that the last service a hairdresser can perform for a customer is to do her hair when she dies."

"Are you sure you want to do that?"

"Why not?"

"Have you ever done it before?"

"Not on a dead person, but I've done Mama's hair."

"You do your mother's hair? All that fantastic stuff?"

"I don't do beads and extensions," she said, "but I do braids and cornrows."

"You going to braid your grandma's hair?" I had a vision of my mother with tiny cornrows. I couldn't help smiling.

"Have you got a picture?"

I got up and we rummaged through the sideboard in the dining room, where she kept scrapbooks and boxes of photos and her camera, an Exacta single lens reflect. I unsnapped the case and showed Cozy. "You look right through the lens," I said, "though sometimes it's too dark to see." I showed Cozy my mother's senior *Tabula*, and the one from her junior year, with Hemingway's signature. Just his name. No best wishes; no fond memories; no promises to keep in touch in the future.

There were no recent photos, but my mother had worn her hair the same way for years, so an old photo of her and my father, shortly after he got cancer, would do. She was standing in front of a new Chevy Impala, the one still parked in the garage. Her hair was pulled back and twisted into a roll.

"That's a French twist," Cozy said. "I can do that."

Back in the kitchen she ran the water till it got hot.

"You should start with cold water," I said.

She gave me a funny look.

"That way the eggs warm up slowly inside. They cook more evenly."

She emptied the hot water out of the pan, covered the eggs with cold water, and put the pan back on the stove. The house was chilly. Barent had turned down the thermostat and I hadn't bothered to turn it back up.

We ate the eggs in little painted egg cups. We ate them with little silver spoons. We salted and peppered them with blue-and-white salt and pepper shakers. You punched down a button on the top and a spray of salt or pepper shot out the bottom. Very effective for soft-boiled eggs, though the spray was just a little too wide, like a shot-gun pattern that needs to be choked in a little.

After breakfast I called Howard Cochrane, Frances's father. He was an old man now, older than my mother. I'd dated Frances once or twice after Corinna disappeared, but it never amounted to any-thing. She was willing, but I held back, and then she went off to the University of Michigan in Ann Arbor and I went to boot camp at Great Lakes and I don't think we'd spoken since. Mr. Cochrane said that Barent had already called him. I should come in the afternoon to discuss the arrangements.

I thought I'd ask Barent to remove the tree that had fallen over the garage, but then I decided I'd do it myself. I needed to do something. But I couldn't get the chain saw started—a French chain saw, a Poulan, that struck Cozy as funny; she'd never thought of the French as hav-ing chain saws—and by the time I went into town for fresh gas and a new spark plug, it was time to go to the funeral home to pick out a casket. Cozy wore her jeans and sweatshirt; I took off Janis's Aran sweater, which was a little too warm, and put on a white shirt.

Howard tried to steer me toward the expensive ones, but I knew the drill, and I knew that they were all the same. Even so, I didn't pick the cheapest one.

"My daughter wants to do her hair."

He looked Cozy over. Not unkindly, just curious. "I believe I knew your mother," he said. "She and my daughter used to be good friends." No challenge here. No response either. "I've already talked to your aunt Bridget," he said. "You won't have to worry about her hair."

"Well I'm sure Aunt Bridget won't mind," I said. I looked at Cozy to make sure this was what she wanted to do. She nodded.

"Certainly, Martin; I'll have Dolores give her a call."

Everything was included in the price of the casket, so there weren't that many decisions to make, besides what dress my mother should wear.

"Have you ever done a dead person's hair before?" Mr. Cochrane asked Cozy.

"No."

"It's a little different. But you'll see. Have you got a photo, Martin?"

I produced the photo.

"Would tomorrow afternoon be all right? Then the visitation on Thursday and funeral on Friday?"

"Fine."

We drove back to Dijksterhuis Corners and then kept right on going, all the way out to the lake—Potter Dunes. No one was checking stickers or asking for money at the little kiosk. The beach was empty.

"It's like the ocean," Cozy said.

We climbed Old Baldy, leaving our shoes and socks in the car.

"This is where we had our class parties, and a big picnic at the end of the year. Your mother was a good swimmer."

"Did she have lots of friends?"

"Yes, I'd say so. She was very popular. Does she ever talk about those days?" *(Meaning, I guess, does she ever talk about me?)*

"She talks about climbing the water tower. She tries to pretend it was no big deal, but I think it was pretty major."

"I should have understood then, but I didn't."

"Should have understood what?"

"That she wanted to leave, to get out of here: 'F—— this town.'"

I remembered standing behind Corinna bending over the railing, rubbing up against her. Rubbing up against her butt. Putting my arms around her. Touching her breasts. Closing my eyes and kissing the back of her neck.

"Maybe I *should* have left it the way it was," I said, as if we were resuming the conversation we'd had in New York two years earlier. "It's not such a bad place, though."

"Grandma didn't like it either, did she? Your mom?"

"She was more interested in books and literature, and history."

"Couldn't she read books here?"

"I suppose, but there was no one to talk to about them. Almost no one. There was Mr. Haptonstahl, and then Mr. Marckwardt, who bought the depot and turned it into a bookstore, but he died right after I left home."

"Did you like books?"

"I liked the books I sent you: *The Three Musketeers,* and *Robin Hood,* and *The Boy's King Arthur. Pooh. The Wind in the Willows.* I didn't know it was a version for boys. I thought it was 'the boys' King Arthur, you know what I mean? Like 'the boys' was what you called the knights of the round table. And I liked Beowulf. He had a grip of steel, and I thought that meant a suitcase."

"A suitcase?"

"My folks always called a suitcase a *grip,* like my RPO grip. You know how you sometimes see one of those metal grips with the straps around them on the baggage carts in the station, and I always think that Beowulf must be on the train. I liked the Hardy Boys too," I said, "but I didn't realize there was a whole series. I had one that I read over and over. It wasn't till my junior year that I found out there were dozens of them. By then it was too late."

"That's sad," she said, but she was smiling. "You know the tape Grandma made?"

"'Babette's Feast?'"

She nodded. "It's a pretty good story. Grandma liked it too. Grandma Williams. She said she didn't know anybody except your mom who'd do something like that. I mean make that same dinner. It must have been a lot of work."

"But worth it."

It was getting dark. We ran down the dune, taking bigger and bigger leaps, until we felt like we were flying. We walked along the edge of the lake, but the water was icy. We drove back to the house without putting our shoes and socks back on.

Aunt Bridget was waiting for us in the kitchen when we got home. There were two casseroles on the table and one in the oven. She'd always been stout, but now that she was in her seventies she seemed to be getting smaller.

"Aunt Bregje," I said, "I hope you don't mind if Cozy does Mom's hair."

"Cozy," she said. "Is that your name?"

Cozy nodded.

"I've done your grandmother's hair for the last twenty years," she said. "Don't you think I'd get it right?"

"Maybe it's time for someone else to do it then," Cozy said, and I could see that there wasn't much fight left in Aunt Bridget. My dad and Uncle Piet had bought the beauty parlor for her after my grandmother died. Aunt Bridget never had a head for business, and the beauty parlor lost money every year, but Dad and Uncle Piet absorbed the losses and made sure Bridget had everything she needed.

"I used to do your grandmother's hair—your other grandmother's—did you know that? And your mama used to work for me, afternoons after school, before she went away. I always said she had a gift for handling hair, and from what I hear I guess I was right. Maybe you've got it too."

Cozy didn't say anything, and I couldn't think of anything to say.

"I wanted to see you," Aunt Bridget said, "and your daddy, of course. He used to come over to see me, but I never could keep him long. He was always off and running."

"I think he still is," Cozy said.

"I wanted to show you something, honey, so you can tell your mom and your grandma that you've seen it too. Would you hand me my purse, Marty? It's on the counter."

I handed Aunt Bridget her large black purse. When she opened it I could see the corner of the framed certificate that had always hung on the wall of her sewing room. She held it up for Cozy to see. "The Fastest Typist in the U. S. Navy," she read aloud. "You see," she said, "your daddy wasn't the only one in the Navy. Look." She pointed. "It's signed by Josephus Daniels, secretary of the U. S. Navy. I want you to tell your mama and your grandma now that you've seen it too."

Uncle Barent and Aunt Margriet came over later and we ate the casserole and a fruit salad. I got out the guitar and we sang a few hymns while Aunt Margriet did the dishes, and then everyone went home.

Cozy and I sat in the breakfast nook and drank the half bottle of wine from the refrigerator.

"I should have come back," I said aloud. "I should have come home when she asked me to. I should have taken over the orchards."

Cozy let me speculate for a while, and then she said, "That's the way Grandma talked after Grandpa died."

"How's that?"

"I should have done this, I should have done that."

"You know, I don't think your grandpa wanted to leave here. I think he would have stayed. It was the women who decided everything. Aunt Flo—your grandma—wanted to take the money and run. But your grandpa had a way with the trees. The new trees—*whips*, they called them—were already grafted, but your grandpa liked to experiment a little. Grafting's an art, you know. You can't just a cut notch in the stock and stick your scion in and expect it to grow. He knew how to do that; and he was teaching me. Pruning too. You've got to shape a tree like a wineglass. You've got to open it up so the sunlight reaches in to the inside of the tree."

"What money?"

"You know about the money. My dad paid your grandma and grandpa to leave town."

"How much?"

"I don't know. I couldn't get it out of my mother. But it was a lot. My dad couldn't pay it all at once."

"I don't believe it."

"Cozy, I'm sorry I said anything, really."

"Does Mama know this?"

"She knows. Your grandma and my mom—your other grandma—made the deal. That's what we were talking about after the spelling bee, remember? On the steps of the library?"

"I guess I didn't understand *what* you were talking about then. So that's the big secret."

"That's it."

"All because of me?"

"All because of you."

In the evening we took a walk through the orchards that were no longer our orchards. They were now being run by a professional management company headquartered across the state line in La Porte, Indiana. In the old part of the orchards—planted by my grandfather right after the First World War—the apple trees had been planted forty feet apart and peach trees had been planted in between them, 108 trees per acre. "When the apple trees matured," I explained to Cozy, "my dad and your mom's dad took the peach trees out. They didn't want to do it, but I guess it had to be done to give the apple trees more space. That was before I was born. We should come here in May when the apples blossom. There are five blossoms in every cluster; the center one's the king blossom, and you have to spray ten days later with NAA to shock the extra blossoms off. You just want to leave the king blossom; otherwise you'll get five dwarf apples, about the size of golf balls."

"What's NAA?"

"Naphthalene acetic acid."

"That would be a crystalline compound of some sort, probably derived from coal tar."

"Right. It's called tar camphor."

"You have to wonder how apple trees ever just grew."

"Like in the Garden of Eden?"

"Right."

"I don't know. Wild apple trees are a real mess. If you let *any* tree go for a couple of years it'll go wild—water sprouts coming out of every branch, the top branches getting all tangled up. You wind up with dwarf apples.

"Maybe they ate dwarf apples in the Garden of Eden."

"That's for sure, if they hadn't pruned the trees and shocked off the extra blossoms. Your grandpa liked to take some fruitwood off wild trees and graft it onto a young tree just to see what would happen."

"What would happen?"

"You get different kinds of apples on the same tree."

She looked at me in disbelief.

"Cross my heart," I said.

"Can we see them?"

"If I can find them."

The Williamses' old home had been bulldozed, replaced with a metal storage shed. Lotte's folks were the only Schyulers left now, and most of the Dijksterhuises were gone too. There wasn't much work in the area, apart from farming. There was still some celery, but mostly farther north, and young people didn't want to ditch and drain the bogs, and who could blame them? It was backbreaking work, and there wasn't much money in it.

"My dad—your grandpa—planted these trees in 1926. Dad and Uncle Piet. He worked for the Featherbone Company then, right through the Depression, and then he and Uncle Piet peddled their first crop out of a boxcar in Chicago. They stayed at a place out in Cicero that was Al Capone's headquarters for a while. They came back one night and the whole front of the place had been shot up. They were trying to kill the guy in the barber chair, but they killed the barber instead. Then they lost three crops in a row and had to live on my mother's salary at the school, Uncle Piet and Aunt Sophie too. Your mom's dad started working for them right after that. Dad met him at the big farmers' market in Benton Harbor. That's the world's largest open-air market. Your grandma worked for the Featherbone Company for a while, before she had Charlie, your mom's brother. He's buried in the cemetery out at Poesy Chapel. We can stop out there tomorrow if you want to."

We walked around in the dark, back to the packing shed. At the edge of the picking camp I showed Cozy where I'd first heard the blues, where I'd kissed her mother for the first time, and then we followed the path up to the house. The path hadn't been mowed, but the nettles and raspberry canes had disappeared for the winter.

"When were *you* born?" she asked.

"Same year as your mom, 1938. My mother was almost forty. It was a long time before they could afford to have any kids, and then my mom had a lot of trouble with me—she was in labor for almost two days.

"Things went pretty well after that, financially—my dad started selling directly to the chain stores—but I can remember Dad and Uncle Piet and Cap sitting around the kitchen table after a freeze with a pile of twigs, cutting open the buds to see how much damage had been done."

"What do you think would have happened if you'd gotten married?"

"I guess we'd all be living here now, wouldn't we?"

"You can't be sure. Maybe something else would have happened."

"That's true."

"And I wouldn't be me, would I?"

"That wouldn't be so good, would it?"

"Do you believe in fate?" Cozy asked.

"You mean like predestination?"

"That's different, isn't it? Like you're either going to heaven or hell no matter what you do?"

"Sort of, I guess."

"More like some power behind the scenes. Making sure that certain things happen. Wanting them to happen. Like wanting me to be born."

"That would apply to everyone, wouldn't it?"

"Like if the parents did it at a different time, the baby wouldn't be the same person. In school we read a story about a butterfly. Somebody goes back in a time machine and accidentally steps on a butterfly, and when he comes back everything's different."

I didn't say anything.

"Or if I wiggle my finger, like this," she said, "it might cause a war a hundred years from now." She wiggled her finger. "Just by moving the air molecules. Each molecule touches another molecule and that touches another . . ."

"I get the idea," I said, "but it might *prevent* a war too. You never know."

"Sometimes I think I would have been born anyway. It's just a feeling I have."

"That's a good feeling," I said. "Like you would have found some way through."

The big door on the packing shed was padlocked. "Tomorrow on the way out to the cemetery we'll go see the Indian mounds," I said, "and the pits."

"What kind of pits?"

"For storing grain. They're about ten feet across and six feet deep. The Indians lined them with dry grasses and then put in grain, and then another layer of grass. Then they covered them with bark to protect them from the rain. They're a lot of them around here— Potawatomi Indians—but we'd have to get across the river, and I suppose it's all walled off by now. Unless we swim, and it's a little cold for that."

We stopped at Uncle Barent's and Aunt Sophie's and drank a cup of tea. Aunt Marilyn asked Cozy about her grandmother and about her mother. I was surprised to learn that Lotte had moved upriver and was living with Miss Prellwitz in the mission at Camp Putnam. Miss Prellwitz had not married after all. Her fiancé had decided he didn't want to go back to Africa with her, so she'd gone back by herself.

The next morning in a small room in the back of the funeral home, Cozy did her grandmother's hair. The little room had been one of the mysterious locked doors of my childhood. Actually, you had to go through a series of rooms, rooms that were always locked. I was more familiar with the upstairs, with the living room, which was different from other living rooms. Christian Science magazines were stacked up on end tables that flanked a silvery sofa. A cuckoo clock from Germany chimed on the wall over an Italian *cassone*. I'd been sitting on that *cassone* when Mr. Cochrane's brother, just back from Germany, brought the clock. He was an undertaker too. In Buchanan, about fifteen miles east. A third brother was also an undertaker, in Niles, and when their father, himself an undertaker, died, they'd all gone to Florida to embalm him.

We'd held our class dances downstairs, in the big visitation room where my mother would be laid out. The wife of one of the teachers at the high school had taught us to dance in that room—the jitterbug and the fox trot and the waltz—and Corinna had danced with her cousin from Benton Harbor as her only partner.

My mother was laid out on a gurney, a sheet tucked up around her neck.

"Her hair's been washed," Mr. Cochrane said.

She was lying on her back, her head propped up on a little adjustable cushioned headrest. Mr. Cochrane had set the features of her face, but something was not quite right.

Aunt Bridget was there too. She'd come just in case. If she was still miffed, she didn't show it. "Have you ever done a white woman's hair?" she asked.

"No."

"Well, it's not the same; it's not the same at all. The texture is different, and it holds water differently. Now Rita had a natural wave, but she always wanted it pulled back in a French roll. You can't get a black woman's hair to sit still like that. It's too thick. And Howard here doesn't even have a decent pair of barber's shears. I've brought a good pair, but I left it in my purse in the car.

"She doesn't need her hair *cut*," I said. "She just needs it fixed up a little." I hadn't thought this through, hadn't thought it would be so complicated. I thought you'd just run a comb through it. Maybe spray it with something.

Cozy ran her fingers through my mother's hair. "All I'll need to do is comb it out."

Mr. Cochrane had set out a tray with brushes, combs, and scissors.

Aunt Bridget sat down on a chair and had a little cry. "Your grandmother was the only one who knew what I went through," she said to Cozy. "I'm just sorry to see her go. She always has a buildup of wax in her left ear. You need to swab it out with a Q-Tip dipped in a little rubbing alcohol. Mr. C. keeps the Q-Tips and the alcohol in that little cabinet behind the door. And there's some of that hand lotion too; you should rub some on her fingers. She had terrible cracks in her fingers. Sometimes she could hardly play her piano."

Cozy combed out my mother's hair, which was longer than I'd

expected. She had propped the photograph of my mother on a stand made for just that purpose. Cozy had her fingers in her hair, pulling it this way and that. I could see that the hair grew out in different directions. One clump of gray hair almost seemed to detach itself from the rest.

"You'll want to start on the other side," Aunt Bridget said.

"Do you think the body's just a shell?" Cozy asked. "That's what Grandma says . . . But I don't know. Look at the bodies of saints and people like that. They've got three pieces of a saint in St. Vincent's on Third Street. In little silver holders. Two teeth and a fingertip."

"Have you been going to the Catholic church?"

"I went with my friend Maureen." She took my hand in hers and put it on my mother's head. "You feel that?" I could in fact feel the tension remaining in the hair.

"Hair keeps right on growing," Aunt Bridget said. "It's the last thing to die. I'm going to get my barber's shears out of the car."

Cozy ran a comb through my mother's hair, pulling it back off her face into a ponytail. "Well, what do you think?"

I looked at the photo.

"I forget which way to twist it." We both looked at the photo. "Looks like counterclockwise." She twisted the ponytail with one hand and pulled it up with the other. "Lift her head up a little, would you?"

I lifted my mother's head, and Cozy tucked the ends of the ponytail inside the twist.

"How'd you do that?"

"You want me to take it out and do it again?"

"No, I guess not."

"Get me a hairpin from the tray."

I handed her a hairpin, one of the real thick ones with one wavy prong. Cozy pushed it down into the top of the twist. "That look about right?"

"Close enough for government work."

"No, really. You think it's OK?"

"It's fine."

"It's not right, is it?" She looked at the photo.

I pushed at the hair a little.

By the time Aunt Bridget got back with a pair of barber's shears Cozy had already sprayed my mother's hair. A fine mist filled the air—a chemical smell—and then dissipated.

She put my mother's glasses on and adjusted them.

I was anxious to leave. Aunt Bridget and Cozy and I went out into the hallway, and Mr. Cochrane locked the door behind us. Aunt Bridget and Cozy sat on a small sofa in Mr. Cochrane's little office at the front while I looked over some papers and then signed them.

"I'll just sit here for minute and chat with Mr. C.," Aunt Bridget said.

Outside it was warm, but not summer warm. You knew it would be chilly in the evening. I was anxious to get on.

"Wait in the car, will you?" I said to Cozy. "I want to go back for just a minute, OK?"

"Sure."

Aunt Bridget had disappeared, but the door of mystery—a little less mysterious now—was open, and I found Aunt Bridget starting to fiddle with my mother's hair.

"She twisted it the wrong way," she said. "I didn't want to say anything, but she had it backwards."

"Thanks, Aunt Bregje, but I think it's fine this way. It gives her a new look. I'd like to leave it the way it is, OK?"

"I guess it's up to you. But at least let me put some lotion on her fingertips. She used to get those awful cracks, more in the winter, when it was so dry, but it's good to put some lotion on now."

"I can do that," I said.

"Mr. C.'s got them pretty well tucked in," she said.

"It's OK, Aunt Bregje." I put my arms around her and kissed the top of her old head. "Now I'd like to be alone for just a minute."

My mother's fingers were stiff. I managed to rub some lotion into her fingertips, but I couldn't get her hands back in place. Mr. Cochrane would have to deal with them later. I removed my mother's piano glasses from her face. She must have been playing the piano when she had her heart attack," I thought. I hadn't asked. A couple of little jewels sparkled in the frames, and when I closed my eyes I could see them sparkle in my memory. I leaned over and kissed her and then held her glasses up to my eyes and looked through them. Everything was a blur, and then I could see her sitting at the piano, silhouetted at the kitchen window, sitting in the big chair in the study, doing a crossword puzzle, her books around her, seated at the small mahogany desk in the living room where she paid the bills, standing on the platform of the station in Niles, waving good-bye as the train pulls out of the station.

I'd thought that she was leaving us behind, but it was the other way around. She wasn't going anywhere now. I was the one who was moving on. Cozy and I, and Corinna and Monroe and Aunt Flo and Reverend Taylor, and Aunt Bridget too. We were the travelers. My mother had gotten off the train.

That night Cozy and I were both restless. We went through the dresses in my mother's closet. I still hadn't called the new minister, who hadn't known my mother, and I put off making the call. And I had to call the lawyer, Richard Freeman, about the will. Freeman was an old man, like Howard Cochrane.

There were two casseroles in the refrigerator. All we had to do was warm them up in the oven. There were salads in Tupperware bowls with the names of the owners taped to the bottom. But we didn't feel like a casserole, or a salad, so we drove in to Raker's Tavern instead. It was now called the Village Pump, but it still served the same old-fashioned hamburgers—wrapped in waxed paper. We had fries too, and a glass of draft beer, and then another, though the drinking age in Michigan was twenty-one, not eighteen as in Wisconsin.

Afterward we walked down Main Street to the gate of the Potter Featherbone Company.

"They moved to Atlanta about ten years ago," I said.

"You told me."

The base of the tower was hidden by the huge buckeye trees.

"They took the ladder off," I said, "after your mom and I climbed it. I think the small ladder's still there, though. At the top."

"You told me that too," she said. "I could squeeze through here." There was a lot of play in the gate in the chain-link fence, which had been secured with a heavy chain.

"Speak for yourself."

"You're not fat."

"I'm not skinny either. We'd have to walk all the way around."

"I think you could make it."

"Cozy."

"Do you mind?"

"I've got to call the lawyer tonight, and we've still got to pick out a dress and take it to the funeral home. The visitation is tomorrow night. And I still haven't called the Methodist minister. I should have let Mr. Cochrane take care of it. He offered to."

She put her arm through mine. I was feeling the beer and had to pee.

"Please?" She squeezed through the opening between the gate and the fence.

I tried to follow, but my belt got caught in the latch of the gate and Cozy had to unhook me.

"Grandma has a corset."

"It's probably made of featherbone. Does she still wear it?"

"I don't think so. I think I'd feel it if she did." We stepped on buckeyes in the silence. "So this is the way you and Mama came?"

"We came around from the back."

She took my arm again. "Were you scared?"

"Very scared."

"Was Mama scared?"

"I don't think she was as scared as I was."

"How did you know?"

"She was the one pushing ahead. I think she would have done it by herself."

"What about you? How come you went first then?"

"Because, Cozy, I was a boy and she was a girl. I couldn't let her go first. And to tell you the truth, I think if she'd gone first, I wouldn't have gone all the way. But since she was behind me, I couldn't go back down, could I?"

"It was just like climbing a ladder, right?"

"Yes, but once you get up to a certain height, everything changes."

The tower loomed over us, blocking the stars and the moon. Then we were standing in the dark shadows at the base. I could see the windows of the Ford agency on the other side of Main Street, through the trees. Old Mr. Harrison had died; Mr. Stone too, The last remnants of the minstrel show. The buckeye trees had gotten larger. Buckeyes everywhere.

"Are you glad you did it?"

"Yeah, it was great. It was fantastic."

I picked up a buckeye. Cozy put a foot in one of the little triangles in the leg of the tower and pulled herself up. I started to peel the buckeye, prying apart the prickly shell with my car key so I wouldn't prick my fingers. It was a double. I held the two stones in the palm of my hand. They were smooth, slippery without being sticky. I held them out to Cozy, but she was gone.

I looked around. Then up. She was looking down at me. Ten feet up. My heart jumped. "Get your butt down here."

"Come on up, the view is great."

"Cozy, seriously. Don't give me a heart attack, OK?"

But she climbed higher. Up into the shadows. "Cozy." I didn't want to shout too loud. "Cozy. Cozy, for Christ's sake, get back down here . . . God damn it, Cozy. There's no ladder. You can't do this. Get back down here."

I could hardly see her at all. Just some shimmering movement in the darkness, not a clear shape at all, but dissolving, like a fade-out at the end of a scene in a movie.

No one was on the street. I waited till I couldn't wait any longer, and then I started after her, cursing softly under my breath.

The climb was much harder without the ladder. You had to put your feet in the triangular holes of the welded steel leg, like the triangular holes in the struts of an Erector set. I gripped the leg of the tower tightly with both hands before moving a foot, planted both feet firmly before moving a hand, wishing that I'd peed first.

I couldn't see her, but I could hear her above me. Just a little scraping. What would she do when she got to the catwalk at the top? There was nothing she *could* do.

"Cozy, there's no way to get up onto the catwalk. Please. Listen to me. You'll have to come back down. The ladder slopes out, do you hear me? It slopes *out*."

No answer.

"Cozy, there is no way."

Looking up, I could see her now, above the shadows of the trees. Black against deep blue.

The triangles hurt my feet, cut right into them. We climbed in silence till we could look down on the tops of the trees. Two more minutes and she'd reached the top.

"Wait there, Cozy. Wait."

Still no answer. I was afraid to upset her.

I looked down. The legs of the tower disappeared into the darkness beneath me. Too frightening. I tilted my face up to look at her. The tank loomed above her, smooth and round. What did they do with all the water?

"Cozy," I called again. "Wait. There're pigeons up there. They'll all take off at once." There was nowhere for her to go. I was close enough now to grab her ankle, but I was afraid of pulling her down.

She put her hands on the ladder and started to climb up, up and out, but the bolts at the bottom had rusted through and the ladder swung out into empty space. I held my breath, waiting for the top bolts to give way as her feet dangled above my head; but they took the added weight. I could hear her breathing over the scraping of the rusty bolts as the ladder swung back and forth.

"Cozy, are you all right?"

She pulled herself up, one rung at a time, her feet kicking in front of my face. When she reached the edge of the catwalk I closed my eyes again. I heard the rush of wings as the pigeons took off and then Cozy scrambled over the edge.

I could hear my own breathing too, as clearly as if I had my head against my own chest.

"Jesus Christ, Cozy, are you crazy?"

It was a long time before she said anything. A full minute. Two minutes. "Daddy?"

"Cozy?"

"Are you there?"

"I'm here. Jesus Christ, Cozy, what are we going to do now? Are you all right? Oh God. You all right?"

"I'm all right," she said. "I just have to get my breath."

"Just take it easy."

"I have to pee."

"So do I," I said. "You can pee on the catwalk."

I could hear her footsteps as she walked around to the other side. I was still having trouble breathing. "Don't try to pee over the edge," I called to her. "Don't trust the railing, do you hear me? Don't lean against the railing."

"I hear you."

I heard her footsteps again. She was above me now.

"I can see them," she says.

"What?"

"The yard lights at Dijksterhuis Corners. You can see the lights of Chicago too, from the other side."

"Cozy, how're we going to get back down?"

"You mean how am *I* going to get back down."

"That's what I mean."

"You can see the funeral home. Mama didn't like Frances Cochrane, did she?"

"I know that."

"Did *you* like her?"

"I liked her all right."

"I didn't get Grandma's hair right, did I? I should have let your aunt do it."

"It's all right. It's fine."

"I think I twisted the ponytail the wrong way when I put it into the twist. It's backwards."

"You gave her a new look, that's all."

"Grandma says death is a journey?"

"I don't think so. I think death is the end of the journey. We're the ones on a journey."

"I guess that's what I mean."

A westbound train went by.

"Was that the train you used to work on?"

"Sort of. That's a New York Central train, but it's not pulling any RPO cars. It's all air mail now. Maybe one car. I don't know."

We waited for the train to pass.

"Cozy," I said, "I'm going to go back down and get some help. I want you to stay right where you are. OK?"

"Daddy. Don't go. You can't climb back down now."

"There's no way you can get back down." The ladder's broken. I don't trust those top bolts. They could give way too."

"I don't want you to leave me."

"We need to get someone with a cherry picker."

"What's a cherry picker?"

"One of those cranes, with a vertical boom. Like they use for fixing phone lines, that sort of stuff."

"I've never seen one that big, I mean that would reach up here."

"Are you worried?"

"Sort of."

"Look up at the stars. Do you know the constellations?"

"Like the Big Dipper."

"The Big Dipper and Andromeda and Orion, the mighty hunter. If you look up there you can see Orion. See the three bright stars? That's his belt."

"I don't see how the constellations are going to help us."

"Well, if they can build the tower in the first place, they can figure out how to get you down."

"But *how?*"

I started to climb down.

"Daddy, I'm coming down."

"Cozy, stay right where you are."

"I don't want you to leave me."

"I'm not *leaving* you. I'm going to get help."

But I could already see her feet sticking out over the edge of the catwalk.

"Cozy, what the hell are you doing? I want you to stay put."

"I don't want to stay put."

"God damn it, get back up there."

I climbed back up. She was coming over the edge. I could see her silhouetted in the moonlight. The moon was in the west by now.

I fought back an urge to pray. I didn't have Miss Prellwitz or Aunt Flo or Reverend Taylor to carry me along. I had to do it by myself: *Jesus, will you come by here.*

"Cozy, get back up there." I closed my eyes.

She's on the ladder, but she can't reach the leg of the tower. She holds out her hand, but I can't reach it, even when I lean out, hold-ing on to the leg of the tower with one hand.

"You need to get back up on the catwalk. I'll get help."

"I'm going to swing the ladder," she says.

"What about the top bolts?"

But she's swinging. Our fingertips touch on the second swing, and on the third. On the fourth I grab her wrist. The ladder reaches the top of its arc and starts to fall back. If I hold on and she doesn't let go, I'll pull her off the ladder. If I let go, now . . .

She lets go of the ladder as it starts to swing back down. She's falling now, swinging in toward the leg of the tower. I've got her wrist, that's all. It all happens in an instant. I can feel her twisting in my grasp. Knowing that if my prayer is answered I will later on explain things in some other way, I pray, not simply opening myself to whatever is out there, not simply affirming that in some mysteri-ous indefinable way that universe is not totally indifferent to us, but asking, begging, humbling myself.

She swings in toward the tower leg. Banging, twisting, scram-bling. Her toe slips into one of the little triangles. One arm wraps around the leg of the tower. I don't want to let go of her wrist, but she pulls away so she can hold on with both hands.

What has she seen from the catwalk? Is it what she expected? Or something totally different? There will be time for questions later. She's below me now. I follow her down into the shadowy darkness at the base of the tower, step by step, the little triangles twisting our ankles first this way and then that, but it feels as if we're climbing up toward the light.

A SCRIBNER
READING GROUP GUIDE

BLUES LESSONS

DISCUSSION POINTS

1. For Martin, growing up with Cory in Appleton, Michigan, was truly paradise. What parallels can be drawn between Martin's life in the orchard and the biblical Garden of Eden? Why is he, like Adam, ultimately expelled from the garden?

2. Vocation is an important theme in *Blues Lessons*. What is Martin's vocation and how does he struggle to find it? Do you think everyone has a vocation? Do you agree with Reverend Taylor's belief that God has a plan for each person, but that it's up to us to choose to follow that path? Or are we more or less at the mercy of dumb luck?

3. The work of Ayn Rand makes a big impression on Martin in high school. After seeing the movie, his mother deftly sums up the main theme of *The Fountainhead*: "You have to live for yourself, heroically, if you want to achieve something for mankind" (page 30). In what ways could Martin be said to succeed—or fail—at living for himself, heroically? How about Cory?

4. Why do you think Martin chose to enlist in the navy and then take a job with the RPO instead of studying at the University of Chicago, as he intended? How do you make sense of his decision, and how do you feel about it?

5. Where did Martin's passion for the blues originate? With what does he connect its sound and its power to move him? The blues is sometimes identified with feelings of disappointment and longing. In fact, as a teenager Martin claims that he's come to regard longing as "the central experience in my life" (page 33). How does this feeling of longing continue to characterize Martin even as an adult? Does his relationship with the blues change and grow over time?

6. Do you agree with Cory's initial criticism that it's inappropriate for Martin to claim the blues as his vocation? Can the blues be played only by a certain kind of person? Has Martin—a young, white, middle-class guy—earned the right to play the blues?

7. *Blues Lessons* unfolds over the course of the turbulent sixties and seventies, alongside the civil rights movement. How does that

time period shape the events of this novel? In what ways does Cory's life path exemplify the changing role of African-Americans in society at that time?

8. Ultimately, do you think it's simply race that separates Cory and Martin? Had their parents allowed them to stay together, what do you think their relationship might have been like?

9. After learning about his daughter, Cozy, for the first time, Martin thinks, "sometimes finding something can be as painful as losing it" (page 156). What does he mean?

10. The nursery rhyme "Humpty Dumpty" appears several times in *Blues Lessons,* and at one point, Martin tells Cory, "Sometimes you *can* put things back together" (page 249). Do you think they could ever go back to the ways things were, making a whole from the broken pieces? What kind of future do you envision Martin, Cory, and their daughter will be able to create together?

11. Climbing the water tower was a profound experience for both Martin and Cory, but for completely different reasons. What did the event mean for each of them, and why did they see it through such different eyes? What does it mean for Martin to climb the tower again as an adult, this time with his daughter? What effect do you think the experience will have on Cozy?

12. Martin's mother prepares a special dinner for herself and her son in which she re-creates "Babette's Feast." What is she hoping to evoke or affirm with this meaningful evening? Why is her trip to Paris important to her, and what does it mean that she never gets to make the journey?

13. Martin and Cory's parents conspired to do what they thought was best for their children. Did they succeed in helping Martin and Cory achieve the brightest possible future? What kind of regrets—if any—do you think they had about their decision? What would you have done in their shoes?

14. As the orchard foreman, Cory's father, Cap, sometimes experimented with apple trees, grafting various kinds of branches onto a young tree. The result was a tree that grew several different types of apples at once. How does this image resonate within this story?

Q&A with Robert Hellenga

1. *Reading* Blues Lessons, *it seems clear that you're a passionate fan of the blues yourself. Can you explain what role the blues plays in your life? You write about playing the blues in considerable technical detail. Do you play the guitar, or is this topic just especially well researched?*

In a way, the blues are the sonnets of the musical world. There's a pretty tight format on the one hand, and room for variations on the other. But I'd trace my emotional involvement to the great themes and images of parting: men and women standing in railway stations as their lovers are carried away; or leaving their lovers behind; or men and women saying good-bye to someone setting out on the highway, or setting out on the highway themselves. My working title for *Blues Lessons,* in fact, was "Key to the Highway," but we changed it because that sounds too much like a road novel.

I've devoted a lot of time and energy to the blues since I took up the guitar in 1975. I play out occasionally, but mostly I play at home, where I do some recording on an eight-track digital recorder. I've learned mostly from books, which is how I learn most things.

2. *The main character in your previous novel,* The Fall of a Sparrow, *is also very drawn to the blues. In fact, the song "Corinna, Corinna" even makes an appearance in that book. Was this the inspiration for* Blues Lessons? *How did the ideas in this novel take shape?*

Rudy, Margot's father in *The Sixteen Pleasures,* is also a blues player, though he doesn't get much playing time in the novel. Woody in *Fall of a Sparrow* gets a lot more playing time, so I guess you could say that from the very beginning I was moving in the direction of a full-time bluesman/protagonist.

The novel didn't really take shape, however, until I hit upon the illegitimate daughter, Cozy. I'd vowed that in the novel no one would go to Italy, and that there wouldn't be a father with three daughters. No one goes to Italy, but I couldn't go without a daughter to move the story along.

3. *Your novels are generously peppered with references to other works of art—books, songs, poems, paintings, etc. How important is the role of art and literature in your life? And how do you think that's expressed in your novels?*

Literature has always played a very important role in my life. My grandmother read the King Arthur stories to me when I was little; my mother read Dickens to me; and I read to my three daughters every night for years. And of course I read on my own. That's what I do. Art and music are more difficult. I feel that I understand literature. I don't have to ask myself, do I like this story or this novel? I do not understand art and music, however, probably because they're nonverbal. I don't know how to deal with them. But in a way that's an advantage: they are mysteries that I don't understand, and so I keep pecking away at them, trying to get a foothold.

4. *What works of art and what other writers have inspired you and shaped your journey as a novelist?*

My favorite novel is Tolstoy's *Anna Karenina.* I always have a copy nearby. I especially like the forward momentum of the novel.

There's an urgency in the narrative voice, something that says, this story is so important that I don't need to fool around with narrative tricks or verbal fireworks. Let me just set things down as clearly as possible.

Three contemporary novels that I return to very often are: Gail Godwin's *Finishing School* and *Father Melancholy's Daughter*; and Sue Miller's *Family Pictures*.

5. *Do you see your books as related? Are there themes that you explore from book to book, with pieces of each novel echoing one another? Are there also motifs that you find recur even unconsciously in your works?*

Yes, and I'm not terribly happy about it, but I don't seem to have any choice. The largest most consistent theme is transcendence vs. immanence. I can't get away from it. All my characters are torn between the desire to affirm that this world is enough and the sense that there's some spiritual realm that calls us away from this world.

There are smaller things, too, about which I don't seem to have any choice. The blues, for one thing. In the novel I'm working on now the impulse to make the protagonist a blues player is hard to resist. And it's hard not to give him a really good fountain pen, too. All my protagonists have a really good fountain pen, and in fact my picture appeared on the cover of *Pen World* magazine in an article about writers who write with a fountain pen.

6. *The Sixteen Pleasures and* The Fall of a Sparrow *were set at least partly in Italy. What draws you to Italy? And what brought you back to the United States—and to Michigan, the state where you grew up—for this book? Will you be returning to Italy in a future work?*

My first taste of Italy came from the men (almost all Italians) who worked for my father on the produce market in Milwaukee (where we spent our summers). They represented a different world, a different set of values, from the small, Protestant town in Michigan where we lived the rest of the year. The Italians valued pleasure, sex, food, drink. Back in Michigan we admired restraint, self-discipline, keeping a lid on things. (Like Lake Woebegone.)

7. *The idea of vocation is a key theme in* Blues Lessons. *Do you consider writing fiction to be your vocation? Was discovering and accepting your vocation as difficult for you as it was for Martin?*

Writing fiction has definitely become my vocation. The importance of story is a key them in all three novels. Margot realizes that without our stories we don't know who we are; Woody believes that what we find at the core of all religions are stories; Martin and Corinna define themselves by their stories, which are, in a sense, two different versions of the same story.

8. *What's your favorite part of the writing experience? How do you manage to balance your writing with your teaching career? Do the two conflict with or nourish each other?*

My favorite part of the writing experience is revising. I think that insight, inspiration, creativity—whatever you want to call it—is more likely to strike in the fifth or sixth draft than in the first.

If my classes are going well, then the teaching nourishes the writing. If they're not going so well, I tend to get preoccupied, and this makes writing more difficult. I taught full-time for thirty-three years, and now I'm shifting to writing full-time and doing a little teaching on the side.

9. *What can we look forward to reading after* Blues Lessons*?*

I'm working on a novel about Rudy Harrington, Margot's father in *The Sixteen Pleasures,* who goes to Texas to raise avocados and to meditate on the nature of reality. Right now it looks like a comic philosophical novel, but we'll see.

Look for *The Fall of a Sparrow*—bestselling author Robert Hellenga's masterful novel about the strength and resilience of the human spirit.

0-684-85027-3 • $14.00

Available wherever books are sold.

Printed in the United States
By Bookmasters